Two delightful Regencies—available for the first time in one volume!

"One of the freshest voices in the Regency genre."
—*Rave Reviews*

Lady in Green
"Barbara Metzger deliciously mixes love and laughter." —*Romantic Times*

Minor Indiscretions
"Metzger's prose absolutely tickles the funny bone." —*L.A. Life Daily News*

[handwritten label] Mary Lou Riley / 45 Fox Dr / Narragansett, RI 02882-4

Lady in Green

AND

Minor Indiscretions

BARBARA METZGER

A SIGNET BOOK

SIGNET
Published by New American Library, a division of
Penguin Putnam Inc., 375 Hudson Street,
New York, New York 10014, U.S.A.
Penguin Books Ltd, 80 Strand,
London WC2R 0RL, England
Penguin Books Australia Ltd, Ringwood,
Victoria, Australia
Penguin Books Canada Ltd, 10 Alcorn Avenue,
Toronto, Ontario, Canada M4V 3B2
Penguin Books (N.Z.) Ltd, 182–190 Wairau Road,
Auckland 10, New Zealand

Penguin Books Ltd, Registered Offices:
Harmondsworth, Middlesex, England

Published by Signet, an imprint of New American Library,
a division of Penguin Putnam Inc.
Lady in Green was originally published by Fawcett Crest/Ballantine
Books, copyright © Barbara Metzger, 1993.
Minor Indiscretions was originally published by Fawcett Crest/Ballantine
Books, copyright © Barbara Metzger, 1991.

First Signet Printing, February 2002
10 9 8 7 6 5 4 3 2 1

All rights reserved

 REGISTERED TRADEMARK—MARCA REGISTRADA

Printed in the United States of America

PUBLISHER'S NOTE
These are works of fiction. Names, characters, places, and incidents either
are the product of the author's imagination or are used fictitiously, and
any resemblance to actual persons, living or dead, business establish-
ments, events, or locales is entirely coincidental.

AUTHOR'S NOTE

To err is human, to forgive divine.
To make corrections is . . . not permitted.

Authors love having their books reprinted. New readers, new sales, and new opportunities to make an old book better. Unfortunately, the economic constraints of publishing the double volumes are such that no changes are possible, in order to keep the price such a bargain for readers. I am, therefore, begging your forgiveness for the mistakes, misprints, and muddled titles of nobility.

I hope the errors do not ruin your pleasure in the stories, and I hope I know better now than to make the same mistakes again. New ones, maybe.

With all best wishes,
Barbara Metzger

Lady in Green

To all my cousins

Chapter One.

$\mathscr{M}$iss Annalise Avery's fiancé was keeping a mistress. If anyone had told her that dependable, solid Barnaby Coombes had a paramour somewhere, Annalise would have laughed in his face. Hearing it from Barny's own mouth was not quite as funny.

Miss Avery had not meant to eavesdrop, of course. Her mother raised her better than that. She was so excited to tell Barny the doctor had finally declared her well again after that dreadful fever, that the wedding plans could now proceed, she fair flew down the stairs when she heard his carriage in the drive. Naturally she first had to don a warm dressing gown, and her maid insisted she wrap a dark wool shawl over her shoulders, too. She definitely had to tie the ribbons of a frilly cap firmly under her chin. Her outfit was not quite the thing for receiving morning callers, to say the least, Annalise acknowledged with a smile, but more of her was covered than in her sheer muslins and clinging

1

silks. Besides, it was only her stepfather, Sir Vernon Thompson, Bart., who would see her, and comfortable old Barny. She'd known Barny since she was eleven, when her widowed mother, Caroline Avery, *née* Bradshaw, had returned with her daughter to Worcester ten years earlier. They'd been promised forever, it seemed, but the formal announcement had been postponed by her mother's death; the wedding itself was put off for mourning first Annalise's maternal grandmother, then Grandfather Bradshaw. This final delay for her illness was going to be the last, Annalise vowed, and so she would announce to dear Barny as soon as she made sure the green-tinted spectacles were secure on her nose, lest the bright sunshine damage her weakened eyes after so long in the darkness. She didn't bother trying to pinch color back into her sallow cheeks; there was hardly enough flesh left to pinch. And good-natured Barny wouldn't mind. Annalise knew he was as eager as she to start their life together, so she hurried down the stairs to greet her childhood beau with her happy news.

Barnaby had already been shown into Sir Vernon's library, so Annalise pattered down the hall in her slippers, smiling in anticipation. She hadn't counted on how weak the fever and its aftermath had left her, though. She was forced to lean against the wall outside the library to catch her breath. The door was slightly open.

"You're sure she's out of danger, then?" she heard Barnaby asking, and was warmed by the concern in his voice.

"Yes," Sir Vernon answered, "the sawbones assures me she'll make a total recovery. We can have the first reading of the banns in a week or so. The wedding will take place next month."

"Thank God."

Annalise could hear the clink of glasses being

raised in a toast. Smiling, she pushed away from the wall, ready now to join the men. Her stepfather's voice stopped her just as her hand was raised to knock.

"What, so relieved? Which is it, are your debts so pressing or does your ladybird in London grow restless while you play the pattern-card suitor for your ailing betrothed here in Worcester?"

Annalise's hand fell to her side.

Barnaby grinned and tossed back his brandy. He held his glass out for a refill. "Both, if you must know. Sophy don't like missing Vauxhall and the Argyle Rooms. Says she attends with some of her girlfriends, but I don't trust her."

"Why? Aren't you paying enough to ensure her loyalty?" the baronet asked sarcastically.

"I'm dashed well paying enough to keep her in style, that's for sure. Now that you tell me Leesie ain't about to stick her spoon in the wall, I'll just toddle off to Town and surprise the old girl."

"Ah, yes, your 'business' in the City. Why the devil don't you just install Sophy in Birmingham or somewhere? Save all that travel time and expense."

"I told you, Sophy likes the nightlife in Town. 'Sides, a fellow needs to get away once in awhile, especially after putting his foot in parson's mousetrap."

"I still think you'd find it more convenient having a . . . convenient closer to home."

"Oh, I intend to, Sir Vernon, I intend to. There's a widow in Stourport who'd suit me like a plum. Do you know the one? Mrs. Yarberry. I can imagine Mr. Yarberry dying with a smile on his face. Then there's Marcy over at the Golden Hare. She's got cheeks like peaches, and melons out to . . ."

Annalise trembled in the hall. Not only did Barnaby Coombes have a mistress whom he intended

3

to keep on after their marriage, he also planned on setting up a veritable fruitbasket of a harem! Miss Avery raised a hand to her mouth to muffle a cry.

"Don't suppose you'd care to make me an advance," Barnaby was going on, "with the wedding so soon and the settlements all signed?"

"Not on your life, my lad," Sir Vernon replied. "Dear Annalise could have a relapse, after all. No, you'll just have to wait for the marriage lines to be signed before getting your hands on even a shilling of her dowry."

Barnaby slammed his thrice-emptied glass down on the desk. "I don't see why you're being such a skint. You made me sign back enough of Leesie's portion as settlements to keep you in clover for the rest of your life."

"Ah, but we all have our little vices. You have your Sophys and I have my gaming debts. You've waited this long, while, I might add, my stepdaughter's dowry has grown considerably from the Bradshaw grandparents' inheritances. You can wait a shade longer."

"While you skim off all you can."

"Wedding expenses, dear boy, don't you know. And all those pricey physicians and specialists I called down from London to guarantee the precious girl's recovery. You cannot argue with that. Nor," he added softly, "can the Bradshaw accountants."

"I'd still like to see some of the blunt now," Barnaby muttered, "before I'm leg-shackled and off on a blasted wedding trip. Ireland, faugh! I know— maybe Leesie'll still be too weak to travel. What do you think? If I suggest we wait . . ."

Not only did Miss Avery's betrothed have a mistress and a few in reserve, he was going to support them all on Annalise's money!

When pigs flew, he was!

Seeing red even through her green-tinted glasses,

Annalise charged into the room. "You cad!" she shouted. "You slime, you slug."

Barnaby gasped in horror, but Annalise couldn't tell whether his dismay was more for her overhearing his conversation or for her appearance. She did not care either way. "So what if I look like something that crept from a crypt? At least my conscience is clear, and that's more than I can say for you, Barnaby Coombes. You don't have to worry about going to Ireland with me; you don't even have to worry about going down the church aisle with me!"

Sir Vernon rose from behind the desk. He slowly raised his quizzing glass to his eye and surveyed his stepdaughter through the horribly magnified orb. "Fetching ensemble, my dear," he drawled. "I'm delighted to see you back in prime twig. I was just assuring Barny here that you were regaining your health and the wedding can be moved forward again."

"Haven't you heard what I said? I wouldn't marry such a bounder if he was the last man on earth and the future of the entire human race depended on me. He'd find an ape to give carte blanche."

"Leesie—" Barny started to protest, so she turned on him again.

"Don't you call me by your silly baby names, Mr. Coombes. I'm not a child anymore to be taken in by your fervent declarations of love and loyalty. Loyalty, hah!" She poked a bony finger in his thick chest. "I heard all about your Sophy, so don't pretend I'm throwing a distempered freak over nothing, you scurvy cur."

Barny tried to grab her hand. "But Lee—Miss Avery, Sophy means nothing to me, I swear!"

"And I suppose my money means nothing to you, either?" Annalise said with a sneer, snatching her fingers away and wiping them on the skirts of her navy-blue dressing gown.

"Dash it, Leesie, you know I'm not a rich man!"

"No, I don't know anything about you at all, Mr. Coombes. I thought I did. I thought we could build a good marriage based on all the years of friendship and trust, even if we did not share any great passion. You have destroyed—"

"That's it, Leesie, passion," Barnaby exclaimed, clutching her words like a drowning man a lifeline. "I do feel passion for you, more than you'll ever understand. I couldn't show you, of course, gently bred female and all that, don't you know, so I had to find an outlet for my, ah, affection. That's all it ever was, just, ah, protection for your maidenly modesty. That's it, Leesie, I swear!"

"Lust and greed, Barnaby Coombes, nothing else. You make me sick."

"You're sick! That's the ticket! You're over-wrought and upset. A few more days' rest and you'll see my little fall from grace is just the way of the world."

"Not *my* world, it isn't, so you can just take your passing fancies and pass right out of my life."

"But, Leesie—" Barnaby couldn't see Annalise's eyes through the dark lenses, but he didn't need her clenched fists to tell him they were sending daggers his way. "Miss Avery, which is downright ridiculous since I've known you since we were practically in leading strings together. Anyway, Miss Avery, you can't just throw me over like this. Sir Vernon can tell you, we've been promised forever, the notice was in the papers, the settlements have been signed. You can't back off from the engagement now."

"Oh, can't I? Just watch." And she started to fumble with the knot on the ribbon around her neck. The ribbon was holding Barny's betrothal ring safe since she'd lost so much weight that the diamond and ruby band slipped off her finger. Now her fingers were trembling with rage and weakness, making her too clumsy to undo the knot. Frustrated, she jerked the whole ribbon over her head, thereby dislodging her spectacles, which fell to the floor at her feet, and her nightcap. She threw the ring, ribbon and all, at Barnaby, who caught it automatically, his mouth fallen open and his eyes popping out of his skull like a sandy-haired carp.

Miss Avery was as bald as the day she was born.

With the slightest pale down sprouting here and there on her head, Annalise might look like a plucked chicken, but Barnaby Coombes was squawking like one. "G-g-gads, L-l—ma'am, y-your hair!"

Near tears, Annalise cried back, "Yes, my beautiful hair that used to reach below my waist! His fancy specialists"—she jerked her head toward Sir Vernon Thompson—"shaved it off. To save my life force, they said, all the while they bled the strength out of me. It might grow back, they said. But don't worry, Barny, you won't have to look at my ugliness over breakfast for the rest of your life. You should thank me."

Barnaby swallowed and made one last try. He pressed the ring into her hand and said, "Your hair will grow back, Leesie, but no matter. You'll always be b-beautiful to me."

"But not beautiful enough to keep you faithful. Not even Sophy is that beautiful. Here, give her this, and may she get more pleasure from it than I did!" She tossed the ring back, hard.

Barny caught the ribbon, but the ring bounced up and nicked his cheek. "Bitch," he muttered, dabbing at the stream of blood trickling down his neck.

"Good," Annalise said, although actually horrified at her own behavior. Quite at the end of her tether, she decided to make a clean breast of things. "And I am glad I don't have to marry you, Barnaby Coombes, because you drink too much. Furthermore, in a few years you'll need a corset and a hairpiece both. And finally, I've seen a sack of potatoes that had a better seat on a horse than you!"

Barnaby's face turned white, then the blood rushed back to give him a mottled, swollen look. "Oh, yeah," he raged, "and just who do you think you'll find to marry a viperish old scarecrow like—"

He was wasting his breath, for Miss Avery's last outburst took more of an effort than she had in her. She quietly collapsed to the floor in a heap of flowing fabric.

Sir Vernon came around the desk and felt for a pulse.

"She ain't croaked, is she?" Barnaby asked.

"No thanks to you. My congratulations on your fine touch with a skittish filly."

Barnaby was pouring himself another shot. "What did you want me to do? Zeus, she must have heard everything we said; there was no use denying any of it." He tossed back the drink, then sank down in a leather chair, looking away from his erstwhile fiancée's shiny pate with a shudder. "Lud, what'll I do now?"

The baronet rose and went to pull the bell for a footman. "I suggest you go visit the fair Sophy for a week or two while my stepdaughter cools down. You might even visit your creditors and tell them not to worry."

"Not worry? Gads, you heard her. She'll never marry me."

"She will if she knows what's good for her. I'll talk her 'round."

Barnaby gave a quick peek at the shaved head

8

and scrawny neck, wondering if Newgate mightn't be preferable after all. Annalise still hadn't moved. "Sure she ain't going to stick her spoon in the wall?"

"All that lovely Bradshaw money goes to charity if she dies without husband or children." Sir Vernon rang the bell again. "She wouldn't dare."

Chapter Two

𝒷roken hearts mended faster than brain fevers. At least on the outside. On the inside, something in Annalise shriveled and shrank, leaving a cold, hard emptiness where love and dreams and hope used to sing and dance. On the other hand, perhaps she was not so disappointed in her engagement's dissolution after all, for a scant two days later saw her ready to receive her stepfather in her sitting room.

Annalise knew why Sir Vernon had requested this visit, and she knew what her reply was going to be. She just hoped this discussion could be conducted with dignity, unlike the last. She felt she owed the baronet that much, for her mother's memory and for the years of his guardianship, although she now suspected his efforts on her behalf to be less sacrifice than self-serving. Of course he had welcomed an awkward thirteen-year-old into his household when he married Annalise's mother; Annalise was a considerable heiress in her own right even then. And of course he had kept her with him at Thompson Hall after her mother's death rather than have her passed about among the Bradshaw relatives; he kept control of her fortune and got an unpaid chatelaine for his manor house to boot! He might have ignored his stepdaughter, spending most of his time in London, but that had always suited her. Still, Annalise acknowledged, she had never been treated as anything less than a lady until two days ago, when her position was redefined as that of a commodity, an investment, a meal ticket. Well, she *was* a lady, her own papa having been Viscount Avery, albeit he was a disinherited ne'er-do-well. She vowed to receive Sir Vernon with the grace of a duke's granddaughter, not the wrath of a ranting fishwife.

Some vows were harder to keep than others. Sir Vernon entered her sitting room, for the first time ever, she realized, and started prowling about. Instead of taking the seat pulled near the chaise longue where Annalise reclined, wrapped around with blankets and shawls, he raised his quizzing glass and inspected her possessions. If she were a dog, her hackles would be up. When he lifted the jade carving of a horse on the mantel, turning it upside down as if to look for a mark of its value, Annalise coughed delicately. "You wished to see me, sir?"

Thompson swung his glass in her direction. "Ah, yes, my dear." He took slow, careful note of her gaunt and pallid cheeks, the heavy coverings pulled up to her chin, the cap pulled low over her forehead. "Not quite the blushing bride."

Annalise started to correct him, but Sir Vernon held up one long, tapered finger. "No, no, my dear, do not excite yourself. Let us keep this a comfortable little coze, shall we?"

She nodded, for that was her intention, too, and

indicated the chair and decanter and glass placed nearby for his convenience. "Please help yourself, sir."

His thin lips twitched into a semblance of a smile as he poured, but he remained standing, so Annalise had to crick her neck uncomfortably to see his face. Finally he deigned to take the seat, flicking a bit of lint off the velvet cushion first. "You have led quite a sheltered life, haven't you?"

Annalise wondered if that was a question. He knew very well that she'd had no come-out and no Season, what with periods of mourning and then no proper female to present her, and of course Barnaby always in the wings. How the situation must have pleased Sir Vernon, keeping her from meeting other eligible beaux, gentlemen who might not be as amenable as cabbage-headed Barny to sharing her dowry. Sheltered? Yes, she'd been kept from all but the local society, but if he meant to excuse Barnaby Coombes on the count that she was a green girl, the baronet was sadly mistaken.

"I have not been so sheltered, sir, that I do not know the ways of a man with a maid, if that is your meaning."

He dismissed her words with a wave of his manicured hand. "No, no, I did not suppose you to be an ignorant schoolroom miss. That's not my meaning. I refer instead to how you have been protected from fortune-hunters and hangers-on, and shielded from slights due to your mother's, shall we say, bourgeois background."

"Mother's parents were wonderful people!"

"And wonderfully wealthy. Unfortunately, that wealth came from trade, my dear, which even your sweet innocence must recognize as offputting to anyone with pretensions to gentility. That is not quite the point I am desirous of making, either. Your mother and your Bradshaw grandparents,

12

with my assistance, I admit, and Barnaby's, have kept you from the harsher realities of life faced by every other well-born female. The fact, drummed into the ears of each and every girl infant blessed with either fortune or breeding or merely great beauty, is simply the necessity to marry well."

Annalise twisted the fringe on her shawl. "I take it you are speaking of arranged marriages, arranged for the convenience of the families instead of for the young people involved. Titles are exchanged for riches, lands are joined, successions are assured without considering the feelings of those who must spend their lives together."

"Precisely. Great happiness is often found in these marriages, and if not"—another casual wave of his hand—"other arrangements can be made. Less regular, but highly rewarding."

"If you are suggesting that I contemplate wedding someone only to . . . to forswear my vows, then I shan't listen."

"Why, I would never suggest you compromise your morals, my dear, I am simply trying to make a bitter pill go down easier. You see, you have foolishly been led to believe that you could marry to please yourself."

"My parents did, and I intend to do the same."

"Ah, yes. Your parents, the perfect example. Sweet Caroline followed her heart—right into disaster!"

"My father—"

"Is dead, so I shall not disparage his memory. Suffice it to say that Viscount Avery was cast off without a farthing for marrying a tradesman's daughter. And not just any trade, but coal, the dirtiest, sootiest trade of them all, considering how the ton hates getting its fingers dirty. Caroline was never accepted in his world, and he despised hers. The viscount took up gaming, you must know, and only his early death saved even Caroline's vast fortune from being whistled down the wind."

"My parents loved each other!"

"That was not enough. At least Caroline had the sense to accept my offer, so that you might be raised away from the smell of the shop."

"And you did not suffer from the marriage, either. I remember Thompson Hall was in shambles when we moved here from Grandfather's, and there were almost no servants."

"Precisely. An advantageous marriage for both parties. Just as your wedding to a well-respected landowner like Barnaby Coombes will benefit all of us."

"*I* do not respect Barnaby Coombes. I do not trust him, and I do not even like him very well anymore. I shall never marry him, no matter what you say. I shall marry for love, as my mother did, or not at all."

Sir Vernon studied his polished nails. "I never supposed you to be so buffle-headed, so perhaps I have not made myself clear even yet. You have no choice, Annalise."

"Of course I do," she said with a laugh. "Other men will be attracted to my dowry if nothing else. I am not quite on the shelf, you know, even if I am one and twenty."

"But I prefer Barnaby." Sir Vernon's words were softly spoken, but Annalise caught the steel behind them.

"You cannot force me to—"

"Yes, I can. That old fool Bradshaw used to be your guardian; now I alone have the right to bestow your hand, and not a court in the land can gainsay my choice. If we were not in such a backwater, I'd have had you wed while you were delirious with the fever. Our own Vicar Harding is above such irregular proceedings, unfortunately. He would be

14

affronted at the idea of a deathbed marriage unless I suggested you and Barnaby had anticipated the wedding night."

"You wouldn't!"

"Of course I would, child. Do not doubt it for a minute. A bit of laudanum ... a tearful plea for your soul's salvation. Had I known you to be such a willful chit, the deed would be done and we'd not need this tiresome little chat. That was my error, thinking you to be a biddable female like your mother." He sighed. "I shan't make the same mistake twice, so I'll have to journey to Town for a special license. So fatiguing, don't you know."

Annalise could not believe what she was hearing. They'd never shared much affection, but this ... this declaration of cold-blooded treachery sent tremors down her spine.

"You'll never get away with such villainy," she declared.

"Oh, no? Who will stop me? The servants whose salaries I pay? Or perhaps you think the Duke of Arvenell will come to the aid of a mongrel granddaughter now, when he wrote his son out of his will ages ago. Your mother showed me the letter he sent when she advised him of the viscount's death. Arvenell *thanked* her, Annalise, for having just the one daughter, so he never had to worry about the succession falling into tainted hands. No, the mighty duke is not about to leave Northumberland to cry halt to an unexceptionable wedding of an unacknowledged chit. Don't suppose any of the local gentry will interfere, either, not when I tell them how unbalanced you are by illness and grief. They'd only congratulate me on finding you such an understanding husband."

Annalise was trembling for real now. Perhaps she was still caught in the fever's nightmares. But no, Sir Vernon was pressing Barny's ring into her clenched fingers, fingers that had unraveled half the fringe on her shawl.

"The choice is yours, my dear," he was saying. "You can accept Barny's offer and have your charming little wedding in the village chapel next month after the banns are read, or you can expect my . . . solution to the dilemma. The outcome will be the same, my dear, never doubt it. I'll have your decision ás soon as I return next week with Barnaby and the special license."

Annalise was going to be long gone by then.

Chapter Three

"*H*ere's some nice gruel, Miss Avery."

"How about a little nap, Miss Avery? Are you sure you should be downstairs, ma'am?"

The servants must have been told Annalise was suffering a nervous decline from the brain fever, for they watched her and followed her about, speaking to her as if she were in the cradle or in her dotage. They were happy enough to humor her, fetching any number of books from the library, fresh flowers from the gardens, the most tempting delicacies from Cook's pantry, but not one would call a carriage for her.

"Oh, no, miss. Sir Vernon said you were much too ill to go afield. Doctor's orders, he said. Perhaps you'd like to see the latest fashion journals the master had sent from London for you?"

At least none of them objected when Annalise wanted to search the attics for old wigs and such. The entire staff knew the fate of her long blond locks and sympathized with poor miss, so gone off her looks that her handsome Mr. Coombes had ridden away in high dudgeon. Her maid and two footmen even helped carry down some ancient costume pieces, stuffing them in satchels and hatboxes, so miss could try them on later in the privacy of her room. Maybe that would raise her spirits.

Annalise raised the bandbox lid and stuffed in one more change of linen and another pair of sturdy shoes. Into the satchel she crammed her jewel box, miniatures of her parents, the jade horse, and her grandmother's journal, all cushioned by two heavy flannel nightgowns. She pulled on one of her old mourning gowns, then another on top of that. She was so thin her new riding habit, a green velvet picked to match her eyes, still buttoned over the two black dresses. A heavy wool cloak went over everything, the pockets weighted with a small pistol, a silver flask of Sir Vernon's finest contraband cognac, the contents of the household cash drawer, and as many lumps of sugar as she'd been able to pick up from the tea tray without drawing suspicion. Her own pin money was stashed in various inside pockets of the several layers of clothing, along with the thin stack of letters Sir Vernon must never find.

Annalise did leave him a note saying that she was running away to Bath to find Signor Maginelli, the music instructor who had begged her to elope with him last Christmas. She also left her entire trousseau, and Barny's ring. Adjusting the wig on her head one last time, she gathered up her parcels and locked the bedroom door behind her. She placed two wig cases outside the door to be returned to the attics, indicating that she was not to be disturbed till morning, then she crept down the stairs while the servants were at supper.

The hard part was saddling her half-Arabian mare Seraphina before the stable lads came back for their nightly dice game. No amount of sugar was going to keep the spirited animal from cavorting around in welcome to her long-missing owner.

"Hush, you silly, hush! I missed you, too. Now stand still, and we'll have a nice long run. Hush, beauty."

At last Annalise was done, the mare daintily sidestepping at the unfamiliar packages tied to the saddle. She whickered softly when Annalise led another chestnut mare into the Arabian's vacant stall. "No, she's not as pretty as you, my darling, but in the dark she'll do. Now come, Seraphina, just a few more minutes of quiet, then we can fly. No one will ever catch us."

Especially not with all the loose bridles locked in a tack box, the key tossed into a pile of manure.

They rode through the home woods, picking their way cautiously around fallen trees and rabbit holes, then cross-country over fields and pastures. At last they were beyond Sir Vernon's boundaries, with the main road just ahead. Annalise laughed out loud and Seraphina reared on her hind legs, then dashed forward, not south toward Bath, however, but north toward the market village of Upper Morden. Annalise laughed again, causing a weary farmer to cross himself and a goose girl to run down the lane, screaming about haunts in the woods. A poacher just setting out at dusk decided to return home. This was not a night to be testing one's luck, not with any White Lady abroad, riding astride like all the hounds of hell were after her and her devil horse. Worse, she was yowling like a banshee, with bundles of souls flapping beside her and a great dark cape billowing behind. She and the horse and the cape were all shrouded in an eerie white fog.

The only wig Annalise had considered suitable for her purposes was a towering edifice à la Marie Antoinette. Well powdered, of course.

She discarded the wig behind a hedgerow outside Upper Morden and tied on a close-fitting dark bonnet. She walked Seraphina right through the main street and tied her to the rear of the Findleys' Two Rose Tavern. Mrs. Findley herself bustled over to the back entry where Annalise stood, drawing the dark woolen cape more firmly over the green of her riding habit.

" 'Ere now, we run a proper establishment. We don't let none of your sort in this—criminy, Miss Avery, is it?" She looked behind Annalise as if the girl were hiding a maid and two footmen behind her skirts. "And out alone? I swann, that's a rare to-do. What's the world coming to, I want to know, when proper young females go racketing about the countryside after dark on their ownsomes?"

Annalise was gently steering the portly landlady down the hall toward the private parlors, away from the public taproom. "Please," she whispered, though not terribly softly, "I need your help. I am running away."

Mrs. Findley's mouth hung so wide, a swallow could have nested there. "I swann."

Annalise tucked a coin in Mrs. Findley's fat hand. "It's not as improper as an elopement or anything. My grandfather is sending a coach to take me north. My grandfather, his grace the Duke of Arvenell, that is. I need to wait in your back parlor for just an hour or so. Will that be all right?" She held out another coin, which quickly followed the path of the first down a slide between mounding bosoms.

"What about Sir Vernon?" Mrs. Findley whispered so loudly that only the passed-out louts in the alehouse missed her words.

Annalise hid her smile by staring at her riding boots. "You mustn't tell Sir Vernon. He . . . he wants to marry me against my will." Which wasn't a lie, just misleading. It was enough to send Mrs. Findley's massive chest heaving.

"Lawkes a mercy! That bounder! That Coombes fellow was bad, always sniffing round the serving girls, but this is outside of enough, I swann! I get my hands on that makebait, he'll wish his parents never met. You come this way, dearie, where no one'll bother you till your granfer comes. A real dook, too? I swann."

Annalise was right where she wanted to be, in the Findleys' own parlor, with its own rear door. She ate the bread and cheese a wide-eyed serving girl brought, and waited for full darkness and a full taproom, judging from the noise. She left another coin, then she stepped outside, asking a passing ostler the way to the necessary.

This time Annalise kept the mare to a quiet walk through the back alleys of Upper Morden. Then she took every deserted lane and cowtrack she knew, keeping to the trees when she heard a carriage or another horseman, until she was nearly back to Thompson Hall. At the edge of exhaustion, she rode through the home woods and down a quiet path that skirted the home farm and the tenants' houses. Annalise could barely keep her head from collapsing onto Seraphina's neck when she finally saw the glow of candles from a cottage that stood all by itself in a clearing. She smiled. Sir Vernon was wrong; there *were* people who would help her.

In times of dismay, disillusionment, and dire peril, a body needed three things: love, loyalty, and larceny. Annalise's old nanny, Mrs. Hennipicker, was sure to provide unquestioned love, unquestioning loyalty—and hot soup. Henny's husband, Rob, was a retired highwayman. What better allies could a fugitive find?

"What are you, girl, dicked in the nob? Stealin'

a horse and the household money, tellin' whiskers up and down the pike, gallopin' like a goblin acrost the countryside. And for what? So's you don't have to marry your childhood sweetheart, 'cause he's been gatherin' his own bloomin' rosebuds, and so's your step-da can't steal the money old man Bradshaw stole from the poor sods who worked his coal mines." Rob spit tobacco juice into the hearth and went back to trimming his beard with a knife. "I thought you had more sense'n a duck. Guess I was wrong, chickie."

"Whisht, Rob, leave the poor thing be. Can't you see she's plumb tuckered? You go on and hitch up the wagon. It's too cold for missy to ride home in her weakened condition."

So much for love and loyalty.

"I'll have a little talk with your Barnaby afore the wedding if you want," Rob offered, holding the shining blade to the fire's light. "Convince him of the error of his ways for you. Worked fine on that nasty billy goat old Trant used to let roam loose. Of course old Trant's nannies ain't had no kids since then. . . ."

And minor illegalities.

Bribery wouldn't work; Rob likely had three times her jewels and coins stashed away in the secret compartments of the cottage, from his days on the high toby. Threats would never do the trick, either; she hadn't cried rope on Rob for thirteen years, and they all knew she'd never go to the authorities now, even if she weren't a runaway herself. Nanny always said, "Crying don't pay the piper," so tears would be useless, should Annalise find the energy to produce them. That left only honor. It was a hard hand to play, and only one trump left.

Annalise put her high card on the table: "You owe me, Rob Hennipicker."

Rob put the knife down and winked at his wife. "I told you she had bottom, Henny, didn't I? You fatten our girl up whilst I go see about hidin' that pretty little mare."

Annalise had to use the corner of her cloak to wipe her eyes. With all the miscellany in her pockets she could not find a handkerchief. "You and Rob were going to help me get away the whole time, weren't you?"

"Of course we were, poppet, we just had to make sure that was what you really wanted." Henny put a steaming bowl of stew in front of Annalise, clucking her tongue about how those fools at Thompson Hall were letting her baby waste away to nothing. She brought over a thick slice of bread and began buttering it. "You wouldn't have called in that old debt if you hadn't been desperate. We all know that."

Many years ago, when Annalise's father was still alive, he rented a place in Brighton to be near the ton's wealthy gamesters for the summer. The viscount and Lady Avery went ahead, with the baggage and their personal servants in a second carriage. Eight-year-old Annalise was prone to travel sickness, so she and her nursemaid, Mrs. Hennipicker, traveled at a slower speed in a hired chaise. Henny was deathly afraid of being set upon by the highwaymen plaguing the Brighton road, but the hired driver and his arrogant young footman made light of her fears.

"G'wan with you," the old coachman wheezed, "most of the ladies is pleased to give their baubles to a gentleman of the road."

"Especially that brazen Robin fellow," the footman added, taking another swig from the jug he refilled at every rest stop. "The one what kisses the ladies' 'ands an' calls 'em 'chickie.' Cock Robin is what they're callin' 'im, on account a' that an' 'ow cocky 'e is, but you don't 'ave to worry none. 'E's only interested in women what got jewels or looks. All you got's an ivory-tuner's brat an' a sour puss."

Annalise stuck her tongue out at the rudesby; Henny let her get away with it.

They were not set upon by highwaymen after all. Instead, the ancient driver wheezed his last right there on the box of their carriage. The footman sitting beside him was so castaway by then, he never even attempted to catch the ribbons as they fell from the coachman's lifeless fingers. He just jumped off the box. What was a bad situation was going downhill quickly. And literally. The horses were panicky, the road was steep with a sharp curve at the bottom of the incline. The horses might make the turn; the coach never would, not without someone's hands on the brake.

Now Robin Tuthill never made it his business to hold up drab and dusty hired chaises. Not worth the risk. And he surely never made it a habit to stop runaway coaches. No money in that at all. But there was something about the screams of a woman and child, coming to him as he sat his horse at the top of the hill, that just ripped away at his heart. Before he could wonder if there'd be a reward, he was digging his heels into his stallion's sides and taking off after the careening coach. With her head out the window, Annalise could see everything, how the caped rider pulled even with the frantic horses and strained to reach the reins. How he stood in the saddle of his own galloping mount, then leapt up to the box of the coach and pulled with all his strength. How the foaming horses made the turn as sweet as pie, and the carriage barely rocked going around the corner.

"You saved us, sir!" Henny was crying as their

rescuer opened the coach door. "How can I ever thank you?"

"Don't fatch yourself, chickie, the pleasure was mine."

Chickie? Henny collapsed in a dead faint, right into Robin's arms. Oh, Lud, that's what a fellow got for not minding his own business. Then he looked up, and it was love at first sight—between his fierce black stallion and a tiny golden-curled moppet who was feeding the unruly beast a peppermint candy from her pocket. Now, what was an honest bridle cull to do? He couldn't go off and leave an unconscious nanny and her little charge out there with a dead coachman and, unless he missed his guess, a broken-necked groom. On the other hand, someone would be coming, there was no cover on this stretch of the road, and his own horse was winded.

At this point the debt was entirely Miss Avery's, until she led his horse back to Robin, looked up at him with innocent green eyes, and sweetly inquired, "Do you really like being a highwayman? If not, I have an idea . . ."

So Robin Tuthill, wearing the footman's livery, drove the ladies into the next village to report that the notorious Cock Robin lay dead on the road a few miles back, having fallen from his horse during an attempt to waylay their carriage. Their poor driver had had a seizure during the holdup. A new driver and groom were hired. Two months later Robin became Rob Hennipicker, Henny's long-lost husband, home from the sea with a comfortable nest egg from prize money, and a fine, full beard. After they'd all moved to Worcester, Rob built Henny a little cottage and set up pig farming.

"So now, chickie, what's to do? We can tuck you away in the tunnel beneath the cottage until Sir Vernon comes to his senses, but with the kind of blunt involved, you could sprout roots and turn into a mushroom quicker."

"It's too damp, Rob. Remember, the girl's been sick."

Annalise smiled, revived by Henny's stew. "No, I'd have to stay hidden away in your bolthole for four years, until I reach my majority. Even marriage to Barny might be preferable to that. I don't have enough money to keep myself for that long, either, not even in a tiny cottage, and no, I will not take any part of your, ah, pension. I have a better idea anyway."

Rob spit into the fire and grinned. "And here I was thinkin' I'd have to take up the profession again, it was gettin' so quiet around these parts."

"I'd take my skillet to the side of your head, Rob Hennipicker, and well you know it. So just hush and listen to what the child has to say."

"Henny, I'm not a child! I'm twenty-one, well past the age to be married and a mother in my own right. That's the whole problem, don't you see? If I hide away until I am twenty-five, I'll never find a husband." She fumbled through one pocket after another, handing the silver flask over to Rob, until she located the packet of letters. She waved them triumphantly and announced, "I am going to go live with Aunt Ros in London!"

"But, Miss Annalise, I thought you never heard from her anymore, not since Sir Vernon forbade your mother to correspond with her. That was years ago, right after they got married."

"No matter, she's been at the same address forever, and she was always inviting me to come visit. And her particular friend Lord Elphinstone is very high in the government. Surely with his influence something can be done about my stepfather's guardianship. So I only need your help in getting to London."

"Only? When every man, woman, and sheriff'll be out looking for you soon as Sir Vernon puts out the word and the reward? A' course here'll be the first place he'll look, so we don't have half to worry about, now do we, chickie? 'Sides, seems to me this Aunt Ros of yourn blotted her copybook onct herself. I'm not sure she's fit to be in charge of you and your cork-brained schemes."

Annalise refuted that argument with a snap of her fingers. "Pooh. That's just Sir Vernon's priggery. And the Duke of Arvenell's. You know what kind of man he is by the way he disowned his children. All Aunt Ros did was refuse to marry the man he chose for her. She *has* to take me in!"

Chapter Four

$\mathcal{U}$nfortunately, Lady Ros was not in London. She and Lord Elphinstone had traveled to Vienna for the peace talks and parties.

This bit of news was one crushing blow too many for Annalise. She was cold, hungry, tired, and frightened. Crying still wouldn't help, so as soon as the helpful watchman went on along his beat, Annalise kicked at the locked door of Aunt Ros's small, tidy town house at Number Eleven, Laurel Street. Then she limped back to the hackney carriage where Henny and Rob waited. The devil fly away with it, she thought, they'd worked so hard just to get to London!

They'd waited at the cottage long enough for Sir Vernon to throw Rob off his land.

"Iffen we leave afore he gets back, he'll move heaven and earth to find us," Rob said. "You can put your blunt on that. The man's mean, he ain't stupid. 'Sides, I got preparations to make."

Annalise didn't ask what those preparations

were; Henny advised her it was better not to know. Rob promised Seraphina was safe and would be waiting in London when they arrived, and that was enough. Annalise slept the time away in her hidden little cubby behind the kitchen pantry, waking only to swallow the hot soup Henny kept bringing.

The retired highwayman was right: the cottage was the first place Sir Vernon looked, after sending men north to Arvenell and south to Bath. He arrived with the magistrate and three brawny grooms.

"Don't see no writ for a search," Rob said.

"I don't need one," Sir Vernon replied, holding a lace-edged handkerchief over his nose. "It's my property."

"Seems to me just the land is yourn, on rent. You know I built this cottage on my own." The magistrate, Squire Bromley, was looking uncomfortable, so Rob went on: "No matter. I got nothin' to hide. Go ahead, boys, look your fill. You find any sweet young thing under the bed, just don't tell m'wife."

So the men made a halfhearted search, Henny following them about, threatening to comb their hair with her footstool if they so much as disturbed her pressed linens and stacked preserves.

"If she's not here, Bromley, then this man helped my stepdaughter escape, a minor female, out of her wits and sickly. I demand you arrest him and hold him till he reveals her whereabouts."

Henny started weeping into her apron, and the magistrate was shifting from foot to foot.

"And when you think about doin' that, Squire, think about what himself's done to make a gently reared female run off that way, and straight from the sickroom, too."

"The chit's dicked in the nob, that's all. Her nerves came unhinged from the fever, so she doesn't know what she's doing. It's obvious the dear girl needs a keeper," Thompson insisted. "I intend to see she's held safe and secure as soon as we find her."

"Aye, clappin' the poor lass in Bedlam'd suit you to a cow's thumb, wouldn't it? Then there'd be no one to ask about all that inheritance money."

"Why, you, you . . ." Sir Vernon looked around and noticed the interested grooms. "I want you off my property, you swine. There's always been something havey-cavey about you anyway. No common seaman I ever heard of made enough prize money to live so well."

The bearded farmer spit tobacco juice, missing Sir Vernon's highly polished boots by a good half inch. "Mayhap I weren't so common. And mayhap I kept back enough of my winnings to hire me a fancy advocate, in case some jumped-up toff tries to bring false charges 'gainst me, or tries to take my land without compensatin' me."

"My secretary will bring the rent refund tomorrow morning. Be gone by the evening." Sir Vernon stomped out of the cottage.

"What about my house that I built with my own two hands?" Rob called after him.

"Take it with you."

"I druther see it burn than leave it to the likes of you."

So they burned the cottage, after packing what they could onto a wagon, and after Henny made her farewells in the neighborhood, leaving her cousin's address in Swansea. "Her man's a fisherman, you know, and my Rob's been missing the sea for all these years. We were only staying to be near Miss Annalise anyways, and with her gone, and bad feeling from Sir Vernon, it's better this way. You come visit if you ever get to Wales."

Henny cried softly despite her own advice as they

drove away from the flaming building, even though there had been no choice. They couldn't leave the cottage standing, lest Sir Vernon come find the hidden chambers.

Annalise did not see the flames or the tears. She was tucked away under the wagon's false bottom.

They traveled slowly west, just another country couple in somber clothes. They bought food in the village shops or from housewives rather than from taverns, and they paid a shilling or two to sleep in barns instead of inns. Before Hereford, Henny got down with her portmanteau and walked the last quarter mile into town, where she purchased an inside seat on the mail coach to Oxford. No one paid any mind to the nanny on her way to a new position.

Rob and Annalise took turns driving the wagon, just another country couple in somber clothes, traveling west for another half day. Then they turned south toward Gloucester, where they traded the wagon for a hooded carriage; Rob shaved his beard and donned a caped driving coat, and Annalise pinned a silk rose in her bonnet, veiled to keep the travel dust from her eyes and nose. They stopped at only the busiest posting houses, Mr. and Mrs. Robbins, off to Oxford to see the sights. They left Oxford in a hired coach, Rob and Henrietta Tuthill, taking their widowed niece to London to meet her in-laws. In the center of London they switched to a hackney, whose jarvey didn't care who the hell they were, so long as he saw the color of their money.

"Henny, have you ever seen so many people? Don't you think the smoke bothers them? Did you see that man dressed all in green?"

"Look, Miss Annalise, I swear that's the spires of Westminster itself!"

Rob frowned. "We ain't never goin' to get away

31

with this if you two can't remember your places. We made it so easy a goose could get it right. Annie and her auntie, and Uncle Rob. Unless you want to put a notice in the papers that Miss Annalise Avery's come to Town, chickie." He settled back on the squabs, his arms crossed over his chest.

"Pshaw, Robbie," Henny chided, "just because you're happy not to be Rob Hennipicker any longer, no reason to have your nose out of joint. I intend to enjoy my visit, see the sights, the Tower and Pall Mall and everything."

"And as soon as Aunt Ros and her friends hear my story, I'll be safe with my own name, Uncle Rob, so you can stop grizzling."

They passed through twisty, dirty streets, then broad avenues shaded with trees and wide thoroughfares choked with traffic. They saw mean slums, then vast open spaces with houses set in parks minutes apart, right in the middle of the city. After a while they left the fancier neighborhoods for narrower houses on narrower streets.

"This don't look like Mayfair," Rob grumbled.

"It isn't," Annalise answered. "Didn't you hear me give the driver the address? We're going to Laurel Street, Bloomsbury."

"Thought your aunt was Quality, knowing all the nobs. What's she doin' out in Bloomsbury?"

Henny looked out the window. "Oh, my, they sell near everything on every corner, don't they? Look at that, Robbie, fresh lavender and milk and—"

"Is Rosalind Avery respectable, or ain't she?"

Annalise answered: "I explained that the duke cast her off, remember? I never knew the whole story; it happened before my time. As far as I understand, Lady Rosalind was beautiful and in love with a handsome soldier, but her father wanted her to marry a crotchety old nobleman whose land marched with his. Aunt Ros tried to elope with her soldier instead, but they were stopped before reaching the border, but not before, uh . . ."

"I know what *uh* is, chickie."

"Papa always said she was just young and in love, like him and Mama. He said the Averys fell in love with their hearts, not their minds, but the Duke of Arvenell never did care about anything but the family name. So the handsome young soldier was sent back to the army, where he died. Aunt Ros refused to marry anyone else, which was of no account, I suppose, for the duke's choice refused to marry her since she was ruined, although there was no child. But Arvenell never forgave her, and she never forgave him, so she left home and came to London."

Henny nodded. "Leastways he didn't cut her off entirely. She had enough income to set up her own establishment, though not the first stare, naturally."

"And it was a brave thing to do, because most of her old friends cut her at first. Not all of them, though, not when they saw she wasn't setting herself up as a cyprian or anything."

Henny squealed, "Missy! What do you know about such things?"

"Enough to know my aunt would never be one! She's not invited to all the ton parties, of course, and the highest sticklers didn't recognize her when Mama was alive, but she is still Lady Rosalind Avery. Maybe they do now."

"And maybe they don't. Them niffy-naffy types have long memories."

"So what? Mama was not received, either, so I have no place in society anyway. Can you see Henry Bradshaw's granddaughter being invited to Almack's?"

"I can see the Duke of Arvenell's, for sure. And that's 'xactly what I thought I'd see when I agreed to this harebrained scheme. Not settin' you down on any primrose path with a fallen woman."

"Now, Rob," Henny put in, "Miss Annalise's mother always spoke highly of her sister-in-law, and she was real upset when Sir Vernon made her stop writing. Lady Rosalind led a quiet life, she said. I suppose she couldn't do much better on the portion she had."

"And I didn't come down in yesterday's rain, chickie. No gentry mort lives in Bloomsbury."

"Aunt Ros *is* respectable," Annalise protested, "and her friends *are* influential. You wait and see. Besides, until everything is settled, I'll be safer there, where it's quieter and away from all the gossip. No one will care tuppence about some hagridden female on the fringes of town."

"And when you get roses back in your cheeks and hair back on your head, chickie, what then? Where're you goin' to find any eligible part-ee to take you in hand, that's what I want to know. Not in Bloomsbury with some—"

"Mind your tongue, Robbie Tuthill."

Rob still grumbled. "Should of taken the womanizer. A little arsenic in his coffee, you could of been free in no time. That's why they call it widow powder, ain't it?"

Annalise could not look Rob in the eye when she reached the carriage and had to tell him what the watchman had said, that Aunt Ros was traveling abroad with a gentleman friend. "Of course there must be some innocent explanation," she added, wishing she had the imagination to conjure one up. More important, what were they to do now? Her friends had already given up their home for her. How much more could she ask? "Do you think we should try to find her in Vienna?"

"Thompson's sure to be having the ports watched.

'Sides, I ain't never been on no boat, and I ain't goin' on no boat now. Good Lord wanted men to swim, He'd of given us gills."

"Pshaw, Robbie, and here I've been telling everyone back home we were off to the coast so you could go fishing!"

"Cut your nattering, woman, and let me think."

"Well, do your thinking in a hurry, Robbie Tuthill, for this coach is passing damp, and Miss—Annie needs to be in a warm bed. All that jouncing around in the cold and wet, and eating what I wouldn't toss to the pigs, why, I can see my lamb fading right away."

Annalise bit her lip. Henny's shorn lamb would fare even less well locked away in some insane asylum for the rest of her bound-to-be-short life. She'd heard of such things, unscrupulous physicians taking money to declare an unwanted family member mad. Right now Annalise was so mad, she could just—

The door of Number Eleven, Laurel Street opened and a young girl in a gray uniform with white apron and cap peered out. "Was it you knocked on the door a minute ago?" she called over to the carriage. "I was on the ladder, doing the chandelier."

The maid's name was Lorna, and she allowed as how the travelers could rest in the kitchen for a bit, the younger female looking so pulled and all. Of course they had to be gone by four o'clock, when a young lord was coming to look the place over to rent, she told them, happy to have someone to talk to. And she wouldn't mind a hand with moving the heavy furniture at all, because she was hoping his lordship would keep her on as daytime help if the house met with his approval. "Of course he'll still need to hire a housekeeper and a cook and a man of all work. Was you folks interested in the positions?"

Chapter Five

*R*oss Montclaire, the sixth Earl of Gardiner, loved women. All women. Tall or small, lithe or rounded, haughty or shy, exquisite or plain. He loved the way they moved, the way they smelled, the way their emotions were written on their faces, the way they played off their charms for a man. Old ladies delighted him; tiny moppets enchanted him. The only females he did not enjoy were the predatory debutantes on the Marriage Mart and their ambitious mamas. Luckily, he never encountered these greedy, grasping representatives of the fair sex in his rambles through London. In fact, he avoided the polite world's piranhas like the plague. Worse, for if there were a plague, he would offer to help bury the dead; Lord Gardiner could not even bear to witness his friends' weddings.

The earl's friends, those still speaking to him after his refusal to attend their nuptials, called him Gard. The broadsides and scandal sheets called him Earl en Garde, because he was always ready. The duels they referred to were not affairs of honor, either, simply affairs: the *duello d'amore*, whose field of honor was a bed, a couch, a closed carriage, or a blanket in the woods, the eternal skirmish from which both combatants rose satisfied, if the *passage d'arms* was conducted properly. Ross Montclaire was everything proper, and he never received a challenge he didn't meet.

Like the bee that goes from flower to flower, the earl visited woman after woman, never bruising the most fragile blossom, never staying longer than the sharing of a sunbeam. He might return, but a single bloom never held him long, much to the rosebuds' regrets.

When Lord Gardiner was not paying homage to his ladyloves with his body, he was worshipping them with his pencil. He sometimes got so lost in the beauties of a woman's form that he forgot her function there in his bed for hours on end. Well, minutes on end. Heirs to earldoms seldom being encouraged to pursue artistic careers, Ross was not as fine a draftsman as more advanced technical training could have made him. Practice, however, made him outstanding in this field, too. The faces of his portraits may have been mere rough likenesses of their models, but, oh, the bodies were perfect in their infinite variations. An unexpected dimple here, a softer fold there; the earl took endless delight in his two favorite pastimes.

Ross Montclaire, my lord Gardiner, was a rake of the first order. Then his mother came to Town.

The earl was as close to his mother as most noblemen with one and thirty years in their dish. Like most of his fellows, he'd been sent off with wet nurses, nannies, and tutors, then to boarding schools and university, grand tours and a stint in the army. His later years were spent between house parties, hunting boxes, and bachelor digs, with occasional appearances at his far-flung properties and his seat in Parliament. Which is to say, Gard might be able to sketch his mother's face from memory. Or he mightn't. He did love and respect Countess Stephania, naturally. She was his lady mother; he was a proper son.

"You are the most unnatural child a woman could bear!" the diminutive dowager screeched, beating her much larger son about the head and shoulders with her cane. "Where are my grandchildren? Where is the successor to your title? Do you think I suffered with your great hulk for nine months just so you could become a byword in the gossip columns? That's not why a woman has children, you dolt! She has them so her husband leaves her alone—from the grave, you jackaninny. Your father is disturbing my rest again!"

Ross tried not to laugh as he easily fended off his mother's thrusts. The late earl, Sebastian Montclaire, often cut up his lady's peace, it seemed, especially when Lady Gardiner was dissatisfied with her allowance, her life as doyenne of Bath society, or, most commonly, her son.

"Sebastian cannot be happy knowing his heir is a profligate here-and-thereian," the countess pronounced, finally accepting an Adams chair in the Gold Parlor. "And I deserve to have little ones playing about my skirts."

The last thing the countess would have permitted, her son considered as he rang for tea, was sticky fingers on her elegant gros de Naples ensemble. Nevertheless, she seemed determined to make Ross's life a misery. She was in London, the dowager announced, to make sure he reformed. This time she would see he attended correct gatherings, met suitable females, settled down to begin his nursery.

"Your past behavior outrages and offends my every proper feeling as a mother," she continued after Foggarty, the butler, wheeled in the tea tray. Eyeing the almond tarts, macaroons, and poppy-seed cake, Lady Stephania slammed her delicate cup down in its saucer. "How can I eat, looking at my only son, knowing he has just recently left some doxie's arms?"

So Gard made sure the dowager's digestion did not suffer. He left. Since his presence seemed to displease the countess, and he was nothing if not a considerate son, the earl stayed as far away from her as possible, which was far indeed in the clubs and stews of London, and the vast reaches of Gardiner House, Grosvenor Square.

The dowager bribed the servants to discover her son's location; he threatened them with dismissal if they divulged his hideouts. Ross came in after she was abed and left before she was awake. Peace reigned. If the fifth earl walked the halls at night, the sixth one never met him in the darkened corridors.

The system worked fairly well until the night of Diccon Inwood's birthday celebration. Lord Gardiner found himself having a late supper at Hazlett's with his closest comrades and half the Royal Theatre's *corps de ballet*, the most comely half. *Esprit* was running high after the sweets course and after numerous bottles of champagne, when the guest of honor turned to his dinner partner and declared, "You're as pretty as a picture, *chérie*." Which wasn't terribly original for a gentleman hoping to entice a female to his rooms for another bit of dessert. Considering how castaway Lord Inwood was at the time, however, his friends were impressed with his finesse as he continued: "Not even Bottle . . . Botti . . . Michelangelo could capture your incredible beauty."

To which Lord Gardiner's best friend Cholly, otherwise known as the Honorable Charlton Fansoll, replied, "Gard could do her justice."

Some of the other revelers remembered Lord Gardiner's clever renderings from their Oxford days and quickly followed Inwood's plea that Gard do a portrait of his *belle amie* with clamors of their own. No one wanted to be behind times with the girls, who seemed entranced with the idea. Zeus, it was cheaper to buy old Gard another round than to spring for a pair of diamond earbobs. But old Gard couldn't do all the fair charmers' pictures, especially when they seemed to multiply in front of his eyes, so he offered an alternative. He'd give the fellows a few pointers, lend a more practiced if no steadier hand so they could each draw their own lady. The suggestion was received with applause and laughter, and quickly evolved into a bet, as was wont to occur among these bucks and sporting bloods of the Corinthian set. The best portrait would win ten pounds from each of the wagerers, half to the artist, half to the model. Gard could judge, since he was too good to compete. The only problem was that they needed more room than Hazlett's private dining parlor could provide, and a few props and drawing materials, all of which were in ample supply at Gardiner House in Grosvenor Square.

The earl was very considerate of his staff, most of whom had been at Gardiner House longer than he had. He always sent his valet, Ingraham, to bed when he left for the evening, scandalizing the old man with tales of how many times he'd be in and out of his clothes that night without his valet's assistance. Lord Gardiner also refused to permit Foggarty to stay on duty all night just to open the door, when Gard had a very fine key in his pocket, so no one met his lordship's party in the marbled hall.

They tiptoed past a gape-jawed night footman on their way to the grand ballroom, miles away from the family wing of the huge pile. The footman's only prior function, as far as Lord Gardiner could tell, was to report back to the countess what time her erring son returned and whether his neckcloth was tied correctly. Tonight the clunch could earn his keep lighting candles, laying fires, and fetching the earl's pads and charcoals. Gard and Cholly made forays to the wine cellar and the conservatory while the other gentlemen shifted a plant stand or two and helped the dancers remove Holland covers from the gilt chairs and satin-covered love seats.

"Gentlemen," Gard finally announced, "in the interest of fairness, I have established some criteria for the judging. Artistic composition and depth of expression shall be counted as well as execution."

"What the deuce are you talking about, Gard?" Cholly asked for the rest, who were shaking their heads and looking more confused than foxed.

"That it doesn't have to look like your ladybird, you gudgeon, it just has to be a good picture. That way you can use your imaginations, if you have any, even if you haven't much skill. You have one hour. On your mark . . ."

Soon there were naked ladies with roses in their teeth, naked ladies draped creatively across gilt chairs. Ballerinas had remarkable flexibility, surprising even the connoisseur earl. One dancer was wearing the gauntlets from a suit of armor and nothing else; one was en pointe on a plaster pedestal. There were more chuckles than concentration on the other side of the makeshift easels.

"Drawing class was never like this," Lord Inwood laughed as the earl made his way around the room, straightening a line, adjusting a pose. He offered a suggestion here, a bit of gauze there, a kiss or a pat of encouragement to all the models. Ah, the joy of Art.

"Cholly, you've given her three arms! Nice pose, Lockhart, but you're not supposed to be in the picture with Chou-Chou; get back to your drawing. Hello, Mother. No, Nigel, you're supposed to draw on the paper, not on the model." Hello, Mother?

More lightskirts went home in Holland covers that night than in the entire history of British shipping. Someone had the presence of mind to extinguish most of the candles. They were just a tad too late, however, to prevent some of London's choicest spirits from witnessing the Dowager Countess Gardiner, five feet from the tips of her embroidered slippers to the curl papers in her silvered hair, attack her six-foot-plus son with a fireplace poker.

By way of remorse, Gard sat through three lectures about not fouling one's own nest and two secondhand visitations from his father's uneasy spirit. In the end, just to win a modicum of peace for his aching head, he even agreed to accompany Lady Stephania to a few tonnish parties and to consider—consider, mind!—looking around for a suitable countess.

The balls were as awful as he recalled, too hot, too crowded, too many rules. The refreshments were more fashionable than filling, the table stakes were low, the dance floor stakes were high. He no sooner asked a young lady for a dance than her name was linked to his in the morning's papers. Her mother was calling him "dear" and her father was telling him when he could call. And the debutantes were as insipid as the lemonade they drank, while their older sisters, the established Beauties, were as cold as the ices from Gunther's every hostess served. Raspberry, lemon, the only difference was in the color of their dresses. As for the dresses themselves, those low necklines and dampened skirts did nothing to reconcile Lord Gardiner to leg shackles. A fellow didn't choose his wife from a row of Covent Garden whores, and the whores at least provided what they promised. The price for these highborn high flyers was too costly.

Those same clinging gowns and plunging bodices did arouse a bit more than Lord Gardiner's ire, however, so he picked up a few of the hankies dropped at his feet by dashing widows and daring wives. He gathered his rosebuds where he may.

A sennight or so later, he hobbled into White's.

Chapter Six

"*D*euce take it, man," his friend Cholly asked; "what happened? Did Lady Stephania light into you again? I thought you were reformed."

Gard carefully lowered himself into one of the leather chairs and signaled for a waiter. One ankle was strapped, one eye was blackened, and, most unfortunate of all in his lordship's opinion, he had a fiercesome rash where he sat. He did not bother answering Cholly's remark about the dowager: less said, soonest mended. Not soon enough for his battered skull.

Cholly was observing him through a quizzing glass. "Can't believe you turned your curricle over, nonpareil whip like you. Does the Four-Horse Club know?"

"Cut line, Cholly. You look like one of those blasted dandies. Put that silly thing away and I'll tell you what happened." Ross leaned his head back against the cushions and sniffed at the aged cognac the servant brought. "Ah," he sighed, swirling the dark liquor around in the glass while his friend waited impatiently. At last Lord Gardiner took a swallow of his drink, savoring the flavor. "I have indeed been a paragon of virtue," he finally confirmed. "No opera dancers, no chorus girls, no bits of muslin."

"What, no females at all?" Cholly nearly choked on his own drink.

The earl looked down his aristocratic nose, which was just slightly out of line. "That's not what I said. At Mother's insistence I frequented the haut monde instead of the demimonde."

"Nearly took a turn seeing you at Lady Bessborough's."

"Precisely. So all of my, ah, companions this past week have been *ladies*." He took another sip. "And see what it's gained me."

Cholly nodded his head in sympathy. "They're the devil when it comes to being crossed. Why, m'sisters—"

"No, the women didn't wreak such havoc on my body, not directly, at any rate. This"—he indicated the leg propped on a footstool in front of him—"I received when I was forced to climb out a window. The *lady's* husband came home unexpectedly. The trellis broke, equally unexpectedly, by George. My face, on another night, was rearranged by footpads."

"Jupiter, I would have thought you were too downy a bird by now to be taken like that."

"And so I thought, too, but it was four in the morning with not a hackney to be seen, if a person could have seen anything through the fog. I had sent Mother off from Lady Bessborough's in our carriage, and then accepted a ride home—her home, naturally—from a certain widow who shall, of course, remain nameless."

"Of course," Cholly echoed, searching his mind for likely candidates.

"A widow who is received in all the best drawing rooms, incidentally. I must say I was delighted with her charms, until she rudely shoved me awake and out of her bed. The servants mustn't see me there when they lit the fires in the morning. The *lady's* reputation would suffer." He took another sip of the brandy.

"But what of the footpads?"

"I think they'll be more careful picking their target in the future. Just because a chap is clunch enough to leave a warm bed in the middle of a cold night doesn't mean he's an easy mark." Lord Gardiner ran his fingers through his dark curls, wincing at the lumps and bruises. He couldn't tell which were from the attempted robbers, which remnants from the dowager's fire poker. "And that's not the worst of it," he confessed.

Cholly refilled his own empty glass. "Deuce take it, there's more?"

The earl shifted uncomfortably on his chair. He nodded. "There was one more *lady*. A regular dasher, with some old dragon living with her to lend countenance. Bold as brass she asks me to take her for a ride in the country while the dragon visits an ailing cousin. She wants me to pull in at a quaint little inn she knows outside of town. *Quaint* wasn't the word I'd have used. Rundown, ramshackle maybe, not quaint. And you know how I never stay at even mediocre inns."

Cholly was starting to smile. "And I know the way your man Ingraham is always following you around with your own bed linen and stuff. Tender skin, ain't it?"

The earl flicked a speck of dust off his dark sleeve. "But the jade says that way she can be sure no one will recognize her, so I take a room. Blast it, quit laughing, she was a convincing armful!"

"And?"

"And those sheets were so filthy, my butt's the color of a baboon's behind!"

When Cholly finished wiping his eyes, he told the earl, "What you need is a wife!"

"I need a wife like your picture of Babette needed that third arm. What's a rash compared to a nose ring?"

Cholly put his handkerchief away. "Mightn't be so bad, y'know."

"What? I can't believe my ears! Never say you're thinking of becoming a tenant for life?"

"Been thinking, that's all. 'Sides, who'd have me? I'm just a second son with a houseful of sisters, and m'brother's already filling his nursery with heirs. Ain't got a fortune, no title to trade for one, so no nabob's going to hand me his daughter. Wouldn't want an heiress anyway; don't fancy living under the cat's paw." He considered his friend's tall, athletic form and chiseled features that were only made more interesting by the purplish bruises. Then he contemplated his own short, stocky body and carroty hair. "Ain't got your looks, and never did have your way with the ladies. Still, we're not getting any younger. All I've got to offer is a comfortable income. If I found a comfortable female, I just might take the plunge."

"Dash it, marriage isn't a bath you can jump out of if the water's too cold! It's for deuced eternity!"

Cholly nodded sagely. No argument there. "If you won't take a wife, then how about a mistress?"

"What, a fixed arrangement? Hell, if I wanted to be faithful to the same woman day after day, I'd get married."

Cholly choked. "You mean you intend to be constant when you're hitched? You?"

"Why not? I'd expect my wife to be." Gard ignored his friend's sputtering. "No, mistresses are more trouble than wives, greedier and harder to please. They're always throwing jealous tantrums and they're impossible to get rid of. No wife of mine would expect me to live in her pocket, and she'd dashed better be too well-bred to get into distempered freaks. No, thank you, the carefree bachelor life suits me fine."

Cholly raised his quizzing glass again. "Looks to me instead like the tomcatting is killing you, creeping down alleys and over windowsills. What you need is an establishment of your own."

The earl resented his friend's inference that he needed taking care of. "Have you forgotten Gardiner House? It's a little hard to miss if you happen to be near Grosvenor Square."

"No, I mean a pied-à-terre, a little place you can come and go, private like. Discreet."

The earl called for another bottle. "A *bijou*. Interesting. I could fix the place up the way I like, even set up a little drawing studio. I could hire a whole new staff of servants who wouldn't carry tales."

Cholly smiled. "And who'd make sure the sheets are clean."

Gard laughed, too. "Can you imagine me asking poor old Ingraham to carry fresh linens to a house of convenience? He'd have a spasm."

"Should have pensioned off the chap years ago if he disapproves of you."

"I can't. The man valeted my own father. Frankly, it would be a relief not to see his disappointment every day. I'm getting to like your idea more and more. Still, I could make the love nest so cozy, the birds of paradise might want to take up permanent residence. They're deuced difficult to dislodge, you know."

"Blister it, you have the butler send 'em to the rightabout if you're too tender-hearted."

They both laughed at the picture of the elderly Gardiner butler giving some courtesan her *congé*. Old Foggarty was another long-time employee who refused to leave the earl's service, he and Ingraham having nowhere else to go. "Lord save me from loyal old family retainers."

Cholly stared at the tassels on his Hessians. "Seems to me you could keep any of the ladybirds from settling in if you told them right out the arrangement was only temporary, that you were just renting the place. I recall hearing that Elphinstone's digs out in Bloomsbury are for let."

"Someone mentioned that he went with the delegation to Vienna. I didn't realize Lady Rosalind went with him."

"Should have. Inseparable, don't you know."

"And you say their house is out in Bloomsbury . . . ?"

The town house could have fit into the entry hall of the earl's principal seat in Suffolk, but it was well maintained and respectable-looking. The street was quiet, with trees and flowers, and mothers pushing prams. The man who came to take Lord Gardiner's horses was middle-aged, neatly dressed, and clean-shaven. He seemed knowledgeably appreciative of the earl's prime-goers.

"Shall I take these beauties back to the mews, gov'nor, or just around the block so's they don't cool down?"

"Can you drive?"

The man carefully aimed a stream of tobacco juice between rows of pansies. "Anything with wheels."

"And can you keep a still tongue in your head?"

"I reckon so," the one-time Cock Robin said with

a grin. "If Rob Tuthill can't keep his mummers dubbed, then no one can."

Lord Gardiner watched Tuthill drive the curricle away with consummate skill. He was liking this notion better and better. He'd have to remember to invite Cholly to his first not-so-intimate gathering.

A dimpled little maid opened the door for him, took his beaver and gloves, and showed him to the parlor. "I be Lorna, milord. I come in days. Would you please to wait in the parlor while I fetch the housekeeper to show you about? We put refreshments out for you, milord." She curtsied prettily, showing the dimples again before she left.

Gard smiled back at the delightful little baggage, not that he ever dallied with servants in his employ, or such young chits, either. A pretty face always being welcome, though, he automatically added the maid to the inventory of the house's attractions.

The excellent strawberry tarts were another. 'Pon rep, he wouldn't miss squiring his barques of frailty to noisy public restaurants if the house boasted a fine cook of its own. Strange, he thought as he sipped a fine sherry and had another bite of pastry, the rental agent had not mentioned the residence was fully staffed. The fellow would have dickered for a higher price if he knew how Lord Gardiner loved strawberry tarts. Ross's blue eyes shone as he looked around the parlor that ran from front to rear of the small home, tastefully furnished yet with enough room for a deal table or two. Even had a pianoforte, although he doubted many of his guests would have the training, or the time, to play. Yes, the house was a bargain.

The rest of the place was just as pleasing. The housekeeper led him to a smaller sitting room across the hall that contained an overstuffed sofa in front of a tiled fireplace. Excellent. Next to that was a dining room that could seat ten, the house-keeper informed him. Two was enough. Beyond the dining parlor was a small apartment consisting of an office for the household accounts and a tiny bedroom, which she hustled him out of so fast, he was sure it belonged to his guide.

Below stairs he was introduced to Rob Tuthill's wife, who blushed when Lord Gardiner complimented her cooking. " 'Tis a joy to cook in such a modern kitchen, my lord." She rattled a stack of dishes nervously, so the earl bowed and moved on, determined not to agitate such an asset. The chef at Gardiner House threw a Gallic fit if a stranger entered his domain. Ross smiled, trying to turn the woman up sweet so he'd be more welcome in her kitchen next time. He gave cursory inspection to the Tuthills' chambers behind the kitchen and pantries. What he wanted to see was upstairs.

He was not disappointed. The master suite consisted of two fair-sized dressing rooms connected to a bedroom almost as large as his in Grosvenor Square. There was an enormous canopied bed and rugs so thick he'd have taken his shoes off right then if not for the housekeeper. Ah, yes.

There were two other pleasant bedrooms on this floor, in case Cholly stayed over. On the attic level were some unused servant's rooms, one of which could make a perfect studio. "Yes," he said, nodding. "Yes, indeed."

"Then you like it?" the housekeeper asked, nearly wringing her hands. "You'll take it?"

Lord Gardiner cupped his chin in his hands, deliberating. The house was ideal for his purposes, close enough for convenience yet almost invisible to the eyes of the Polite World, ergo, his mother. The place itself was charming, inviting. He mentally saluted Lady Rosalind's taste. Only one thing bothered him: the housekeeper, Annie Lee, *Mrs.* Annie Lee, by George, was the ugliest female he had ever seen!

Chapter Seven

$\mathcal{T}$he *Mrs.* had to be a courtesy title. Love might
be blind, Gard reasoned, but this was asking too
much. The woman had jaundiced skin and a chest
so flat you could iron a neckcloth on it. She wore a
black dress obviously made for someone two sizes
larger, and a grayish mobcap with lappets that covered whatever hair she might have, except the three
long ones growing out of the mole on her cheek.
Dark spectacles most likely hid an awful squint or
worse, and, since she never smiled, the earl assumed her teeth were as bad as her eyes. She stood
perfectly, rigidly erect, except for the one shoulder
that was permanently higher than the other.

Love would have to be deaf and dumb besides to
settle on Mrs. Annie Lee. The notion of an unfortunate Mr. Lee offended the earl's sense of justice.
The unfortunate notion of Mrs. Annie Lee in his
cozy little love nest offended his aesthetic soul.
There just had to be a way of getting the house
without this housekeeper from hell.

"You seem young for such a responsible position," he began with a lie, having no way to guess the woman's age with so little of her showing. At least she had not gotten out of breath on the stairs.

"I have been holding house for years," Annalise quickly replied, happy to be telling the truth. She'd been managing Thompson Hall since her mother's death. "Hen—my aunt Henny trained me. That's Mrs. Tuthill, in the kitchen," she added. "Her, ah, rheumatics make it too hard for her to manage anything but the cooking."

Blast, the witch was a relative to the Tuthills. That meant he'd have to give up the treasure in the kitchens and that man who was a dab hand with the horses, too, just to be rid of her ugly phiz. It was worth it.

"Have you been here long?" he asked, preparatory to mentioning that he had an old family retainer in mind for the position.

Annalise knew she'd be found out as soon as he made inquiries, so she answered, "Not personally, but the family . . ." She let her words trail off.

Ross knew all about lines of service passing from father to son, mother to daughter. Hell and tarnation. Well, if he had no grounds to dismiss her on issues of loyalty or longevity, he still had the matter of remuneration. He could just refuse to pay.

"The rental agent mentioned nothing about your salary being included in the terms. I am not prepared to—"

"Oh, but we have nothing to do with the land agent. It's more a private arrangement with Lady Rosalind. Here." She whipped a letter out of her pocket, held it under his nose for a moment, then snatched it back. As far as he could tell, Lady Rosalind had abominable handwriting, but her signature was there, all right, under a line that seemed to have read, *Annie* (something), *Always welcome. Stay as long as you want. Fondly.*

"Lady Rosalind took her butler and abigail along with her, of course," Annalise went on, thinking that sounded likely, "but meant for us to stay with the house. She said any gentleman hiring the premises could be expected to honor her commitments."

That tore it. Gard was trapped with the subtle emphasis on *gentleman* and *honor*, the hag's intention, of course. He'd have to keep her on. At least his mistresses wouldn't have any jealous complaints. And she seemed surprisingly well spoken for a servant. See, he congratulated himself, there was something to admire even in the homeliest woman. "Yes, yes, I'll take the house."

"Excellent. Our salaries amount to eighty pounds per annum. Thirty for myself, twenty for each of the Tuthills, ten for Lorna, the maid. That's twenty pounds quarterly, payable in advance. Uniforms not included. Vacations and half days as per custom. Additional wages for extra servants for heavy cleaning or large parties shall be determined later. Housekeeping expenses cannot be estimated until we know the style you wish to maintain. Oh, and we require advance notice for company."

On the other hand, Lord Gardiner told himself, there was nothing whatsoever admirable about an ugly woman with the mind of an accountant and the arrogance of the royal *we.* He swallowed a sharp retort. The demands were not outrageous. Gads, he spent more than eighty pounds on a pair of boots. He simply was not used to dickering prices with servants—that was Foggarty's job, or his man of business's. He had certainly never haggled with a female employee in his life. The women he usually had dealings with were never so vulgar as to mention money at all, merely hinting at a pretty brooch

55

they'd seen or a diamond pendant. That was obviously not suitable in this instance. He nodded curtly.

Annalise released the breath she'd been holding. "Fine. When shall you be bringing Lady Gardiner around to inspect the premises?"

"Lady Gardiner? Mother? Here? When hell freezes over, Mrs. Lee!" Gads, he wondered if the woman was queer in the attic besides being ugly as sin.

"I meant your wife, my lord," she offered hesitantly.

His bark of laughter shook the hairs on her cheek. "I'm glad to see you have a sense of humor, Mrs. Lee. You were bamming me, weren't you?" She was wringing her hands again like something out of *Macbeth*. He laughed again. By all that was holy, the woman was a prude! Here he had the perfect solution, a way to get rid of the cloud and leave the silver lining. "I thought you understood, working for Lady Rosalind and Lord Elphinstone as you did. I shall be bringing lady friends here, daily, nightly, whatever. Of course I'll give notice when possible, as I agreed."

He got no response. Blast, he wished he could see behind those tinted lenses! "And I shall expect you to make my . . . friends welcome. You know, flowers, bonbons, bath salts, the kinds of things women like." Then again, perhaps she didn't know. Damn, she was nodding mutely. The woman was as hard to get rid of as a toothache. So be it.

The earl took out a roll of bills and peeled off a small fortune in pound notes. "Here are your wages, and uniform and household expenses. As you can see, I do not wish to stint on anything. I'll make separate arrangements with Tuthill about acquiring a carriage to leave here, but I wish you to purchase personal items my friends might forget to bring with them, robes, hairbrushes, et cetera. Do you understand?"

The woman was clutching her stomach as if she were about to be sick. Gard refused to feel sorry for her. Be damned if he was going to go shopping for negligees and perfumes when he was paying such a handsome wage. If she wanted the position so badly, she'd just have to earn her keep. "Oh, yes, and fetch me a dressing gown, a banyan or something. Can you do that?"

She grunted her assent, or groaned. He couldn't tell which, but she took the money from his hand. "I'll send over a change of clothes later. It will be a relief to have fresh linens on hand. I do like things clean, Mrs. Lee. That's one of the reasons I decided on this house, your excellent housekeeping. Keep up the high standards and we'll get along just fine." He could swear her lip curled, but he went on anyway. "There's just one thing more, Mrs. Lee, and then I will let you go about your duties. Understand this: you are all sacked if a single word of my involvement here reaches my mother's ears."

If a single word reached past Annalise's lips again, she'd be surprised. She was so shocked, so utterly dumbfounded, she could only nod as the elegant nobleman retrieved his high-crowned beaver hat and gloves from the table in the hall. She only just remembered to curtsy when he left to speak to Rob about a carriage.

"Try to have everything ready in a day or two," he'd said on his way out. "I'll send a message when to expect me."

"He can send his message to hell!" Annalise exclaimed, finally finding her voice twenty minutes later when Rob came back into the kitchen. "I'm sure they are expecting his lordship's arrival daily! Let him just see what kind of welcome they give

57

him!" Not even hot tea and the last of Henny's strawberry tarts could calm Miss Avery's rage. The dastard had eaten all the rest!

Rob straddled one of the kitchen chairs and lit a pipe. "What did you think a fancy young buck like him wanted with such an unfashionable address?"

"I never thought he wanted it to set up a . . . a bordello!"

"Tain't that at all, chickie. Just somewheres cozy for him to be private-like, away from all the rattlin' tongues of Mayfair."

"He talked about bringing friends for cards and such! He'll be throwing orgies next thing you know!"

"Now, what do you know about orgies, huh, chickie? Anyways, the gov told me as I'd be fetchin' young ladies from Drury Lane and such."

"Ladies, hah!"

Rob took a deep pull on his pipe and watched the smoke rings rise. "He don't seem evil to me, just a young buck sowin' his wild oats."

Annalise pounded her fist on the table. "Not in my house, he won't!"

"But it ain't your house, chickie, that's the point."

Henny stopped banging her pots and pans around and took a seat at the table. "But, Robbie, Miss Annalise's reputation! No young lady should even know about such things, much less be living amid such carryings-on! We'll have to leave, that's all."

"Can't do it without makin' people wonder what happened and why. No, no hope for it. 'Sides, it's safer this way. Even if Sir Vernon happens to locate Lady Rosalind's address, there won't be a trace of any Miss Avery, just a swell and his sweeties."

Annalise grimaced, but she knew Rob had the right of it. "I have no reputation left anyway,

Henny, not after running away and spending all those nights on the road. No one would believe I'm innocent of nothing worse than avoiding marriage to a womanizer. Hah! This philanderer is worse. At least Barny kept some loyalty to his Sophy!"

"Maybe we won't have to stay too long," Henny said hopefully. "Just till we get word to your aunt."

"I already sent letters through the foreign office and the embassy. One of them has to reach her. I know she'll come or send for me, and I'm sure Lord Elphinstone can have the guardianship overturned. He has to!"

Henny patted her hand and poured more tea. "He will, dearie, he will."

"And meantime his lordship ain't so bad," Rob commented.

"Rob, he's a libertine!"

"He's generous with his blunt, knows his cattle, and likes Henny's cookin'. That's enough for me. I've worked for worse."

"He's a despicable, lust-ridden whore-monger!" Annalise insisted. "And you don't have to work at all if you don't want to!"

Rob made another smoke ring. "I wouldn't leave you alone here, chickie, even if Henny'd let me. 'Sides, I've a mind to see the fancy lord's fancy pieces."

Both women glared at him.

The next morning Henny was humming while she baked enough strawberry tarts for an army. Rob was whistling when he went off to the livery stable to see about Seraphina and a coach for his lordship. Miss Avery was loudest of all, gnashing her teeth.

"Ain't he the handsomest thing that ever lived?" the maid Lorna rhapsodized, skipping along at Annalise's side as they went to the shops. "He's got the broadest shoulders in all of London, the bluest eyes, and the nicest smile I ever seen."

"The man's a rake!" Annalise stormed back. "An unprincipled, immoral rake."

"Me mum says they're the only sort worth having."

"Hogwash," retorted the ladylike Mrs. Annie Lee. "You'll want a nice, steady fellow when you're old enough, not one with a roving eye."

"Yes'm," the little maid replied doubtfully, ready to agree with her new benefactress. She'd never had so much money to bring her mum at once, with the promise of a new dress and some pretty ribbons for her hair, and good smells coming from the kitchen. If this lady wanted his lordship to be Old Nick himself, Lorna would help look for his horns and tail next time he came.

Lorna had no doubts whatsoever that the housekeeper was a lady, a real lady, no matter what rig she was running. Lorna had watched the sickly looking miss who called for Miss Ros turn into the hideous Mrs. Lee, even helping tear up one of the lady's fine petticoats to making a binding for her chest and a hump for her shoulder with the rest of the muslin. She'd gazed in wonder as the cook mixed up a batch of flour and stuff to make a yellowish powder for her skin and then added a little sugar and water to affix the mole. Whatever hugger-mugger was going on, this was better than the Punch and Judy show at the ice fair. And Lorna was getting paid for being in it! She danced along at Mrs. Lee's side.

"Get ready for his friends, he said," Annalise was muttering. "I'll get ready, all right."

"Ma'am?"

"I don't care what Rob says, I refuse to live in a bawdy house! I'll show that bounder the error of his ways, or die trying!"

"Oh, ma'am, you can't be thinking of worriting his lordship. He'll up and leave!"

"Exactly. If I discourage him enough, he'll get out. We'll find proper renters next time, a family or a pair of retired schoolteachers or something."

"You'll get us fired!" Lorna wailed.

"No, I won't be so obvious."

She did not buy him a hairshirt instead of a dressing gown, for instance; she just bought him a robe at least two sizes bigger than she estimated he needed, and slippers two sizes smaller. She did not purchase dowdy flannel nightgowns for his lightskirts, just lacy ones with about a million tiny buttons. And robes with ostrich boas whose feathers got inhaled up your nose if you wore them. And the heaviest, most cloying perfumes she could find. She bought tooth powder that tasted like garlic, a hand mirror whose slight distortion just happened to add a few pounds to the reflection, a lovely bedside carafe that was sure to drip, and exquisite blown wineglasses that were so fragile, they were bound to break at the first use.

No, she wasn't obvious, but the dastard wasn't going to find Laurel Street any bed of roses, either.

There was no way on earth Annalise Avery was going to let another despicable man and his lascivious ways ruin her life.

Chapter Eight

*W*ednesday night. Almack's. The wages of sin. Gads, he'd promised the dowager he'd escort her a few places, not lay down his life for one minor indiscretion. Yet here he was, martyr to a mother's pique, clad in knee breeches, with his neckcloth starched so stiff and tied so high he'd have a rash under his chin by morning.

If this was the Marriage Mart, he'd do his shopping elsewhere—when the time came, of course. He doubted he'd ever be on the lookout for a silly female who giggled and batted her eyelashes like the one in his arms right now. The chit's only conversation consisted of her clothes. Hell, the widgeon would be a damned sight more attractive without all the ruffles and ribbons. Without any clothes at all, in fact. Firm, high breasts, soft skin . . . my lord Gardiner entertained himself throughout the remainder of the Sir Roger de Coverley picturing his mother's best friend's goddaughter naked.

Lady Jersey babbled in his ear during the waltz,

trying to get up a flirtation. She was a little ripe for his tastes, but then he envisioned himself swimming, sinking, lost in pillows of warm flesh. No bony hips, either.

Miss Kelsall romped energetically through the country dance beside him, but he saw only her enticing derriere jouncing, bouncing, joyously bare.

The stately quadrille brought him statuesque Lady Moira Campbell, aspiring widow of a spendthrift Irish laird. Lord Gardiner hardly noticed the speculative gleam in the widow's hazel eyes, his own blue eyes firmly fixed on her low neckline. It left little to the imagination. His creative mind subtracted the rest.

Another waltz, and his hand was at Miss Compton's tiny waist. Two hands could span it, Gard estimated, two hands that could stroke and caress the Pocket Venus till she reached Olympus.

The boulanger, Miss Beaumont's legs. The lancers, no. He'd embarrass himself on the dance floor with that image. So Ross drifted through the bastion of the upper crust, mentally undressing every doyenne, dasher, and debutante right down to their drawers. He floated toward the refreshments room, picturing them all in their altogethers. Shifts, chemises, petticoats disappeared like magic in his mind's eye. Laces, ribbons, buttons went flying through the assembly rooms. Alabaster flesh came tumbling out of corsets. Acres of velvety skin lay yearning for his touch, posed for his pen and pad, poised for his pleasure.

Lord Gardiner ate three pieces of stale cake with such a wide grin on his face that his mother was picking names for grandchildren. His friends were shaking their heads at the next benedict. Bets were being made on which of the lovelies had caught his interest, since he'd not danced twice with any of his partners. Every one of those partners was sure the earl's glorious smile was just for her. Every one was right.

By the time Countess Stephania was ready to leave, Gard was so randy, he leapt into the family carriage next to her and ordered Ned Coachman to spring the horses. Stopping at Gardiner House only long enough to call out his curricle, he kissed his mother's cheek, told her what a delightful evening he'd had, and that he'd be sure to accompany her next week. Foggarty was waving a vinaigrette under the dowager's nose when Ross hurtled into his curricle. He nearly ran over an urchin, a mongrel, and a streetlamp in his eagerness to get to Laurel Street.

Foresight was everything. That afternoon he'd counted on a night at Almack's being such a bore that he'd deserve a reward. Instead, it was such a ... stimulating evening, he thanked his lucky stars for Corinne.

He'd thought to share his first night at a new place with an old friend. Not Cholly. He sent an invitation to Corinne Browne, an occasional lover who was rarely too busy to answer an invitation from a warm-blooded, deep-pocketed earl. As soon as her affirmative reply came, Gard sent a messenger to Laurel Street. Tuthill was to pick up Corinne at her rooms, rooms that often smelled of other men's colognes, to the earl's displeasure. Not tonight. Tonight Corinne would be waiting in his own rooms, just for him. Life was sweet.

"Did Miss Browne arrive?" Ross asked the housekeeper, who must have been waiting for his knock, she answered the door so promptly.

"Yes, a few hours ago. She decided to wait upstairs. You said to make your guests welcome, so I offered her some wine. Was that acceptable?"

"Perfect. You are a jewel." He was already on the

stairs. Not even the depressing sight of Mrs. Lee in her yards of black could dampen his enthusiasm.

"Mrs. Tuthill made a supper for you and the young lady," she called after him. "Filet of sole stuffed with mushrooms, duckling in oyster sauce, and a trifle."

"That sounds delightful. Thank Mrs. Tuthill for me." He took another two steps.

"I saw no reason for Aunt Henny to stay up, my lord. I hope I did right?"

"Fine. Whatever. You know best." He started to loosen his neckcloth.

"The supper is keeping warm on the stove. Shall I serve it now?"

"Deuce take it, no! That is, please hold it for later, Mrs. Lee." He took the rest of the stairs two at a time, tearing at his shirt buttons. Gard never even felt the housekeeper's scornful glance. If looks could kill, that one would leave him a soprano.

Only one candle was left burning in the large chamber. By its soft light he could see Corinne's long, dark hair spread out on the pillow. A bottle of wine stood nearly empty on the bedside table. He smiled. The flame in the hearth and the fire in his loins weren't to be the only glows this evening.

"Corinne?" She didn't move. "Corinne, my sweet?"

He leaned over the bed. Her red lips were curved up in a smile, but she was fast asleep. "I hope you're dreaming of me, my pet. I know just how to awaken a sleeping beauty."

Once in the dressing room, the earl couldn't get his clothes off fast enough. He didn't bother lighting another candle; the fireplace from the bed chamber offered enough light for him to find a maroon velvet robe carefully draped over the back of a chair. Its satin lining next to his skin heightened

65

sensations already at fever pitch. So what if he had to roll the sleeves back a bit? The velvet in his fingers made his toes quiver. He quickly slipped his feet into the matching slippers. And winced. Ah, well, he'd go barefoot. The rug was thick, the rooms were warm. . . .

"Blast!" He immediately tripped over the hem of the robe, stubbing his toes and slamming his shoulder into the edge of the dressing table. By George, he thought, rubbing the painful joint, it would take a giant to fill this robe. He was right: Mrs. Lee knew nothing about men. Luckily, Corinne did.

"Corinne?" he called softly. Then he pulled back the bedcovers and discovered Corinne's ample charms laid out for him in a nearly transparent gown. He forgot all about housekeepers and hurt shoulders. Something was aching, and it wasn't his toes. He climbed into the bed next to her and kissed her awake.

"Huh?"

"Corinne darling, it's Gard. Wake up."

Corinne rolled away from his seeking mouth, whacking him on the chin with a limp hand as she turned. This was not quite the reception he had in mind. He put his hand on her nearly bare back, and the girl made a soft, moaning sound. That was more like it.

He trailed kisses where his hand had been, and she moaned again, louder. This time she followed the sound with a disgruntled "Oh, go away."

"Corinne?"

She pulled a pillow over her head. "I said go away. I have a headache."

A headache? He thought only wives got headaches.

Perhaps she'd feel better after a nap, he reasoned, deciding he may as well assuage another hunger while he waited. Gard vaguely recalled eating a few pieces of stale cake in King Street. He only hoped Mrs. Tuthill's cooking was as good as he'd imagined; Lud knew he deserved that something should be this night.

He considered changing back to his clothes to face Mrs. Lee downstairs but, dash it, this was his house. If she was offended by his immodesty, she could leave. Then again, no one told the old besom to wait up; she was most likely contentedly asleep on her cold, narrow pallet. Good. He was certainly capable of serving himself. If he didn't trip over the damn fool robe on his way down the steps.

He was holding up the hem like a belle making her come-out, feeling a total nodcock even before he caught sight of the housekeeper sitting by a candle in the hall. She adjusted her spectacles and put the book she was reading in a pocket before he could catch the title. Sermons, no doubt.

"You needed something, my lord?"

The blasted woman was staring at his bare feet. He released the fabric in his hand. "Miss Browne isn't feeling quite the thing."

"I am sorry, my lord. Shall I send Uncle Rob for a physician?"

"No, no, I doubt that will be necessary. She says it's just a headache."

Annalise nodded. "Perhaps she had a bit too much to drink." Then again, Annalise thought, perhaps Miss Browne had just enough laudanum. She couldn't help the tiniest of smiles from escaping. "I noticed the bottle was half empty when I checked the fire. Perhaps I should have removed it. I am sorry."

Deuce take it, the crone didn't look sorry. She looked like a cat in the cream pot. He cleared his throat. "Yes, well, I thought I'd try a bit of Mrs. Tuthill's cooking. No, you needn't fix a tray or anything, I'll eat in the kitchen."

Lord Gardiner took a step in that direction and tripped over the robe again. This time he caught himself on the hall table, merely tipping a vase of flowers which splashed cold water on his feet. Annalise continued on her way to the kitchen, pretending not to see. "Damnation!" he cursed, which she pretended not to hear. "Do you sew?"

"Of course, my lord. All housekeepers sew."

"Do you think you might hem this up for me? I'm afraid I'm not the man you thought I was," he said, trying to make a joke of it while she laid out a place setting for him at the heavy oak table.

Or perhaps you're not the man you thought you were, Annalise silently commented, wondering whether he'd have an apoplexy if a pin should accidentally be left in the sewing.

There was that smirk again, Gard noted. The witch was laughing at him, he knew it! Well, he'd have a bit of fun himself.

"I was wondering about your name, Mrs. Lee. I cannot help noticing that you wear no ring. Is the honorific merely because it is customary for your position?"

Some of the wine she was pouring spilled over the edge of the cup. Now *he* was smiling, which made the already frazzled Annalise forget her role even further. Here was this half-naked man, dark hairs showing all over his chest where the robe lay open, who had just left his doxie upstairs, making sport of her, Annalise Avery! "That's none of your blasted business. My lord," she added belatedly.

That wiped the smile off his face in a hurry. *No one* addressed the Earl of Gardiner in such insolent tones, especially not some hatchet-faced harridan who seemed to delight in his discomfiture. "Who the bloody hell do you think you are?" he bellowed. "I pay the—"

"I apologize, my lord," Annalise hastily interrupted before he could waken Henny. The fat would really be in the fire then, her old nanny seeing her charge alone with a belligerent, bare-chested man. She'd most likely reveal it all, landing them in the basket for sure. "I . . . I forgot my place, Lord Gardiner. Of course you have a right to know something about your employees. I am afraid I'm just . . . sensitive about my ring," she told him, improvising madly. "You see, after my husband fell at Corunna, I gave my ring to buy medicine for the wounded soldiers. I . . . I prayed that someone did the same for my Jamie."

Her thin, work-worn hands trembled, and she brought her apron up to cover her tears. My God, what had he done? Ross thought in dismay. He stumbled to his feet. "Don't give it another thought, Mrs. Lee. Please accept my apologies. I never wished to bring back unhappy memories, I swear. I, ah, I'll be going now," he decided, his appetite having disappeared altogether. He grabbed up a handful of the robe, inadvertently revealing muscular calves in his hurry to be gone.

Annalise only peeked a little, sobbing even louder into her apron.

Upstairs, his lordship quickly changed his clothes after checking on the still-sleeping Corinne. He left her a handsome *douceur*, for her time if nothing else, hoping she wouldn't spend it on Blue Ruin. The ring he'd intended giving her, a pretty pearl and sapphire affair, he left in the pocket of the maroon robe. The blasted thing only reminded him of poor Annie Lee and her lost ring, and the misery he just caused her. Fiend seize all women and their megrims!

Downstairs, Annalise was helping herself to his lordship's supper, falling to with the best appetite she'd had in weeks. At this rate, she'd have her weight back in no time. At this rate, she'd have that scoundrel out of her life even sooner.

Chapter Nine

"*Y*ou're mighty chipper this mornin', chickie."

"Hmm," Annalise answered, peering in the corners of the stable behind the town house, where Rob was lovingly currying the horses he'd selected for Lord Gardiner's new landau. The coach was comfortable but undistinguished, just the way the earl wanted it, and the grays weren't flashy, either, just the way Rob wanted them. He'd picked the geldings more for strength and stamina, just in case he and Henny and Missy had to show London their heels in a hurry. It didn't appear that Miss Annalise, Annie as he'd better remember, was worried.

"Get a good night's rest?"

"The best in ages."

Rob figured he'd give his eyeteeth to know what went on after he went to bed last night. The dollymop he drove home this morning had hardly enough energy to make it up her stairs. Seemed happy though, and gave him a tip. Now, here was their Annie looking merry as a grig. It didn't figure after the fuss she'd made yesterday. "Guess you've got it all straight in your head now about Lord Gardiner and his bits o' fluff, eh?"

"You might say I am resolved."

"That's all right, then," Rob said, returning his attention to the horses. But Annalise was shifting bales of hay. "Did you want something there, chickie?"

As nonchalantly as possible, she answered, "Oh, no, I'm just trying to catch mice. You wouldn't want any in here with these beauties, would you?" She came over and stroked one velvety nose.

Rob looked across the gray's broad back and saw that she had an old cheese box in one hand and a broom by her side. He shrugged. Never could figure women. "Got a message from the gov'nor this mornin'. Company again tonight."

"The same woman?" she asked sharply. The horse stamped its feet. "Sorry, boy. Corinne again?"

Rob shook his head. "No, this one lives at St. James's Street. He says to ask for Catherine."

"But St. James's is where all the men's clubs are. Ladies cannot even walk there!"

"Didn't suppose she was no lady."

"And I didn't suppose she was a . . . a dealer or something from a gambling den. Actresses and dancers are bad enough."

He spit a stream of tobacco juice out the door. "Could be worse. Lot of high-priced fancy houses are set up near where the gents are like to be."

The cheese box hit the floor. "F-fancy houses? You mean . . . ?"

"Ain't for me to say." He looked closely at her, close enough to see that red was creeping into her cheeks, even under the yellowish powder she wore on top of her own still-sickly color. "And ain't for you to say, neither!"

"I do not intend to speak one word to that reprobate who calls himself a gentleman," she snapped back, snatching up her broom and the empty crate. "I intend to find me a mouse. No, a rat. The bigger the better."

Rob could only scratch his head at that. "I know Henny ain't goin' to let you serve up any rodents on the earl's dish, so I don't need to know nothin' more. 'Sides, I misdoubt you'll find any vermin here. I got me a ratter." He whistled, and a small dog trotted into the stable.

Annalise took off her dark glasses and inspected the ragged little mongrel, who was busy scratching its ear. "That? It looks more like an overgrown rat than anything. No, it looks just like a fur muff I once had that the moths got into."

"Genuine Clyde terrier he is, from Scotland. Guaranteed to catch mice."

"Catch fleas more like." She laughed as the dog performed acrobatics to get at an itch near its tail. "Wherever did you find it?"

Rob gave the horse's rump a pat. "I didn't need to go lookin' for him, I swear. Poor tyke must of been livin' off the rats here after Lady Ros cleared out. He ain't skin and bones, but he was happy enough for a biscuit and gravy. I mean to give him a bath this afternoon when I wash the carriage. Get rid of some of his stowaways, then I figure Henny won't mind him in the kitchen."

Gold flecks sparkled in Annalise's eyes behind the spectacles as she watched the mongrel scratch some more. "You're so busy, Rob, why don't I give the dog his bath?"

"You're sure you don't mind?"

"Absolutely positive. Come on, Clyde."

Clyde had the most thorough scrubbing of his short life—after he'd been fed and put to rest for the afternoon in the Earl of Gardiner's bed.

Catherine was too totty-headed to be a dealer; she said she couldn't deal *vingt et un* because she didn't know French. She was more a decoration at Fremont's gaming parlor, sometimes a distraction for the less reputable doings at the tables. Sometimes she wasn't even at the tables, taking certain high rollers upstairs for private games. Fremont didn't mind. Why should he? He got a portion of everything that went on under his roof. He got an even larger fee, in advance, when Kitty prowled under someone else's roof. She was good for business, he insisted, explaining the exorbitant price.

Her name was Catherine but they called her Kitty for her playful ways. She was small and sweet and silly, a fluffy armful with big brown eyes in a heart-shaped face. She was just what the earl needed after a musicale at Marlborough House where all the guests were as solemn as creditors at a poor man's funeral.

He'd gone to Fremont's after the debacle with Corinne. White's was too sedate for his mood; unfortunately Gentleman Jackson's was closed. Instead of getting thoroughly disguised, which was his intention, the earl became enamored of little Kitty as she stood on tiptoe to whisper in his ear, rubbing against him.

He could have had her then and there—heaven knew he was ready—but Corinne was sleeping off her drunk in Laurel Street, and the idea of trailing a strumpet up the stairs in full view of a roomful of hardened gamblers no longer appealed to him. They'd be taking bets on how soon he returned, he knew. He'd have done the same a fortnight ago. Gard supposed his mother's stay in town must be having some effect after all. Tomorrow, then.

"The wait only makes things more enticing, eh, *chérie*?"

"Oh, you wanted *sherry*. I thought you wanted an hour with me." She stuck her lower lip out in an adorable pout.

An hour wasn't going to be enough. He wanted Kitty purring the whole night, no matter Fremont's fee.

Lady Gardiner decided to leave the entertainment at the intermission, Handel be praised, so her son was able to dash across town earlier than he thought. He reached Laurel Street before Kitty and scurried around, getting ready. First he happily dismissed Mrs. Lee for the evening. The woman made him so uncomfortable, he was glad to see the last of her, even if he did have to open every cabinet door in the kitchen to find fresh wine goblets. The first two broke off in his hand, spilling wine on the lace cuffs of his dress shirt. He shrugged and drank a glass of the excellent vintage to steady his nerves. He wasn't any young sprig taking a lass out behind the barn for the first time. There was no hurry.

He still bounded up the stairs to snuff out candles and turn down the bed. Putting on his robe, he was pleased to note that it was neatly hemmed and the ring was still in the pocket. The ring was for Kitty if she pleased him, since Fremont was most likely keeping the lion's share of the night's fee.

Then he scampered back down the stairs, getting stabbed in the back of his calf only once by an overlooked pin. Well, the woman did have such terrible eyesight, it was a wonder she could sew the thing at all. He had another glass of wine. It wouldn't do to leave too much in the bottle for Kitty, not after his experience with Corinne.

At first Kitty was disappointed in the house. "I thought an earl's would be bigger." Then she giggled as Lord Gardiner chased her all the way upstairs, the belt to his robe in her hand. "I was right."

He grabbed for her right there by the hearth—the rug was soft enough; the wooden floor of the hall landing was soft enough, by George—but she danced away.

"The wait only makes things more exciting, eh, brandy," she laughingly echoed his words, pirouetting out of reach. Then she proceeded to show him how exciting the wait could be. First she kicked off one shoe, raising her hem to show nicely turned ankles, then the other. The watered-silk gown was shortly in a puddle at her feet. Gard felt he'd join it soon, so slowly and sinuously did she move, like a cat stretching. He groaned.

She tossed her petticoat over his head, after spending at least an eternity untying the tapes. He dragged the soft muslin down, then clutched it to him, as much to cover his excitement as to uncover his eyes, lest he miss an instant of her performance or an inch of her rosy skin. Kitty wore no corset—her sweet young body required none—so only her lace-edged chemise covered her from swelling breast to dimpled knee. She reached for the ribbons, winked at him, then lifted the chemise to untie one of her garters.

"No!" he growled, so she smiled and went back to the ribbons on her shift. What a painting she would make, he thought an instant later when he could breathe again, bare skin reflecting the fire's glow, the pink frills on her garters the only prop she needed. No, what a lover she would make, his body insisted, refusing to wait an instant longer. Those silly garters and silk stockings could stay on till the cows came home, for all he cared.

Ross scooped her up and tumbled her to the bed, where she still played the coquette, tickling and teasing, nibbling and nipping. Her hands were everywhere, her mouth was everywhere, his wits had gone begging ages ago. Finally he pulled her down on top of him for a deep, deep kiss. Still she made tiny pinches up and down his legs, little bites on his buttocks. Only her lips were clinging to his lips and her hands were stroking his—

"Yeow!" Ross shouted, throwing Kitty off him, jumping up and beating at the bed. "I'll kill her," he raged, flailing at a pillow so hard it ripped, turning the room white with feathers, where it wasn't already blue with his cursing. "I'll tear every hair out of her head for this, I swear."

Now, Kitty might have more hair than wit, but even she was instantly able to ascertain that his lordship was no longer interested in her services. As a matter of fact, where certain parts of him were swelling up like sausages with angry welts all over, other parts of him were trying to disappear altogether. That seemed smartest to Kitty, too, who scrambled into her clothes and fled outside to call a hackney while his lordship was still calling for his housekeeper's blood.

Chapter Ten

*G*ard couldn't find the blasted belt to his robe. *It would serve that beldam right if I go downstairs like this,* he raged. Then he tugged the bellpull so hard, it ripped right off the wall. He tied *that* around his waist and stomped down the stairs, still bellowing with fury.

"You rang, my lord?"

There she was, waiting at the foot of the stairs, still dressed although he distinctly recalled dismissing her for the evening. Still wearing that shapeless black sack and hideous cap, that same infuriating smirk, Mrs. Lee was his own personal Fury, Erinys come to torment him for his sins. He hadn't done anything terrible enough to deserve her—yet.

"No, I didn't ring, blast you. I didn't call and I didn't send a message!"

"No, my lord, you shouted." Now, Annalise had never seen a man so enraged in her entire life. Sir Vernon had been cool and restrained in his anger, not like this inferno of ire. Could he get violent? Employers beat servants all the time, according to Lorna. Annalise took a step back. But no, she told herself, she was made of sterner stuff. She wasn't about to let any great, roaring bear of a man intimidate her. She'd faced her first naked chest the evening before and survived; she was not about to be sent scurrying off to her room by a wrathful earl, especially not over a few pawky flea bites. Even if half of his body was uncovered again.

Annalise was too tired for all this nonsense anyway. She refused to go to bed with all the muck on her face, and feared to remove it until his lordship left the house. With just cause, as events proved. The sooner he got it all off his chest—and some proper clothes on his chest—the sooner Miss Avery could find her own rest. She kept her eyes lowered, but she did step closer to the earl to inquire, "Was there something you wanted?"

"Yes, Mrs. Lee, there was something I wanted!" The framed prints in the hallway vibrated from the force of his shout. "I wanted to wring your scrawny neck! I *wanted* a clean house! Just look at this!" And he made to whip aside his dressing gown.

Annalise shrieked and threw her hands over her glasses.

"For the love of—I am not quite that depraved, Mrs. Lee." But he was red-faced all the same. "Take your hands down and look at my legs. No, I wouldn't want to offend you. Look at the welts instead. Do you know how they got there—and everywhere else? Bedbugs, that's how! After I particularly told you to make sure the house was immaculate. You are relieved of your position, Mrs. Lee, and I don't care how many appeals to my honor you make."

Annalise had nothing left to lose except her temper and her pride. She raised her chin in the air.

"Honor? You talk about honor? Then look a little further before you place all the blame, my high and mighty lordship. You said yourself you rented this house because the premises were spotless. Well, they were before you started bringing your straw damsels here. You want to know how those bedbugs got in your bed? I'll tell you: You lie down with dogs, you wake up with fleas!"

"What the devil is that supposed to mean?"

"It means that it took me hours to scrub the face paint off the sheets after Miss Browne, and now this! It means that if you bring home girls of the night, you have to be prepared to pay the consequences. Be thankful it was parasites and not the pox!"

Annalise clapped her hand over her mouth, shocked at the words that had spewed forth. The earl never noticed her action, being too outraged to see anything beyond his own shaking fist. He'd never in his life struck a woman; there was a first time for everything.

"How dare you!" he thundered instead. "Not even my mother would dare to speak to me like that!"

"Perhaps she should have!"

"You are an insolent old bat!"

"You are a licentious, loud-mouthed fribble."

And they continued to stand in the dimly lighted hall, glaring at each other, until Lord Gardiner felt an unavoidable urge to scratch his nether regions. He couldn't, not in front of this green-glassed she-dragon. A gentleman could curse and carry on in a female's presence under certain circumstances, but some things were simply beyond the pale. The housekeeper crossed her bony arms over her flat chest, almost challenging him. So he did it, he scratched his arse, right there in front of her. Then he was ashamed when he heard her gasp at this ultimate insult.

"Told you I had sensitive skin," he muttered, looking away and so missing the smile Annalise couldn't hide.

"Oh, stop whining about it like a sulky child," she told him, almost feeling sorry for what she'd done. "I'm sure Henny has something in her kitchen for the itching, or else I can mix something up from Grandmother's book of receipts."

He grunted something that may have been a thank-you.

She didn't wait for him to follow. That way he couldn't see the grin on her face; she didn't feel quite so bad, now.

Gard sat down in one of the kitchen chairs, and immediately jumped up again, squealing like a stuck pig. Or peer. He pulled a needle out of the back of his robe.

"Oh, is that where I left the silly thing? I searched high and low for it, too. Thank you," Annalise said sweetly, putting a pot of water on to boil before returning to her search through Henny's medicine shelf. "I'll have to consult Grandmother's book. She kept an excellent stillroom, so we can only hope Henny—Aunt Henny—stocks the right ingredients. Tea will be ready in a minute."

"Wine," he grunted, scratching his leg.

"I'm afraid alcohol will only heat your blood, making you itch more. How about some lemonade? And don't scratch, that makes it worse, too."

What was it they used to do with witches, Gard wondered, burn them at the stake? That was too good for Mrs. Lee. Here he was, in the middle of the night, in his charming little love-lodge, swollen and spotty and being lectured at by a shriveled old prune. He leaned back in the chair and closed his eyes, defeated and disheartened. And despising Mrs. Lee the more for seeing him thus.

Still, the lemonade did cool a throat parched by

shouting, and the damp cloth she placed on his forehead while she mixed her potion was refreshing. Maybe a heart did beat in her narrow chest after all.

"I think you are supposed to bathe in the stuff, but we don't have enough of some of the wild things, like dock, so I'll just spread some on, like this."

"Like this" was burning hot. His lordship yowled and jerked his foot away.

"I thought men were supposed to have a code about stoicism, stiff upper lip and all that. Why, you're worse than a colicky infant."

So the earl sat there, suffering as silently as he could, while his housekeeper tortured his already agonized limbs. He muttered almost to himself: "I bet Mr. Lee threw himself in front of the French cannons on purpose."

"You leave Jake out of this," she said, applying a measure of the hot salve with unnecessary vigor.

"I thought his name was Jamie."

"It was. James Jacob Lee." She kept spreading the stuff on his feet and ankles.

"He must have been a rake of the first order."

"That's a shameful thing to say, my lord. Why ever would you think a thing like that? Don't you believe any man can be constant? Or do you just doubt that any man could be faithful to me?"

"You're putting words in my mouth. I just thought he must have been a womanizer, to have you so set against the breed. You obviously do not approve of me or my life-style."

"That's not for me to say, my lord."

"And that hasn't stopped you before. What, did you suddenly remember your place? I'm asking you, Mrs. Lee, as your employer, why are you so bitterly resentful of a man having a bit of fun?"

"I am not in your employ any longer, my lord. You dismissed me, remember?"

Gard remembered. But that stuff she was spreading on his legs was working on the itch, after the initial sting, and Mrs. Lee apparently had a gentle touch when she wished. Besides, he noted as he watched her work, the housekeeper's wrists were perhaps the thinnest he had ever seen on a woman not begging in the streets. If she lost this position, no one would hire the harridan, and then what would become of her? The earl did not want her wasting away on his conscience. "Perhaps I was a bit hasty. I'll reconsider, if you swear to rid that room of its wildlife. And if you answer my questions."

Annalise nodded. "Very well, I shall fumigate the bed chamber, and no, I do not approve of your ways."

"You do not believe in innocent fun?"

"Innocent fun is sleigh-riding and picniking, not your hellraking. My lord."

"Come now, hellraking? I don't go around raping innocent women and ravishing the countryside. My, ah, companions are all willing, nay, happy to spend time with me."

"So happy that Kitty flew out of here as if she'd been scalded, and Corinne had to drink herself into oblivion before facing you?" Annalise got up to mix a fresh batch of the ointment.

"Those were two instances out of many." He spoke angrily, to her back.

"Many. Exactly. You make a travesty out of what should be a sacred act of marriage. You have no faithfulness, no loyalty, no real love."

"Lud, how did a moralist like you ever get on with Lord Elphinstone?"

"I, ah, had few dealings with his lordship, but Lady Ros always spoke highly of him. Trust and respect, that's what they share. And friendship, of course."

"Friendship? You cannot be bacon-brained enough

to think that's all Lady Ros and Elphinstone share!"

Annalise had nearly convinced herself such was the case. She absentmindedly dabbed at the earl's knees with the freshly heated salve as she explained: "Lady Rosalind lost her heart many years ago in a tragic romance. She remains true to her first, dead love. That's why she and Lord Elphinstone could never marry."

"You've been reading too many novels, woman," he said through gritted teeth. "That's a touching story. Perhaps you should tell it to Elphinstone's wife."

"Wife?" Annalise let the cloth she was using fall into the bowl. That explained a lot. Poor Aunt Ros was being exploited by another no-account libertine, just like the one grinning at her discomfiture now. Annalise thrust the bowl into his hands. "You can finish the rest yourself."

He kept grinning. "I was wondering when you'd reach that point. Do you think you could force yourself to put some of that stuff on my back, though, where I cannot reach?"

Annalise could not refuse such a reasonable request. She took the bowl while he turned around, straddling the chair, and shrugged the robe down over his shoulders. Annalise tried not to think of those broad shoulders or wavy muscles. "Lady Ros is no trollop!" she stated instead.

"I never said she was. I never heard a rumor of her going with another man, Annie."

Miss Avery stiffened, there behind his back. First he was half naked, now he was getting familiar. In her most haughty, lady-of-the-manor voice she declared, "I did not give you permission to use my given name."

He laughed. "I don't need your permission,

ma'am, now that you're back on my payroll. Lud, you're not like any servant I ever knew."

And the situation was like no other he'd been in since he was five and some nursemaid or other had pulled nettles out of his hide. She'd put on the same smelly concoction, too, most likely. She never aggravated him or taunted him or made him feel like the lowest kind of reptile. He could feel the housekeeper's antipathy through the slaps on his back. "By George, I'm only being friendly. You'd think I was asking for droit du seigneur or something."

"I am finished, my lord," she said, slamming the bowl down on the table. "And of course you can call me what you will, my lord. As you said, I work for you. However, I do not wish your glib friendship. Save your honeyed words for the women who accept money to listen to them, *my lord.*"

Gard turned around in the chair again and began to daub at the welts on his chest. "Don't be so quick to condemn those women and the men who support them. You have an honest job now, but where would you be if you had no position and no family to help you?"

"I'd find some way other than selling my body!"

"You'd have to," he said without even looking up to see the rigidity in his housekeeper's stance.

"If men would keep their minds more on their business and less on their pleasures," she snarled at him and his bare chest, "they'd be better able to provide for their daughters." Affront was interfering with Annalise's breathing, that and knowing the robe was draped just across his hips and thighs. She took a deep breath. "For men to use women so is deplorable. There is no excuse for lives based on satisfying lower appetites, lives ruled by vulgar passions." She gasped as his hand moved beneath the robe's covering. "And don't think you can force your unbridled lust on me!"

85

Lord Gardiner laughed till tears came to his eyes. "You can rest assured, Annie Lee, that is the last thing in the world I'd ever do!"

Chapter Eleven

*H*is lordship went to Suffolk to nurse his wounds while the Laurel Street lodgings were being de-infested. "Estate business," he claimed to Lady Stephania, making his excuses to visit a place where he could wear loose clothing.

"But Lady Martindale and her daughters are coming for dinner Tuesday next, and we are promised to the Ashford-Farquahars' come-out ball on Friday. Twins, you know. Both well favored and fabulously wealthy. And that Irish widow, Lady Campbell, called again this afternoon. She said she wanted your advice about buying a carriage. Encroaching female, coming to tea as if she were one of my boon companions, but you did make an offer to help, it seems. What shall I tell them?" Her cane rapped the floor, fractions of an inch away from his toes. "What shall I tell your father when he wakes me in the middle of the night to ask why you are not paying court to any of the reigning Toasts?"

"You may tell Lady Martindale and her fubsy-faced daughters to go hang. And that goes double for the Ashford-Farquahar twins. You may tell Lady Campbell that I shall call as soon as I return, although a visit to Tattersall's is not quite what I offered. And you may respectfully tell my father not to worry about finding his ice skates. Hell will freeze over before I dance attendance on one of the spoiled society darlings you keep tossing at my head."

"But you gave your word to look around for a countess!"

"I gave my word to show more responsible interest in the earldom, my lady. That's what you wanted, and that's what I shall be doing in Suffolk."

This time the cane caught him firmly in the ankle. "I meant in providing it with heirs, you lobcock, not giving the estate managers advice they neither want nor need!"

Miss Avery, meanwhile, was stalking rats. She'd burned pastilles in the master bedroom, boiled all the linen, beat all the rugs, changed the mattress. Now she and Clyde were on the hunt.

Mangy rats, she sought. Plague-carrying rats. Red-eyed, yellow-toothed rats as nasty as the vermin who had the nerve to laugh at her. There she'd been feeling sorry for the cad, all lumpy and swollen. Then he'd called her Annie. What was she supposed to call him? Gard, as his friends did, according to Lorna? He was so arrogant, so self-assured, he most likely preferred to be called God. Heaven knew he had the same morals as those old Greek basket-scramblers. He even looked like a god with his dark curls and ripply muscles and finely detailed features, flea bites notwithstanding. Still, he was a rodent.

"Why'n't you just put down some poison, chickie,

if you're so worried about pests gettin' into the house? Get rid of the problem onct and for all."

So she consulted Grandmother's stillroom book, took her market basket, and stomped off to the apothecary. When he read her list, the assistant there gave her an odd look, undecided whether to call for the manager or the constable. Annalise glanced over both shoulders, the high one and the low one, to make sure no one overheard, then whispered, "Mistress runs a school for wayward boys. Springtime, don't you know."

The assistant put the powders and salts in a sack. "This should take care of the problem for her."

Her house in order, or soon to be, Miss Avery went riding in the park. Smuggling Napoleon out of Elba had to be less complicated.

At seven o'clock in the morning, Rob walked Annalise the three blocks to the Holborn road. No one in the neighborhood who was awake at the time saw anything unusual about the new servants from Number Eleven setting out on their errands. They were used to Tuthill the stableman and his widowed niece who kept house because she was too ugly to get lucky twice.

The pair was met at the Holborn road by a hackney carriage, a former associate of Rob's at the ribbons. The housekeeper entered the coach, a black cloak covering her from collar to toes, a black coalscuttle bonnet concealing most of the rest of her.

When the carriage pulled up at a livery stable behind Cavendish Square, an establishment also owned by a friend of Rob's in his earlier days, an elegant young woman stepped out. There was no question that this was a lady, not with her noble bearing and obviously expensive green velvet riding habit in the latest military style, which she filled to admiration since the habit's alterations.

She wore a veil over her face, attached to a shallow-crowned beaver hat with green feathers at the side; only the tiniest hint of silver-blond curls peeked out beneath the brim. Just in case there was any doubt of the Fair Incognita's status, the biggest, brawniest groom in the stable bowed low, assisted the lady onto the back of her prancing mare, and followed her down to Oxford Street and hence to Hyde Park. The fraternity of the road was a loyal bunch, or Rob would never have let Annalise out of his sight.

Miss Avery had a glorious ride, feeling freer than she had in ages. It was almost as if she could outride her problems, just gallop away on Seraphina and leave all of the distress and uncertainty behind. Nothing could destroy her sense of release this morning, not even the gentlemen just returning home from an evening's carousal who were stopped dead in their wobbly tracks by the vision of a goddess flying past on her Arabian mare. They may have been tempted to try to stop her, to talk to her, but the fellow riding behind on a rangy bay looked like he'd be more at home on a gibbet than on a jaunt in the park. If Clarence's scarred face and thick arms were not discouragement enough, the pistol tucked in his waistband was. The wastrels doffed their hats and reverently watched her ride away.

One fellow was not so polite, or so wise. A sporting mad young buck out exercising his stallion decided to make a race of it with the veiled equestrienne. He tried to pull ahead on his barely controlled mount so he could cut her off and force her to a halt and an introduction before any of the other early morning riders got to her. Ignoring the warning from the lady's groom, he made a grab for her reins, shouting suggestive offers at the same time.

Annalise could not have been more disgusted if

one of the park pigeons had left its calling card on
her shoulder. She reached over and brought her riding crop down on the scoundrel's gloved hand, then,
when he pulled back, down on his horse's flank. At
the same time a pistol shot rang out. The unruly
stallion snorted, lifted all four feet off the ground,
did an about-face, and departed a few days early for
the Newmarket meets. His rider didn't make it as
far as the park gate. He stood, rubbing the part of
him that had landed hardest and contemplating the
bullet hole in his hat. He made one last try as Annalise rode past: "You could kiss it and make it
better, sweetheart!"

At least no one could see the scarlet color creeping into her cheeks. Her pleasure in the day had
been stolen by the insufferable coxcomb, however,
another male with as much control of his passions
as over his horse. Men! Faugh!

She returned home by Rob's prescribed circuitous
routes, confirmed in the righteousness of her plans.

The earl's problem was not getting Lady Moira
Campbell alone; it was putting the fiery redhead off
long enough to send a message to Laurel Street to
make sure the place was ready.

"I don't think this afternoon is the proper time
to discuss your new carriage, my lady. My mother
frowns on discussions of horseflesh over tea. Why
don't we wait for after Mrs. Hamilton's card party
tomorrow evening? That should break up early, so
we'll have ample time to make sure I know what
you want."

"I like my horses big and dark and not too tame,"
the lady murmured. The dark-haired earl stirred
his tea with added vigor. "Strong ones that can run
all night."

Lord Gardiner blotted at the tea on his fawn

inexpressibles. "I'm certain we can find just what you're looking for."

Lady Moira was statuesque, Junoesque, Reubenesque—one escargot away from plump. She was also one escapade away from being cut from polite society and even closer to drowning in River Tick. She couldn't afford a coach and four. She couldn't afford a bag of oats. And she definitely couldn't afford to let Ross Montclaire, Lord Gardiner, slip through her fleshy fingers. The earl was said to be on the lookout for a bride. With his reputation, no milk-and-water miss would suit him, not like a mature woman who could match his passion, yet still bear him sons. Stranger things had happened than a well-breeched young nobleman falling for a well-formed young widow's lush charms. He might just succumb. If not, he was known to be generous to his ladyloves. She might stave off her creditors a bit longer; she might even put off forever her acceptance of that rich old satyr with damp lips and clammy hands. She much preferred a lusty young centaur with deep pockets. Oh, yes, Moira Campbell was eager to please his lordship.

"Good evening, my lord, my lady." The earl's message to the house had stated very clearly that he was bringing a lady; Annalise was not impressed that he was associating with a higher class of doxie, although she did wonder if his choice reflected their last conversation.

The housekeeper curtsied deferentially as she took the woman's wrap. This blowzy female may be a lady, but she was certainly no better than she ought to be, with her black crepe gown cut down to there. The widow's vibrant coloring looked spectacular in black, Annalise thought sourly, looking at her own hanging black bombazine with disgust. She might look like the hag she meant to imitate, but at least she was decently covered. "You must be chilled, my lady, it's such a damp, cold night. There's a nice fire in the small parlor. And, my lord, I think I made a good find in some excellent Burgundy. I'll need your opinion, of course, before purchasing the case. If you'll come this way?"

The parlor was snug; the Burgundy was superb. The earl had two glasses finished and half Lady Campbell's buttons undone when he heard a scratching at the door.

"Yes? What is it, Mrs. Lee?"

"I'm sorry, Lord Gardiner," she said from the doorway, her eyes carefully averted, "but Robbie thinks there might be a swelling in one of the horses' forelegs."

"Blast!" But he went to check his precious cattle.

"Would you care to wait upstairs, my lady? Perhaps you'd enjoy a relaxing bath while his lordship is busy with the horses? These things can take awhile, as I am sure you know. I can have hot water upstairs before you can say Jack Rabbit."

When Gard came back, complaining that he found no swelling and no stableman, either, Annalise was quick to tell him that Rob must have gone to the livery stable to fetch ingredients for a poultice. "You know he would not take a chance with the horses. Oh, and Lady Campbell is having a bath."

She only raised her pointed chin a little, as if to say this was part of her tidy housekeeping. He nodded curtly and went to stand by the fire, cold again. He welcomed the glass of wine Annie put in his hand.

Annalise ran upstairs to help Lady Campbell with her bath, downstairs to tell the earl just a few minutes more and pour him another glass of Burgundy. Upstairs, downstairs. "Will that be all, my lord?"

"Yes, thank God. Ah, thank you, Annie. I'll see to the lady now."

Annalise's lip curled. He'd see her, all right. The trull was lazing in the tub surrounded by bubbles, waiting for Lord Gardiner to watch her leave the water, like Venus rising from the sea. Or a fat pink sow shaking off a puddle. Annalise went back to her own rooms. Gard flew up the stairs.

Now, there was a sight that could warm any man's blood. Except that Ross was still a trifle chilled. He held the towel and Moira flowed into it, not so quickly that he couldn't see she was a natural redhead after all, disproving his doubts. But that rosy skin, that fiery triangle. Ah, the heat rose in his face, at least.

"Come to bed, my centaur," she urged, unbuttoning his marcella waistcoat, letting the towel fall to the floor between them. Soon his shirt followed. "Hurry, my charger, I want to ride." And his dove-gray pantaloons. "I want to gallop with the wind, my noble mount, my stallion." Finally his small-clothes. My gelding?

Moira shrugged. The earl took another drink from the bottle he'd carried upstairs. "Just a little cold," he apologized.

"I'll warm you soon enough," she said, getting into the bed and holding out her arms.

'Faith, she was inviting. Not just a tasty morsel, she was a whole feast, laid out just for him. Why was his appetite not rising to the occasion? Because instead of her lush charms he saw his blasted housekeeper's sidewalk-straight chest. Instead of flowing auburn locks he saw an awful, dingy cap. And instead of Moira's full red lips he saw Annie's pursed-up, pinched-together mouth, frowning in disapproval. Or worse, smirking in secret enjoyment. Let the old stick enjoy this, he thought, throwing himself into Moira's eager embrace, returning kiss for kiss, caress for caress.

Soon they were both damp and breathing hard. Moira had twice crested the great steeplechase hurdle and feigned a third. The earl had not yet left the gate.

"My Earl en Garde," Moira panted in his ear. "I have yet to be pierced by your famous sword. Show me your weapon," she gasped. "I long for your forged steel."

Unfortunately, that particular dagger stayed in its scabbard. The earl's lance couldn't have made an indentation in a feather pillow. Blade, bayonet, broadsword—there wasn't enough mettle to make a butter knife.

Moira did not give up. Her hair hanging in moist tendrils, she tried tricks no Haymarket whore would do, to the embarrassment of them both. Nothing. Then she laughed. And kept laughing all the way down the stairs, where Annie held the door open for her.

Chapter Twelve

*H*is life was over. There would be no pleasure. Ever. No children. Ever. So this was his punishment for a life of sin, being cut down in his prime. He should have listened to his mother and ensured the succession years before. Now, most likely his father would come visit *him* in the middle of the night. Lord knew, no one else was going to.

Gard checked under the covers. No soldier stood at attention. "Traitor!" he cried. "Deserter!" Near tears, he drank straight from the bottle of wine, not bothering to find a glass. Maybe he should see a physician? Maybe he should join a monastery. Lord, the closest he'd ever get to a woman again was with a drawing pencil—one with lead in it! If he got up, he could go visit the foundling hospital on the other end of Bloomsbury, see all the little nippers no one wanted—no one but a man who would never have his own.

No, he thought, if he got up, he might have to

face Annie and her knowing smile. His life was hard enough. It was the only thing that was.

Jupiter, how was he ever going to face Lady Campbell? She wasn't some chance-met cyprian he'd never see again. She was part of the beau monde. He was bound to encounter her at every ball, rout party, and breakfast his mother dragged him to. The theater, the opera, not even the farthest-flung of his properties was far enough away to make a safe haven. The woman was always invited to country parties. What could he say? What could she say? Then again, she might find a lot to say—to everyone else. What if Moira Campbell were a gossip?

Oh, God, all women were gossips!

It was all Annie Lee's fault, of course, that he'd picked a prime article from the polite world instead of his usual opera dancers and actresses. Hell, Corinne could have slept through the whole debacle and woke with a smile on her lips. But no, there was Annie with her long-nosed insinuations that his soiled doves were befouling her roost. Her roost! He laughed, but it came out more a sob. Quit whining, she'd said when he complained about the flea bites. Would she tell him to keep a stiff upper lip now, too?

Gard drank the last of the wine and lay in a sodden stupor, telling himself that he'd get up and go home when he was sure the old bat had gone to sleep. He stayed awake, breathing in the nauseating mixture of sweat and heavy perfume, afraid to shut his eyes. He knew he'd hear Moira's laughter in his nightmares, that and Annie's "Good night, my lady. Thank you for coming."

"All right, missy, I want to know what you did to that poor bloke. I brought me a peacock and his game pullet to the house, and I took home a cackling hen. Hours later I get to half carry a bird what's like to cock his toes up. Plucked and ready for the pot, he looked. I want to know what's going on, chickie."

Annalise was in her riding habit, the black cape buttoned securely over it so no green showed. She was getting warm in the stable, warm under the ex-highwayman's steady regard. "Don't be silly, Rob. I just keep house, remember?"

"And I've known you since you was in pinafores, remember? I mistrust that dancin' light in your eyes. Tells me you've been up to no good. Just how bad have you been, is what I want to hear." He made no move to follow her when she stepped impatiently to the door, just stayed seated on an upturned keg, polishing harness.

So Annalise told him. About the sleeping powder in the wine and the fleas in the bed.

"And?"

"And . . . I gave the earl an inhibitor."

"An inhibitor?" Rob sounded it out. "You gave him something to inhibit his—gor blimey, you didn't, girl!"

She nodded and picked up the harness he'd dropped.

"You took the charge out of his pistol? The wind out of his sail? The fire out of his furnace? That's downright evil. Why, I knows body snatchers as wouldn't sink so low."

Annalise shook the reins under her friend's nose. "He is not going to carry on in this house while I am under this roof!"

Rob shook his head. "Little harmless fun is one thing. Give him somethin' to think about besides his rod. But diddlin' him out of it altogether is a whole nother kettle of fish, chickie. I ain't going to be party to filchin' any fellow's manhood."

"Gammon. I didn't steal anything. I didn't even

borrow it! That insufferable man's manhood is the last thing I'd want! I simply discouraged him, temporarily, so maybe he'll go away and leave us in peace."

"And maybe he'll kill hisself. You didn't see the look on his face. A fellow loses his pride, his confidence."

"Oh, pooh. You're making too much of it, Rob."

"And you're making too little." His face split in a grin, till he remembered the unfortunate earl, and his audience. "Deuce, chickie, you don't know what you're talkin' about, innocent miss like you. You ask Henny. At least she appreciates a man for what he is. No matter. Whatever old-maid notion you've got in your pretty head, I won't stand for any more of this tinkerin' with his, ah, virility. You find some other way of keepin' his bed empty or him out of it, you hear me, missy?"

"I hear you, Rob. Now can I go for my ride?"

He went back to polishing the tack. "That's another thing. You're stirrin' up talk with your rides in the park."

"But I don't speak to anyone, and I have your friend Clarence with me. No one has bothered us since that first time."

"No, but they've noticed. Can't help it, you ridin' neck or nothin' like you was born in the saddle."

She smiled. "Well, I was, practically. And you taught me everything else." Clyde came in, so Annalise bent down and scratched behind the little dog's ears.

Rob looked up, and his weathered face creased in a grin. "Howsomever, you do look a picture on your horse. And all veiled like that, you create a kind of mystery for the paper-skulls with naught else to do but gawk."

"Those fops and fribbles are harmless enough.

99

The others who are out exercising their horses know better than to come near."

"Aye, but they're talkin'." He turned aside and spit into a bucket halfway across the floor. "London's a great place for talkin', you know. Clarence says he heard mention of a lady in green in the pubs."

"So let them talk." Annalise kept petting the dog.

"Thing is, I have one of my chums on the lookout. Sir Vernon's sent orders to the Clarendon, where he keeps rooms and a staff. Keepin' it mum about any missin' heiress so far, but he's got men out askin' questions."

"But none of his London people know me, and he's never seen this green habit. And I make sure every morning that Clarence remembers to paint the three white stockings and blaze on Seraphina. There is no way Sir Vernon's people can recognize me."

"Ain't many women ride like the wind, chickie."

"Oh, Robbie, don't say I shouldn't go!" she pleaded, taking the harness away from him. "I cannot attend parties or the opera. I must not visit the fashionable shops or booksellers where the ton gathers. I can't even go sight-seeing except dressed as an old crone. Please don't say I have to stay indoors all day, feeling as depressed as I look!"

"Reckon you'd only get up to more mischief that way, anyhow. Suppose it'll do, leastways till we hear Sir Vernon hisself comes to town. I'll have Clarence take another groom along. And maybe you should get to the park an hour earlier, afore the young bucks get there."

Annalise laughed. "Then we'll certainly have to convince his lordship to go home early at night, won't we?"

The earl went home and soaked in a hot tub to get rid of the stink at least, if not his despair. His spirits did not rise, however, nor anything else.

He sent his disapproving valet for a bottle of brandy. "But, my lord, it's barely gone seven."

"Morning or evening? No matter. Just fetch the liquor, Ingraham."

Then Ross decided he'd never drink again. Men were often ruined by strong spirits; he'd always heard it was so. Who'd have thought it could happen to Lord Gardiner, though? He'd been a three-bottle, four-barmaid man in his salad days. Obviously his salad was wilted.

Hell, he reconsidered, if he could never go wenching anymore, he may as well drink himself into oblivion. He started as soon as his man returned with the bottle.

Ingraham was shocked. "But, my lord, we have an appointment with Gentleman Jackson for this morning, and we are promised to attend a Venetian breakfast this afternoon with Lady Gardiner. Then there is dinner at White's with Mr. Fansoll."

"*We* aren't going anywhere. Certainly not to be pummeled by any sparring partner or fawned over by those simpering misses. And as for White's . . ." He shuddered, thinking of listening to the latest *on-dit*, knowing there was a special place in tattle-monger's hell reserved just for him. "You can make my excuses, Ingraham. Tell them I'm below par, out of sorts, under the weather. Incapacitated." He shuddered again.

Ingraham attempted to put his hand on the earl's forehead to feel for a fever. He was roughly pushed aside. "Shall I call a physician, my lord?"

"No, just leave me alone." Then Gard regretted the real concern he saw on his old retainer's face. "I just need a few hours' sleep. Been trotting too hard, is all. Don't worry, I'll be right as a trivet tomorrow."

Ingraham smiled in relief. "That's all right, then.

A day's rest should put the starch back in your step."

Too bad that wasn't where he needed it.

Annalise put the mare through her paces, wishing there were a jumping course, a real challenge. As it was, her mind was only half on controlling the playful chestnut. The other half of her thoughts were on Rob's words, what he'd said about his lordship.

Taking the lustful Lord Gardiner down a peg or two was as satisfying as this morning's hard gallop on the deserted paths. On the other hand, even she had to admit he was a handsome devil, exuding manliness with every breath. It would be a sin to cause such a virile man permanent damage, even if he was a rogue. Gelding a fractious stallion was one thing, but Annalise never meant to end Lord Gardiner's career as a rake altogether, just while he was in her vicinity. His morals or lack of them were his own affair, as long as he kept his affairs out of her house.

Unhappily for Miss Avery's conscience, her grandmother's directions were not quite as explicit as Annnalise could have wished. Most likely the older woman never had occasion to use that particular formula.

Annalise was thinking so hard about his lordship's condition that she never heard her name called.

"Miss Avery? Miss Annalise Avery?"

By the time the name registered, she and Seraphina and their two escorts were far beyond the caller. Clarence and his cohort were not aware of her real name in any case, just knowing her as a connection of Cock Robin's. Ma'am, she was to them, or Miss Robin. They never looked back.

Annalise knew the danger and was able to ride on without registering the slightest start at hearing her name, not the smallest jab at the reins to disturb the mare's easy gait, not the tiniest stiffening of her own erect carriage. She did turn back at the fork in the path, though, cantering effortlessly the way she had come, trying to spot her adversary in order to get a good description of him for Rob. The man called out again as they passed, and she looked right through him, through her veil, with the same haughty rise of her chin she gave the few pedestrians who sought to engage her in conversation. One man whistled and another rudesby tipped his hat and offered compliments on her riding. She kept going, knowing that anyone who sought to follow would be deterred by her companions.

Annalise knew better than to flee the park immediately, so she continued with her ride although her peace was cut up. She thought she'd acquitted herself well, but now she had something else to worry about in addition to Lord Gardiner's sex life.

Chapter Thirteen

*L*ord Gardiner slept the clock around. He awoke at dawn refreshed and optimistic. The morning waters always—no, the tide was still out. He decided to go riding despite the dismals. A horse just might be the only thing he'd ever mount again.

Expecting to have the park to himself, he was astounded at the small knots of riders and carriages he saw along the tanbark. Even Cholly Fansoll was out, and Cholly never stirred before noon.

"What's toward, Cholly?" Gard asked, pulling his black stallion to a halt alongside his friend's curricle. "A race or something starting here?"

"Where have you been that you haven't heard the latest—oh, forgot. Sickly, your man said. How are you feeling, then?"

"Fine, fine." He didn't want to talk about it. "What's this about, some new marvel?"

Cholly just smiled. "Wait."

All eyes were directed toward the avenue along the Serpentine, so Gard looked that way, too, holding his restive horse in check with a firm hand. "I know you want to run, Midnight. Soon, boy."

In a few minutes a collective sigh went up from the gathered gentlemen as a perfect vision cantered down the path.

"My word, what a magnificent creature," Gard exclaimed.

"And the horse isn't half bad, either. Part Arabian from the neck and the small head. She's got enough speed to give even your Midnight a run for it, I'd guess from the way she's been showing all the chaps her heels."

"Who the devil is she?" the earl demanded, interrupting Cholly's continuing enumeration of the chestnut mare's fine points, from the three white stockings to the white blaze on her forehead.

"Dashed if I know. That's what all the commotion is about. Fellows are determined to find out. Intrigue fires 'em up, don't you know. Lady in Green, they're calling her. Don't talk to anyone, won't stop for anything. Bets are on whether she's just another pretty horsebreaker trying to stir up interest and a higher price, or visiting royalty trying to remain incognito. Eccles has a monkey riding on her being someone's runaway wife. Alvanley thinks she's just some demirep with a horrible scar, and that's why she stays all covered up."

"I'll lay my blunt on the princess."

"But you can't see her face!"

"She's just got to be beautiful. Look at that figure. Besides, only a beautiful woman carries herself with such assurance. And none of the Fashionable Impure would ever be seen with two such thatch-gallows in tow. Or a veil. Or without her manager, if she's looking for a new protector. No, she's a lady."

"Someone's wife, then?"

"No one in his right mind would let her out of

his sight, and someone would have identified her by now if she was married to any of the peerage. She's a princess, all right. There's just something about her." And something else about her, perhaps the defiant way she raised her head and ignored the stares and whispers, perhaps just the silly green feathers trailing along the cheek he couldn't see, appealed to him so much that he felt a current stir in himself he feared was dead. He shifted in the saddle and grinned. "I think I'm in love."

"In rut, more like," his friend commented ruefully, out of long habit, "though how you can be without ever seeing the female is more than I can say. Still, glad to see you're takin' an interest. Some odd stories going a—"

Gard rode forward, to see better. He knew the path the lady was on, but so did the others. He couldn't get near.

Annalise was getting nervous. All those men, all the carriages. Her tension was reaching Seraphina, making the high-strung animal jittery. Annalise turned to her escorts to tell Clarence to close ranks, to ride closer, they'd be leaving the park. But a high-perch phaeton somehow darted into the narrow path between her and her companions. When she looked forward again, a racing curricle was sideways across the roadway in front, and riders and men on foot lined the grass verge on her right side, with the river hemming her in on the left. Seraphina pranced in place uneasily. Annalise stroked the mare's neck, but her own tension was like a hammer pounding between her ribs.

"A moment of your time, pretty lady," the driver of the curricle called to her. He was what Robbie would have called a curst rum touch, she could see from his snuff-stained shirt, the pouches under his eyes, the evil grin that showed blackened teeth. She said nothing, allowing Seraphina to back and circle in her fidgets.

She could hear Clarence bellowing behind her, and the sounds of a scuffle where her other guard, Mick, should have been. She did not take her eyes off the dissipated driver in front of her.

"Your name, fair one, that's all."

At first Annalise did not understand what kind of game the men were playing. Surely these gentlemen—and she labeled them thus from the expensive equipages she saw and the unmistakably Weston-tailored apparel on many of the leering pedestrians—never meant to offer harm to a well-bred female in broad daylight. Robbie was right, she concluded. She had made herself too mysterious to these profligates with nothing better to do than tease an unprotected woman. They were just curious. She could give them Miss Robbin or something, and they would let her pass.

Then a man in a puce waistcoat, on a winded bay, shouted to the man in the curricle, "No, Repton, that ain't all. Ask for her price."

One of the other men who bordered the path, cutting off a possible retreat through the wooded area, yelled, "I'll match it, whatever you bid."

Her price? Were they thinking Seraphina was for sale?

Then she heard another voice from behind her. "I say we get a look at her face, see what we're bidding on."

Dear Lord, they were discussing her, Annalise Avery, as if she were a horse on the block! She looked again at the man in the curricle blocking the roadway. His eyes were glinting and he licked his lips. He actually thought she would go home with him if he paid enough! Annoyance gave way to insult, tinged with fear. That man, Repton, they'd said, did not look like he'd accept a polite refusal.

One of the riders darted out of the crowd. "I'll uncover the masterpiece," he bragged, reaching for her veil.

Annalise backed Seraphina again and raised her whip.

"Watch out, Hastings, she already caught Jelcoe with the whip." There was coarse laughter from the group nearby.

The man called Hastings answered, "That's all right. I like a woman with spirit. I don't mind using a whip myself on an unruly filly."

More crude comments and advice were sent to Hastings and Repton, most of which Annalise did not understand, blessedly. She had heard more than enough, however. Anger overcame her fright. "Animals!" she screamed. "You are all worse than beasts! Have you no respect, no honor? Not all women are for sale, you dastards!"

Lord Gardiner had managed to push his way forward through the ranks of horsemen. "Bloody hell," he swore when he saw one of the lady's bodyguards on the ground, wrestling with four times his number. The other was still on his horse, but with a pistol held to his head.

Some of the other men were turning back, shamefaced and muttering. Like Cholly, they'd come only to see the latest comet in London's sky. No one wanted to have it out with Repton, though. He was hot at hand when it came to issuing challenges, and he was a crack shot with a pistol. In addition, he held a lot of the younger men's vouchers. They started drifting away.

Gard, however, was determined to go to the lady's rescue. If this wasn't a damsel in distress, he'd never played at St. George. Besides, he owed her for the boost to his morale. Then, too, he'd do his damnedest to get any female, even his housekeeper Annie Lee, out of the clutches of this pack of dirty dishes. Peep-o'day boys and ivory tuners, they were all loose screws. Repton was the worst.

The earl's plan was simple: beat the hell out of Repton and move the curricle from the lady's path. Before he got near enough, she let loose a stream of invectives that stopped him in his tracks. Then, while he and the others were still absorbing her magnificent fury and vitriolic message, the woman pulled back on her reins, causing the mare to rear. The chestnut backed up, still on her hind legs only, until her tail was almost touching the phaeton behind. With the lightest of touches the lady brought the mare down to all fours and then, with a leap and a bound and burst of speed forward, the two sailed right over Repton's curricle and away. If the old roué hadn't ducked, they'd have taken his head with them. As it was, his hat went flying.

Lord Gardiner leaned down from his stallion and retrieved the hat while most of the other spectators were still staring at the cloud of dust kicked up by the lady's departure. One or two started clapping. Ross turned back to them and sneered. "Would you have clapped so hard if she'd broken her neck trying that amazing jump? What if she'd lamed the animal, trying to get away from you?" Eyes shifted to study the ground. "And you call yourselves gentlemen. I am ashamed to be one of your number."

"Come now, Gardiner, just a bit of fun. No harm done." Repton was sitting up again, getting his color back. He held his hand out for his hat. "Since when has Earl en Garde developed such nice scruples when it comes to women anyway?"

Someone, Hastings, he thought, snickered. Lord Gardiner studied the hat in his hands. "Scruples?" he drawled. "Do you know, in all my years I never

109

had to terrorize a single defenseless female into agreeing to warm my bed. I wouldn't quite call that scruples. Not even common decency. I don't suppose you'd recognize either, Repton. By the way, I don't like your hat. It's filthy and smells rank." And he threw the offending article as far as he could, into the Serpentine. "If you have any complaints, I'll be happy to oblige."

Repton was not about to challenge the earl, not with Gardiner's prowess with a sword. Cloth-headed gapeseeds who didn't know an épée from an epergne, those he would challenge. They had to choose pistols. Of course, if Lord Gardiner challenged him ... "Want her yourself, do you?" he taunted.

The earl did not take offense. "I might not be the beast the lady called you, Repton, but I am still a man."

"Are you? I heard rumors ..."

Gard clenched his fists. The muscles in his jaw worked so hard, they twitched. He'd kill the bastard. Then he'd strangle Moira Campbell. He started to dismount. "I won't call you out, you muckworm. The field of honor is reserved for gentlemen. You'd make a mockery of it. I'm just going to beat you to a pulp."

Repton did not need another invitation. He cracked his whip over his cattle and was gone before the earl's foot touched the ground.

Gard turned to the other men. "Anybody else have any questions about my manhood?"

No one answered. Ross Montclaire had challenged Oxford's champion boxer while at school, and won. He still sparred with Gentleman Jackson himself. No one forgot that.

"Then let go of the lady's escort before I forget that I am a *gentle*man."

The man who was covering Clarence put his pistol away and stood back, but not far enough or quickly enough that Clarence's heavy boot didn't catch him in the jaw, knocking him flat on the ground. The rowdies who had tackled Clarence's partner hurried into the woods, some with spilled claret, some with daylights already darkening.

A spotty-faced sprig in yellow pantaloons brought the fellow's horse. He coughed and stammered an apology.

Lord Gardiner nodded. "We all, and everyone who considers himself a gentleman, owe you an apology. And the lady, of course." He directed his words to the two grooms, but spoke so all of the remaining members of Repton's plot could hear. "Please convey our humblest regrets for this deplorable event. And please tell your mistress that she will be perfectly secure in the park from now on. 'Twould be a shame if such a spectacular horsewoman were denied her ride. Inform the lady that I, the Earl of Gardiner, guarantee her safety." He looked around, frowning awfully, making sure the makebaits all understood that he would exact dire retribution on anyone who caused her more distress. The cowed expressions he read satisfied Gard. "The Lady in Green can ride as unmolested as my own mother. If she is still fearful, tell her that I stand ready to escort her, with no expectations or demands or disrespect. On my word of honor."

Chapter Fourteen

Annalise was shaken. She didn't know how she got home, by which route she made her way back to the livery stable, or what she told the men when they asked for Clarence and Mick. There were more insults along the way, she recalled, for a solitary woman with no escort who was galloping madly down the street as if all the hounds of hell were at her heels. They were, as far as she was concerned. Lord, was there no safe place for a woman in this whole city? If two reformed hedgebirds were not enough to protect her in the public park, she could never ride again. Now, when her looks were finally coming back so that she didn't frighten herself in the mirror, she could never come out of her crone's guise. It wasn't that she was vain about her looks; she never considered herself a beauty or anything, though Barny had been wont to call her pretty. She simply hated being the antidote Annie Lee, from whose appearance grown men turned and little children hid behind their mothers' skirts. Annalise hated being ugly. She hated being afraid. She mostly hated the feeling that she was a fox forced to go to ground, with the hunters waiting at every burrows' end, day after day.

Rob had taken Henny on errands, luckily for him, for Miss Avery was damning every male alive. She wouldn't even share her uneaten, crumpled roll with Clyde the dog.

The day got worse. As Annalise sat with trembling hands around a cup of steaming tea, looking fully as ugly as her mood, Lorna reported a man at the door.

"He's nobbut a cheeky footman, I'd guess, passing hisself off as some nob's secretary or something, all so's he doesn't have to use the back door. He's asking for the mistress, and I 'spose that's you, ma'am. I tried to send the fellow away, seeing as how you're looking blue-deviled, but the coxcomb says he won't leave a message or anything, and he'll come back another time. Thinks a lot of himself, this Stavely."

Stavely was a moderately good-looking knave with slicked-back hair and padded shoulders. He was also the man who had called her name in the park yesterday—was it just yesterday? He was Sir Vernon's man.

If she gave him short shrift, Annalise considered as she watched him preen in the hall mirror before he was aware of her presence, he'd be suspicious, wondering why his questions were going unanswered. A pretty fellow like this would be used to getting his own way among the serving girls. Also, even if housekeepers like Annie Lee were often autocratic, deeming theirs among the highest rungs on the servants' ladder, it would never do for Annalise to come over as haughty or arrogant. She didn't want this popinjay going back to her stepfather saying he was shown the door by a housekeeper who was putting on the airs of a lady. Sir Vernon was too clever. So Miss Avery gathered her shaken poise and gushed like a moonstruck tweeny as if her life depended on it. It most likely did.

"Come along, dearie. We can talk about your errand over a nice cup of tea. Or else maybe you'd fancy some of the stable man's ale. I was just saying to myself, Mrs. Lee—I'm a widow, don't you know—wouldn't it be cheery to have some company on a chill morning like this? Handsome company, too."

The footman gulped. His Adam's apple bobbed above his necktie. There was a nice reward if he found any information for his employer, but no tip was worth cozying up to an old hunchback hag like this. "No, ma'am, thanks for the offer, but I can't stay. On important business, don't you know. I'm after news of a young miss what might of come your way."

The witch cackled. "We get a lot of young misses hereabouts. A different one every day, or night. The master's a regular billy goat, he is. Of course, he's not to home right now, so don't feel obliged to stand out in the hall." She made to take his tricorne with her emaciated fingers. He snatched it out of her reach. "What did you say your name was, ducks?"

"Ah, Stavely, just Stavely. Thing is, I've got a lot of places on my list to ask."

"Oh, yes, your missing gel," the housekeeper said with disappointment in her voice.

"I only wish," he replied, equally as disappointed. "The wench is way above my touch. She's a lady, a real lady."

Annie sniffed. "No real lady would be caught dead here. There's some as calls themselves ladies, but I ask you, would a fine, well-bred female come to bachelor quarters like this?"

"No, but this one's a relation of some kind to Lady Rosalind Avery. She's got nothing to do with the buck you've got sporting here now."

"Ah, now, that's a different kettle of fish. I'm right sorry I can't help a likely looking lad such as yourself, Stavely, but I wasn't in charge here until Lady Rosalind left. I had no call to pay attention to the comings and goings of the company."

"And no young ladies have come looking for Lady Rosalind since she left?"

"Nary a female comes looking for anyone but Lord Gardiner. But I'll keep a lookout for you, Stavely my boy. How old is this lady and how'd she come to be lost?"

"She's twenty-one, used to be a real Diamond, they tell me, but maybe fallen off her looks. And she left her stepfather's household 'cause she's all about in the head."

Mrs. Lee clutched her flat chest. "Lawks a-mercy, should I call the Watch, then, if I see her?"

"No!" George Stavely exclaimed. "That is, no, ma'am. She ain't considered dangerous. The family wants her back, is all."

"Seems to me they're well rid of her if her attics are to let. What do they want her back for?"

"Sir Vernon says he wants to take care of her." He put his finger alongside his nose and grinned. "Word below stairs is that she's an heiress. Sir Vernon locks her away—for her own safety, don't you know—and there's no pesky husband to claim her dowry."

"Ah, that's a man after my own heart!"

"Here's his card, if you hear anything. There's a nice bit of silver in it for you if you find the chit."

"Hmm, might be I'd claim my reward in other ways, eh, bucko?"

George left in a hurry.

* * *

Annalise didn't bother with tea this time. She went straight for the Madeira. Near spasms, she decided she must have become another person with this disguise. In less than twenty-four hours she'd stopped a seduction, been the intended victim of a seduction, and simulated the seduction of a slimy footman. In her whole twenty-one years she'd never even contemplated such a thing. She hardly recognized herself at all! Four more years of such deception and she'd be depraved indeed.

Her friends told her she did well. Henny clucked her tongue and busied herself at the stove, but Rob thought she had a great future in the criminal world.

"Never seen a sweet young gal turn to cheatin', lyin', cussin', and committin' mayhem with such a flair. We sure could of used you in the old days. And just think, you get tired of hidin' out here in Bloomsbury, you can make a career on the stage."

"Don't tease, Rob," she said tearfully. "I know I've made a rare mull of things."

Rob lit his pipe, since Henny refused to let him chew his tobacco in the kitchen. He could chew it, that is, but he'd have to swallow the stuff. She wouldn't tolerate spitting in this fancy house. When he got the pipe going to his satisfaction, after much puffing and poking, he winked at Annalise. "Things is workin' out for the best. They allus do."

"For the best? You didn't hear about the incident in the park. I'll never be able to put off these blacks again. Poor Seraphina. No more rides for her, either."

Henny put the bottle of wine back on its shelf and substituted a cup of coffee in front of Annalise. "That's just the wine talking, missy. We'll come about. You'll see."

"Oh, no, Henny. You weren't there. Those men . . ."

"Ain't goin' to bother you again," Rob told her, pulling on his pipe. "We had the story from Clarence. Pay it no never mind, chickie. You have a protector now."

"A protector? Who in the world . . . ?"

Rob slapped his knee and grinned. "Lord Gardiner, that's who! Our very own rake is after protectin' some unknown lady's virtue. Yourn!"

Annalise just shook her head. "I have no idea what you're talking about. How could Lord Gardiner protect me—and why?"

"Seems you left the park in a hurry. Missed the gov'nor tryin' to come help you. By the time he got close, you'd already saved yourself and got away. He stayed to give them clodpates a regular beargarden jaw about honor and stuff. And he vowed to watch over you from now on."

"Me?"

"That Lady in Green they're all talkin' about. Claimed you'd be safe as houses and dared any of them to say him nay. He nearly ate them alive if they blinked, says Clarence. All the milksops backed right down, he's got such a reputation for a handy set of fives. So nary a one of them—and none of the other gents at the clubs—will dare touch a hair on your head."

Annalise didn't credit a word of Rob's story. "Have you seen it, Rob? It's finally growing back. My hair, that is. Except it's silver, not blond anymore."

"Pay attention, chickie. This here's the answer to your problems."

She sat up straighter. "What, I should become his lordship's convenient? That would certainly save me the effort of scuttling his romantic interludes. And think how . . . convenient for him: a housekeeper by day, a bed partner at night. I could have been married to Barny. That's all he wanted, besides the money."

"There wasn't no mention of any arrangement like that. In fact, the gov'nor swore he means to be your escort only, nothin' more."

"And King Arthur is asleep in a cave somewhere! Robbie, chivalry is long gone, and Lord Gardiner wouldn't recognize it if Sir Lancelot bit him on the nose."

"I'd bet his word is good. But don't be so hasty either way. Think on this: After today your steppa's bound to hear about the dasher in the park, the one with the good seat and no connections. But he won't think twice if he hears she's in Earl en Garde's keeping. No way that piece of easy virtue could have anything to do with a female who left her fiancé in a huff over his particulars. You'd be safe as the Bank of England."

"But safe from Lord Gardiner?"

"I ain't suggestin' you accept a slip on the shoulder, chickie. He gave his word as a gentleman. I trust him."

Suddenly Annalise felt better; things weren't so bleak. For some ungodly reason, contrary to all the evidence and everything she believed, she trusted Lord Gardiner, too. Then she laughed out loud. Sir Vernon must be right: She was ready for Bedlam after all.

The topic of the conversation, meanwhile, was sitting in his book room with a sketchpad on his knees and a dreamy smile on his face. He was trying to capture the graceful, soaring flight of the woman and her mare as they leapt the curricle. Of course he had no face to put on the female's form, but he recalled enough of her trim waist and rounded bosom to fire his imagination. Hell, if he had no face to depict, he might as well leave off the clothes, drawing just the female at one with her mount.

Zeus, he needed a woman!

Chapter Fifteen

The beau monde went on the strut in Hyde Park at four in the afternoon. So did the demimonde. The ton came to see and be seen; likewise the muslin trade. The ladies of fashion came to make plans to meet their gallants at the evening's parties. The Fashionable Impure came to make sure their dance cards were also filled, so to speak.

Both groups of females gathered in little knots along the paths or sat in carriages under the trees. One group had more color to their faces and gowns, fancier coaches, and no dowagers, dragons, or dogsberries among them. They also had more of the young gentlemen surrounding them.

Lord Gardiner tooled his curricle along the roadway, studying the various delectables like boxes of bonbons set out in a sweet-shop window. He doffed his hat and bowed to his mother's friends and their milk-and-water misses. He nodded and smiled at a few widows with waving hands and a few wives with wandering eyes. The curricle picked up speed.

There was no way the earl was going to dally with a lady. Not till his confidence was back, at any rate. He looked, though, with a connoisseur's eye at this one's swanlike neck, that one's narrow waist.

If truth be told, Lord Gardiner was searching for the lady from the morning. He didn't think she'd show herself here, not after her efforts at concealing her identity, but she might be playing some deep game after all. She might even be someone of his acquaintance, or soon-to-be acquaintanco, if he had any say. There were females with erect postures and stylish ensembles, but none he could identify as the elegant horsewoman who rode through his mind. Gard followed a lady wearing a feathered bonnet over short-cropped curls that turned out to be brassy blond. He halted the curricle when he saw a flash of emerald green behind a hedge: the foppish Viscount Reutersham was relieving himself.

Finally the earl's eyes lighted on a maiden sitting on a bench, twirling her parasol. She was nothing like that other female, being shorter and rounder and brunette. She was also entirely alone. Something about her appealed to Lord Gardiner, reminding him of another quest in the park that afternoon. Perhaps it was her ready smile mingled with the touch of wistfulness he saw about her eyes. Perhaps it was just that the sunlight playing on the folds of her lime-and-jonquil-striped muslin reminded him of spring, and sap rising. She'd look pleasing on canvas. She'd look pleasing on a bearskin rug.

The earl got down, handing the ribbons to his tiger. "*Bonjour, mademoiselle*, may I join you on your bench?"

It was not long before the earl had his *belle de nuit* and the female had hopes of her month's rent being paid, although nothing as vulgar as money was mentioned. Addresses were exchanged, times were arranged, and both parties were eminently satisfied. Except the lady did not want to be confused with Haymarket ware.

"I don't want you thinking I do this regular like. It's just that my usual beau is below hatches right now. I ain't looking for a new protector, either, my lord. He'll come about soon enough, I'm sure."

The earl grinned wickedly. "Let us hope not too soon, eh, *chérie*? At least not till tomorrow morning."

If oysters were the food of love, kindly Mrs. Tuthill was offering Lord Gardiner sustenance enough to pleasure a harem. Or she knew about his equipment failure. And Annie knew, who was bringing course after course to Lord Gardiner and his companion. Raw oysters, oyster bisque, smoked oysters, roast duck in oyster dressing. And Tuthill knew, having mentioned with a wink that he'd made a special trip to the fish market that morning. They all knew. Gard's hand shook.

In addition to the oysters, very little wine was served, not enough to enfeeble a fly. Gard wondered if he should check for ground-up rhinoceros horn. Rob's fellow feeling he could understand, but why did Annie Lee suddenly feel sorry for him, sorry enough to provide encouragement, when she was the one who deplored his wenching? Did she take pride in her household, like his valet refusing to send him out in anything less than prime twig, claiming it was a reflection on the man's skills? Gads! It was bad enough the polite world discussed his performance; Annie Lee keeping score was enough to dull any man's desire. He almost choked on his last forkful of prawns stuffed with oysters.

Gard couldn't imagine what dessert might be. If there were oyster tarts, he'd dismiss them all. Still, his dinner partner seemed to be taking it all in good part, licking her lips, licking her fingers, licking his fingers. He might be mortified, but he was still interested, thank heavens.

"Do you wish dessert, Sophy, or shall we wait for later?"

Sophy? No, it couldn't be, Annalise considered, a bubble of hysterical laughter welling up inside her. London was just too big a place for that. This girl looked younger than her own twenty-one years—though Annalise had never considered the proper age for a man's mistress—and she was not the great beauty Annalise assumed Sophy would be. Still, her name was Sophy and she was a lightskirt.

So Annalise spilled some of the oyster sauce on Sophy's sleeve. "Oh, I am so sorry, miss! The plate just seemed to slip. Please, if you'll just come with me, I can sponge that off in a trice before it stains. Oh, do forgive me, miss. Right this way." Then she added for Lord Gardiner's sake, "Mrs. Tuthill is preparing a special dessert right now, one that won't keep. She just needs ten minutes more. I'll be sure to have Miss, ah, Sophy restored by then."

They were gone before Gard could offer to see about Sophy's dress himself, and to hell with dessert.

While she worked, Annalise was profuse in her apologies. "I could not be more sorry, ma'am. Such a lovely gown, too. I once saw one like it on a woman in Drury Lane and said to myself, what a handsome frock, especially with the lady's brunette coloring. Why, now that I think of it, it could have been you. Did you ever wear this gown to the theater? Not that I mean to pry, mind."

While Annalise worked, Sophy was surveying the amenities in the lady's dressing room of the master suite. "Some women can afford a new gown each time they go out," she answered with a hint of petulance, examining the silver comb-and-brush set laid out for visitors' use. She was not immune to the housekeeper's flattery, though. Poor old dear likely never got any thrills but for seeing her betters at the theater and such. "I may have worn it to the Opera House a time or two."

"No, I never go there. Can't understand the words they're singing."

"La, no one listens to the music. They just go to be seen."

"For my money, I like to see a show *and* the nobs. Still, the lady I recall at the theater was with a right handsome gentleman. Of course, I was just in the pit and they were in the boxes, but he seemed fair-haired and solidly built. Lovely couple, I thought at the time. Wouldn't that be a coincidence if it was you, and here I am wiping your sleeve."

"Oh, that must have been me and the Barnacle. Barny Coombes, don't you know. I call him that 'cause he's a clinger. When he was flush, that was fine. We used to go to all the fanciest places."

"And now?"

"Oh, now he's badly dipped. Rusticating until he can find an heiress or something. Aren't you done yet? I don't want his lordship getting restless, not with him swimming in lard."

"Just finished." Annalise held up the gown for inspection. "As good as new."

"Nothing is as good as new, ducks. I'll tell you what, if his lordship keeps me around a bit, I mean to get a whole new wardrobe. You can have this rag, since you seem to like it so much."

Annalise could hardly bear to touch it, but she helped Barny's mistress into the gold sarcenet. So Lord Gardiner could help her out of it. Miss Avery seethed behind her dark glasses. "Too generous, ma'am," she murmured.

Sophy clapped her hands and cooed when the housekeeper carried in the dessert, a peach flambé, blue flames licking at the edges. Lord Gardiner had the idea of feeding Sophy himself, sharing his dish, his spoon, and bitefuls of the brandy-soaked fruit, then sharing her tasty kisses. A dessert leading into the real dessert, as it were.

Annie had other ideas, quickly shoveling two servings into dishes and slamming them down at their places at opposite sides of the table.

A manservant would have known better, Lord Gardiner thought. Tarnation, a woman with any blood in her veins would have known better. She stood now at the sideboard with arms folded across her non-chest, waiting to see if they needed anything else. Like a carrion crow at the banquet, Lord Gardiner reflected sourly. "That will be all, Annie," he told her.

"Poor thing," Sophy said, wiping a gob of cream off her chin as Annie curtsied and backed out of the room.

Poor thing? What about him, who had to put up with the Friday-faced, cross-grained creature? Ross did *not* want to think about her tonight. Especially not tonight. "Can I offer you more of the sweet, my sweet?"

Sophy did not need his fingers drumming impatiently on the tabletop to hurry her along. Evidently his lordship's hunger had not been satisfied by the meal. "No, thank you, my lord, I've had enough. My compliments to your chef. Shall I, ah, leave you to your port?"

"Not on your life," he growled.

"Then perhaps you'd be kind enough to give me a tour of the house," she said with a wink. "I just love seeing how various rooms and things are decorated."

The drawing room got decorated with his neck-cloth and her shoes. The smaller parlor was soon strung with silk stockings, and the hall stairs received a hail of hairpins along its length. The guest bedrooms each received a cursory visit, and a bit of muslin here, a waistcoat there. By the time Gard and Sophy reached the large bedroom, there was very little sight-seeing left to be done.

Sophy's body was as luscious as his mind had imagined, and his own—well, his mind and his body were both ready, willing, and able, thank whatever saint watched over weak-kneed womanizers. Thank the oysters. And thank Sophy for molding her contours so exquisitely to his.

Intending to show Sophy just how grateful he was, Gard stepped out of her embrace to fix the bed. She swayed against him, though. "A moment, my pet, let me turn down the bedclothes."

She stared at his naked body, and her eyes snapped shut.

He kissed her and she groaned.

He touched her breast. She clutched her stomach. He turned to extinguish another candle. She turned green.

"My lord, I . . . I think I'm going to be . . ."

She was. On the bed, on the floor, on the fastidious Lord Gardiner.

"Annie!"

The earl tried to help at first. But the smells, the sounds . . .

Annie took one look at him and raised an eyebrow in scorn. "I know, you have a sensitive stomach, too."

Gard shrugged his shoulders helplessly. "I'm a regular Trojan when it comes to blood and broken bones. But this—my stomach gets tied in knots. I'm a fine sailor, until everyone else starts hanging over the side."

Sophy started making gagging sounds again. Gard fled downstairs before he looked worse in Annie's eyes, although he didn't know why he should care what his housekeeper thought. He found that he just did, especially when he saw how hard she worked all night, making frequent trips up and down the stairs with slop jars and buckets and mops and fresh linens. All he could do was wait and see if a physician was needed. Tuthill could have ridden for the doctor, of course, but the earl had too fine a sense of responsibility for that, even if he was useless in the sickroom.

Annie tried to tell him to leave, saying she did not even need Mrs. Tuthill's assistance, for the stairs would be too much for her aunt. Besides, according to Annie on one of her trips from the kitchen, the older woman was devastated to think that her cooking may have been responsible.

"She checked the oysters ever so carefully, my lord. But you never can tell with them."

"Nonsense, I feel fine—except when Sophy makes those noises. And oysters are chancy. Everyone knows that."

Close to morning Annie reported that he should take Sophy home now. She might be more comfortable in her own bed.

Annie looked so exhausted, it appeared to Lord Gardiner that even the hump on her raised shoulder was drooping. She had every cause to be tired, he thought thankfully, for he couldn't have done half what she had this night. He tried to express his appreciation.

"I'm dreadfully sorry you had to go through this, Annie. I don't know what I'd have done without you, and that's a fact. I won't be bringing company tomorrow, so you can rest, and I'll leave something extra for you to buy yourself a gift."

Annalise smiled at him, more in charity with the rakeshame earl than ever before. He didn't have to stay, she knew. Most other men would not have made themselves uncomfortable for a straw damsel they hardly knew, not when they had paid servants to do their dirty work. That's what servants were for, she'd heard Barny say time after time. She repeated it now, "That's what servants are for, my lord. I was just doing my job," so he wouldn't feel the least guilty. After all, what had he to feel ashamed over? He wasn't the one who'd given poor Sophy a dose big enough to purge a pony. She smiled at Lord Gardiner again.

So astounding was the occasion—a smile from Annie Lee—and so sweet was the smile that Gard took special notice. Her lips were not quite as thin and parched, and her cheekbones no longer stood out like a skeleton's. He couldn't see her eyes, of course, and there was still that three-hair mole on her cheek and the dreadful mobcap, but Annie was definitely looking better.

Hell and damnation, he swore to himself later. He'd been without a woman so long, even the hag of a housekeeper was beginning to look good to him!

Chapter Sixteen

*H*e sent Sophy home in the closed carriage with Tuthill driving after all. She sat huddled miserably in the corner of the carriage, wrapped in blankets and one of Annie's black gowns. She wouldn't look at him, not even when he tucked a roll of bills into the blankets.

Gard went home, bathed, shaved, put on his buckskins and boots, and rode to the park through a thin mist. She never came, the woman he was sworn to protect, but he gave himself and his stallion a good workout, searching. No woman who would jump a carriage from a near standstill could be hen-hearted, he convinced himself. She'd be there tomorrow. The drizzle must be keeping her away.

The weather did not discourage that dirty dish Repton and his cronies from gathering near the park gate, making assignations with the pretty exercise girls parading their horses and their wares.

"What happened, Gardiner, your little bird flown so soon?" Repton called over.

Gard turned his back on Repton's taunting grin.

"Maybe she didn't take him up on his noble offer," Repton gibed to his passenger, another loose-screw lordling, but in a rasping voice loud enough for Gard to hear. "I wouldn't be surprised. I understand our eager earl is losing his touch."

Lord Gardiner went home and went to bed. Alone. Again.

His mystery lady was sleeping the sleep of the just. Well, if not the just, at least the satisfied. Lord Gardiner's nefarious designs were foiled for another night—two if he was staying away this evening also—and Sophy was well paid for her avarice. And for one night's agony, according to Rob, who carried in the roll of soft for the bedraggled baggage. Sophy was already recovered, but Lord Gardiner could never be interested in her again, not after seeing his would-be paramour looking like something even the cat wouldn't drag in. Vengeance was sweet.

And a whole day and night without worrying about the devilish lord! Annalise was too tired for her ride, but if she slept the day away, then maybe she'd get to Drury Lane or the Opera House after all. She'd be dressed like a scarecrow and seated in the pit, but it was time Miss Avery got to enjoy something of London.

The Earl of Gardiner was in his box at the theater. He was definitely not enjoying himself. Where the ton was used to seeing the most stunning of dashers at his side, dressed in jewels to rival the crystal chandeliers, they now saw a tongue-tied young chit in pastel-pink muslin with a white net overskirt that was covered with bows. She wore a

130

lace fichu lest anyone's blood be roused to lust by the sight of her insignificant attractions, and a single strand of pearls around her short neck. She may as well have *virgin* written on her forehead.

In case someone in the audience this evening missed the significance of seeing the earl with a demure young miss, her parents sat behind them, beaming. The Duke and Duchess of Afton were having a delightful time of it, waving to their friends, planning the nuptials of their Araminta to this nabob of a nobleman. Gard's mother was also in alt, sitting on his other side, pinching his arm in its blue superfine whenever his attention wandered, which was often. Unlike his usual demireps with their scintillating flirtations, this chit had no conversation at all. She was so overawed by his presence, she answered all of his polite efforts at setting her at ease with monosyllables, except when she said, "Whatever you think, my lord."

He thought he'd rather be at Laurel Street, eating tainted oysters. Maybe he was losing his touch after all.

Lady Araminta did provide a moment's divertissement halfway through the farce. She fainted when a little chorus girl blew Lord Gardiner a kiss as she made her exit. Countess Stephania nearly wrenched her son's arm off in her outrage when he suggested perhaps the wench may have intended her gesture of affection for His Grace, Lord Afton. That's when Her Grace, Lady Afton, fainted, too.

After Their Graces' departure, Gard just smiled angelically, nodding to acknowledge the crowd's delight in this tempting morsel for tomorrow's scandalbroth.

The next interval brought him an invitation to the Green Room which he would have ignored, except for the desire to escape his mother's continuing diatribe on his wastrel life. On his way out of the box, Ross managed not to trip on the cane she extended in his path.

The brazen chit wasn't waiting for him in the Green Room as he expected; the theater manager was, with an offer offensive even by Lord Gardiner's standards.

"I'm giving you first choice," the man, Bottwick, oozed. " 'Cause the gel seems taken with you."

"With my money, you mean." Gard did not like dealing with procurers. Women earning their way giving pleasure was one thing; men living off their labor was another. He knew this man took an interest in more than his actresses' welfare, and was repulsed.

"I prefer to make my own arrangements, thank you." He was polite, but he was not interested.

"But this one's different. She don't know how to make those kinds of arrangements, so she asked me to help. Her first time, don't you know," he added slyly.

Gard was even more disgusted. The price would be skyrocketed for the dubious pleasure of deflowering a virgin. He thought of Lady Araminta. "Sorry, innocents don't appeal to me. I don't believe in ruining maidens, not even opera dancers."

"Everybody's got to have a first time." Bottwick rubbed his stubbled chin reflectively. "And Mimi can't make her rent on what I can afford to pay her. She's just a chorus girl, after all. Some talent, but needs training. Lessons cost money, too." He shook his head regretfully. "It'll have to be some swell or other, sooner or later. May as well be one as has the blunt to pay for the privilege. Too bad it can't be a real gentleman like your lordship. Guess I'll have to take Lord Repton up on his offer, then."

Repton? With that saucy bit of fluff? Gard hadn't studied Mimi until she blew him that kiss, but he remembered a taking little thing with flowing blond curls, big eyes, and shapely ankles as she pirouetted off the stage. Mimi in Repton's arms was a sacrilege.

"Very well, and I'll meet your price, but never again. I never want to hear about your sordid little transactions or your supposedly chaste young ingenues. Do you understand?"

Bottwick bowed. " 'Twas Mimi's choice, not mine."

"Very well. Tomorrow. I'll have a carriage meet her after the performance." He turned away, then gave the man another dark scowl. "And don't think to sell her to Repton tonight, or I'll have your hide. Her maidenhead won't have time to grow back by tomorrow, so I'll know."

Annalise loved the theater, except for Lord Gardiner's making a buffoon of himself during the farce. The notion that she disliked his looking foolish in front of others did not bear close examination, especially since she seemed to devote her own energies to that very end. That was different, she told herself.

The fact that the man was a prize fool besides being a prime profligate didn't keep Annalise from her ride the next morning. Both she and Seraphina needed the fresh air and exercise, and she did not have to talk to the nodcock anyway.

He was astride a large black stallion, waiting by the park gates. Annalise gave the merest nod, barely acknowledging his presence, although she did note how other riders stayed away and none of the early morning strollers made comment, as had been their custom. Clarence and Mick fell back at a glance from the earl, who took his place at her side with a "Good morning, my lady." When she simply moved her head, he let the silence fall between them, not hostile or awkward, simply accepting that was the way she wanted it. He followed her lead, kept her pace, all without another word. Annalise could feel his gaze trying to penetrate her veil, but he made no effort to press her into conversation, thankfully, since his curiosity would have put paid to the excursion. The ride was exhilarating, even for a tame park outing, yet Annalise was constantly aware of his presence at her side—and the note that had come for Rob first thing that morning. Company tonight. There were preparations to be made.

She made a jerking motion with her head, indicating the ride was over, then nodded again in dismissal when they reached the gates.

Lord Gardiner bowed from the waist. "My pleasure, ma'am. Tomorrow?"

Annalise made her voice low, hoarse-sounding. "Yes, please. Thank you."

Gard watched her ride away, memorizing every detail of this intriguing woman and her horse. The mare had the three white stockings he recalled from his first view of the superb pair, two in the front, one in the rear. Oddly enough, he could have sworn they were the other way around the day she jumped the curricle, one in front, two in the rear. His incognita might be a lady, but there was something deuced havey-cavey about her. No matter. He had plenty of time to unravel the mystery, a mystery that only added to his fascination.

At an excruciatingly boring reception at Carlton House that evening, Lord Gardiner's main entertainment was fending off flirtatious matrons, since the fledglings and their mamas were giving him a wide berth after the Drury Lane incident. He'd have to remember to reward Mimi for that bit of deliverance. His other amusement was in seeking his riding companion among the assembled ladies of Quality. Too short, too round, too dark, too blasted talkative—none had her innate dignity or grace of carriage or that delicate, almost fragile look that was belied by her easy handling of the spirited mare.

Oh, well, she would keep till morning. Mimi wouldn't.

No one answered his eager knock at Laurel Street. He pushed the door open and stepped inside. No cheerful fire glowed in the parlor, no wine stood ready to be poured. Only one candle burned in the hall. In the kitchen no pots bubbled on the stove, no enticing aromas came from the ovens. The only food in sight was a big wedge of cheese being shared by a pair of mice in a cage on one of the chairs. It looked like the mice were going to have a better supper than he was, unless the mice *were* his supper.

"Annie?"

The housekeeper met him at the bottom of the stairs. She was wearing what he was coming to recognize, to his regret, as her damn-your-eyes pose: immovable, implacable, stick-thin arms crossed over nonexistent breasts, pointed chin up in the air, spectacles twitching on wrinkled nose as if she smelled something rotten—him.

"Filthy lecher," was her evening's greeting.

So much for the warmer, kinder feelings of two nights ago.

Chapter Seventeen

"Debaucher! Despoiler of children!"

Evidently, Mimi had arrived.

Gard had thought her a trifle young himself, and he never had been entirely comfortable with the situation. Still and all, dash it, he wasn't going to give his head for washing to some blasted servant. A servant, moreover, who was not some old, loyal family retainer. A servant he didn't even like!

"Enough, woman!" he thundered. "I am not in short pants to suffer your scold. Nor am I a child molester, dammit. The girl is old enough to know her own mind. She chose me and she chose this way of life!"

"She had no money and no family and the manager threatened her position at the theater if she did not take a lover to bring in more cash," Annie raged right back, not backing down an inch from the black anger in his scowl. Grown men might take cover at Lord Gardiner's temper, but Annalise Avery was made of stronger stuff. Besides, she was right. And somehow she was not frightened by this towering storm of male wrath, even if she could see his hands clenching and unclenching at his sides, knowing they were aching to get around her neck. She had principles on her side, Annie reminded herself, going on: "She had to have food and clothing and a roof over her head. Do you call that a choice, sirrah?"

"She didn't have to choose the life of an actress, deuce take it! She could have gone into service, a hundred things. Instead, she decided to use her looks and what talent she possesses to better herself."

"Better? You call this"—wildly waving her arms at the house, the darkened hallway—"better? You call selling a young girl's body better than honest work?"

"I call it the way of the world! And your sanctimonious ranting isn't going to keep her out of my bed, because that's where she wants to be. If not mine, someone else's."

Annie stamped her foot. "How can she know what she wants? She's just a frightened little girl. But that man is forcing her into prostitution! He gets a share! Did you know that?"

Gard knew he was on shaky ground here, so he blustered even louder, shaking his fist in front of Annie's spectacles in case that old bat was even more nearsighted than she was narrow-minded. "Of course I know the man is paid. It's deplorable, but that's how these things are handled, the same as an agent takes a share from an actress's salary for getting her the role. That's his job, to handle the details. The theater manager will keep any rough customers away from her"—at the thought of Repton, Gard was not even sure of that—"when he can."

"And give her to villains like you instead!"

"Otherwise she'd be in a brothel, giving a bigger share to an abbess, or walking the street, prey to every pimp, pervert, and footpad." He was satisfied with Annie's horrified gasp. At least he'd managed to shock the virago into silence. "You might find that terrible to consider, but I find it outrageous when one of my own employees considers me so steeped in sin that nothing is beneath me! I'd dismiss you in a minute if I thought you'd leave. You're like a burr beneath my skin, Mrs. Annie Lee, and I've a mind to end my irritation!"

"That's right, pick on me when your position is indefensible." She sputtered in outrage. "Oh, you are so righteous in your indignation, so noble, so honorable. By all that's holy, my lord, what did you plan on doing with that child, read bedtime stories?"

He flushed, but gamely persevered. "I didn't plan on raping the chit, you shrew. I wasn't even looking forward to taking her maidenhead, if it truly exists. Some men thrive on being the first, you know, so a virgin is considered a delicacy; the fee is commensurately higher. There are even specialty houses that cater to such desires, houses which I have never visited, blast you for thinking the worst of me. I happen to prefer women who know all about pleasure and pleasuring a—"

Annie clapped her hands over her ears. "I couldn't think that badly of you! I didn't even know such horrors existed," she screamed like a fishwife. "I have learned more about debauchery in this last sennight than I've known in all my twenty-one years!"

That took him aback. "Twenty-one years? You are one and—"

"In all my twenty-one years of service, of course." Annie took a deep breath to calm herself before she made any more errors. Before the earl could ask another question, she went on the attack again. "How can you live with yourself, leading an innocent into your life of sin?"

"Deuce take it, the girl isn't as pure as driven snow. Your chaste little Mimi blew me a kiss in front of half of London. All this nonsense about her innocence is pure fustian."

"She was raised in a convent!"

"Gammon. You fell for her Banbury tale, that's all, and you are quick to blame me. Why she sought your sympathy, I don't know, except she must have figured you'd take anyone else's side but mine. She'd have done better to come to me if she wanted to inflate the price."

"This is not about money, you . . . you . . ." His raised eyebrows belatedly reminded Annie that she was theoretically in this man's power. "Your lordship."

He shook his head, half in wonder that he didn't beat the infuriating female. "I'll never understand how you keep your naive morality in this house, Annie, but money is precisely what this is all about, not any act of conscience or otherwise. There is no way in hell that woman—not child, mind you—does not comprehend and approve what she is doing."

"Then why is she upstairs right now, crying her eyes out?"

Lud, the girl did look like a babe, lost in the big bed. She was sixteen at the most. Hell, maybe fifteen. Ross's stomach twisted. She was sleeping and her flowing blond locks were in schoolgirl braids on either side of pale, tear-stained cheeks. She was wearing a voluminous flannel nightgown—undoubtedly one of the housekeeper's—instead of the flimsy lace thing laid over a chair.

"Damn and blast!"

The girl's eyes snapped open. They were as large

as he remembered, a pretty blue even, but red and swollen. He took a deep breath. "Mimi—"

She sobbed once and reached out for Annie, who gathered Mimi into her thin arms and sat on the bed, glaring at the earl. At least he supposed she was glaring through the spectacles. He would be, in her place. Tarnation, the chit was afraid of him! "Mimi, *chérie,* please do not be frightened. No one will harm you. I swear."

She looked up uncertainly, clutching harder at Annie. "Mignon, *monsieur.* That is my name. Mignon Dupres."

"Mignon? You are the same girl who waved to me from the stage, aren't you?" Maybe there had been a terrible mistake. And maybe the theater manager would live till next week. Both were doubtful.

"*Oui.* They called me Mimi."

The earl looked triumphantly at Annie, still holding the girl's hand on the bed. "And you knew what that meant, that I might seek your company?"

"*Oui, monsieur.*"

She spoke softly, but he made sure Annie heard. "Why did you do that, *mademoiselle,* if you didn't want to, ah, become—"

"*Monsieur* Bottwick said I must, to pay for the voice lessons, *n'est-ce pas,* so he could give me a bigger part in the next play."

"Was there no one else to help with the cost? Your family?"

"Gone," she whispered. "Papa was a wine merchant. But he was a royalist."

It was a common enough story, except the Dupres family were not decadent members of the aristocracy, they were solid, middle-class citizens. The ones with all the morals. Oh, Lord. Annie was wearing that smug half smile he hated. Ross had to be sure. "This"—indicating the bedroom, the filmy negligee, his own presence—"is not what you want?"

While Mignon sobbed again, Gard felt his same presence looming larger and larger in the room, clumsy, overbearing, *de trop*. Annie handed the girl a handkerchief. After Mignon blew her nose, she looked up at him with watery eyes, full of fear.

"You can tell me, *petite*, tell me what you do want."

"I want to marry a nice man and have babies of my own."

Gard ran his hands through his already disturbed dark hair. He turned, not able to look in Annie's direction, and muttered, "Why the bloody hell did you have to choose me?"

He thought it was a rhetorical question, but Mignon answered, "Because they said you were, how do you say, *impuissant*?"

"I know how to say it, blast it! And it's not true!"

Annie staggered into the dressing room, her hand to her mouth. Gard couldn't tell if she was laughing or embarrassed or merely sparing his blushes. He grimaced, feeling the heat in his cheeks. Blushing at his age, and in front of a puritan and an infant! What a damnable coil.

Mignon hiccuped and sniffed and gave him a valiant smile. "Then if it's not true, *monsieur*, I shall try to be brave." She scrunched down in the bed, her eyes screwed shut, her arms rigid at her sides.

"Blister it, I don't take unwilling women! Or children."

"Then that *chien* Bottwick will find someone else," Mignon told him in a pitiful little voice.

It was true. That's how the whole hobble began, trying to keep her from Repton. Devil take it, the girl's fate was sealed anyway, he could at least make it as pleasant for her as possible. At this moment, however, he felt about as much desire for the chit as he did for Annie.

"No, dash it, there has to be another way. I'll find one somehow. Heaven alone knows where. You don't move from here till I decide what to do," he ordered sternly, making it plain that while he was taking responsibility for her, he was not best pleased. The door slamming behind his departure reinforced the message.

Annie came back into the bedroom and hugged the girl, not even noticing when her eyeglasses became dislodged, she was so relieved. There was nothing she could have done for the girl, nowhere she could have sent her, and not enough money to keep her from harm's way for long. Lord Gardiner had done the honorable thing. He may have needed a nudge in the right direction to get his attention above his britches, but true nobility won out. "He'll take care of you, Mignon," she reassured the girl. "You can trust him, once he gives his word."

She knew it to be true. She smiled and went down to give the mice another bit of cheese.

Cholly was concerned about Lord Gardiner's problem. Not Mimi, just the odd rumors, and now this French ladybird Gard couldn't talk around.

His round face puckered in consternation. "Wasn't expecting to see you here tonight." "Here" was White's, where the earl found his friend sprawled in a comfortable leather chair with a book, a glass of port, and a cigar. "Mean to say, I've got a houseful of sisters, nowhere I can go to blow a cloud. Thought you had other plans."

"They didn't work out." Gard sighed as he lowered himself into the chair and signaled for a glass.

"Want to toddle over to Mother Ignace's? I hear she's got some new girls."

Gard shuddered, thinking of those new girls,

tender young females, crying their innocence away.
"No!" Cholly looked startled at his vehemence, so
he explained, "Imagine your sisters lost and hungry. Maybe in a place like that."

Cholly sat up and frowned. "That's revolting,
Gard. I'd call a man out for saying such things if
he wasn't my best friend. And a better shot."

"No offense meant, Cholly. Just, oh, blast, that
little French warbler turned out to be a littler
French Cit. Selling herself instead of starving, with
that bastard Bottwick's help. I just can't stomach
it."

Cholly loosened his neckcloth. "I see what you
mean about m'sisters. I might wish them to the
devil, but still and all, mean to take care of them."

"Still and all, they are all somebody's sister! Or
daughter, or something! I never thought about it
much either till this blasted Mignon turned into a
watering pot in my bed."

"So what are you going to do with her?"

Gard took a sip of his drink. "Damned if I know.
Imagine if I took her home to the countess. She'd
skin me alive. And if I adopt the chit, pay for her
singing lessons and stuff, no one will believe I'm
not keeping her anyway. She'll never find that husband she wants. For sure I can't throw her back to
that shark Bottwick, either." He had another drink.

"What can she do?" Cholly wanted to know.

"You mean besides stir up hornets' nests? She
sings a little, and that blasted convent must have
taught her something. Needlework, pianoforte, I'd
guess." He laughed. "If you're thinking of recommending her for a governess, I'd add that she
speaks French like a native."

"Not a governess, exactly," Cholly deliberated,
puffing on his cigar. "You know, m'sisters could use
a little polish. Trying to fire all five off at once was

a mistake. Told my mother, but they're all of an age, or near enough as makes no difference."

"I danced with one of them at Almack's, didn't I? Sorry, I can't remember which. She had your color hair, though."

"Carroty. They all do. And no one can tell them apart, and not just the twins. They're pretty enough, and all have respectable dowries, but they've got no style. Just country girls, after all."

"Young misses aren't supposed to cut a dash, Cholly."

"Yes, but m'sisters get lost there with the Incomparables and the heiresses," he noted dismally. "They need something to set them apart."

"Something like a French doxie? Your wits have gone begging!"

"You said she's innocent, and I never did see a Frenchwoman without a good sense of fashion. Told m'mother the chits needed dressing up, but she's more interested in her roses and dogs."

"You really think you could hire Mignon on as some kind of fashion adviser?"

"Got to do something if I'm not going to have all five of them around the rest of my life! She'd be more like a companion or something. You know, go about with the girls, show them how to go on, music lessons, a little French. M'mother won't care that the chit's been on the stage; she ain't so strait-laced. She's only concerned with bloodlines for her hounds."

"But what about the expense?" He knew his friend wasn't plump in the pocket, but Gard couldn't give insult by offering to pay Mignon's salary, although he'd gladly pay it, twice over.

"Well, m'brother—he's the head of the family now, don't you know—holds the purse strings for the girls' come-outs. Guess he'd be as happy as I am to do anything to get them off his hands. I could tell him it's an investment."

"And I'll convince Mignon she'll be happy as a grig." Gard leaned back in his chair, his muscles finally relaxing. "What would I do without you, Cholly?"

Cholly was still thinking. "Can't take her around to parties and the like, but maybe we can find her a clerk or something to marry."

"And I'll throw in a portion for the chit!" the earl declared happily, raising his glass to Cholly's in a toast to their plan. "I'll send her round in the morning, then, after my ride."

"Still seeing that veiled charmer in the park? Have you found out who she is yet? Everyone's waiting for the word so they can settle the wagers."

Lord Gardiner smiled, a slow, sensuous grin. "No, not yet."

Cholly smiled back in relief. "That's more like it. You had me worried there, old boy." The earl cocked an eyebrow in inquiry. "You know, how your name is coming up a lot in conversation."

"But, Cholly, my name is always coming up a lot in the gossip. What's the worry?"

"Worry is, seems your name's the only thing coming up."

Chapter Eighteen

*W*as she wearing the same green habit so he would recognize her, or because it was the only one she owned?

How long before his honorable intents gave way to his lustful nature and he made her an improper offer?

So many questions, so few answers. They rode silently again, enjoying the ride, but very aware of the other's presence. As they neared the park exit Lord Gardiner spoke up: "We have never been formally introduced, ma'am, and I should not want you thinking I am some unmannered brute. I am Ross Gardiner, at your service. My friends call me Gard." He looked to see if she was acknowledging his offer of friendship. Blast, what was with women these days? They were all making themselves unreadable in their spectacles and veils.

Here it comes, Annalise thought, disappointed but not surprised. Here is where he starts casting his net. She ignored him, pretending to adjust her skirts.

Ross laughed. "Very well. I may be Gard later. Today I am merely the honor guard, sworn to shield you from insults and advances. I am, indeed, honored that you accepted my offer to lend you protection. I hope that someday you will honor me with your name."

The silver-tongued devil! "I—"

The earl held up a gloved hand. He could tell by her hesitation that whatever name she gave would be a lie. He was jumping his fences. "No, I am not asking. I gave my word to respect your privacy. I find I do not like addressing my riding partner as miss or ma'am, however. May I call you Miss Green?"

Annalise kept her voice low, husky. "That will be fine, my lord."

"And your horse?"

Her horse? Why should he want to call her horse anything, except as a way of tracing her identity? Regrettably, Seraphina was too uncommon, and the mare was not likely to respond to an alias. "Beauty," she whispered a pet name for the horse softly, and Seraphina blessedly flicked her ears.

"Perfect." The earl nodded approvingly. "Although I might have thought you'd call her Socks, or Bootsy."

"My lord?"

"Her white stockings. If I might be so bold as to offer a word of advice, strictly in my role as protector, do have a word with your grooms, Miss Green. I know they are loyal, courageous chaps; I saw them fight in your defense. But I think they have taken too many blows to the head. Yesterday Beauty had one white stocking on her rear legs, her right rear leg to be exact. Today her left leg is white. It's a wonder she hasn't four stockings, or two."

Annalise laughed. What else could she do? "I am afraid I have no aptitude for hugger-mugger either. Thank you, my lord. I shall be more careful in the future."

Her chiming laughter was a delight, lighthearted yet refined. Youthful. Not childish, he amended to himself, thinking of Mignon, just young. But a young lady of breeding, riding out with two ruffians as guards? He was no closer to solving the mystery than he was yesterday. More important than that, he realized, was his real desire to win her trust— and to keep her from harm if the reason for her secrecy was actually perilous. "Miss Green, I know that we are hardly acquainted, but I believe the deceptions and disguises you are forced to practice are against your nature."

If he only knew, Annalise thought, laughing again, this time to herself, in despair.

"If—nay, when—you come to trust me, please believe that I will do everything in my power to assist you."

To assist her into his bed, Annalise still believed. The man had endearing moments of nobility, though, for a cad.

"I have recently come to a better understanding of women's plight," he continued, and she believed him. Now, if he just stopped using her home as a house of convenience, if he found a lady from his own class, married, and stayed constant for thirty or forty years, she just might change her opinion of him.

While he was out, Lord Gardiner decided to ride over to Drury Lane. Bottwick was not well pleased to receive an irate nobleman, nor the information that Mimi would not be coming back, except to fetch her belongings.

"You can't do that, no matter who you think you are! I got my rights to the wench!"

"Oh, yes? Rights such as slavery? I believe there are laws about that, as well as regarding child prostitution," the earl quietly informed him, eyeing the smaller man through lowered brows. "I should not like to hear of another underage chit being pushed along that path." Gard flicked his riding crop against his highly polished Hessians, giving Bottwick time to digest the unspoken words. "Have I made myself clear?"

As clear as any member of Parliament, a patron of the theater, and a pupil of Gentleman Jackson's needed to be, especially when he held a whip in his hand. Bottwick mumbled his assent, not loudly enough for Lord Gardiner's satisfaction. The earl punctuated his disapproval with a quick right jab that got him the desired promise.

On Gard's way out of the theater, one of the actresses not quite accidentally bumped into him. He automatically reached out to steady her, and somehow found his hand on a bit of flesh that would tempt any anatomy student.

"Oh, la," she squealed, "sure and I should watch where I'm going."

Gard looked into brown eyes with soot-darkened lashes, under hair a yellow color never seen in nature. The amplitude of her endowments, however, were more often found in dairy barns. He grinned. "Sure and you didn't see a wee fellow like me."

She winked, laid a hand on his arm, and drew him aside. "I couldn't help overhearing your arglebargle with that spalpeen Bottwick, me lord. 'Tis a shame, it is, about the young 'uns, and I admire a fine gent like yourself for not taking advantage. Bessie O'Neill, I be, and I didn't come down in the last snowfall."

Or the one before that, he'd wager. Bessie was

definitely not a child, definitely not a lady, and definitely not unwilling. And he was needing something to get his mind off the woman in the park before he became totally obsessed with her and her intrigues. Besides, Bessie's bountiful curves would be spectacular on canvas. He'd hardly done more than a sketch, Gard calculated, since the night of the infamous drawing party in the ballroom. By all that was holy, he hadn't had a woman since then either!

"Are you free tonight after the performance?"

"Free? No, not even for a bonny laddy like you, but I'll be waiting for you after the show."

Next he went to discuss Mignon's future with the girl. Leaving his stallion with Tuthill in the stable, Gard walked through the back door of the town house. Mrs. Tuthill was busy at the stove, and Annie sat at the kitchen table having her breakfast, her back to him.

"Good morning," he called, noticing the way Annie snatched up her spectacles from the table and shoved them on her face before jumping up to curtsy. "No, don't let me interrupt your breakfast. I just wanted to tell Mignon I think there's a solution to her dilemma."

Annie remained on her feet, looking regretfully at her plate. "She's still asleep, poor child. Should I go wake her?"

"No, I can explain to you, and you can tell her when she gets up. Do eat your food while it is hot."

He looked so enviously at Annie's piled plate that she was forced to offer him something to eat before she could enjoy her own meal.

"Thank you," he said when Mrs. Tuthill brought him a cup of coffee and two slices of dry toast. He looked over at the housekeeper's plate, where reposed fluffy eggs, warm muffins, a rasher of ham, a helping of kidneys, then back at his spartan fare. So he was still in Mrs. Tuthill's black books, was he? At least she was feeding Annie properly; the woman no longer looked as if the first wind would blow her over. He watched her butter her muffin with the delicacy of a duchess and wondered again about this peculiar woman. He shrugged. Give him a female like Bessie any day.

"You were going to tell us about Mignon, my lord," Annalise interrupted his musings. "Have you found a place for her then?"

"I think I have the ideal solution." And he proceeded to relate his conversation with Cholly, about the five plain sisters and negligent mother, the absentee heir who paid the bills. "So she'll have a home and companions and an income. Perhaps she'll find she has a flair for being a ladies' maid or companion. Cholly thinks we ought to be able to find a husband for her. He's the best of good fellows, so you needn't worry on that score, or that there might be anything harum-scarum about his household. I'll keep an eye on the infant myself, of course."

"An excellent solution, my lord," Annie congratulated him, and Mrs. Tuthill placed a large steak in front of him. Now this was more like!

"Yes, and I've already been backstage. No one will bother Mignon when she goes to pick up her things. Make sure Tuthill goes inside with her anyway, just to make sure. I would take her myself, but it wouldn't do for her to arrive on Cholly's doorstep in my curricle. Not even Mrs. Fansoll is that open-minded."

Next Ross had the unprecedented honor of basking in the glory of Annie Lee's approval. He was clever and kind and wise. Gads, that it should come to this, that he cared what an ugly old housekeeper thought of him! "Oh, yes, I've already informed

Tuthill about the company this evening. He'll fetch the lady. I may be delayed. I know you'll make her welcome; you were very kind about Sophy and again with Mignon. We do not always agree, Annie, and I still believe you are an odd kind of employee, but I do appreciate your efforts."

Annalise ignored the flummery and Henny's cough. "A lady?"

He found himself coloring. "Her name is Bess. She's from the theater."

Annie stood. "Well, then, there's a lot to be done. If you are finished, my lord?" And she took his plate away before he could protest. He had not gone halfway through the excellent steak, cooked precisely the way he liked it, and now she was feeding it to the ugliest little dog he had ever seen. It figured.

Mignon was tearfully thankful when Annalise told her of the plan. Those were her very favorite things: fashions and sewing, music and speaking French! How could she not be happy, with five young ladies to teach how to flirt! "And I shall do such a fine job of it, they will all marry dukes, no? But not so soon, I think, that I find myself with no position. Ah, *mademoiselle*, I owe you such a debt!"

Annalise was annoyed with the earl, to put it mildly. Still, she had to give him the proper credit. "You owe me nothing. It is Lord Gardiner you must be sure to thank."

"Milord is the true *gentilhomme*, no? Yet I think he would never have come to help Mignon without you. Please, what may I do to repay your kindness? I would do anything for you."

"Anything? Very well, you may tell your friends in the cast, especially the one called Bessie, that his lordship has the pox!"

Mignon's eyes grew round. "The pox? *Mon Dieu!* That is better than the other thing, I suppose. But milord has been so good to me, *n'est-ce pas*, how can I play him such a trick?" She studied Annalise, tugging the spectacles and the awful cap away. "You pull the lamb over his eyes, no?"

"The wool, Mignon. Yes, but you mustn't tell. There are good reasons."

"My lips, they are sealed. But how can I tell such lies about the *grand monsieur*?"

"It's for his own good, I swear! You'd be saving him from a life of sin, the way he saved you."

Mignon looked doubtful, a world of wisdom in her young eyes. "I don't think it is the same, *mademoiselle*. I don't think it is the same at all."

Chapter Nineteen

*B*essie came prepared. When Annie led her upstairs to show her where she might wait, the bleached and painted actress plucked two sausage casings out of her reticule. At least they looked something like sausage casings to Annalise. She averted her eyes.

"In case that rumor is true," Bessie said with a loud laugh, noticing where Annie couldn't look.

"His lordship ... that is ..." Annalise began, forcing herself.

"That other muckle rumor? A brae, lusty lad like himself? Don't worry, m'dear, Bessie's never lost a patient yet." She slapped her knee and laughed herself into a coughing fit.

Between trying not to glance at the items on the nightstand and trying not to stare at Bessie's expansive figure, wondering how a scrap of lace at the neckline could keep all that quivering flesh restrained, Annalise had nowhere to focus her eyes. So she looked under the bed. And behind the dresser, in the water closet, beneath the chintz-covered boudoir chair.

"What's that you're after, dearie?" Bessie wanted to know.

Annalise's muffled reply came from inside the wardrobe. "Mice. We're overrun with the pesky beasts. You're not afraid, are you?"

"Bessie O'Neill, afeared of a wee rodent? No, we have them in and out of the dressing rooms all the time. Takes more than that to send me scurrying. Now, snakes is another thing. I cannot abide the slimy things. Can't even be in the same room with a picture of one. Makes my skin crawl."

Snakes? Where was Annalise to get a snake in the middle of the night? In the middle of London? She might be able to locate an eel, perhaps, if she could bear to handle it. Somehow she doubted that Lord Gardiner would believe that one just happened to appear in his bed chamber, like the plagues falling on Egypt. If he ever suspected—no, that did not bear thinking on. She'd seen the man in a temper, and it was bad enough, thank you. One of his rages would be nothing compared to what would happen if he discovered her conniving against him. But this vulgar woman was taking her shoes off and sprawling on the bed, appendages bobbling about like melons in a basket.

"You know his lordship might be very late, don't you? Surely you'll have to get back for rehearsal."

"Not to worry. Rehearsal's not till three tomorrow, and I know my part so well, I can skip it. Now, beauty sleep is another matter. I'll just catch me a little nap while I wait, dearie. Be a pet and blow out some of the candles, won't you?"

"Ah, miss, you wouldn't by chance believe in ghosts, would you?" It was worth a try.

"Nary a bit, dearie. Old Bess believes in two things: having a good time and getting paid for it."

So Annalise paid her. She always hated that bracelet anyway.

The earl strode up to the door with a jaunty tread, a large pad under one arm and a box of charcoal drawing crayons in the other. He'd made a special trip to the art supply dealers on New Bond Street to find just the right shade of yellow for Bessie's hair. He also purchased a new pencil of emerald green.

Annie opened the door to his eager face, wiping the smile right away with her words: "I am sorry, my lord. Miss O'Neill was called away. A sick relative, I believe."

Gard looked at the pad in his hand, then he turned and pounded his head on the open door. He never even got to touch this one!

"My lord?"

He straightened up and adjusted his neckcloth. "Yes, Annie. Thank you."

"Mrs. Tuthill is fixing supper. Buttered crab, vol-au-vents of veal, braised duckling, and one of her special custard puddings. Will you be staying?"

It was better fare than he'd get at his club, and the temperamental master chef he kept at Grosvenor Square would resign if Gard woke him to cook a late-night snack. It did occur to the earl, and not for the first time, that in some ways he was more at home here than he was at home. Of course, he'd never spent the night upstairs in that bed which looked so inviting, but there wasn't all that kowtowing and ceremonial toadying, either. Even the outrageous tirades from his ill-behaved housekeeper were more mentally challenging than his mother's nagging harangues. At least Annie never dragged forth his father's ghost. At Laurel Street Ross could eat in the kitchen if he wanted—which was what he decided, in fact—instead of dining in state at Gardiner House. He ruefully acknowledged that if he kept eating instead of partaking of his usual exercise, he'd be fat as a flawn in no time.

He sketched Mrs. Tuthill while she bustled around the kitchen.

"Why, it's me to the inch! What a gift you have indeed, my lord. My Robbie will think it's a treat! Why, you could be one of those fancy portrait artists, I swear."

"Most likely no one would pose for me, either," he mumbled under his breath, not realizing Annie was beside him, setting the table for his meal. She camouflaged a giggle with a cough. The earl looked up. "Should you like me to do your portrait, too, Annie?"

Her exultation fled. She did not want him staring at her. Even his quick glances made her uncomfortable, and not just because he might see through her disguise. He was so handsome; she was homely. She slammed the plate down in front of him so hard, the sturdy table shook. "What for? I know what I look like, and no one else cares to look at an ugly old hag."

"I think your face might show a great deal of character, Annie, if you removed the spectacles. At least consider it."

"Mrs. Tuthill will serve your dinner, my lord. I have accounts to look over."

"I didn't mean to insult her," the earl told a frowning Mrs. Tuthill after Annie left.

"She's sensitive about her looks," the older woman replied, banging pans together.

"I suppose it cannot be easy, seeing beautiful women come and go"—mostly go, he mused—"in a place like this. I wonder if that's why she's so prickly, if it's not jealousy instead of moral indignation after all."

"Beauty is as beauty does," Mrs. Tuthill advised

tersely, then exclaimed, "Oh, drat, the custard burned. You weren't waiting for dessert, were you?"

Then again, in Grosvenor Square he wasn't sent to his room without dessert for being naughty. The earl sighed and got up. "Thank you for an excellent dinner, Mrs. Tuthill. I think I'll have my port in the front parlor, by the fire."

He *thought* she grumbled, "You'll do as you please and be damned for it," but he had to be mistaken. Servants just did not behave that way, not even in Bloomsbury.

Gard lounged on the sofa. He was comfortable, warm, moderately well-fed, and bored. He was restless—hell, he was frustrated! He felt like a stallion who knows there's a mare in season somewhere, if he could just get out of the blasted stable. Staring at the flames, drumming his fingers on the inlaid table next to him, the earl contemplated a visit to Mother Ignace's after all.

"Your port, my lord," Annie said, putting the tray down with an audible thud that startled Ross into wondering if the witch could read his mind. He sat up and caught himself reaching to check his cravat. No, no deuced servant was going to reduce him to schoolboy status once more, in his manners or his morals. He sprawled back again, satisfied. Except that she was leaving, and he'd have no one to talk to at all, blast it. Even her viperish tongue was better company than his own unsatisfied thoughts.

"Have you finished the accounts? That is, must you go?"

"My lord?" If bats had established residence in his belfry, she couldn't look more surprised, glasses or no.

He stared around in desperation, till his eyes alighted on the pianoforte. Sheets of music were unfolded on the stand, sheets that had not been there the last time he looked. "Did, ah, Bessie play the instrument?"

"No, my lord," Annie replied, cursing herself for being a skitter-witted noddy, leaving the music out that way. She knew what was coming next.

"Then it was you," he stated, not asking a question at all, and not the least astonished that his housekeeper could play, no matter that no servant in his experience had ever done so. Annie hadn't done the expected yet. "Will you play for me?"

Annalise surprised even herself by agreeing. Why give his suspicions more foundation? Why spend one instant more in the skirter's company than she had to? Possibly, she answered herself while sorting through the music, because he looked so pathetically forlorn there on a couch made for two, and so devastatingly handsome with his collar loosened and his dark hair tousled. As she struck the first tentative chords, she told herself this was the only charitable thing to do, since she had bought off his evening's entertainment.

"I am out of practice, my lord," she apologized beforehand.

"I am no expert, to be criticizing your technique, Annie. I just like to listen."

She nodded and started off with a few country ballads, a delicate Irish air. He relaxed against the cushions, shutting his eyes in quiet enjoyment of her pleasant competency. Then she switched to Mozart and Handel, and played well. Better than well. Better than any servant with a few hours of free time to practice. He sat up and studied Annie, even as she became lost in the intricacies of the piece she played so masterfully.

Gard quietly took up his pad and a pencil without disturbing her concentration. The pencil stayed poised in air. From his angle the flaps on her cap hid most of her face, whatever the rims of the spectacles did not cover. And the sagging black gown only emphasized her figure's deficiencies. So he focused on her hands as they flowed over the keys.

The fingers were long and elegant, easily reaching the spread of ivories, not the bony talons they used to resemble. Her hands were not as red or work-roughened as he recalled, nor were they the cracked and lined and spotted hands of an older woman. Annie Lee was not old enough to have been in service for twenty-one years. He doubted if she'd worked very long at all, since she definitely had not managed to acquire a servile attitude. Most likely her soldier had left her in dun territory. How long since Corunna? "Do you miss James very much?" he asked when she reached the end of a piece.

Annalise was caught up in her music, the first time she'd really had to play in ages. And she was trying to play her best, for him. "Hmm? James who?"

"Your husband. James Jacob."

Her fingers hit a discordant note. "Oh, yes, him. Of course. Um, yes. That is, not so much anymore. Why?"

"No reason in particular. I was just wondering if the redoubtable Annie Lee ever got lonely like us poor mortals. Then, too, you don't appear quite settled in your life of servitude."

Annie shrugged. "I'll do." And she immediately swept into a piece by Beethoven, playing louder than necessary, eliminating the possibility of conversation. He sketched.

When she reached the final deafening crescendo, Lord Gardiner applauded. "Excellent, Annie, excellent. Rest awhile," he told her, placing a glass of wine in her hand, then sitting back down, his legs crossed in front of him. "I had a visit from the real estate agent," he mentioned casually, then paused as she choked on her wine. "He wanted to know if everything was satisfactory here."

Annalise put down the glass lest she spill it. "And what did you tell him, my lord?"

"That all was up to snuff. There was some puzzlement about the household staff. The man seemed to think Lady Rosalind took her servants with her."

As nonchalantly as she could, Annalise responded, "I believe I mentioned that Lady Rosalind did indeed take her butler and footman and abigail with her." She waved her hand, dismissing the man's confusion as beneath notice. It was a gesture more in keeping with a marchioness than a maidservant, if she but knew it.

The earl ran his finger around the rim of his glass. "He was also curious about some missing heiress. A relation to Lady Rosalind. Do you know anything about that?"

Annalise's hand accidentally struck the keyboard. She winced at the sound. "Only what I heard from a man who called here for information. He said he was looking for the stepdaughter of a Sir Vernon Thompson, who was also Lady Rosalind's niece. I told him all I knew, which is nothing really. Lady Rosalind has not been in contact with us, and neither has the niece."

"I see."

As he turned the pages of his drawing pad, Annalise wondered how much he really did see. "Seems a pity," she commented hurriedly, "about the girl, I mean. Dicked in the nob, the man said."

"Not to be wondered at if she's any connection to Thompson. The fellow's a curst loose screw. I pity the chit even more for that. Of course, it was a goosish thing to do, a young girl running off like she did. Any protection is better than having a gently bred female out on her own. Just look at what happened to Mignon. The girl's most likely bachelor fare by now, especially if she's knocked in the cradle, as you say."

Annalise returned to her music, pounding the keys into submission, her back even more rigid than usual.

Gard started to sketch her that way, in hard, jerky lines mimicking her agitated motions. He put in the cap, ear wings flapping like a hound's in the wind, and he put in the flat chest. He started on that stiff back which was not quite as flat as her front, due to the hump over her right shoulder. But wasn't it over her left shoulder yesterday? He tried to picture Annie sitting with Mignon on the bed, or giving him what-for in the hallway. Gard shook his head to clear it. First those white stockings on the mare, now the housekeeper's deformity. Lack of sex must be addling his mind.

Chapter Twenty

"*L*ack of sex addles a man's mind, chickie. Let me tell you, the fellow's wastin' away with unfulfilled desire."

"Fustian," Annalise replied as she and Rob Tuthill walked toward the hackney waiting to drive her to the livery stable. "It's good for his soul. Think of all those monks and saints and martyrs."

Rob spit at a streetlamp. "Them holy sorts chose that way of life. The gov'nor didn't. And I say keepin' a man from his pleasure ain't good for him, besides bein' cruel and heartless. It ain't like you, chickie," he said, shaking his head in sorrow.

"I say it builds character, and his needs it! Did you get a look at that last harlot, that Bessie O'Neill?"

Rob grinned. "An eyeful, all right. But frustration don't build character, missy. That's just a tale the preachers made up to keep the peasants from overpopulatin' the countryside like rabbits. Hell, all frustration builds is aggravation and aggression—

like two male dogs meetin' in a dusty street. I don't like what you're doin' to him."

"I haven't touched him! I promised I wouldn't." Annalise kicked at a pebble in her way. "Besides, you can stop worrying about your randy friend. I am running out of ideas to discourage his particulars. I can't keep giving my jewelry away to every loose woman in London." She kicked harder at the pebble, sending it flying into the roadway. "And I'm sure he'll find every last one of them."

"It's good that you're givin' up. We'd be seein' the whites of his eyes soon else, and then watch out. Red-blooded fellow like the earl's bound to explode from pent-up feelin's and unused energies. You can't mess with life's drivin' forces, chickie, without stirrin' up a mare's nest of trouble."

"Oh, pooh," Annalise pronounced, but she did ride a little farther away from Gard that morning, as if he were a bonfire about to go up in smoke with the slightest touch. He was quiet, thoughtful, paying little attention to her after his usual polite greeting. His lack of interest should have contented her since she did not want him getting up a flirtation with her, nor asking questions to ease his curiosity. Neither reason sat well. Piqued, she even considered initiating conversation.

Then a man stepped onto the path and called, "Miss Avery? Miss Annalise Avery?" It was that same man again, Sir Vernon's unctuous footman, Stavely. Outwardly Annalise stayed calm, but Seraphina took exception.

"Are you all right?" the earl asked when she had the mare under control again.

"Yes, that peculiar person just startled my mare. I, ah, wonder what he was about."

Grimly, the earl declared, "I intend to find out." He gestured to her bodyguards to close ranks around her and the mare, then rode back along the path and dismounted, tying his stallion's reins to a park bench. In three long strides he was next to the pomaded footman, who shrank back, but not in time to avoid being grabbed around the neck and shaken like a rag. "What the bloody hell do you think you're doing, jumping out in front of horses that way?" Lord Gardiner demanded. "You could have caused a serious accident."

"Not if she's Miss Avery, I couldn't," the dangling servant said, valiantly trying to defend his actions. "She's supposed to be the best horsewoman in the shire."

"What shire might that be, sirrah?"

"W-Worcester, where she and Sir Vernon Thompson reside, my lord."

"Well, I assure you, and Sir Vernon, that the young woman with me is not his ward. I do not now and never will dally with wellborn ladies. Next thing I knew, some maggot like Sir Vernon would be demanding I marry his repulsive relation. This lady—and I am informing you just to make things clear, not that I have any intention of discussing my personal affairs with the likes of you or your obnoxious employer—is Miss Green, and she is in my keeping. I will take it seriously amiss if you disturb her again. Do you understand?"

How could the man not understand, with a fist like iron wrapped around his neck and his feet off the ground? "I'll tell Sir Vernon, my lord. Your lady's not a lady."

There, Annalise thought, watching from a distance, Robb was wrong. Lord Gardiner didn't explode, just quietly restricted himself to minor mayhem, which was not entirely undeserved, in her estimation. She smiled and rode on, missing the murder in his eyes when he joined her.

"Excuse the disturbance, my dear, it will not happen again."

See? He was the perfect gentleman. She was building his character after all.

She smiled cheerfully during the rest of their ride. His lordship gnawed on the inside of his cheek.

Rob's news about more company that evening destroyed Annalise's good humor. Not even a visit from an exuberant Mignon could restore her mood, nor the young girl's news that Bottwick had a broken nose. Instead of showing noble restraint in not skewering the scoundrel, Lord Gardiner's actions now seemed to reflect his lordship's savage nature, a nature that gave in to every base instinct.

"That dastard!"

"Bottwick?"

"No, Lord Gardiner."

"*Monsieur* the earl? But no, he saves my life, *vraiment*. He makes that pig Bottwick give my back wages. And he sends me to stay with my new family, the Fansolls."

With an effort, Annalise managed to get her mind off the invidious earl. "You are content with your new position, then?"

"How not?" Mignon said, grinning. "My young ladies are *très charmantes*, and I have a room all to myself, so I can come and go like tonight, once they are out to their balls and parties. *Madame* Fansoll is *aux anges* to be relieved of worrying over the fashions and invitations and dancing lessons. Me, I take charge." She giggled and whispered confidingly, "Someday I plan to take charge of *Monsieur* Fansoll, too."

"Charge of him, the earl's friend, Cholly?" Annalise echoed, unwilling to voice her fears.

"Oh, la, marriage, *certainement*. But he does not know it yet."

"Lord Gardiner admires him exceedingly, and I am sure he is a praiseworthy gentleman, but do you

166

think ..." Annalise was not sure how to proceed. She did not want to hurt the girl's feelings; neither did she want Mignon to get her hopes up.

"That he will marry a penniless orphan who once acted on the stage?"

"And who now is in his employ as companion to his sisters, yes," Annalise concluded sadly. "Don't you think you might be flying too high?"

Mignon settled back with her chocolate, one of Henny's macaroons, and a grin. "Ah, but Cholly is a second son."

"Whose brother is a marquis."

"Who has as many sons as Cholly has sisters! *Mon cher* Cholly says he wants only to be a farmer on his small property, once his sisters are settled. He is not high in the inseam."

"Instep."

"Whatever." The girl shrugged and had another macaroon. "*Eh bien,* now we have settled my future, what shall we do about yours, *mademoiselle*? This disguise is abdominal, no?"

"Abominable, yes. But necessary. I do not want to get you involved, Mignon, so I cannot discuss it."

"Can you not go to milord for help? He was kind to me, no?"

Annalise sipped her tea. "Yes, he was, but this is different. He'd be furious, not just that I tricked him, but that I am a lady he might feel honor-bound to offer for, since I have been living under his roof. And if my real identity became known around, I'd be ruined forever." She didn't mention that she'd be hauled back to Thompson Hall and locked up. That was too dismal a burden to lay on Mignon's young shoulders.

"I think there is much you don't say. *Tiens,* my head aches from these complicated matters. Still, I do not understand why you ruin milord's pleasure."

"I cannot live here in a house of sin if I am to

have any reputation at all. Surely you must see that! Besides, his pleasure seeking is wrong! Every child learns he cannot have every desire gratified. It is time Lord Gardiner learned temperance, moderation, patience. It is good for his soul."

Mignon nodded wisely. "*Enfin*, you want him for yourself."

The cup Annalise was holding clattered back in its saucer. "That's outrageous! I despise the man. He is nothing but a wicked, wanton sinner. What do you know anyway? You are just a child."

"I am not so much younger than you, *oui*? I think I have seen more of the world. Milord Gardiner is a nonpareil, no? How could you not want him? If not for Cholly, I might set my sights on him myself. But no, milord is too proud for one like me."

"He is as proud as Lucifer. An arrogant, swaggering, insufferable man. Having his wishes thwarted once in a while will make him more humble, more human."

Grinning again, Mignon asked, "And you have a plan?"

Well, no, Annalise was forced to admit, she was fresh out of plans. She had this pair of mice, fat and friendly little fellows, but the women Lord Gardiner seemed to choose were made of coarser weave. And her plan to pay them off and send them on their way before he ever got near enough to smell their cheap perfume was not working. In fact, now the tarts thought they could earn an easy wage just by showing up at Laurel Street! One of the other actresses at Drury Lane had had the nerve to write to Lord Gardiner, suggesting a liaison. Rob had taken the perfumed note around to Grosvenor Square and waited to carry the return message. Now he was assigned to convey the hussy to Bloomsbury this evening.

"Which actress is it, do you know?" Mignon asked.

"I think her name was Lilabette. Do you know her?"

"Ah, that one. She had leading roles, so was too grand to notice us poor girls in the chorus. She had to have her own dressing room, and a carriage to pick her up and take her home. Do not worry, my friend, Mignon shall get rid of her for you."

Annalise stared uncertainly at the gamin grin on the petite blonde's face. "How?"

"I think you do not want to know, my dear Annie."

"May I show you upstairs to refresh yourself before dinner, ma'am?" Annie asked the Exquisite in the hallway, taking her ermine wrap.

"I'll be right back, darling, don't go far," Lilabette told the earl, not deigning to acknowledge the housekeeper's presence except for an abrupt "I am sure I can find it myself" as she slithered up the stairs in her red silk. Annie busied herself in the parlor, poking at the fire and fluffing up sofa pillows, taking surreptitious peeks at the earl in his form-fitting evening clothes that accented his broad shoulders and well-muscled legs. Then she heard the shrieks.

"What the blazes?" Gard yelled, starting for the hall. Lilabette met him, coming down the stairs. She smacked him across the cheek, grabbed her fur from Annie, and flounced out of the door.

"What the blue blazes?" the earl repeated, rubbing his cheek, but Annie was already up the stairs before him. Following, he halted at the doorway to his chamber—his unused, unchristened chamber—to see Annie's black-clad derriere sticking up from under the bed.

Bemused, he asked, "What the devil are you doing?"

"Mice" came back the muffled reply. "Maybe that's what frightened her."

So she slapped him? She must have hit him harder than he thought, for he was content for now to contemplate his housekeeper's hind end.

Annalise meanwhile was staring at Mignon, but a Mignon she hardly recognized, with painted lips, rouged cheeks, frizzed hair, and a diaphanous nightgown. To her horror, this jezebel whispered, "I told her we'd share!"

Now Annie shrieked. The earl ran over, she jumped up, they bumped heads.

"What is it? What the deuce is going on? Mice, you say?"

"No, no. Just a spider. I was frightened when it ran over my hand, is all. I am sorry, my lord." She looked around, making sure he noted that not a cover was out of place, everything was as it ought. "The lady must have seen it, too."

So she slapped him?

After another excellent repast—this time he even got a syllabub for dessert—Lord Gardiner tried to relax on the sofa while Annie played. Relax? His body was as taut as a bow string! And all Annie was playing were jolly, lilting country songs. What the devil did she have to be so blasted cheerful about?

And by all that was holy, what in tarnation was happening to him? Once or twice in his later years he'd been disappointed in an assignation. Zeus, carriages broke down, women became ill. But *every* woman? *Every* night? Something was dreadfully, absurdly wrong. He'd get to the bottom of this tomorrow night or his name was not Ross Montclaire. If he didn't, he'd likely slit his own throat shaving.

Gard was promised to his mother for Vauxhall Gardens the next evening. Surely he'd find a warm and willing companion down one of the dark walks there.

That comforting thought was all he had to take to bed with him that night, along with the refrain of Annie's music.

Chapter Twenty-one

So, was his riding partner the missing heiress? Gard rather thought so. Rumors were starting to percolate around town, and while no one actually claimed to have seen Miss Avery, her description was on everyone's lips. Tallish, a Diamond of the first water although recently ill, a superb horsewoman with golden hair and green eyes. The woman riding so handily next to him had silvery curls, from what he could see—perhaps bleached?—but that emerald habit had to have been created for a green-eyed wench. No one else suspected, it seemed, for once the Lady in Green was firmly established as his mistress, she was ignored by the ton.

The real coil was what he was going to do about it. The best solution, Ross told himself, was to marry the chit. Somehow the idea did not stick in his throat as it usually did. His mother was right, it was time for him to set up his nursery, especially after that last scare. And he'd never fall in love with any of the brainless twits his mother paraded past him with such regularity. At least this lady would not jabber his ear off, he considered, finding that he liked her quiet, reserved ways. Miss Avery's breeding was not quite what an earl might consider, but the taint of a grandfather in trade was balanced by a grandfather who was a duke, albeit an unaccepting one. The merchant connection was also deceased, leaving Miss Avery a considerable fortune, both of which were frequent causes of memory lapses among society. The heiress might be his answer.

As for Miss Avery, her reputation would be restored and her deliverance guaranteed from whatever scheme that muckworm Thompson was plotting. And she'd be getting one of the premier bachelor catches of this and many a London Season. Yes, it would serve. Unless the woman at his side really was a Bedlamite, or had run away to join a lover, or was not the missing Miss Avery at all. The first thing to do was place the chit under his mother's chaperonage, which would eliminate any chance of dalliance as well as calm the gossip. In truth, one did not wish one's future countess considered fast.

"I am getting up a party for Vauxhall this evening, Miss Green," he told her. "Many ladies there wear dominoes, even on non-masquerade nights. Might you consider attending with me?"

Annalise knew all about Vauxhall, thanks to Lorna and Mignon. How dare he ask such a thing of her after his promise of respect? She raised her chin in a gesture Lord Gardiner was coming to recognize as affronted dignity.

"With my mother, of course, as chaperone. No insult intended, ma'am."

Annalise was astounded. "You would invite a stranger to sit with your mother?" she asked, try-

173

ing to remember in her incredulity to lower her tone of voice. "What if I am not respectable?"

"I refuse to believe that. I think you must need some diversion, an evening of fun, no matter what hobble you are in."

"Thank you. I should enjoy it, I think, but I must refuse. It would be too dangerous, and unfair to expose your mother and guests to possible unpleasantness."

"Spoken like the true lady I know you to be," he approved. "Perhaps you will reconsider when they hold a true masquerade there, just the two of us?"

She shook her head sharply no and tapped Seraphina lightly to pick up the pace. Gard stayed right beside her. "I do wish you would let me help you, my dear, whatever the problem is."

"I cannot. But thank you. You have already given me a great deal of pleasure by accompanying me on my rides. I will understand if you wish to discontinue the association, however, since nothing can come of this. No other relationship is possible."

"Deuce take it, I am not pressuring you into anything you dislike. I told you I would not. I am satisfied with your company, Miss Green." For now, he told himself. "I am not a wild beast, you know, who needs a physical relationship with every female he meets."

Annalise almost fell off her horse, which effectively cut the ride short.

Maybe she wasn't the missing heiress after all, Gard thought.

Annalise rode home more frightened than she had been since leaving Sir Vernon's house. Her reputation was already in shreds, no matter as a housekeeper in a rake's house, or mistress in the

174

same rake's keeping. Everyone assumed the latter anyway, she knew, from the smiles she received when he was by her side and from the way the occasional lady out exercising her horse looked away when they passed. She had no future anywhere, except perhaps with Barnaby. There was nothing her aunt could do, either, especially not with Lady Ros's own blotted copybook.

Her worst fear, though, was one that had kept her up all night and stood fair to muddle her dreams for many a night to come. She was sorely afraid that Mignon was correct, that besides losing all hope of happiness, she really had lost her heart to an unprincipled rogue.

Lord Gardiner did not have to seek a woman for the night among the frail sisterhood who haunted the Dark Walks of Vauxhall Gardens. One of his mother's guests, the only female over eighteen in the box, was Mrs. Throckmorton, whose eyes smoldered into his over the arrack punch. Whose bare toes massaged his thigh under the table during the shaved ham. Whose hand—whose husband passed out before the fireworks.

Why wait to get to Bloomsbury? the earl conjectured. The small Greek pavilions were scattered about the place for just such occasions. Zeus knew, he'd used them often enough. But Mrs. Throckmorton professed that she was there to chaperone her niece, one of the beruffled belles his mother had in mind for Gard. Mrs. Throckmorton insisted on discretion, which was fairly impossible for his lordship at this juncture anyway unless he remained seated.

So he scribbled the Laurel Street address on a card and whispered that they should meet there as soon as he dropped his mother at Grosvenor Square and she delivered her husband into his valet's hands. "Oh, yes," he added while another starburst went up. "Let me know if you notice anything peculiar about the place."

Having arrived just moments earlier, Mrs. Throckmorton was taking sherry in the parlor, according to Annie, who took the earl's cane and gloves, curtsied, and disappeared. For once she was acting the proper servant for the situation, Gard noted with relief, joining his guest.

The parlor was fine, too, he figured, eyeing the thick rug by the fire as Mrs. Throckmorton's clever hands continued their explorations. But, "Why don't you give me a minute or two before joining me upstairs?" she murmured to him, chuckling softly. "Hold the thought," she cooed, "but not too tightly, mind."

Those were perhaps the longest two minutes of his life, so he cheated. At the count of sixty Gard was up the stairs and on the landing outside the bedchamber, where Mrs. Throckmorton stood clutching her magenta dress together and screaming: "Peculiar? I'll give you something peculiar, you unnatural animal!" And she kicked him.

At least he wouldn't be wanting a woman for the next day or two, was his last coherent thought.

Annie stepped over the earl as he lay writhing and groaning on the wooden floor, with nary an ounce of pity for his plight. This time Mignon winked at her from inside the wardrobe, and bowed. Which was not inappropriate, since the grinning minx was wearing nankeen shorts, a schoolboy's jacket, and a short, curly wig.

"Anything?" Ross managed to grit his teeth and ask when Annie stepped over him again on her way out.

"No, perhaps the colors clashed with her gown."

* * *

One of Lord Gardiner's more fervent prayers was answered the next morning. No, Annie did not get on her broomstick and fly away, and no, Miss Green did not send him a billet-doux begging for an assignation. Instead, it rained. It rained so heavily that there was no chance of a ride in the park, thus no need to try to explain why Lord Gardiner was not in the saddle. He stayed in bed.

By midday his dreams were of the emerald rider and the mare: the perfect conformation, the supple movements and muscular strength and stamina, the graceful neck. And he wouldn't mind having the mare in his stable, either. Such dreams quickly gave rise to the conclusion that the good Lord obviously loved a sinner, for Gard suffered no permanent damage.

"Do we have an engagement for this evening?" he asked his mother over tea.

Hers must have had too much lemon in it, from the sour look the dowager gave her only son. "We were supposed to entertain Lady Barringdon and her granddaughter for dinner. The gel is a baroness in her own right, from one of those old land-grant titles that can pass through the female line, along with acres and acres in the Downs. They cried off for some silly reason." She looked at him through her lorgnette. "You didn't do anything to give 'em a disgust of you, did you?"

The earl couldn't imagine what. "I've been a paragon of virtue. And I don't even know the chit. Have we been introduced?"

The dowager struck him across the knuckles with her glass. "Scores of times, you clunch. A mother is always the last to know, but you must have done something terrible to keep Lady Barringdon from coming. The chit would have to be half dead before they'd give up a chance at a wealthy earl. Your father is not going to like this."

Lord Gardiner was not listening, sucking his knuckles and already planning on how to spend his delightfully free evening. There was nothing he could do about the Avery business, but he could positively get to the bottom of the problem at Laurel Street. All he needed was a willing woman.

The first three courtesans he approached in the park turned him down. Two had prior engagements, one a permanent jealous protector. Felice, a one-time associate of Harriet Wilson's, had an inflammation of the lungs. She cleared her throat a few times to prove it. At least the flower girl on the corner winked at him. How the mighty were fallen, he thought, considering the wench. She was pretty and reasonably clean, but he couldn't do it. Instead, he bought all of her wares and had a boy deliver them to Felice with his get-well wishes.

Two of the actresses at Drury Lane slammed their dressing room doors in his face, and one of the chorus girls laughed at him for asking if she was busy. What was wrong? Had he suddenly lost his fortune and no one told him? He caught a glimpse of his reflection in a shop window as he walked down Bond Street. He still had all his hair and all his teeth. Had the world and all its females suddenly gone daft?

And speaking of females, where the devil was he supposed to find one for tonight at this late hour? A shopgirl, a tavern wench, a denizen of one of the finer bawdy houses? Was that what Lord Gardiner was reduced to? He was the one who was so fastidious, he had to invest in his own love nest! He was determined to have a bed warmer tonight at any cost, because he couldn't think straight or keep his mind on the various intrigues that surrounded him. All he could hear was his own body's insistent clamoring.

Then he noticed a woman, an attractive woman,

staring into a millinery-shop window. She was dressed in the kick of fashion, and she was alone. She looked vaguely familiar, although Gard believed he'd last seen her wearing a ribbon around her middle—and nothing else—as she posed in his ballroom. The earl seldom forgot a pretty waist.

"Maudine, *ma belle*?" It was as easy as complimenting her taste in hats, assuring her no lady ever looked finer in that bird's nest of a bonnet, and paying for same. As down payment, it was understood.

He did not send a message to alert the staff in Bloomsbury of his arrival; he did not send for Tuthill to fetch the lady. Gard handed her into his curricle, sent his tiger home, and drove across town himself, determined not to let the female out of his sight. Maudine sat stiffly, one hand nervously clenched around the seat rail, but she smiled gallantly at him and touched the feathers on her new bonnet when the earl reassured her they were not likely to overturn.

Annie was polite, to Gard's surprise, despite the lack of notice of company. Dinner was undistinguished, mutton and kidney pie, served with a stony demeanor indicating this was the Tuthills' own meal, and now Mrs. Tuthill was going to have to start over again. She'd most likely start with the ingredients purchased for his dinner, the earl surmised from her pursed lips. Let the staff eat lark's tongues and pigeon's feet, he didn't care. Just let Maudine finish her raspberry trifle before he burst.

Just when she'd licked the last pink drop off her soft pink lips, just when he was about to lead her upstairs, Annie waylaid him with a message about a note being delivered. His mother came to mind immediately, right after Miss Avery. Gard followed Annie back to the door, where a small lad in short pants with brown curls and an oversize cap handed him a folded note in exchange for a coin. Gard started to open the message on his way to join Maudine then stopped with a curse. "Blast, this note is for a Lord Gortimer, not Lord Gardiner. You go on up, my dear, I'll just bring this back to the housekeeper to get rid of."

He met Maudine in the middle of the stairwell. He was going up, she was going down, fast. The wide-eyed look on her face made him pause. She raised her hand, he immediately took his off the stair rail to protect his privates. She put her hand to her mouth, gasping, "Don't touch me!" The chit was petrified—of him! Gard automatically took a step backward. And toppled down the stairs.

He knew he was alive because he could feel the breeze where Maudine had left the front door open and because someone had placed a damp towel on his forehead. He didn't bother getting to his feet in a hurry; there'd be nothing to see upstairs anyway.

So he missed watching Annie scurry around the bedroom stuffing whips and chains and manacles back into a cloth satchel.

Chapter Twenty-two

"You look like the devil. What happened, did the dowager light into you again for not coming up to scratch with one of her choices?"

"Cut line, Cholly," the earl said as he carefully lowered himself into one of White's most comfortable chairs. "I do not wish to talk about it. I need a drink."

"Ah, another rash," his erstwhile friend concluded knowingly as they waited for the waiter to come take Gard's order.

"No, I do not have another rash. I fell down the stairs in that blasted house you convinced me to let for the season."

"What, Elphinstone's little hideout? Mean to say the place is decrepit?"

"No, I mean to say the place is haunted!"

Cholly shook his head. "You've been getting some deuced odd notions lately, and daresay I'm not the only one to notice." His round face cleared when the waiter brought a glass and two bottles. Cholly already had an empty one in front of him. "I bet the second bottle is a gift from Calthorpe, for winning his wager for him."

Gard lifted his glass to the foppish Calthorpe, who bowed back from across the room in a flourish of lace. Gard wrinkled his aristocratic nose. "What wager might that be?"

"You needn't put on that high-toned act with me, you know. It won't wash. Thought we was friends, though. Least you could have done was let me have a hint."

"Hell and damnation, Cholly, are you castaway so early in the night? What are you blathering about? I swear, I'm in no mood for anything to do with that queer nabs Calthorpe."

"Devilish glad to hear it, old fellow, though I never believed half the—" He caught the earl's lowered brows and changed tack. "Uh, the wager. You remember, I told you they were laying odds on the Incognita in the park."

The brandy was not sitting well on Lord Gardiner's stomach. "And?" he asked quietly, menacingly.

"And Calthorpe bet she was just some rich man's exotic bird of paradise. He followed her back from the park yesterday when you were done with your ride. Seems she leaves her horse near Cavendish Square and gets in a hackney, which meanders around a bit. You'll never guess where the hackney drops her, eh? You could have told me when I asked you, don't you know. Pockets are always to let and all, I could have used the extra blunt. All you said was not yet! Fine friend, Gard, be damned if I let you have one of m'sisters after all. Not sure anyway, with all the stories flying 'round."

Ross pushed the decanter out of Cholly's reach. "You've had enough. If you do not tell me where the hackney dropped the lady, I shall personally pull out every red hair on your head."

"Why, to your little love nest, of course, or did you think the ladybird was playing you false already?"

"And Calthorpe?" the earl ground out through clenched jaws.

"Well, you are as rich as Golden Ball, so he won. He's over there collecting now, counting his money."

Gard slowly stood and poured Calthorpe's bottle into one of the ferns. "You can tell him for me, Cholly, that if he ever goes near the lady again, or mentions her name, that he'll be counting his teeth next, in a glass beside his bed."

So Annie and the Tuthills were hiding Miss Green at Laurel Street, Lord Gardiner deduced. This conclusion explained a lot, especially if Miss Green was indeed the missing heiress, which was more and more likely. The fact that everyone else considered Miss Green his mistress was all that kept them from making the connection, while he knew for certain the woman had no ambitions along those lines. Heaven knew he'd dropped enough hints.

The real estate agent was right then; Lady Rosalind had not left any of her staff behind. The Tuthills and Annie must be Miss Avery's own loyal servants, that they would lie through their teeth for her. That also explained Annie's instant antipathy toward himself: The old family retainer deemed him a threat to Miss Avery. Naturally Annie also wished to discourage any inquisitive females from snooping around the premises, hence his disappearing demimondaines. Gard had no idea how Annie and the others were getting rid of his companions, but was certain they figured eliminating the women would eliminate his own troublesome presence. He rubbed the lump on the back of his head. Ha! They weren't going to deter him so easily!

Miss Avery knew of the plot all along, then, might even have been hiding in a cupboard somewhere while he toppled down the stairs. She must have been laughing up her sleeve at him every time she saw him. Blast, the chit was not so innocent after all. Perhaps marriage to her was not such a downy notion.

Ross was determined to have it out with Miss Avery that very morning during their ride, promise or no. Blister it, if she wished to stay at Laurel Street, let her do so openly. Everyone already believed he had installed her there. Then he thought of the parade of women through the house. Granted, they never stayed long—not nearly long enough—but, Zeus, that was not what a fellow wanted his future wife to see. 'Twas a poor reflection on his character, he supposed. Then again, he'd never considered himself good husband material, and a little conniver like Miss Avery would be satisfied with his wealth and title. If he decided to offer them to her.

Annalise arrived at the park before Lord Gardiner, so she decided to trot some of the fidgets out of Seraphina on the carriageway right by the gates. She was circling to come back when a man jumped out at her again, grabbing for the reins. This time Clarence was off his horse and had the man pinned to the ground before he could shout her name. The man was not a frippery footman, however; he was stocky and sandy-haired and full of bluster.

Annalise signaled Clarence to let the man up. "Hello, Barnaby. What brings you to London?"

"Jupiter, Leesie, you know dashed well what

brings me to London! I've been searching high and low for you, out to Bath and halfway to Wales, and here you are, bold as brass, riding in the park!" He angrily wiped the seat of his pants, which were now mud-streaked. "Or did you think I wouldn't recognize Seraphina, even with those ridiculous painted stockings that come off in the dew, when her sire was my own Altair?"

"Frankly, Barnaby, I didn't think you'd care."

"Not care? Not care when the woman I love is making a byword of herself in Town, even if no one knows your name?"

"That's a farrago of nonsense, Barny. You never loved me at all."

"I am fond of you, Leesie, more than that reprobate you've taken up with ever could be. I cannot believe you'd get in a pother with me over Sophy and then attach yourself to the most depraved man in all of London! The stories, Leesie! Why, they say the Hellfire Club is child's play compared to Gardiner's debauchery."

"That's ridiculous. His lordship has led an exemplary life since I've known him"—not with his cooperation, true—"and has always treated me like a lady."

Barny ran muddy hands through his hair in exasperation. "You never used to be such a goosecap. The man hasn't an honorable intention in his body."

"And you do?" she asked scornfully. "I suppose you think it more honorable for a betrothed man to keep a mistress than for a bachelor?"

Barny flushed, the red color blending into the dirt on his face. "I always intended to marry you at least. Still do. I gave up Sophy, I swear it."

"You mean you can no longer afford Sophy without my money. No, Barny, we shall never see eye to eye on this." She started to back the mare away from him.

"That's right, ride off, enjoy your tryst with the evil earl while you can. Just how long do you think it will take Sir Vernon to get back from Northumberland?"

Annalise again halted the mare, who pranced in place. "What is Sir Vernon doing in Northumberland?"

"Making sure you didn't take refuge with your grandfather. Not even Thompson would dare call a duke's granddaughter batty, at least not to his face. Arvenell was your only safe refuge, Leesie. Now I am. Your stepfather has the right to lock you away, and he means to do it. I expect he'll be here by week's end. You can't hide in London, and he'll chase you down anywhere else. Don't you understand, people notice veiled women as easily as they notice beautiful ones! And the mare! You might as well send out notices of your new address to the newspapers. Marry me and at least you'll be able to ride at will. You'll have a home and a family, your freedom."

"But what about respect?" she started to say, when she saw Lord Gardiner approaching at a furious pace, thinking she was being harassed.

Barny didn't see him. "I'll take care of you, Leesie, you know I will."

At which words Lord Gardiner leapt off his horse, grabbed the other, heavier man by the shoulder, spun him around, and planted him a facer. Barny went down in the mud again. He took one look at the blood in Lord Gardiner's eye and decided to stay down. He did call out one more message to his former fiancée: "I'm at the Clarendon, Leesie. I'll give you three days, then I'll tell Sir Vernon where you are myself. Three days."

* * *

"You know you are going to have to let me help," Gard shouted to Miss Avery's back as she tried to outride her devils. "Shall I call that nodcock out for you?"

Annalise pulled Seraphina up sharply. Distraught, she cried, "You wouldn't!" Dear heavens, if she had to fret about Lord Gardiner losing his life or being wounded on top of her other worries, she'd have a seizure for sure. "I forbid it!"

The earl raised an eyebrow. "I do not think you are in a position to forbid me anything, Miss Avery."

Her quick gasp told him his barb had hit home. "Yes, I know your identity and I feel certain everyone else shall in—what? Three days, was it?—when Sir Vernon comes to town and starts making louder inquiries. I really can help, you know. I have properties where no one could find you, a yacht to get you out of the country if you are set on bolting." He grinned. "A handy set of fists and excellent aim if you wish to stay to face the challengers."

"You do not know what you are saying. There is no reason for you to get involved in this coil for me."

"There is every reason, none of which I feel like discussing on horseback. The only reason you need understand at this moment is that you need help."

Annalise put her hand to her head. "Oh, I cannot think now!"

Gard reached across the horses to take that hand and give it a comforting squeeze. "And no one shall force you to. You have today and tomorrow to decide what you wish to do. All I ask is that you hear me out before you decide. Will you come with me tomorrow? We could ride out to Richmond, with your guards, of course, to play propriety. No one will know you, no one will distress you. Fresh air,

187

flowers, we'll pack a picnic lunch. Things will look better there, I swear."

Annalise knew she shouldn't, knew with every drop of blood that raced through her body at that slightest touch of his hand that she should stay at least a mile and a half away from this man. She knew it would be harder to marry Barny after one more minute in Gard's company, much less an entire day. And marriage to Barny was looking more and more like her only choice. It wouldn't be a terrible marriage, she told herself. He'd be pleasant enough most of the time, and leave her in peace the rest. And he would not break her heart.

But.

How many times had Annalise contradicted her own reasoning with that slippery *but*? She hated this charade, but she came alive matching wits and words with Lord Gardiner. He was a rake and a rogue, but she ached to wipe the lines of worry from his face. He'd leave her soul in tatters, but she had to have one last day with him.

"Yes, I will ride with you to Richmond."

Chapter Twenty-three

Gard had no intention of letting matters rest until tomorrow. Miss Avery, Leesie—what the deuce kind of name was that?—might not be safe, no matter what the chawbacon in the park said. What if the stepfather came early? He could snatch her away and Gard might never know where she was. Nor did he have any intention of letting Miss Avery make up her own mind about fleeing or marrying the lobcock, despite his assurances to her. Seeing her in supposed peril had quite settled the question in his own mind, after the blood lust drained enough for him to think clearly. The woman was his. That's all there was to it, primitive male possessiveness toward his mate. He'd tell her tomorrow. Today he had to make sure she was protected.

While he was outside the park gates debating whether to go to the Clarendon and beat the towheaded fellow to a pulp, or go to Laurel Street and ascertain that Miss Avery was, indeed, staying there, a woman on a showy white mare winked at him. As a matter of course Gard noted that she had a good seat, nicely rounded. She had the magnolia skin and jet-black hair that some Spanish beauties possessed, set off by a black habit and shako-style hat with a red feather. An altogether fetching study in contrasts.

"Señor?" she queried.

His stallion Midnight neighed in greeting. "Me too," Gard seconded. "Si."

Considering that he expected to be a betrothed man in another day, and considering that he intended to do his damnedest to keep his vows, the earl felt entitled to one last fling. If Miss Avery did find out, she deserved the setdown for making a fool out of him at his own lodgings. She could take it for a lesson that he was not to be trifled with.

First he went to Bloomsbury, ostensibly to advise them of company that evening. No one was at home but the maid Lorna, polishing the banister, so he took the opportunity to look around the attics and cellars, searching for signs of occupancy. When Annie returned home, market basket full of fresh lavender for the linen closets and drawers, Lorna directed her upstairs, for " 'Is nibs is acting mighty strange."

Ross was reduced to tapping the wainscoting for hollow sounds, lifting the rugs for trapdoors, feeling like the most caper-witted cocklehead in nature, when he noticed Annie silently observing him from the doorway of the master bedchamber. "Looking for ghosts," he hurried to tell her. "Making sure nothing frightens away the lady I have coming tonight."

Annie left just as quietly. The glasses hid the tears that trickled down her cheeks, leaving paths through the yellowish powder. How sad, she thought, he was making a heartfelt assignation with one woman for tomorrow, yet he had to have another tonight. She was right to decide on Barny. Ross Montclaire couldn't go one evening without a female in his bed.

So let him go to hell in a harlot's handcart. Annalise no longer cared, and her bag of tricks was empty.

Until Maudine came back.

Gard repaired to the stables to see what he could discover from Tuthill. The man was as close-mouthed as a clam, except for the stream of tobacco spittle he managed to get on Gard's Hessians.

"Sorry, gov'nor. Didn't see you standin' there."

"You wouldn't know anything about any mysterious young ladies, would you?"

Tuthill scratched his head with the sharpening stone he was using on a wicked-looking knife. "You want one in a mask tonight? I doubt my Nan'd approve me goin' out lookin', gov'nor, but since that's all she lets me do, I'll try."

"Devil take it, you dolt. You know I meant a real lady, coming here."

"You bring a real lady here, my Nan and Annie'd have your hide for sure. You'd be eatin' stone soup and cinders for days. And they'd take the lady and wash her mouth out with soap and march her off to church or sommat."

The earl twitched his crop against his leg. The stableman was more like to tap his claret than tell the truth. "I am not happy with this situation, Tuthill."

"Not by half, I'll warrant." Tuthill tossed the knife to test its haft, accidentally slicing off one of the tassels on Gard's boots. "Sorry, gov. Needs more work."

Nobody answering Gard's description of the man who accosted Miss Avery was staying at the Clarendon. That is, they had no tavern-mannered, tub-of-lard jackanapes lout with straw-colored hair. There was a Mr. Barnaby Coombes staying there who was blond and stocky, but he was out for the day. No, my lord did not wish to leave a message. He *wished* to tear the man's heart out, but he said he'd return another time.

Angelita was whispering sweet nothings in Gard's ear on the way up the stairs. They were nothings indeed—the sultry wench didn't have a particle of sense, and not much English, either—but they felt good, until they entered the bedroom and she let out a piercing scream that was like to reverberate through his brain box for days. He turned as she began pummeling him with her reticule. "I did not do it!" he yelled, not knowing what he was denying, since he couldn't see beyond the beaded missile and he could not understand the Spanish curses she was raining on his head along with the blows.

Annie pushed past him, grabbed up the washstand pitcher, and tossed the contents at Angelita. "*Basta*, you ninnyhammer. Of course he didn't do it. How dare you think he did! Now, get out. *Vamos usted.*" Annie held the pitcher over her head, ready to throw that, too, if necessary. Angelita vamoosed.

Gard was already at the bedside before Angelita was out the door, screaming of *los locos*. He gently examined Maudine's blackened eye and split, bloody lip.

"I swear to you, whoever did this will be fortunate if he lives to see tomorrow's dawn."

"No, you must not, my lord. It was my man. He'd only beat me worse."

"Why did he do this to you, my dear?"

"Because I ran away from you yesterday and

brought no money home, only the lovely bonnet. He said I had to come back, so I did. Annie says you're not a brute after all, it was all a hum." Looking up at him through the one eye that opened, she confessed, "I don't understand the joke, but Annie says you'll fix things right."

Gard looked at Annie, so confident, so trusting. Oh, Lud, how could anything make this right?

Eventually he promised to find Maudine somewhere safe, perhaps with Mother Ignace. Zeus knew, not even Cholly's mother was *that* broadminded. He gave her the ring that had gone begging in his robe pocket all these nights, knowing how she liked pretty things, and the promise of whatever blunt she needed, until she was settled somewhere, somewhere her so-called protector could never trespass. He also vowed to teach the scum of a procurer what it felt like to be pummeled by a stronger force. Meantime Maudine should stay right where she was as long as she wished. Gard wouldn't be needing the bed; he'd never bring another woman here. The house was jinxed.

Later, when the girl was asleep with the help of a little laudanum, and Gard's fury was eased with a little cognac, he asked Annie to play for him, to calm his nerves.

While Annie sorted through the music, the earl reviewed the day's events. Mostly he pictured Maudine's battered face atop Miss Avery's vibrant body, under that damnable veil. The thought of his Lady in Green in the hands of a vicious, greedy man made his pulse pound louder than Annie's tentative practice chords. B'gad, he *had* to keep her safe!

"Annie, I know—"

"I know I should not have put the girl in your bed, my lord," she interrupted, turning on the stool so he could see himself reflected in her dark glasses.

193

"But she was so frightened. I had to prove to her there were no . . . ghosts there."

"No, I wanted to discuss—"

"I don't suppose you can find her a position as a lady's maid?"

"Not for any lady I know. And I do not think Maudine is suited for a life of service. That type of service. She likes fancy clothes and jewels too much. But what I wanted to ask you was about Miss—"

Annie hit a few wrong notes in succession, then stood up. "I am sorry, my lord, but this has been a distressing evening for me. I cannot concentrate on the music. Will you please excuse me? I must see about Miss Maudine at any rate. Good night, my lord."

"Wait, I need to know—blast!" She was gone. That woman and Tuthill obviously shared a family distaste for the truth. The only difference between them was that Annie didn't spit and Tuthill didn't have a mole on his cheek.

Aggravated beyond reason, Lord Gardiner went to one of the new gambling dens, hoping to lose himself in a game of cards. None of his acquaintances seemed eager for his company at their table, however.

"Sorry. We're just playing the last hand." Or "Too bad, we already have a fourth." Ivory-tuners were at the craps tables, and Kitty was presiding at the roulette wheel, which left only the hardened gamesters playing faro, never his choice, never among such unsavory company. He left and went to White's.

The Duke of Afton got up and left when Gard walked in, not even nodding to the younger man in passing. He'd cut the earl since the night at the theater, so Gard did not even blink, until other gentlemen turned their backs to him.

"What's going on, Cholly?" he asked his friend.

His complexion as red as his hair, Cholly got up from his comfortable seat in the quiet corner. "Sorry, old chap, promised m'mother to make an early night of it. Busy day tomorrow, don't you know."

The earl lifted a brow. "What, you too, Cholly? My best friend?"

Cholly sank back down. "Ain't it time for you to have a look-see at your Suffolk property?"

"I just did, not a fortnight ago."

"Then a cruise on your yacht? You ain't been out sailing in ages."

"There's been a war going on. I don't wish to be blown out of the water by any eager Revenuer, either." He looked around at the heads turned away, the eyes not meeting his. "Why?"

"You just looking peaked, is all."

"I meant, why am I being treated like a leper?"

"You know how it is, the rumor mill and all. I don't believe a bit of it m'self. Not about the boys, leastways. Or the whips and chains. I mean, it was hard enough believing Don Juan was in decline."

"Boys? Whips and chains?" he asked in a fading voice. *That* was how Annie discouraged his light-skirts? By all that was holy, and a few things that were not, Gard swore he'd see that woman burn in hell.

"It'll all blow over, don't you know. Always does. Some noble will run away with a coal-heaver's daughter or something and they'll forget about your little peccadilloes. Uh, supposed peccadilloes. You might consider a change of scenery, meantime."

Gard considered returning to Laurel Street and causing a furor that could be heard back in Berkeley Square. Instead, a weasel named Fred received the brunt of Lord Gardiner's fury. Fred would not be bothering Maudine or anyone else any time soon. The minor altercation left the panderer waiting for the sawbones, and left Lord Gardiner winded and too muzzy-headed to confront Annie. Another day, he thought, wrapping a handkerchief around his torn and bloody knuckles. As for the rumors, Ross decided a change of scenery was indeed needful, starting with tomorrow's visit to Richmond.

Chapter Twenty-four

The road to Richmond was nearly empty at such an early dawning of the morning. The polite world made their jaunts to the nearby countryside at a more respectable hour, after their chocolate and sweet rolls. Only draymen and drovers were on the road, starting their daily treks into the City. They waved and nodded to the attractive couple and their grooms, on their way to the famous gardens. The working journeyers thought nothing of Miss Avery's veil, the roads being so dusty and all. Gard thought everything of that accursed scrap of netting, enough so he found the most secluded spot, among some trees, on a knoll where they could see anyone coming. While Clarence tethered the horses some distance away and Mick unpacked the blankets and pillows and hampers, Gard held his breath. Miss Avery seemed to be admiring the view from their grassy hill.

"It's much too early for nuncheon," he said finally, "but my cook packed us some hot cider.

Should you like some now, to take away the morning chill?"

"Please."

Gard pawed through the baskets, searching for the jar wrapped in towels, and two mugs. "Here, ma'am."

Annalise looked at the inviting steam rising from the cup, then at the mesh covering her face down to the chin. No one was near, and Lord Gardiner already knew her identity, this one at least, so where was the harm? If she only had this one last day to enjoy, let it be as herself. Annalise held her mug out to him; Gard held his breath. She started to remove the hatpins. Gard started to sweat. Then she removed the hat, veil, and all.

"By all the blessed saints." The earl took a hasty swallow of his cider, burning his mouth, tongue, and esophagus. "Heaven help me" was all he said when he could speak again. She was an angel with a silvery halo of tiny ringlets, the sweet, gentle smile of a madonna. She was a temptress, though, a siren with the sea-green eyes of a mermaid. Green eyes he expected, but not the dancing gold flecks that spoke of joy and laughter. She had fine bones and a perfect nose, not too sharp, not too tilted. There was a beauty mark—a real one, not a patch— beside her mouth that just invited kisses. "I'll be damned."

Gard's eyes were dry from not blinking. His mouth was dry from gasping. Everything else about him was damp from the two cups of cider he'd spilled as his brain caught a glimpse of paradise and forgot its job on earth. Her lips were twitching at his moonstruck attitude, so he gathered what wits he had left, poured two more mugs, offered one to Annalise, and promptly burned himself again.

"Why don't we take a stroll while the cider cools?" she suggested, amused and at the same time incredibly elated that she could have such an effect on this worldly man. No wonder he was a womanizer, if a comely face could so impress him.

They walked where there were few people, saying little, admiring the early spring blooms. Gard was thinking that the idea of marrying the girl for righteous reasons alone had gone begging, along with his mental faculties.

"Miss Avery, I know something of your difficulties," he began. "The prattleboxes have been busy, and I . . . I would deem it the greatest honor if you would permit me to safeguard your future."

Annalise hid her face in a cluster of daffodils, inhaling their scent, convincing her heart not to shatter. "I am sorry, my lord, I cannot accept. Thank you, but your solution will not wash. Sir Vernon is still my legal guardian and has the right to dispose of me and my money as he sees fit. I do not think he will see his way clear to letting me become any man's mistress."

"Do you think so little of yourself," he asked angrily, "and of me? I am asking for your hand in marriage, Miss Avery."

Marriage? Lord Gardiner was asking to marry her? Annalise may have dreamed such an event; never did she hope to hear it. Never would she have, either, if he knew how she had made such a fool of him by playing at his housekeeper. With deepest sorrow she had to refuse this offer, too. "But I am underage, my lord. Sir Vernon will never permit it; he will never release my dowry. I would be coming to you penniless and worse, with a background in trade, a scandalous family history, and a tattered reputation. I would only bring shame to your family."

"Somehow I do not think that matters these days," he said dryly. "I fear my own reputation, unsteady at best, has gone aground on gossip island."

"But you are an earl, time will erase the memories. I am a country nobody and I am ruined."

Now Annalise meant her reputation. Lord Gardiner thought she meant that clunch Barnaby Coombes. He swore to murder the dastard. Nor was he going to bother doing the thing up properly by issuing Coombes a challenge, no more than he had called out Maudine's pimp. Still, Miss Avery's giving her innocence to that boorish Barnaby was a definite facer. Coombes was a slowtop for letting this gossamer creature slip through his hands like fairy dust, but how could she not be enough for a man? Any man.

And was Gard going to let her fly away, too? He never minded a previously owned horse, but a wife? Good grief, he even brought his own sheets to strange inns. He never considered that when he eventually married he might have to worry about his heirs being of his flesh and blood, but a woman who was tempted before the vows was just as likely to be tempted after. He never thought Ross Montclaire would wear horns. Those fashionable arrangements where spouses went their own ways had never appealed to him, and less so now, thinking of sharing this divine body, that heavenly smile. Hell! He never used to be jealous. He never used to care.

Annalise understood his silence. He had offered for her out of kindness, but her difficulties were too much for even his broad shoulders to bear. His was an ancient title; he owed his ancestors a better bargain than a tarnished bride. But how could she simply walk away from him, the honorable thing or not? Honor be damned if it meant a lifetime of misery!

"My lord," she said into the quiet, "I have reconsidered. I should like to become your mistress if we can go away somewhere Sir Vernon cannot find us."

Another facer! "My dear, you cannot have considered. There has to be a better solution than that."

"Why? Marrying Barny would be selling myself anyway. I'd simply become a prostitute with a license. I am sorry. I can see I have shocked you, but that is how I would feel." She may have shocked Lord Gardiner, but she half surprised herself, too. On reflection, she realized she did not think so poorly of the women who traded their favors, not after knowing Mignon and Maudine. There were so few ways for a woman to be honorably independent.

Mostly, Annalise admitted, Mignon had been correct days ago. She did want Gard; she did hate seeing him with those other women. She was willing, even eager, to taste the forbidden fruit of his passion for herself. She wanted to be able to touch his firm strength, to feel the wiry curls on his chest, to caress his lowered brows, to know his kisses. The thought of kissing Barny made her gag. If love were the greatest deterrent to promiscuity, and if Gard grew to love her a little, maybe he could be faithful. He must care some already, to offer her his name.

While Annalise searched her heart and came up a wanton, Lord Gardiner also plumbed his soul. Incredibly, he found honor.

"No, I could not. You are gently born, a lady. It would be wrong."

"I never thought to hear Lord en Garde discourage a woman," Annalise said with a laugh. "What difference can my being a lady make to a rake like you?"

"I may have the name, but I swear I have not had a woman since I met you."

"I know. That is, I know how you must feel. I could not let another man touch me."

Ah, those were sweet words to Lord Gardiner's

ears. "I hold the lease on a place in Bloomsbury, by the bye," he offered tentatively. Of course she knew.

But Annalise answered noncommittally: "It is common knowledge that you rent my aunt's house. Sir Vernon will hear of my being there before the cat can lick her ear. I have to leave London, with you or without."

She'd leave London without him when cows sang the national anthem. "Very well, I'll make arrangements." He lifted her hand and pressed a kiss at the wrist, above her riding glove. Annalise was sure she'd made the right decision, if such a simple touch could make her toes tingle in her boots. It needn't be permanent anyway. When she reached her majority she'd be wealthy enough to live on the interest and her memories. Four years, unless he tired of her first.

"I think the cider should be cool enough to drink," he was saying, although he was thinking that he needed something cold instead, to chill the fever in his blood from her closeness. She smelled of roses and lavender and horse, all his favorite things. "And I am devilish sharp-set"—though not with hunger—"so perhaps we might open those hampers."

They ate cold chicken and Scotch eggs and sliced ham and fresh bread and cheese and tarts. Their hands touched and their eyes met and Annalise's cheeks grew flushed. They spoke of her parents, his childhood, books they had read, places he had traveled. They did not speak of tomorrow or the days to come.

When Annalise yawned after the meal, Lord Gardiner suggested she take a nap, for yesterday had been trying and they still had the maze ahead of them, then the long ride home. She demurred, not wanting to waste a moment of his company, but she did lean back on the pillows. Soon her eyes drifted

closed and her breathing became even, albeit Gard
tried not to notice the rhythmic rise and fall of her
chest. He withdrew a small drawing pad and a pencil from one of the baskets. Although he thought he
could stare at her forever, memorizing every detail,
he wanted a record for that night, and any night
they were apart, in case his brain ever doubted the
existence of such perfection.

No, she was not perfect, he noted as he drew. Her
chin was a trifle too pointed, reminding him of Annie and that harpy's stubborn streak. He quickly
put all thoughts of his wretched employee from his
mind. Not Annie on a day like today, he swore, getting back to his sketch.

Some might consider Miss Avery's beauty mark
an imperfection, too, he considered, studying to get
the placement of the mark exactly right, near her
mouth. His hand stilled as he deliberated on her
soft lips, slightly open as she slept. No man alive
could find fault with those lips. Of course he'd have
to feel them under his to make sure.

Her skin was too milky, even for one with such
silver-blond hair. Of course every blush colored her
pale cheeks delightfully, telling Gard that his touch
affected her, too. She'd been sick and indoors or
veiled, he reminded himself. Country sunshine
should have her looking not so ethereal, not so fragile that he'd have to worry about holding her as
close as he ached to. Disposing of her stepfather
and that jackass Coombes should also eliminate the
dark shadows of worried sleeplessness from under
her eyes.

Too bad her eyes were shut. He wanted another
look into those green depths, and he didn't even
have his colored pencils. Too bad she had clothes
on. Lud, he wanted her so badly, it hurt. How was
he going to manage until he made her his?

And how soon could he manage the thing?

"Tomorrow," he told her when she woke up, her cheeks tinged with pink when she met his intent gaze. "I'll meet you tomorrow for our ride and discuss what I'll have planned. I have already asked Clarence and Mick to keep watch over you tonight, just in case. They can reach me at Grosvenor Square or my club, or at Laurel Street. I am sure you'll wish me to consult the staff there about our plans."

Sure, was he? Annalise did not want to consider the outcome if he mentioned making Miss Avery his mistress. Henny'd be like to poison him and Rob would have his guts for garters. And Annie? Annie was aghast at the moral depravity—and delighted. It should be an interesting conversation all around.

Chapter Twenty-five

*W*hen the world turns its back, a fellow can always count on his mother to stand by him. There she was, the dowager countess Gardiner, Lady Stephania, standing by her only son in the entry hall of Gardiner House amid mounds of luggage, waiting for her coach.

"I would not stay in this sinkhole of venery if your father's ghost danced naked on my bedpost. Especially if he danced naked on my bedpost. I am going home to Bath, and I pray God I get there before the gossip, so I can still hold my head up in church."

"Mother, I can explain. Please wait."

"Wait?" she screeched, punctuating her outrage with jabs of her cane's gold-studded tip to his midsection. "Why should I wait, you codshead, to see the last hope of the Gardiner family locked away in Newgate prison?"

"Come, Mother," he said, pushing aside the cane before his waistcoat had a permanent indentation, to say nothing of his stomach. "Things cannot be as bad as all that."

"Oh, no? Then why are two Bow Street Runners waiting for you in the library?"

"I have no idea, as hard as you may find that to believe. I suppose I shall have to speak to them to find out, my lady, so feel free to go about your business of washing your hands of the head of the household. Of course you'll miss meeting your new daughter-in-law, but we'll get to Bath sooner or later, I am sure."

The dowager didn't bother asking anything about the girl, for all the good it would do, with her son's back disappearing down the hall. Lady Stephania didn't care if the chit was respectable or not, as long as she was willing to marry Ross. At this point the countess was glad enough he was bringing home a female, any female. She gave the orders to have her bags unpacked.

Two men with red waistcoats were indeed waiting in the library, watched over by Foggarty the butler and a footman, just in case the minions of justice saw fit to take the law—and whatever else they found loose—into their own hands.

"Gentlemen?" Gard nodded dismissal to the servants, who left reluctantly.

"Yer worship," one of the Runners greeted him in return. "Would you mind comin' along wi' us to Bow Street? Seems 'is 'onor the magistrate 'as some questions to put to you."

Gard offered his humidor around, then lit a cheroot. "Do I have a choice?"

The Runner who was doing most of the talking scratched his balding pate. "Well, you does an' you doesn't. We could get a writ of arrest on suspicion, 'owsomever we don't 'appen to 'ave it right now. On t'other side of the coin, most nobs don't like 'avin' their names broadcast about as'd like to occur, iffen we process a warrant. Don't suppose it'd bother you much, what with the talk already goin' the rounds."

"And too late if it did." The earl tapped the ash off his cigarillo. "What's this all about anyway? What am I supposed to have done now? Let me guess. I had an illicit relationship with Princess Caroline? No? Then with Napoleon, or his horse, or his grandmother."

The Runner scratched his head again. "Gor'blimey, you been busy, ain't you."

The matter actually concerned a bracelet, a gaudy but expensive bauble of multicolored stones set in gold medallions which the magistrate's secretary dangled in front of Gard's eyes in the shabby office at Bow Street. It was stolen property, according to Lord Ffolke, the gentleman-turned-law-officer in charge of the investigation.

"Very interesting, my lord. But what does it have to do with me?" Gard wanted to know. "I do not recall ever seeing it before."

"There's a reward out for this and a list of other pieces taken from an estate in Worcester. A jeweler brought it in for the money. He says he bought it from an actress at Drury Lane. Does that refresh your memory any, Lord Gardiner?"

"With due apologies, Lord Ffolke, I know *many* actresses at Drury Lane."

Lord Ffolke slapped his pudgy knee and chuckled. "I'm sure you do, my boy. Anyways, this one, Bessie O'Neill, reports that she received the trinket from you, for services not rendered, so to speak."

Gard shook his head. "I have no idea to what you are referring, my lord."

"Well, here's the bite with no bark on it. Word is that you're not much between the sheets, that you'll try anything to stir up a little interest. Bessie didn't do the trick, but she got paid anyway."

Gard was wondering if it was too late to book passage on the next ship bound for the Orient. What with the long journey, exploration of hidden temple sites and vast unknown regions, he might be gone for ten or twelve years. Which was about how long it would be before he'd dare show his face again in London.

"My lord?"

"Oh, yes, sorry. Woolgathering. You say I gave Bessie this bracelet?"

"No, your housekeeper actually handed it to Bessie, she said. You aren't going to give us some folderol about your servants having expensive gewgaws to distribute to doxies without your approval, are you?"

His housekeeper, Miss Avery's servant, most likely had access to a king's ransom in jewels. The she-witch was using Annalise's wealth to buy off his paramours!

He picked up the bracelet from the cluttered desk and pretended to study it once more. "Oh, *that* bracelet. I left it with the housekeeper for safekeeping because I had no use for it, I thought. It's too vulgar for my usual birds of paradise. They prefer diamonds or rubies, it seems," he said with a wink. "I won it in a game of cards, don't you know. And I, ah, did not fail Bessie. I failed to keep the appointment. My staff must have felt she deserved recompense for her time—I always insist they be courteous and generous to my particulars—and this was the only thing of value around. You must not believe everything you hear, you know, especially a man in your position."

"Indeed, indeed." Lord Ffolke was nearly convinced. This story tallied much better with the handsome devil seated at ease in front of him than did the idle chitchat of a bunch of old windbags at White's. "Then you won't mind telling us from whom you won the bracelet?"

"Only if you'll tell me what this is all about."

So Lord Ffolke told him how Sir Vernon Thompson had put up rewards for information leading to the recovery of his stepdaughter, an escaped Bedlamite. She took the family jewels and raided the household account, not that Sir Vernon was looking to press robbery charges against the girl or anything. She was too addled to know right from wrong. Sir Vernon merely wanted her back, where the family could look after her. He was also willing to overlook any irregularities in the jewelry's arrival at Bow Street, in exchange for information.

"Is Sir Vernon in town, then? I don't seek the reward, of course, I just wish to see the unfortunate girl taken care of. I'll go talk to him myself, and give him what assistance I can."

"Kind of you, my lord. Sir Vernon arrived in the City today. I already had my secretary visit him at the Clarendon, where he keeps rooms. I wish we had more to report, to relieve his worries. Now, if you'll just give us the name of the gentleman you played cards with, we'll be on our way with the investigation. You did give your word, my lord."

"So I did. Unfortunately I am not positive who actually put the bit of frippery on the table in the first place. Too much to drink, don't you know. Of course you do, if you heard all the other rumors. In fact, just between us, that's how most of the tittle-tattle started." He leaned closer, so only the magistrate could hear. "I was entertaining a regular dasher, a lady of the ton, a widow, don't you know. But I had overindulged, and fell asleep before I could, ah, entertain her properly. In a fit of pique she gave out that I was, shall we say, as responsive as the warming brick she had to put in her bed."

The magistrate slapped his knee again and Gard sat back, satisfied he'd done the possible to scotch some of the rumors, the important ones. Let this doddery fool think he was drunk; Gard realized now he'd been drugged!

He went on with his testimony. The sooner he got this over, the sooner he could knock a few heads together. "I think I won it the night I sat in for a round with Repton and his crowd. Eccles, Hastings, Jelcoe, I believe. I don't usually gamble with those Captain Sharps, but there you have it. Drink makes a man do strange things."

Before going to the Clarendon, Lord Gardiner stopped off home to place one of his dueling pistols in his greatcoat pocket, to exchange his cane for a sword stick, and to slide a thin stiletto inside his topboot. And to accept a folded note from his silent valet.

"What's this, Ingraham? I'm in a hurry."

"My resignation, my lord."

Gard ripped the thing up unopened. "Balderdash. You cannot leave now. Who else can make sure I am bang up to the nines for my wedding in a day or two?"

Gard left as soon as Ingraham regained consciousness.

Sir Vernon and Barnaby Coombes were having dinner in one of the private parlors. Lord Gardiner invited himself to join them.

"I believe you have lost something of value," he commented as he selected a slice of beef.

Sir Vernon chewed his own meat slowly, gesturing the already red-faced Barnaby to remain in his seat. Thompson noted the earl had not removed his greatcoat, nor handed his cane to the footman. It paid to be observant about these things, he had learned in many years of gulling the pigeons, just as it paid to listen carefully to the blockhead oafs he'd sent in search of Annalise. One of the fools even managed to recall a description of Lord Gardiner's housekeeper. Tallish she was, with a pointy chin and a wart, and all her hair pulled under a cap. Oh, yes, the man had added under Sir Vernon's patient questioning, she'd been wearing green-tinted spectacles, the same spectacles his dear stepdaughter had worn when he last saw her. The baronet did not know about the woman in the park—Barny had kept his word to Annalise so far— but he knew all about Lord Gardiner's housekeeper. He just hadn't had time to get her away from the house yet. The earl was no greenhead flat, though, nor doltish footman.

"Did you come for the reward, my lord?" he asked, playing his cards as close to his chest as the earl. "Are you below hatches at Gardiner House, then? Odd, that's one rumor I haven't heard."

Gard helped himself to a scallop of veal. "Not at all. Just wanted to find out how the recovery of the heiress was going."

Barnaby sputtered until he recalled the earl's punishing right. He subsided, gulping down his ale. Sir Vernon sipped from his glass more slowly. "I believe I shall have happy tidings shortly."

"Yes, I believe you shall. I am henceforth taking over the search for Miss Avery, and responsibility for her welfare." The earl put down his fork and stood to his considerable height, the capes on his greatcoat making him loom even larger over the others seated at the table. He was no longer the amiable dinner companion; he was a bird of prey. "Understand this, both of you. You have nothing more to do with the lady. You"—he addressed Barny, who was eyeing the distance to the door— "shall not talk to her, threaten her, or make any

211

effort to see her. If you are thinking you can kidnap her and elope to the border, think again. You'll be dead before you reach Gretna Green. Do you understand?"

Barny understood he hadn't a snowball's chance in hell of getting Leesie's dowry now, not with this handsome, well-heeled, and titled bastard sticking his aristocratic nose in. He finished his ale and nodded.

"And you, sirrah," the earl ground out, turning to Thompson, whose eyes were narrowed in anger, "will agree with my terms."

"What, give that innocent child into your keeping? No one would deny my right to keep her from such a dissolute libertine."

"I deny your right. You are no better than a pimp, selling her to this mawworm. And if you think to declare her insane so you can lock 'that innocent child' away forever, I'll make sure Parliament takes up the debate." When the other would have spoken, he went on, staring at Sir Vernon with deadly intent. "I have the means and I have the influence to get what I want. You'll have to meet me on the dueling field if you choose to get in my way. Miss Avery shall be free to live her own life if you hope to live yours."

Chapter Twenty-six

"*I* have decided to accept the earl's carte blanche," Annalise quietly announced to the Tuthills before dinner, in case Lord Gardiner arrived that night to discuss the arrangements with them. "I cannot keep hiding and running, feeling threatened all the time. Nor can I marry Barny, feeling as I do." She went upstairs to her room.

Without making a sound, Henny took the pot off the stove—lamb stew, Rob's favorite—and threw the entire contents out the back door to the hogs. The fact that the hogs were in the backyard of her cottage in Worcester made no never-mind.

A bit later Rob sat picking cold chicken from his teeth with his knife. "So Missy falls from grace and I go hungry," he complained to the replete and somnolent dog Clyde at his feet in the stable, to which he'd been banished. " 'Is nibs gives the chickie a slip on the shoulder and I get to sleep in the barn. Seems to me the gov'nor has a lot to answer for when he shows up."

Ross was at home, thinking about going to Laurel Street that evening. From what he knew of the baronet, Sir Vernon was not one to throw in his hand until all the cards had been played, including those dealt from the bottom. If Thompson was going to make a move, it would have to be soon, before Gard finalized his arrangements. This was contingent, of course, on Miss Avery's stepfather knowing her whereabouts.

Gard decided that Bloomsbury was his own best chance at finding the elusive female. Either she was on the premises or he could persuade Annie to divulge her location, after he convinced the housekeeper of the girl's danger. Annie owed him something, by Jupiter, after making micefeet of both his social life and his social standing.

In any case, he could not call on Miss Avery in all his dirt, stinking of horse and needing a shave, so he called for a bath. Trying not to fret, telling himself that Clarence was looking after her and so were the Tuthills and Annie, he paced the floor while waiting for the cans of hot water. Ingraham was humming contentedly in the dressing room as he laid out the attire he deemed appropriate for a visit to the future Lady Gardiner: black satin evening knee smalls, sparkling white linen, white brocaded waistcoat, and midnight-blue swallowtails that would take himself and a footman to fit over his lordship's broad shoulders.

The man's cheerful humming was grating on Gard's already sensitive nerves. Impatiently he picked up his sketch pad and thumbed through it to the end. Could she really be as beautiful as he remembered? If the picture from Richmond was accurate, she was even more so.

Idly he flipped back through the pages until his fingers paused at the drawing of Annie playing the pianoforte. Nice hands. Then he turned the page to stare at the other likeness of the housekeeper, the one that depicted the ugly cap, the flat chest ... and the pointy chin, the mole to the right of her mouth. He ripped the page out of the book and held it next to the last portrait, the one where he'd worked so hard to position Miss Avery's beauty mark correctly, to the right of her mouth.

Annalise. Annie Lee. An ass of an earl. His bellow of rage caused the footman to spill the two cans of hot water he carried.

Hot water be damned. Ross plunked himself down in the cold. Not even that cooled his blood. "The hell with clothes," he told the dismayed valet, pulling on his buckskins again, grabbing the frilled dress shirt from Ingraham's arms and buttoning it any which way. If not for the frail old man trembling in consternation, Gard would have dispensed with a neckcloth altogether. He snatched up a starched length of muslin and tied it in a rough knot. "À la Jack Ketch," he snarled at poor Ingraham as he stuffed the dueling pistol in his waistband and dragged on an old hunting jacket.

"Shall ... shall I have your carriage brought round, my lord?"

"No, I'll walk. By the time I get there, maybe I'll be rational enough that they won't add *strangler* to my list of sins." And if Sir Vernon got to her first, Gard raged, the baronet would merely be saving him the effort.

Ingraham was searching in the trash for his letter of resignation.

Clarence was across the street, watching out for the Lady in Green. Of course he was. Any looby could have figured it out. Any looby but a moonstruck rakehell. How could he not have seen? All those inconsistencies, all those coincidences! He

215

waved Clarence off, telling the man that he'd look after her. Ha! He hadn't looked after her when she was right under his nose! The earl wanted to bang his head against the lamppost for being such a noddy. Instead, he banged Tuthill against the stable door a few times for being a lying, cheating, scheming snake. He desisted when he felt the tip of Tuthill's knife pressed dangerously close to his inseam.

Tuthill spit to the side but did not move the blade. "I told her lack of sex'd make a man violent." He pressed the knife a little harder. "Lack of these might cure the problem. Works on horses all right."

Gard released his hold on the smaller man's shoulders, cautiously stepping back out of range. "Insolent bastard."

"Arrogant lecher."

They traded insults like boys in a schoolyard until Rob turned his head to spit, taking care to avoid Clyde. As he turned back, a pistol fired, the ball taking his knife right out of his hand. "Just an accident," he called out to the shouted queries, and "Damn good shot," to the earl. Then he went on. "Way I see it, my sticker's gone but your rattler's empty. What do you want to do now?"

"I want to go inside, and I am bigger, stronger, and younger."

Rob nodded. "You might get in, or you might not. Either way, you won't get out to see the dawn. I got so many crimes in my dish, killin' a nob won't make the noose any tighter."

"I'll bet you do, you old horse thief. Lucky for you I'm not a violent man."

"Too bad for you I am. And you might be bigger 'n all that, but I know more dirty tricks."

"I'll bet you do," Gard said again, losing patience with the stable hand, if that's what he was. "So are you going to try to stop me or not?"

"Depends on what you're lookin' for in there." Rob jerked his head toward the house.

"Revenge, mostly."

"Can't argue with that. Figure you've got a right. What else, though?"

Gard snarled, angry at the thought of an earl seeking permission to go courting from a thatch-gallows horse groomer. "What are you, her father or something, that I have to declare my intentions?"

"Someone's got to, looks like."

"Oh, stubble it already. Enough. I am still a gentleman."

Tuthill was satisfied with that, enough to curl up in his makeshift bed in an empty stall with Clyde for company. He wished the earl luck.

Ross went around to the front door and knocked. Annie opened the door and curtsied, then looked beyond the earl for his companion.

"No, Annie, I have no lady friend with me tonight, but I am sure your diabolical mind had something planned for our entertainment. What was it to be, poisoned toadstools? Leaking roof? Rocks in the mattress?"

Drat, she wished she'd thought of half of those! All she had were some overfed mice that wouldn't scare a grasshopper. Then she realized he was standing in the parlor, legs spread apart, arms crossed across his chest, scowling fiercely from under lowered brows like some seafaring brigand. "Are . . . are you very angry, my lord?"

"Angry? No, I wouldn't call it anger. Mind-numbing blood rage is more like it, Annie. You know, when all you can see is red in front of your eyes and smoke starts pouring from your ears and you—"

He had no hat or gloves for her to take, but he

did have a pistol tucked in his waistband. Annie started backing toward the door. Gard stepped that way, blocking her retreat.

"I have another idea for this evening, since you have frightened away all of my other interests." His voice was low, measured, implacable. "I thought you might provide the night's entertainment."

Annie glanced toward the pianoforte and licked her dry lips. "I don't think I could—"

"Oh, no, Annie, music wasn't at all what I had in mind." He took a step toward her, close enough for her to see the twitching of his jaw muscles. She backed up until her legs hit the sofa. When she couldn't go any farther without putting herself in an even more disadvantageous position, Annalise crossed her own arms over her own chest. She refused to be intimidated, she told herself, trying desperately to keep her knees from knocking together so loudly that he must hear them. She raised her chin defiantly. "I do not want to—"

"No. Tonight we do what I want. What I've been wanting to do since the day I met you." He put his strong hands on her shoulders, dislodging the shoulder pad that made her look deformed. Then he moved his fingers closer to her throat.

"My lord?" Her voice was at least an octave higher than normal.

"What, Annie, frightened? Just as those women were frightened by what they saw? Just as I was frightened, thinking I could never—"

"What . . . what are you going to do, my lord?"

"This," he declared, pulling the green-tinted spectacles off her nose and throwing them into the hearth, where they shattered with a tinkle of glass. The fear in her eyes sent a twinge of remorse through Gard, but only a twinge. This was ugly Annie, sharp-tongued Annie, Annie the trickster, who had made his life hell. "And this." He grabbed that awful cap off her head, releasing the silver curls, but he did not stop there. While one hand stayed fastened to her shoulder in an iron grip, the other used the muslin fabric to scrub her face. He did not even try to be gentle as he rid her of the disfiguring mole and the yellowish powder. "And this," he moaned, pulling her into his arms at last. She was brave and beautiful Annie, clever Annie, Annalise, who was his. "Oh, God, I have waited so long to—" Holding her in his arms was not the unalloyed delight he was expecting. In fact, it felt somewhat like embracing a boy, he imagined. He jumped back as if scalded. "Damn and blast, whatever you've done to your body, undo it!"

Annalise blushed. Or was her face red from his scrubbing? "Here, my lord?"

"It's Gard, dash it. And I refuse to call you Miss Avery, not when you've led me such a dance. I'll try for Annalise if you wish, but I'm afraid you'll always be Annie to me."

"Annie sounds fine." Always sounded better. "I'll, ah, go fix my gown," she said with a shy smile.

"You'll get rid of that monstrosity altogether, my sweet, or I'll throw it in the fire along with your cap. And hurry. We have a great deal to discuss."

In a daze Annalise unbuttoned her gown and unwrapped the binding around her chest. She was alive and he still wanted her. Two miracles in one night! She grinned, standing there in her chemise, thinking that the night was still young. Then she took to wondering what to wear. Not another of her black gowns, for she had no desire to kindle Gard's rage, and definitely not her heavy riding habit. Her flannel nightrail? Never.

She slipped up the back stairway and surveyed the selection in the lady's dressing room off the

219

master bed chamber. Not even for Ross Montclaire was Annalise Avery going to put on one of those filmy, transparent bits of harlotry. Not the ostrich-feathered robe, either. Finally she went to the other dressing room and put on his robe, wrapping the maroon velvet nearly twice around her and cuffing up the sleeves.

She started down the front stairs, being careful not to trip, and then she did not have to worry at all, for she was in his arms, being carried down.

"Oh, Lord," he breathed in her ear, "I have waited so long for this. I want you so badly."

"I know, Gard," she said from her place tucked against his chest on his lap on the sofa. "You've been so long without a—"

He shook her gently. "Little goosecap. Don't you know the difference between wanting a woman, any woman, and wanting one woman so badly, no other will ever do?" When she shook her head, tickling his chin with her soft curls, he told her, "I'll have to show you, then. Uh, just how much do you know about men anyway?"

"Only what I've learned from you this past few weeks."

"Then you and Barny didn't . . . ?"

"Of course not!" she proclaimed, which statement required another lengthy embrace, one that left her robe partly open and his shirt partially unbuttoned. Annalise had finally gotten to feel those dark curls on his chest.

Breathing heavily, Gard asked, "Will you come upstairs with me?" The sofa pillows were slipping around, and he could only picture that virgin bed upstairs, with his virgin bride lying beside him. She wasn't his bride yet, his conscience told him, but his baser self answered that she would be soon enough, and with her swollen lips and dreamy eyes, she'd follow him anywhere.

But what if she regretted it later? the inner debate went on. She deserved a little torment for his suffering, was the reply. Annie, his precious Annie? Gard sighed and compromised. Very well, he'd take her upstairs, where he could touch her, look at her, feel her warmth against his skin—and that was all. Perhaps he might sweeten his retaliation by bringing her to the brink of passion, then telling her he was too noble to continue. After all, he was no rutting beast, no adolescent. He could hold her soft, luscious body in his arms and still keep control of his own passion.

And for his next act he'd hold back the sun.

Chapter Twenty-seven

*W*hile Annalise and Lord Gardiner were so pleasurably involved, Sir Vernon, from his carriage parked across the street, was pleasurably watching the candles go out one by one. First his minion came around to report that the lights were out in the kitchen and the rooms below stairs. Stavely returned in an hour to report a candle to the rear of the ground floor, which was extinguished shortly thereafter. Finally the front parlor grew dark except for the fainter glow of a dying fire, and lights bloomed upstairs. Sir Vernon told his dark-clad assistant to wait half an hour, then get busy. The smarmy footman gathered his equipment and silently crept away, eager to exact retribution for being duped so badly, even more eager to earn Sir Vernon's gold.

The baronet was willing to pay whatever it took to get rid of his little problem—tonight. By tomorrow the interfering earl could present the girl to the ton, as the ordinary, well-behaved female she was, not a raving lunatic. Worse, he could marry the chit.

The haut monde—and the authorities—might conclude that the missing heiress was indeed the veiled horsewoman he finally heard about from Stavely, but they might never realize she was also a lowly servant. So if the housekeeper met an unfortunate end, one, moreover, that left her body unidentifiable, then to all intents and purposes Thompson's ward was still alive, just waiting to be returned to the bosom of her loving family. And he'd have at least four more years to milk her estate, especially if Lord Gardiner and those Hennipicker people also perished. Sir Vernon filed his nails while he waited.

It was a kiss to make every other kiss feel like an uncle's. It was the Marco Polo of kisses, going where no kiss had gone, opening worlds of wonder. It heated their bodies and clouded their minds, ringing bells in both their ears. And they hadn't gone past the bedroom door.

Bells? his lordship thought. Bells? It was a fine kiss indeed, but bells? Then he heard a dog barking and someone calling "Fire!"

"Blast it, Annie, if this is another of your tricks, I'll—"

"No, Gard, I swear!"

They both realized the room really was warm, not just their bodies overheating, and their minds were not fogged at all, they were full of smoke. Annie started to cough. Gard pulled a blanket from the mattress to beat at the flames if necessary, giving the still-chaste bed only one melancholy glance. Annie ran to the washstand and poured a pitcherful of water over them both before they dashed down the stairs. The earl had to steady her frequently, as she lost her footing in the trailing robe.

The front hall was engulfed in fire, so they made for the rear stairs and the back door.

"You go make sure Henny and Rob are out," Annie called, shoving him down the first few steps while she ran back to her own room to gather her jewels and her reticule and her riding habit.

"You fool," Gard shouted, wrenching the stuff from her and dragging her out. "As if I'd leave you!"

"But Henny and Robb?"

"Are already out. I heard them shouting. Now, come before they try to get back in to save you!"

But the kitchen door was also in flames; there was no exit that way. Annalise managed to grasp the mouse cage before Gard hauled her along after him upstairs again, where the fire was starting to travel along the hall carpet, licking up at the wood paneling and the wallpaper.

"Damnation!" Gard swore, not releasing his hold on Annie's wrist. He made for the smaller parlor before the flames could reach the draperies, and shoved Annie facedown onto the love seat. "Stay there!" he ordered while he searched around the room for a fireplace poker, a chair, a heavy stool to throw against the window.

"Why don't you just unlock it?" Annie demanded from his side, suiting action to word before Gard nudged her aside and threw the window open, then jumped down, holding his hands out for her. First she passed down the mouse cage while he swore. Then she retrieved her jewel box and reticule and riding habit from where he'd tossed them.

"For heaven's sake, woman, you are taking years off my life with every second's delay! Get yourself out here *now*!"

Annalise looked down at him, with soot on his face and his shirt open and untucked, appearing more like a buccaneer than ever. "I do not like it when you shout at me that way, my lord."

"My God, Annie, do not get on your high horse now. Please don't torture me this way!"

She read the anguish in his eyes and sighed contentedly as she jumped into his arms. "You really do care."

The fire brigade managed to save some of the house, but not from smoke and water damage, naturally. The Watch declared the fire suspicious. How could they not, when it arose in two separate locations at the same time? None of the neighbors saw anyone lurking about. In fact, no one saw or heard anything until the dog's barking awoke the neighborhood again after the pistol shot. Clyde was the hero of the hour and Henny the heroine for making Rob sleep in the stable, where he could hear the little terrier and alert everyone before they were overcome by the smoke. Annalise, Rob, and Henny were still hugging one another and Clyde when the fire engines rolled away. The earl came in for his fair share of exuberant affection, too, although Rob merely shook his hand.

They were alive. They were also damp, dirty, exhausted, and homeless. "Enough," Lord Gardiner declared. "Tuthill, harness up the carriage. It's time we got out of here. It's beyond foolish to survive a fire and perish of pneumonia. Besides, whoever set the deuced fire might still be about, getting up to who knows what other mischief." He stood closer to Annalise, shielding her with his larger body while his eyes tried to pierce the shadows.

Annalise agreed. "I am certain one of Rob's disreputable friends must own an inn or someplace with rooms to let. No respectable hotel would accept three such ragamuffins as we appear, nor Clyde, of course."

"Gammon. You are all coming to Gardiner House in Grosvenor Square."

"Now who is being a nodcock? You know you cannot take me to Grosvenor Square. I don't even have any shoes!"

"What the devil have shoes got to do with anything? You'll be safe there, that's all that matters," he insisted.

Annalise took his arm and pulled him away from Henny's hearing. "Gard, you cannot take me to your house," she hissed in his ear. "Your mother is there, isn't she?"

"Of course she is, or else I'd take you to Cholly's or Aunt Margaret's."

"Has all that smoke shriveled your brain, my lord?" Annie stomped her foot, then recalled she was barefoot and got even angrier that Gard was being so obtuse. "You cannot bring your mistress home to your mother, my lord earl."

"Stop throwing the title in my teeth, little shrew. You are not my lover at all, or did I miss something between 'Oh, Gard' and 'Fire'?" He put his finger to her lips when she would have protested that the intent was there, if not the deed. "I am not bringing my mistress. I am bringing my fiancée. Mother will be delighted."

"Gard, you cannot tell your mother such a Banbury tale!"

"No such thing, my pet. It's true, and always was. I have intended to make you my wife for ages now. That's the best way to protect you permanently from fortune hunters, be they relatives or suitors, and to restore your reputation. My mother is one of the highest sticklers. No one will dare criticize her daughter-in-law." And, he said to himself, she'll make damned sure there will be nothing to criticize while we are under her roof. He determined to get a special license as soon as possible.

"No, Gard, I cannot let you do this. We can simply go to an inn. My reputation be hanged!"

"That's very well for you to say, my dear, in your chameleon disguises, but what about me? A respectable wife is about the only thing that can salvage the micefeet you've made of my good name! We're going to Gardiner House, and that's all."

Ross was right: His mother was thrilled to welcome the prospective Lady Gardiner and her servants even though the hour was late. An emergency, he explained, a fire having destroyed Miss Avery's lodgings.

Miss Avery, the heiress? An earl could reach higher on the social ladder, but the gel was Arvenell's granddaughter, and that counted for nearly as much as the fortune. Lady Stephania was liking the match better and better, as long as the chit wasn't the moonling gossip was claiming. Gard was able to reassure her on that score, and that Miss Avery was respectably chaperoned by her old nanny.

The dowager floated down the stairs in a drift of chiffon, delighted with the news she could relate to her husband's spirit. Maybe now the old fool would let her sleep in peace. She smiled as she let Ross lead her to the Adams drawing room, where Miss Avery was waiting.

The smile died a painful death when Lady Gardiner finally confronted her promised replacement. Annalise stood by the fireplace, her boyishly short hair in damp tendrils, her skin as soot-darkened as a blackamoor's, her feet bare, and her body barely covered by a man's oversize robe. And she was clutching a cage of rodents.

"Mice!" the countess shrieked, throwing herself into the nearest pair of arms, which happened to belong to Ingraham. The ancient valet had come to see if he could assist his master after the harrowing events, and to get a good look at his lordship's intended. One look was enough to drain the blood from his head and send it to his feet. Being embraced by the countess was one shock too many. He collapsed onto the floor, taking the countess with him, where she remained screaming that the fifth earl was spinning in his grave, that, with a Bedlamite for a mother, the seventh earl was like to have two heads or think he was Nero, that if the rats were not destroyed immediately, she'd have the sixth earl drawn and quartered.

Gard was not sure which was worse, the fire or his mother's tantrum. He knew the latter left Annalise more shaken. For that reason, and others too base to consider, he did ask Henny to sleep on a pallet in the room assigned to Miss Avery.

"She'll feel better having someone familiar nearby in a strange house," he explained, "and there will be less bibble-babble about us arriving in the middle of the night if the servants know you slept with her."

Henny was a bit intimidated by the grandeur around her, and the earl in his own surroundings was not the handsome lad who ate in her kitchen. He was a peer of the realm, all right, aristocratic down to his bare toes. She curtsied. "Yes, my lord. As long as you think it's necessary."

The night had been hell except, of course, for the few moments of euphoria with Annalise in his arms. Gard reflected that sending that Tuthill scoundrel off to find a bunk in the stable was nearly as enjoyable.

"So you ain't above a few dirty tricks of your own, eh, gov'nor?" Rob muttered on his way to another hard, itchy, lonely bed in another cold, smelly stall.

"You better not think it's necessary for too long if you know what's good for you."

Lord Gardiner just grinned.

Chapter Twenty-eight

*A*nnalise couldn't stay. She couldn't sleep, either, so she lay in bed, listening to Henny's soft snores, counting all the reasons she had to leave Gardiner House and its owner, instead of counting sheep. The sheep would have looked back at her with their placid woolly faces as they marched across the landscape of her dreams. Instead, she saw Gard, with one dark, raised brow, an unruly curl hanging on his forehead, and that soft, one-sided smile.

She couldn't accept his offer of marriage. Except the infuriating man had not actually offered, he had ordered their engagement the same way he ordered dinner or ale or a hot bath, without a by-your-leave for Annie. He was too used to having his own way, was my lord Gardiner, too arrogant and domineering for her taste, Annalise tried to convince herself. He was also kind and noble, with a deep-seated sense of honor that often collided awkwardly with his rakish, raffish ways. Like now, when he was planning to marry a girl who had agreed to become his mistress.

Annalise knew he was intending to marry her to keep her safe and to keep her name from the gutter. Oh, he liked her, too, and desired her, she was well aware, but, heavens, the man was a rake. He liked a different woman every day. He was infatuated with her now, but how long before the bonds of matrimony became a noose? How soon before he resented being forced to do the honorable thing, resented her? How long before he strayed? She did not think she could bear it when his eyes no longer gleamed when she entered a room, or he started to find pressing business elsewhere. If only he loved her . . . but that was a sheep of a different color.

And she'd never be accepted in his world, no matter what he claimed. Annalise saw the way the dowager responded. If his own mother could not welcome with equanimity a scandal-ridden hoyden, the rest of society was sure to be even less accepting of coal-king Bradshaw's granddaughter. She'd be cut; he'd be ostracized from the life he enjoyed. Or else he would still be invited everywhere—without her.

All of that was assuming, of course, that they lived long enough to face the ton. Sir Vernon was not like to give up, not even if they married. He'd fight for the money, dragging the sordid case through public trials, or else he'd resort to more villainous efforts like the fire. Annalise had no doubt as to the blaze's instigator, nor that he'd try again. If the baronet was never to see a groat of her fortune, he'd want to get even. Annalise was already responsible for the destruction of her aunt's little house in Bloomsbury; jeopardizing this magnificent mansion was unthinkable. Besides, earls made large targets.

Gard could never be convinced to go into hiding,

she saw that now; the earl was just fool enough to challenge Sir Vernon, or do something equally as nonsensical. Sir Vernon was not constrained by the rules of honor, so she'd never have a moment's peace, worrying for Gard's very life. Her friends were already in danger, especially Rob, whose past could not afford scrutiny, and every minute they remained with her magnified their peril. She had to leave.

At dawn Annalise rose, washed, and donned her riding habit and a pair of boots that had been placed in the dressing room for her. The boots were too big, but she stuffed some handkerchiefs from a drawer into the toes. When Henny went off with Rob to see if any of their possessions could be salvaged from the fire, Annalise sat down and wrote a note. She was going to Northumberland, she penned, where she should have gone all along. The duke was bound to accept her rather than see her go into service in his own neighborhood. She had enough money for the coach ride, and she'd be long gone before Sir Vernon stirred from his bed, so they were not to worry or try to follow. She sealed the note and marked "Henny" on the front.

No words came to fill the blank sheet she intended for Lord Gardiner. Her hand could not possibly form the letters to spell good-bye, and her tears would have smudged the ink anyway.

Shutting the bedroom door firmly behind her, Annalise went down the marble stairwell and asked the venerable butler standing at attention there the way to the stables.

Foggarty bowed and gave her the direction. Miss Avery *looked* a proper lady, he judged, which just went to show how deceptive appearances can be. Everyone knew you didn't do anything to excite a madwoman to violence, though, so he did not comment that proper young ladies never left the door without an escort and they always waited for a horse to be brought around to them. She didn't ask about the mice; he didn't ask her destination. Having closed the door behind her, Foggarty wiped his brow. Ingraham was right: It was time they retired.

Annalise turned the corner for the Gardiner House stables and kept on going. She was familiar enough with London to know she could find a hackney stand at the next intersection; the jarvey was bound to know the coaching inns. She regretted having to leave Seraphina behind, but Rob was sure to take good care of the mare and Annalise would send for them all when it was safe. She regretted having to leave the earl even more. Who will take care of him? she wondered. Certainly not his high-strung mother or doddery retainers. Not a one of them was liable to tease him into laughter or make him lose that awesome dignity. Of course there was an entire continent full of women just waiting to smooth back his hair and erase the longing from his sky-blue eyes.

With tears in her green eyes, Annalise did not see the coach and four following her progress.

It wasn't much of a struggle. Sir Vernon threw a blanket over her head from behind, then Stavely carried her to the carriage. The baronet held an ether-soaked cloth over her face until she stopped thrashing about.

When she woke up, her mouth was dry, her insides were in an uproar, and Sir Vernon was across the coach from her, reading a newspaper. "Good afternoon, Annalise," he greeted her politely, setting down the paper and pouring her a glass of wine from a bottle by his side. "Here, have some of this. It will help settle your stomach. Unfortunate side effect of the stuff. Nasty, but effective. Oh, and thank you. That was very kind of you to keep to your early hours, especially after such an eventful evening."

She took the glass and drank most of it down, hoping the spirits would clear the muddle in her head, too. The baronet refilled her glass and leaned back, smiling. It was not a smile to warm an abducted heiress's heart.

"Where are you taking me?" Annalise demanded. "I won't marry Barny no matter what you do!"

"I'm afraid that is no longer an option, my dear. Nor is my plan to keep you under lock and key. Your noble protector promises to put a spoke in that wheel, also. Too bad. Those were the more pleasant choices. No, my dear, you've been a bit too much trouble already. I thought first we might simply dispense with your company somewhere along the road, but that's too chancy. So we are going to Dover right now, and then on to Vienna. My poor ailing stepdaughter needs a change of scenery, according to the doctors' recommendations. Where better than the gaiety of the Peace Congress, where all of Europe is convened?"

"You are taking me to Aunt Rosalind?" Annalise asked optimistically.

"That is who you wanted to visit, isn't it? Regrettably, somewhere between Calais and Vienna, my unfortunate, deluded ward, you shall run away with the footman Stavely, who is, incidentally, driving this carriage."

Annalise made an unladylike noise. "I wouldn't have Barny. What makes you think I'd wed that scum of a servant?"

"Oh, there needn't be any wedding, although I am afraid Stavely might insist on his conjugal rights. No, I'll go on to Vienna, mourning your loss but washing my hands of such a hopeless case. I won't have to give up your estate until you reach your majority, naturally, since you made such an unsuitable match and without my permission."

"And when I do reach twenty-five?"

"Oh, I am sorry, my dear, I thought you understood. You won't see twenty-two. Stavely will be able to settle handsomely in the colonies, and you?" He shrugged and picked up his newspaper again, holding it to the window for better light. "Whoever knows what finally happened to that demented Miss Avery?"

"And you think I'm just going to sit here all the way to Dover and not make a fuss at every toll and changing stop?"

He looked at her over the top of the paper. "Oh, I don't think you'll cause much of a problem. That wine you just drank was dosed with enough laudanum to put a horse to sleep."

By eleven o'clock Gard was in possession of a special license, thanks to his godfather the bishop; a ring, an emerald, naturally, surrounded by diamonds; and promises from three modistes to deliver within the afternoon everything a lady of fashion needed and dressmakers to make sure it all fit.

By twelve o'clock he was at the Clarendon, asking after Sir Vernon.

"I'm sorry, my lord. The baronet checked out early this morning."

"Did he happen to mention where he was going? I have some information for him."

A coin helped the clerk recall: "He didn't leave anyplace to send messages, if that's what you mean, but he did ask to see the shipping schedules from Dover."

Excellent. The cur was leaving the country and saving Lord Gardiner the effort of encouraging his departure.

235

Not so excellent. By one o'clock he realized Annie was gone. So did the rest of Grosvenor Square, when he was finished shouting. How could his butler have let her go out unaccompanied? How could Henny and Rob go off and leave her in a strange house? How could his mother sleep all morning on his wedding day? How the hell could he make up Thompson's lead?

Thompson had a cumbersome coach and four that had to stick to well-traveled highways. Lord Gardiner on Midnight and Tuthill on Seraphina had no such restrictions beyond resting the horses occasionally. These horses were bred for stamina besides, not like the tired nags Sir Vernon had to hire at the changes. At each posting inn where the earl or Rob inquired, they were closer to their quarry, close enough by late afternoon to stop for some bread and cheese and ale. One more hour of hard riding should put the coach in sight.

"There she is," Rob finally shouted, taking the pistol out of his waistband. The earl followed suit and would have ridden straight after the carriage, but Rob indicated they ride across a hill and come out ahead of the coach, face on. "And let me say it, gov'nor, please?"

Before Gard could ask what the deuce Tuthill wanted to say, they were coming down the slope. Rob fired his pistol, then he yelled in an awesomely authoritative, menacing voice: "Stand and deliver!" He ruined the effect for an astounded Gard by following his command with "Damn, that felt good."

Any coachman worth his salt would have known he could never outrun two mounted horsemen, armed and in front of him to boot, but Stavely wasn't a real coachman. What he was, was ready to face near death instead of the certain death he saw looming ahead in the person of Lord Gardiner.

He was already having trouble controlling the frightened cattle after the gunshot, but he lashed them with his whip anyway to get more speed.

The carriage horses bolted forward, sending Gard and Rob flying out of their way and then after them again.

"Pull up, man!" Gard ordered, brandishing his pistol at Stavely, but the footman couldn't have stopped those horses if his life depended on it, which it did. As chance would have it, there was a sudden bend in the road. Without a steadying hand at the ribbons, those wild horses were never going to make the turn. As the earl swore from one side of the leaders' heads and Rob cursed from the other, Stavely decided to save himself from the inevitable accident and the implacable earl. He jumped. If he'd waited a few more seconds, he'd have hit some bushes instead of the rocks.

By dint of incredible skill and a measure of luck, Rob and the earl were able to turn the horses after all. They couldn't stop them yet, but the frenzied beasts would be winded soon. Meantime Rob wiped his forehead as he rode alongside the left leader. "Just like old times," he said, grinning at the earl. "Damn, I forgot how much fun this is!"

Inside the coach, all the commotion and being tossed around had roused Annalise from her stupor. Her head ached and she was more nauseated than ever from the effects of the ether, the laudanum, and riding backward. She never had been a good traveler.

"Stop the coach," she cried weakly, and ridiculously, under the conditions. There was no one to hear her, however, for Sir Vernon was standing up across from her with his head and upper torso out the coach window, trying to get off a clear shot at the earl from the jolting coach.

If she were a man, with a man's strength, Annalise considered hazily as she absorbed the situation, she could lift Sir Vernon's legs and hoist him out the window. But she could barely lift her head, much less Sir Vernon. If she were less a lady, or perhaps less dizzy, she could take a page from Mrs. Throckmorton and kick him, but her booted feet seemed miles away, all four of them.

So she did what she could, since it appeared no one else was going to stop this hurtling vehicle before she cast up her accounts. She picked up the heavy bottle of drugged wine and swung it with every ounce of strength she could gather, slamming it against Sir Vernon's leg with a satisfying crack.

Luckily for Annalise, Thompson dropped the pistol when he smacked his head on the carriage roof, trying to get back inside to collapse on the seat, clutching his shattered leg. He would have killed her for sure right then if the gun remained in his hand.

Annalise stared in amazement at the still-intact bottle in her hand, then at the blood dripping down her stepfather's face and oozing between the fingers on his leg. She clamped her hands over her mouth just as the carriage stopped and the door was flung open.

"Annie, my darling! Are you—"

"Get out of my way, I'm going to be ill," she managed to say, running to the other side of the carriage.

So much for grateful maidens swooning into the arms of their gallant rescuers.

Chapter Twenty-nine

They did not reach Dover that night at all, what with having to locate the magistrate, a surgeon for Sir Vernon, and an undertaker for Stavely. Squire Josiah Nutley, the magistrate, was a florid-faced, friendly man, delighted to invite nobility to accept his hospitality for the night. His wife gathered Miss Avery to her ample bosom, weeping over the sad story and vowing to make sure the poor girl had everything she needed, once Squire whispered into her ear that he'd actually seen the special license in his lordship's pocket.

Fanciful tales of abductions and evil stepfathers were all well and good for the Minerva Press; Mrs. Squire Nutley liked happy endings, which to her meant orange blossoms and church bells, not any young couple riding off into the night with naught but an unsigned scrap of paper to keep them respectable. No, she wouldn't hear of them traveling on to Dover, not when Miss Avery could share a bed with her oldest girl and the boys could bunk together so Lord Gardiner could have their room.

After the briefest of rests and a bite to eat in the kitchen, Rob Tuthill volunteered to ride back to London that night to reassure the earl's household and to fetch Henny with Miss Avery's new wardrobe. There was no way Rob was staying in a magistrate's stable. There was also no way Annie was going to return to London without Lord Gardiner, she insisted, and no way he was leaving without seeing Sir Vernon embark on a ship bound for anywhere far away. They'd all meet tomorrow in Dover, it was decided.

While Rob was riding by moonlight on a borrowed horse, just wishing he'd be set upon by one of his old friends, Annalise was upstairs, gritting her teeth, listening to girlish giggles and rapturous sighs over her handsome betrothed, who had already reminded her at least thrice that if she hadn't been such a peagoose as to run away in the first place, she would never have been abducted. His lordship, meanwhile, was drinking inferior brandy with the genial squire and settling Sir Vernon's fate.

The baronet was induced, by the simple expedient of withholding his laudanum, to sign a confession in the magistrate's presence. The crimes enumerated included the abduction, the fire, embezzlement of trust funds, attempted murder, and enough other legal-sounding terms to have him clapped in prison if he ever set foot—or crutch, as seemed likely—in England again. Gard was satisfied, or would be as soon as the dastard was carried aboard a ship, and the squire was almost satisfied that justice was being tempered with the right amount of mercy for such a blackguard as Sir Vernon. He was getting off easy, feared the squire.

"One thing puzzles me, my lord," Nutley complained when the baronet was securely locked up for the night. "If the young lady broke his leg with a bottle, and he broke his head on the carriage, how did his jaw get broke and his gun hand get a knife through it?"

"Oh, didn't I tell you? He tried to escape on the way here."

With a busted leg and a banged head? Now the magistrate was happy. Justice was served best with a firm hand, he always said.

Sir Vernon was deemed well enough to be transported to Dover the next morning, if one didn't have to listen to his moans. Squire and Mrs. Nutley lent a driver for the coach and a maid for Miss Avery, but the maid had the unhappy task of tending the baronet instead, for Miss Avery refused to share the coach with him. She much preferred to ride a well-rested Seraphina next to his lordship's Midnight.

Lord Gardiner installed Annalise in two rooms and a private parlor at the Three Sisters Inn before seeing Sir Vernon aboard the packet for France. He sent the Nutleys' servants home in a hired coach with a generous tip and a finer bottle of brandy than Squire was used to drinking. This one even had excise labels on it. He also sent a smoked ham from the inn's kitchen along to Mrs. Nutley, to thank her for the hospitality. Then he went in search of a vicar, but the nearest man in orders was at a deathbed vigil.

"Dash it, the wedding will have to wait for tomorrow after all," he announced to Annalise in the private parlor, going to warm his hands by the fire.

"There will be no wedding, my lord. I thought I made that clear."

The chill reached his toes. "You did not deny it to the Nutleys when I said we were engaged."

241

"I couldn't let those nice people think . . ."

"What everyone else is going to think," he completed. "And worse, if Tuthill and his wife do not get here soon. You widgeon, you *have* to marry me."

"No, *you* have to marry *me* because of your confounded honor, which you may now consider satisfied by the offer. Thank you, but I do not want an unwilling husband who has to be forced into marriage." Annalise was proud; her voice hardly quivered at all.

"But I am not unwilling." Gard insisted. He held out his arms. "Come, I'll show you how much I am looking forward to the wedding."

"That's lust," she said, keeping her distance. "You don't love me."

Gard blinked. "I don't? Then why have I gone around milling down everyone who looks at you sideways? Why have I moved heaven and earth to get the special license so I could have you next to me forever, without waiting another day?"

"You do? You really love me?" Tears started to well in her eyes.

The earl gathered her into his arms. This time she went eagerly. "Of course I do, you adorable ninny." He addressed the curls on the top of her head. "I loved you from the first day I saw you in the park. I thought you were royalty, you know, so proud and elegant."

"And then you discovered I was just a hobbledehoy coal-miner's granddaughter. You must have been disappointed."

"Never, I just found how right I was. You are the queen of my heart, Annie. Please say you care for me?"

She looked up, eyes shining, without leaving the warmth of his embrace. "I must have loved you forever, I was so jealous of those other women. You were calling me Miss Green and them 'sweetheart.' I was green with envy!"

"There will never be another, I swear," he declared, and sealed his vow with a kiss.

When Annalise could speak again, she smiled and said, "I know."

Gard raised an eyebrow. "You know what? That I'll never have another woman? Just what are you planning, Annie?" he asked suspiciously.

"Just this." She wrapped her arms more firmly around him and raised her lips for another kiss, telling him without words that she'd bind them together with love and passion enough for any man.

Some moments later Gard cupped her face in his hands and gently kissed the beauty mark to the side of her mouth. "Then it is all settled? The vicar can come in the morning and you won't have flown away before the ceremony?"

"Well, that depends. You haven't asked me."

Gard was confused. "Asked you what, my love?"

"You haven't asked me to marry you, my lord. You simply told me. You informed me that I had to marry you or you had to marry me. I believe those were statements, not requests. Either I have equal say in this marriage, which means my wishes are consulted, or I won't do it."

Gard tossed a cushion from the sofa onto the floor at her feet and kneeled on it. "Lud, what I don't do for you. And you wonder if I love you?" Then he took her hand and brought it to his lips. "Miss Avery, my dearest Annie, will you do me the greatest honor, make me the happiest man on earth, by accepting my heart and my hand in marriage?"

"Yes, my dearest Gard, I will," she said with a sigh, tugging on his hand.

He stayed on the ground, when she wished him up for another embrace. "Tomorrow?"

She pretended to consider. "That depends on one condition, my lord. Can we have our wedding night tonight?"

He laughed and pulled on her hand until she was in his arms, on the floor. "My endless delight, you can have whatever your heart desires, as long as it's me." He loosened his hold on her only long enough to unwrap the neckcloth borrowed from Nutley, which left a rash under his chin.

Annalise was very near to having her conditions met when a banshee's wail split the air. Even before turning to the doorway, Lord Gardiner cried out, "Lord have mercy, am I never going to get la—"

"Aunt Rosalind!" Annalise scrambled up and into the embrace of a tall, blond-haired woman in sable and rubies. "Oh, Aunt Ros, I am so glad you've come home, but everything is all right now. However did you find us? Oh, there's Rob, and Henny!" Annalise was so in alt over seeing her aunt again, she forgot the civilities for a moment, which gave Lord Gardiner time to button his shirt and run his fingers through his hair while Tuthill looked on, grinning.

"Aunt Ros, may I present my fiancé, Lord Gardiner? Gard, Lady Rosalind Avery."

"Not anymore, dear," her aunt informed them all, dragging forth a small, bespectacled man from behind her. "Elphy's wife finally expired—in her lover's arms, I might add, lest you think I'm being disrespectful of the dead—so it's Lady Elphinstone now."

After exclamations and congratulations and more embraces and handshakes, the new Lady Elphinstone went on: "Now that we're married, Papa has decided to forgive me, the old curmudgeon. He wrote me in Vienna, telling me to come home and bring Elphy for his blessing. He also charged me to see what Sir Vernon was nattering on about."

"He was dreadful! I am sorry about your house, Aunt Ros."

Lady Elphinstone waved one beringed hand in careless disregard. "Oh, Elphy has a grand place right in Mayfair. As soon as we all get back from visiting Papa, we'll hold your presentation ball there."

Gard spoke up for the first time. "*We* are returning to London tomorrow, after the wedding. My Lady Gardiner shall be presented from Grosvenor Square."

"What, after some hole-in-corner ceremony nobody will believe happened? Not on your life." Lady Elphinstone crossed her arms over her bosom and raised a familiar pointy chin in the air. "You haven't asked her grandfather's permission, either, I'll wager. Pray, do you want to complete the chit's ruin? We got here just in time as it is, I swear. No, you'll come along to Northumberland, meet Arvenell, and get his blessings. Then we'll call the banns and have a lovely wedding in the Arvenell chapel with half the shire present. That should do the trick."

"That should take months!" Annalise and the earl chorused.

Lady Ros patted her niece on the cheek. "Don't be so impatient, dearest. I waited all these years for my darling Elphy."

"Like hell you did," Lord Gardiner said with a growl before turning to his betrothed. "We can be remarried in Northumberland in a chapel or in a turnip patch, however many times you wish, Annie, but we are first getting married right here. By special license. Tomorrow morning," he firmly declared. Then he added, "Aren't we, Annie, please?"

She looked at him and smiled. "Whatever your heart desires, my lord, as long as it's me."

Minor
Indiscretions

This one is for Dottie,
Diane, Donna, and Eileen
with love

Chapter One

The bags were packed; the hired chaise waited outside. It remained only to sit through the headmistress's parting speech, and Miss Melody Morley Ashton would be free. After ten years of enforced education, Melody had learned patience along with grammar and globes, dance steps and deportment. She sat in perfect dignity and composure, her back straight, her fine green eyes lowered in respect, prepared to swallow Miss Meadow's own blend of tea (far superior to that served the students) along with the old windbag's own brand of niggling nastiness. Miss Meadow was small in stature, smaller in mind, and smallest of all in human kindness, according to the students at the Select Academy for Young Ladies, located outside of Bath, which Melody would soon be leaving, praise be!

"All young things must eventually leave the nest," the dumpy little matron recited, waving her pudgy hands around. "They must try their wings, take to the air."

The young woman on the other side of the desk

1

still wore a demure smile, wondering if Old Meadowlark was going to have her digging for her own worms before she was at last excused.

"Of course you are a trifle underage. We do prefer our young ladies to attend classes until they are eighteen. Those final courses in decorum are so crucial, don't you know."

Miss Ashton knew it nearly broke Miss Meadow's nipfarthing heart to return the unused tuition. As for the roll of guineas now wrapped in a handkerchief secured in Melody's reticule, tears had almost come to Miss Meadow's beady little eyes at having to hand over the money set aside for a student's incidental expenses.

"And yet, I do not feel I need worry about you casting shadows on the school's fine reputation. As I wrote to your dear mama, you have been one of our least troublesome, ah, best students. True, your musical abilities will never grace a drawing room, but that cannot be held against the school, now can it?" She tittered.

Melody tilted her head, her thick chestnut curls braided neatly into a coil at the back of her proudly held neck. She remembered agonizing, humiliating hours of practice, and folded her hands in her lap.

"No, as I told your mother, now that you have matured past a tendency to show inordinate temper, you are not one of the flighty girls with all their fits and starts who are no more suited to make an early debut in the ton than the cook's pot girl. I would be embarrassed to have some of them pitchforked into the haute monde. Poor reflection on the academy, don't you know." Miss Meadow plopped another almond tart into her pouched cheeks. "When your mother wrote that she wanted to introduce you at some small local gatherings and a house party or two before the Season officially started, I was not terribly concerned. After all, you will not be alone and untutored if you find yourself

2

at a loss in the wider range of polite society. Your mother will be there to guide you, and you must consider yourself fortunate indeed. Your mama turned out to be a fine lady. After a regrettable beginning, of course."

Ah, so there was to be a final examination after all. Miss Ashton bit down on her pride and temper, while Miss Meadow bit down on a macaroon. Melody nodded, her outward composure not touched by the gratuitous innuendo. Not after ten years.

She returned Miss Meadow's squinty black stare with a cool green gaze. "As you say, only the most narrow-minded of gossips would reflect on an age-old scandal. And Mother has certainly proven her gentility a hundredfold, not merely by being a cherished member of society, but with her truly noble charitable acts: running an entire orphanage by herself since Aunt Judith passed on, to say nothing of making a life for herself and her daughter with the passing of my father, and staying loyal to his memory. . . . I shall try very hard to live up to her good name."

Yes, Miss Ashton was mature beyond her seventeen years. If she could not be rattled by mention of the family's dirty linen, she would have no problems with those haughty Almack's patronesses and those other high-in-the-instep keepers of the ton whose approval was so necessary for a girl's success on the Marriage Mart. "Your own loyalty does you proud, my dear. Just maintain your values and the lessons we have drummed—ah, imparted to you, and do not let yourself be infected with all those romantic notions harum-scarum young girls are so prone to. Novels—" she shuddered at the word "—put more foolish ideas in more empty heads than a hundred teachers can displace in a lifetime. I am sure you will not succumb to such dire temptations."

Miss Ashton crossed her fingers and assured the

3

old besom that she wouldn't think of such a thing, aside from the four purple-bound volumes smuggled into her luggage by her classmates.

To guarantee that a promising young mind was not corrupted, at least until in her parent's care, Miss Meadow then handed a small book to Melody as a parting gift. No larger than her hand, it was a hefty little tome, with pearl-inlaid wooden covers, embossed gold corners, and sticky fingerprints.

"I am sure you will find it comforting and informative on your journey home. Please accept it with our very best wishes for your success."

Miss Ashton stood, her medium height at least six stately inches above the dumpy headmistress, and gave her best curtsy. Then she stuffed Mingleforth's *Rules of Polite Decorum* into her reticule, although the weight made the strings dig into her arm, and left before she was betrayed by a very girlish giggle indeed.

The bags were loaded; the hired chaise was off. Miss Melody Ashton tossed back the hood of her new velvet cape, green to match her eyes, and shook her head, loosening tiny reddish-brown curls to frame her cheeks.

"And good riddance," she shouted joyfully at her last glimpse of the ugly brick building. Then she quickly reached over to clasp her companion's hand.

"I'm so sorry, Miss Chase. That was thoughtless of me, for you are not free of the place as I am."

Her fellow traveler, one of the younger instructors at the academy, begged her to pay no mind. "I cannot blame you for high spirits, my dear. I am only pleased I was selected to accompany you to your home. Even three days . . ." She bit her lip, having said too much.

Melody squeezed the limp hand she held before sitting back on her own side of the carriage. "I know, I shall ask Mama if you cannot accompany

4

us when we go up to London. She won't want to visit the Tower or Westminster or all the lending. libraries I am anxious to see, and I cannot go by myself, of course. It will be perfect."

"Yes, dear," Miss Chase answered without conviction, five years at Miss Meadow's having left her with little hope and fewer dreams. The expectation of days in a jouncing carriage, indifferent food, and unaired sheets at various inns, and then a return journey alone on the mail coach, was a positive treat compared to a junior mistress's life at the school. She was happy enough to sink into an exhausted slumber.

Left to her own devices, Melody untied her reticule's strings and, with a smile that showed one quicksilver dimple, drew forth Miss Meadow's gift and read the inscription inside the front cover: *The child who is shown the path, and knows the path, will follow the path.* She chuckled softly, thinking of primrose paths and paths to hell. Trust Miss Meadow to adopt addlepated profundity when *With our best wishes* would have done. Melody closed the book and fumbled with the window latch.

"Oh no, my dear, you mustn't," Miss Chase murmured.

"But I was just going to—"

"The dust from the road and the cold, you know." Miss Chase shivered in her threadbare pelisse.

Melody hurriedly fastened the window and tucked the lap robe around her companion, who promptly closed her eyes again. Melody ruefully stuffed Mingleforth's *Rules of Polite Decorum* back into her overloaded purse. Perhaps it would come in handy someday for propping up a chair leg, or providing kindling, or lining a canary's cage. Not that Miss Ashton owned a canary, but she had always hoped to. She had always hoped for pretty gowns, balls, and jewels, putting her hair up, sipping champagne, and meeting the Prince. She

5

pulled her cape closer around her and settled into her own comfortable corner, her green eyes drifting shut, a smile on her pretty face.

For Melody Morley Ashton, levelheaded, dignified, and mature, had more than a few romantic notions. A love match, that's where her dreams always led. She knew she was supposed to marry well; what girl at Miss Meadow's didn't know the point of her existence? Each proper female's mission was to add consequence to her family, to join her name to someone with a higher title or deeper pockets, preferably both. That fact of life was taught to even the youngest pupil, along with drawing room accomplishments, and everything and anything to attract this most eligible of *partis*.

Let him be wealthy and well connected, Melody prayed, but mostly let me love him. Let me know a grand passion, like Mama.

Of course, Melody did not wish to marry a ne'er-do-well, sporting-mad gambler as her mother had. She barely remembered her handsome father, dead on a muddy field due to too high a fence and too deep a bottle, leaving her and her mother impoverished. But at least her mother had had her grand passion, a runaway match, a love that survived parental disapproval and society's strictures, if not an unbroken gelding. Lord Ashton's untimely death—and unpaid bills—had left his wife and young child homeless and hopeless.

Please, let him not be a second son, Melody's prayers continued.

Lady Jessamyn Ashton's only course was to throw herself and Melody on the untender mercies of her much older sister, Judith Morley, a moralistic, man-hating spinster who had inherited the Oaks, the Morley ancestral home at Copley-Whitmore. Aunt Judith devoted her life to good deeds and her ward Felice, the daughter of Sir Bostwick Bartleby, the nabob. Felice devoted her

6

life to making Melody miserable. Felice was two years older, china doll pretty, and graceful. Melody was sallow faced then, scrawny, and awkward. She was a brown study, quiet child. Blond-haired Felice was not.

"Your papa gambled all his money away; *my* papa is in India, adding to his fortune. You'll have no dowry; I'll have diamonds and rubies and pearls. You'll marry a farmer; I'll marry a maharajah, if I choose."

Somehow Lady Ashton found enough money to send Melody to school, and somehow she found the means to reenter society, floating from country house party to Irish hunt meeting, from seashore excursion to London Season, during Melody's vacations at the Oaks or not. Even after Aunt Judith's death, Lady Jessamyn continued her social rounds and yet maintained Judith's good works. Melody dreamed of making her mother proud, this mother she hardly knew, who was everything a lady should be.

Now was Melody's chance to have it all, the Season, her mama's company, true love. Unfortunately, Felice was waiting with Mama at the Oaks.

So let him not prefer blondes.

Chapter Two

$\mathcal{D}$aydreams are peculiar, taking on lives of their own. Think of the inveterate gambler who is positive his horse will win the next time. He'll lay all his blunt on the nag, even borrow on his optimism. He'll decide to pay off his bills, treat himself to a fine dinner on the winnings, even hand his wife a few of the flimsies, maybe. The money is all spent before the horses leave the starting line. Just so, by the next morning Miss Ashton was the Season's Incomparable, the belle of every ball, in her mind's eye. London beaux were at her feet writing sonnets to her eyebrows, while one gentleman in particular . . .

As for Miss Chase, the downtrodden, colorless schoolteacher, she was delighted with an ample, hot meal at last night's inn, and the fact that there were no creatures sharing her bed.

So the next morning, who was most devastated by the change in plans? On being informed that she was to return to Bath with the hired chaise, Miss Chase was only mildly affected. She would miss another day or two of freedom, but she was richer by a good night's rest, a full breakfast, and two of Miss Ashton's precious guineas. Perhaps she was correct: hope for little, and you won't be disappointed.

For there, at the first change, along with Mama's note that Melody should proceed in the family carriage, was the death of all her fantasies. This killer of dreams, slayer of wishes, sat like a dark specter in the inn's parlor: Nanny. Melody's nanny, her mother's nanny, perhaps Queen Guinevere's nanny, she'd been at it so long. Nanny in her starched black gown, black bonnet, black mustache, with her ubiquitous knitting, was truly the hangman of hope.

"Cow's dry. Well's dry. You be wanted to home."

Doom.

The bags were unloaded; the hired chaise pulled away.

"Nanny?"

"Money's gone. Can't get blood from a turnip, I says."

"From a stone, Nanny. You cannot get blood from a stone. But what—"

Nanny shook her head and kept on knitting. "All that learning. A body can't eat stones, missy. Nor books nor fine ideas. Head as hard as rocks. Hard times."

"Do you mean we're . . . poor?"

"We were always poor. What's worse than poor?"

"But, but Mama and the orphans and—"

"Your mama's in a decline, children running wild. Servants gone. Constable's nosing round. We'll be digging acorns next, I told her. Tried eating toads, missy?" At Melody's gasp she guessed not. "Bein't all bad, howsomever. Some of us got our health. Not Ducky nor little Meggie, a course, who's never been a strong 'un, and some of the boys is sniffling. Your ma hardly gets out of bed these days. Then there's my rheumatics and—"

9

"But what happened? What about all the plans for house parties and a London Season?" Melody plucked at the folds of her new, expensive cape. "My new clothes?"

Nanny turned her nose up at the green velvet. "Here, you'll need this."

This was a wool scarf she uncoiled like a rope from her workbasket and wrapped around Melody's throat. It was that same scratchy, undyed wool Nanny always used, with the smell of sheep still in it. Melody could feel rashes on her chin already. "But—"

"Air dreams, your mama always had her head filled with air dreams. She'll tell you. You're needed to home, is all I'm supposed to say." And Nanny pursed her lips, gathered up her knitting, and stomped out the door.

Heaven help us, the bags were being loaded. The rickety, ramshackle, crumbly old family carriage stood waiting. In Melody's memory only chickens had used it, for roosting. The neighborhood of Copley-Whitmore was small enough to get everywhere on foot, and Aunt Judith had been a firm believer in healthful exercise—rain, sleet, or snow. An ancient driver was at the reins, muffled to the eyes in another undyed wool scarf.

"Isn't that old Toby from Tucker's farm? Why, he's more used to driving—" Yes, now that she looked closer, those were indeed plow horses between the traces, huge, placid beasts that had one gait, a ponderous, plodding walk. "Why, it will take forever to get home behind those animals."

The old man cackled. "Aye, but they'll go in the prettiest, straightest line you ever seen." Then he scratched his chin.

At least she was not going to hell in a handcart, Melody decided, wrinkling her nose. She was getting there slower, in a henhouse on wheels.

The horses plowed on. Urging Toby to greater speed was fruitless, for the old man was quite deaf when it suited him. Nanny knitted, like the Fates weaving Melody's future in itchy skeins. There was no budging Nanny from her decision to stay mumchance on everything Melody wanted to know either. Conjecture was pointless, so Melody tried to settle back on the odoriferous squabs, but loose horsehair stuffing kept pricking into her back, and the badly sprung carriage kept rocking her head and shoulder into the unpadded door. Life at Miss Meadow's was taking on a rosier cast.

At least they would not starve. Nanny had brought a huge hamper of food along, filled with fresh bread, cold chicken, thick chunks of cheese, apples, a jug of cider, and even Melody's favorite gingerbread.

"There's so much here, Nanny; surely your tales of woe must be exaggerated," Melody noted hopefully.

"Out of the mouths of babes . . ."

Melody stopped chewing. "You cannot mean the children are going hungry? I couldn't eat another morsel if I thought so."

Her chick withering away without proper nourishment? Nanny relented. "Nay, we brought our own rather than pay ransom prices for a bit of victuals from those highway robbers pretending to be honest innkeeps. Dirty hands they have, too; you never know if they be mucking stables or serving dinner." Nanny bit into an apple. "At least I know whose orchard these were stole from."

Melody choked.

Needless to say, the travelers were treated less than royally at the inn where they spent the night. The women would not order dinner, and the horses did not require changing or a postboy's attentions, just feed and a rest. And not only did Nanny haggle with the owner over the price of a room, but she

11

accused the poor man of watering the wine, brewing the tea leaves thrice over, making improper advances to his serving girls, and burying the bones of unwary wayfarers out back. And she did all this, standing as rigid as a masthead on a man-of-war, in the only public room the inn offered, in full view and hearing of two local dairymen, a merchant of some sort in a checkered waistcoat, and a party of four rowdy young bucks on their way to a mill.

Melody pulled her cape's hood down over her eyes and prayed for a bolt of lightning. Instead she got snickers and guffaws and the tiniest of attic rooms with the narrowest of thin mattresses, which she was to share with Nanny. There was not even a chair, nor room to sleep on the floor. There was no hot water to wash in, which really was all of a piece, for Nanny would not let her change into her nightclothes, or sleep beneath the covers. Who knew what pox-ridden fiend slept there last?

Not Miss Ashton, that was for sure, cold and crammed between Nanny's angular bulk and the even more rigid wall, listening to the raucous young men in the taproom and Nanny's snores.

The following day dawned cold, cloudy, and very, very early. Workhorses rise with the sun. So, it seems, do disgruntled innkeepers who see no reason to cater to jug-bitten nobs who take to smashing chairs, toplofty old harridans with tongues like vipers, or schoolgirls who really should have had more beauty sleep.

Miss Ashton needed a hot bath, her morning chocolate, and someone to help braid her thick hair. What she got was advice: "Don't you go putting on airs like some I could mention."

So cold wash water it was. Then Nanny took the brush and scraped it through Melody's hair like a garden hoe through creepers. Melody hurriedly tied her hair back in a ribbon while she still had any,

12

and straightened her dress as much as possible. Nanny retied her muffler, despite Melody's protests, saying, "Fresh air is what you need to get rid of that peaked look."

"Nanny, I'm a grown woman now. You can't keep treating me like an unruly child!"

"Humph. Birds don't fall far from the tree."

"That's apples, Nanny."

"If you want apples to break your fast, that's fine with me, Miss Book-Learning. I'd just as soon not give that thief another groat for lumpy porridge."

Old Bess and Thimble were right fresh, Toby informed them. "They'll be setting a lively pace this morning, see if they don't."

"Maybe they could be encouraged into a trot now and then, do you think? Nothing that might tire them out, of course."

Toby cupped his hand to his ear. "What's that, miss?"

Melody gave up and took a deep breath of the last unfouled air she would get for a while. She smiled that it should be *unfowled*, and climbed into her seat across from Nanny. The bread was not quite as fresh this morning, and the cider was a touch vinegary, but at least her hunger was satisfied. Melody's need for sleep came next. She made herself as comfortable as possible, using her hood as a pillow, and drowsed off to the steady clops of the horses, the sway of the carriage, and the click of Nanny's needles.

She awoke to angry shouts and curses, and Nanny's hands clapped painfully over her ears.

The horses were keeping their steady pace, it seemed, straight and true down the center of the road, to the disgust of other travelers.

"Halloo, the carriage! Move off to the side, blast you, and let someone pass. By all that's holy, you don't own the whole bloody highway!"

Toby was still deaf this morning. Nanny put her

13

head out of the window and shouted back, "You ought to have your mouth washed out with soap, young jackanapes. This is the King's highway, and there be ladies present."

That carriage passed them, two of its wheels dangerously close to the ditch, and then a few others went by, sporting vehicles with raffish young gentlemen at the ribbons, from what Melody could see from her position, scrunched down in her seat as small as possible. It wouldn't matter if there was no money for a London Season; her chances there would be immediately ruined if any of these town-bronzed gentlemen recognized her.

The next voices on the road behind were familiar. The four revelers from last night's inn were on the road earlier than usual, before they'd had a chance to sleep off the evening's effects. They had just completed their private wagers on the coming mill, so quite naturally, by these bloods' standards, the only thing left to enliven the drive to West Fenton was a contest between their two racing curricles. It made no matter that the roadway was becoming crowded with other vehicles headed for the same destination, or oncoming traffic, or farmers herding sheep by the verge, or the great lumbering relic of a coach. It certainly never occurred to any of the young gents that their judgment might be the slightest diminished.

"It's the old hag from the inn," called out the driver of the leading carriage to his passenger's, "Tallyho!" The other curricle drew neck and neck, and Miss Ashton could hear bets being laid, wild sums being wagered on which vehicle could pass the old coach first. They both pulled wide, to either side of Melody's carriage.

Melody tried to shout to Toby to pull over, but Nanny was waving her knitting out the window and ranting about how someone should take sticks to such care-for-naughts.

"Catch the prize!" one driver roared, while his whooping passenger leaned dizzyingly off the edge of his seat.

"Twenty guineas more if you can snabble it!" came from the other side.

Melody shut her eyes. Nanny squawked. There was an ominous crunch as one of the curricle's wheels scraped by, and then the old coach came to such a quick halt that Melody was thrown forward right off her seat, onto the floor that was still littered with chicken droppings.

Now Old Bess and Thimble knew their job. If there was a rabbit in the field, it was the rabbit's job to scamper off. If the plow was stuck on a rock, it was Toby's job to free it. They weren't bothered by silly fools darting by, or loud laughter, or even Nanny's squalls of divine retribution. But snakes, long, flappy white snakes trailing across their backs—that was not their job. They whoaed all right, with another crunch of the wooden axle.

Nanny stood clutching her empty workbag, shaking her head in disbelief, while Toby and Melody walked around the carriage.

"Wheel's took a whack, I swear, no telling if it'll last. Axle's got a crack, prob'ly. Worse, horses is spooked. These two ain't going to budge right aways. I know them. After a bit, maybe we could go real slow, see if she holds."

Slower than they'd been going? "Perhaps you should walk ahead and send a blacksmith back," Melody suggested.

"What's that, miss? You and Nanny want to step along to the village coming up? That's a fine idea, ma'am. Could be hours else, and you'd likely have to walk it anyway, if t'wheel comes off. There's a posting house on the square, so there's bound to be a smith. I'll just give Old Bess and Thimble here a chance at some of that new spring grass, then be along after you."

15

In little under an hour, Toby caught up, leading the pair, the coach creaking behind. Just when the road was really congested with all manner of sporting gentlemen heading for West Fenton and the mill, Melody's little procession wended its slow way onward, following the path of—and meticulously rewinding—a thread of hoof-marked, mud-caked, crinkled wool.

Chapter Three

This time Melody was determined to get to the innkeeper first. It was the innkeeper's wife, though, who spied the bedraggled group entering her establishment and sent her husband away to tend to the crowded taproom. In Mamie Barstow's experience, sporting nobs always attracted a certain type of women, and she wasn't having any of it, not at her inn. She stood guarding the front door, arms folded across her chest.

"Good day, ma'am," Melody began. "Your inn looks to be a pleasant place, and my companion and I are sorely in need of rest and refreshment. I hope that you can accommodate us."

On closer examination, Mrs. Barstow recognized quality. The young woman with such cultured accents was standing proud as a queen, just as if she didn't look like she'd been dragged through a hedge backward, and the companion was brandishing a knitting needle aloft like a saber charge. The old wreck of a carriage would have been in fashion thirty years ago, but the driver would have been old even then. Whatever this odd lot was, they weren't loose women; light-skirts fared better. Still, they did not belong at her inn, not today.

"I'm sorry, miss, but you can see there's a big to-do this afternoon. The place is overbooked as it is, and some of the gentlemen are like to get above themselves, if you know what I mean."

Nanny snorted. "Hanging's too good for the likes of them. Attacking honest women in broad daylight. Ravaging the countryside. Spare the rod, and use a butcher's knife, I say."

Mrs. Barstow's mouth hung open, and the door was about to shut. Melody quickly withdrew the roll of coins from her reticule. As she unwrapped her bona fides she raised her chin. "I believe some of your guests are already castaway, but we have no choice. There has been a mishap with the carriage, and we are left here until it can be repaired."

"Oh dear, and no work likely to get done soon, with every man jack in the town out to watch the fight. Still, every bed is spoken for, and some doubled as it is."

"Heathens," Nanny muttered.

"Please, ma'am, we just require a quiet place away from the public view." Melody jingled a few coins together.

"I suppose I could let you have our own rooms for a bit. Mr. Barstow can bunk with the stable lads, and I'll share with the maids, for all the sleep we'll be getting this night. It won't be what you're used to, I swear, but you'll be safer here than out on the road."

Melody was used to sharing a room with four other girls; last night she'd shared a bed with Nanny. "I'm sure that will be fine."

"And mind, I haven't got a spare girl to be fetching and carrying for you, and I'll be too busy cooking and serving, what with all these gentlemen to feed."

18

Nanny puckered up her mouth as if she had swallowed a lemon. "No way I'd let some tavern wench take care of my chick." Melody quickly added another coin to the handful she rattled.

"There's some pigeon pie left from luncheon, nothing fancy. And there's always stew and a kettle on for tea. I suppose it will do, if you just stay out of the public rooms."

Nanny swore to lock the windows, put chairs across the doors, lay her body across the sill if need be, to keep her lady in and all the depraved sons of Satan out. Shaking her head, Mrs. Barstow led them down the hall past the taproom. Nanny pulled Melody's hood so far down over her eyes she couldn't see, and so as a result nearly stumbled right into a broad gentleman in a spotted Belcher tie. He put up a quizzing glass and asked, "What have we here?" He got an enlarged eyeful of Nanny's Gorgon glare and a sharp knitting needle in his breadbasket.

Mrs. Barstow hustled them through the dining room, thankfully empty now, and beyond into the kitchen where two young girls in neat aprons were peeling vegetables. Past the pantry was a half landing and there, to everyone's relief, was the door leading to a tiny sitting room with a sofa and chair, and an even smaller bedroom. Mrs. Barstow twitched a faded quilt into place on the bed, and Nanny pulled all the curtains closed. Soon there was food and blessedly hot water and Nanny's snores almost drowning out the commotion in the taproom and the rattle of pots and pans in the kitchen.

Melody spent some time trying to sponge off her cape and unsnarl her hair before lying down to nap. Her mind was too unsettled, though, and the noises were getting louder and more distracting. She wished she had her luggage from the carriage so she could change her gown, or at least retrieve one

19

of those Minerva Press novels from her trunk. Perhaps if she could just locate Toby in the yard, she could find out how long repairs would take or if he could fetch in the bags. Mrs. Barstow was still in the kitchen, however, up to her arms in pastry dough. She waved the rolling pin in the air and gave Melody such a scowl that the younger woman scurried back to her rooms. Maybe she could spot Toby from the window and get his attention.

When she opened the curtains in the sitting room, Melody had to take her shoes off and stand on the sofa to see out, the window being so high. Because the little apartment was up a landing, she found herself looking down on the inn's rear courtyard, with stable blocks forming the other three sides to the square, and, good grief, the entire clearing was filled with shouting, shoving men! She leaped off the sofa. What if anyone looked up and saw her?

Don't be a goose, she told herself, they are all more interested in what's going on than in looking around at the scenery. Furthermore, enough of them must have seen her walking at the head of her little caravan en route to the inn for her to be a laughingstock as it was. So just what *was* going on? She hopped back up.

One man was standing in an open area at the center of the courtyard, ringed by rough wooden benches all filled with workingmen in coarse smocks sitting next to gentlemen in lace-edged linens. Behind them stood more so-called sportsmen, and in the last rows the carriages were arranged, with the Corinthians in their top hats and many-caped driving coats looking down on the proceedings from their lofty perches. Melody could not pinpoint the two racing curricles from the morning anywhere; perhaps they had landed in a ditch. She did see serving girls carrying trays of mugs, and men collecting sheaves of paper, and one person in a frieze coat making marks on a big board.

And still the man in the clearing stood curiously alone.

He was an enormous man, she could see even from this distance, with a red face and black mustachio. The crowd roared when he took off his leather jerkin and shook one huge fist at them. The muscles in his arms and chest poured over each other in layers, dark, hairy, sweat-dampened layers. What an education Miss Melody was getting!

"Al-bert," the crowd chanted, "Al-bert." Albert, obviously the local favorite, circled his little clearing, waving. Then he stood, his hands on his wide hips, waiting. And waiting some more. The noises from the benches grew louder, with whistles and foot-stampings joining the shouts. Some of the men started tossing their mugs at one another. Scuffles broke out, and the serving girls ran back toward the kitchen, screeching. The man Melody identified as the innkeeper, the one wearing an apron and tearing his hair out, tried to separate the brawlers and get others back in their seats.

Then, when it looked like the inn yard would turn into a free-for-all, a stern voice that was obviously used to command called "Halt!" There was a moment of silence, and Melody could see a high-crowned beaver hat come gliding into the clearing next to Albert. It was easy to tell where the hat had come from: all heads were turned toward the back where a gentleman was standing in an elegant high-perch phaeton. He was handing his coat to his companion, untying his neckcloth as he stepped down from the carriage as casually as if he were going for a stroll in the park. He was fair-haired and tanned and, although the distance was too great, Melody just knew he was bound to be handsome, with such assurance.

The crowd took up a new chant now: "Cor-ey, Cor-ey, Cor-ey," and she lost sight of him in the mobs. When he reappeared, he was stripped to his boots

21

and buckskins, and Melody was right. He was beautiful. Where Albert was all hulking thew and flab, Corey was like a Greek god in a garden, rock hard, sculpted, sun kissed.

He was also inches shorter than Albert and half his girth. He was going to get killed.

As the two men squared off with their fists raised, and the chanting turned to a thunderous uproar, Melody scrambled down from her perch. She went into the bedroom where Nanny still slept, shut the door, got into bed, and pulled the quilt over her head.

Chapter Four

"*H*ere you go, my lord, nice and easy now. You can rest here, private like."

"Mmunh . . . wife . . ."

"Never you mind the missus. She's just in a pother, what with all the argle-bargle. Feared for her rug, likely, is why she kicked up a dust about me bringin' you in here. You, uh, ain't about to cast up accounts, are you?"

"Hunh . . ."

"Good, good. Don't worry over my Mamie. Nothin's too good for you, and I'll tell her so. Saved my bacon, you did, my lord. They would have torn the place to splinters when the Irishman didn't show. You just lie back now whilst I go send a boy off for the doctor. Be here before the cat can lick its ear. I'll fetch some towels and hot water, meanwhile. We'll have you right as a trivet, my lord, don't you fret."

"Mumunh?"

"Brandy? Of course, my lord. Nothing but the best for you."

Mr. Barstow left, and Melody checked to make

sure Nanny was still sleeping. Then she tiptoed to the bedroom door and ever so quietly opened it a crack to peep out. Mr. Corey—Lord Corey, it seemed, which she should have guessed—was sprawled out on the sofa, what was left of him anyway. He had survived, but barely, from the looks of it. His blond hair was plastered to his forehead in damp curls, blood was dribbling down one brow into an eye already swelling shut, and he held a length of cloth, likely his neckpiece, over his nose. That was why she could not hear his words to the innkeeper, Melody realized, her eyes traveling lower. Lord Corey's shirt was draped over his broad shoulders, trailing in streams of blood, some dried, some not, which ran between huge red welts on his chest and down his sides. His buckskin breeches were blood spattered and torn, one knee shredded.

Melody shuddered and closed the door. Then he moaned, and she peeked out again.

Lord Corey took the cloth away from his nose—it was soaked through anyway—and muttered. "Hell and damnation," Melody could hear quite distinctly. "No reason to get blood all over the woman's couch." He levered himself up and took one cautious step toward the wooden chair before his foot skidded on something. Lord Corey fell, hitting his head soundly on the pine end table.

"Blast!" he swore, rubbing the back of his head and then grabbing for the sodden linen when his nose started gushing again. Still on the floor, Corey reached behind him for what had tripped him: Melody's slipper. "What the bloody hell—"

Melody just had to go to him. He obviously needed help, but not as much as he would need if Nanny woke up and found a half-naked man spouting blasphemy in the sitting room. Another round with Albert would be a waltz by comparison.

She only stopped to snatch up her reticule with the extra handkerchiefs and the vinaigrette Miss

Meadow insisted the girls carry, before softly pulling the door shut behind her. "Ssh," Melody whispered.

"Who the—?" Only one blue eye opened, but what a sight it beheld! Lord Corey, better known as Lord Cordell Inscoe, Viscount Coe, looked up to see a shapely young woman in a high-waisted sprigged muslin gown, with dark hair that curled in red and gold flickers around soft, peach-tinged cheeks, and eyes so green they should belong to a mermaid or a forest dryad or . . . He held up the slipper in his hand and noted her stockinged feet. "Cinderella. Ah, and I am not dressed for the ball." To use boxing cant, Lord Coe had been tipped another settler.

He tried to rise, to gather his shirt closed, to dab at the warm blood on his upper lip. With Melody's help, he made it to the chair, but he had to sit still a moment, gasping and clutching his ribs, and her hand. Melody stared around desperately. She couldn't just leave an injured man, could she? Even Nanny must see that.

Mr. Barstow saw it when he brought a loaded tray into the room. "Lawkes, where'd she come from?"

"Heaven, my good man, heaven. Where else would an angel come from?"

"Well, there'll be hell to pay, an' my wife catches you at it."

Melody resented that. "I'll have you know, sir, that Mrs. Barstow herself was kind enough to permit me and my companion the use of these rooms." She nodded her head toward the adjoining room, as if another closed door would prove her respectability when a bare-chested man held her hand in his.

Barstow scratched his head. "I don't know. She said somethin', but with all the commotion in the kitchen . . ."

Corey took over. "Come now, man. I'm in no shape for anything your wife would disapprove. I only ravish maidens on Fridays. Wednesdays are my days for being beaten to a pulp. And you can see that Miss—ah, the young lady is properly reared and properly chaperoned." He, too, nodded to the other door, having no idea whatsoever who or what was behind it. "So why don't you pour me a glass of that fine brandy I see there, and then go on back to tend to all of the pub business before your clientele decides to reenact that last round in your common room?"

"But you need doctorin'. Our local sawbones might take a while to get here, it seems. Martin Reilly's wife, you know. Jake the ostler's a dab hand with injuries, howsomever. He'll be glad to strap them ribs up for you."

Corey tossed back the glass and held it out for more. "Thank you, friend, but I'll wait for the doctor."

"I got some salve for them cuts, my lord. I'll just—"

"From Jake the stableman?"

Melody was already dipping one of the towels into the can of hot water and gingerly dabbing at his forehead. "My angel's ministrations will be a lot more tender than yours, Barstow. Go feed the masses, fill the coffers." Glass broke somewhere down the hall. "Save the good bottles."

Barstow backed out of the room quickly, and Melody continued with the towels and water and salve. "I am, you know," she said quietly, pushing his head back and laying a dampened cloth across the bridge of his nose, which was still bleeding slightly.

"You are what, *mon ange*?"

"Properly reared and properly chaperoned."

"I never doubted it for a moment. Of course, I have never known a chaperone to be so accommodatingly invisible, or a debutante to go barefoot at her come-out ball—Ouch!"

"I'm sorry, my lord. Did I hurt you? I think this should be stitched. Perhaps Jake . . . ?"

"You've made your point, Miss—Ah, our host seems to have failed to make the formal introduction. No, don't say anything; it's all to the good. You may find the need someday to deny the association. This way I can swear I never met any Miss So and So, only a kind-hearted seraph."

"Silly, I know you are Lord Corey."

Few people had ever called the viscount silly. Fewer had fussed over him with such sweet, selfless concern. "My friends call me Corey."

"You seemed to have a great many out there shouting for you."

"I just had better odds. The underdog, you know."

She was concentrating on getting a sticking plaster to his forehead, her tongue between her teeth. He never felt the pain. She did, and her eyes grew moist.

"What's this, Angel, tears? Don't worry, head wounds just bleed a lot."

"That's not it. All those people were *cheering* while you were getting hurt."

He touched her cheek with a bruised knuckle. "An angel, indeed."

"No, I'm not," she said angrily, trying to get the dried blood off his chin, which she could see was very strong and square. "It's just that you were so . . . so . . . handsome is not the right word. A lot of men are handsome. You were perfect, like some kind of hero. Now look at you!"

Melody felt herself blushing. However could she have said that to him, a total stranger?

Corey had forgotten such innocence still existed. His heart thumped—or was that just a twinge from a cracked rib? He smiled as best he could with a swollen lip. "Well, I'll admit I am not a pretty sight right now, sweetheart, but I doubt any of the mess is permanent. The ribs are the worst of it, and

27

they'll heal. I still have all my teeth, and if that doctor does a halfway decent job of stitching, there won't be much of a scar on my brow. It wouldn't be the first anyway, after the cavalry." He moved the cloth and carefully touched his nose. "Luckiest of all, my nose isn't even broken."

"As if that makes it right!"

His nose had finally stopped bleeding; his eye needed a slab of liver or something. Her inspection continued down—No, mopping at a man's chest was still beyond her daring. She'd never even seen one before today! For goodness' sake, she'd never been alone in a room with a man before today. Melody dragged her eyes back to Corey's, and caught an amused, knowing smile. She took his hand and poured brandy over the torn knuckles.

"The deuce!"

"Sorry, my lord, but spirits are the best thing to keep a wound from infection."

"And a waste of fine liquor. I can see by that martial look in your eye that you disagree and are about to do your worst to my other poor hand. Do you think I might have another glass while there is a drop left?"

Her hand shook slightly when she poured, he noticed, along with noticing the graceful tilt of her neck, the soft curve of her gown's bodice. His own hand shook slightly. "Perhaps you should have a sip also. This cannot be pleasant for you."

"Thank you, my lord, but I am not used to spirits."

"I'll warrant you aren't used to nursing fallen gladiators, either. You have my gratitude, of course, and also my respect. Every other young lady I know would have fainted long ago, and some gentlemen, too."

"Paltry fellows," she said, to cover her embarrassment at his praise. She certainly could not admit to the queasy feeling in her stomach. "And

Monday is my day to be a vaporish female, not Wednesday."

His hands were dried and loosely wrapped in torn strips of linen. That left his chest to be tended, his taut-skinned, well-muscled chest. Melody took a deep breath.

Corey chuckled. "Are you sure you wouldn't like a drink? Dutch courage, don't you know."

He was altogether too knowing.

"I'm, ah, afraid of hurting you further. Shouldn't you do this?"

He held up his bandaged hands and just smiled. The dratted man was enjoying her discomfort.

"Ow!"

"Sorry."

"Like hell you are."

Maybe if she distracted him, and herself, she could consider this just another job, like polishing silver or rinsing a fragile teapot. Of course no teapot of her experience had soft golden hairs or firm—

"Why did you do it? I mean the, ah, fight. It could not have been for the money, I know." At his raised eyebrow, the good one, she admitted to spying out the window and seeing his expensive equipage. Then there were his clothes, and the deference of Mr. Barstow.

"Have you never heard of punting on tick, little one? No, I can see from your face you haven't. No matter, I am well enough to pass that I need not hire myself out for a sparring partner. And no, I am not so noble a character to sacrifice myself to save Mr. Barstow's inn from an ugly melee. It was the challenge of the thing. The locals were boasting that Irish Red had gone fainthearted, and no one could best Albert. I took the dare."

"You did this for a *dare*?" She rubbed more vigorously; the viscount clenched his teeth. "Of all the irresponsible, reckless, cork-brained notions. Isn't that just like a man."

"How much could you know about men, from your great age? What are you anyway, eighteen, nineteen?"

Melody chose not to answer that. "I know that my father was just such a one, gambling on duck races, taking every madcap challenge, thinking no farther than the excitement of the moment! Why, you could have been killed!"

"So little faith, my angel. But I did weigh my chances, you know. After all, there is science involved. Albert is the product of barroom brawls, while I have studied with Gentleman Jackson. Albert had strength, I knew, but I had speed. He may have the brawn, but I have the brains."

"And the conceit! I should have thought the brains of a flea would tell you not to get in the ring with a man twice your size. Just look at you!"

"Ah, but you haven't seen Albert."

"You mean you won?"

Her look of incredulity struck a blow to his pride, possibly the only part of the viscount not yet injured. Then she smiled, with dimples and sparkling eyes, and it was almost worth it, even the aching ribs. Gads, what a little beauty! Young and unsophisticated, she was unaware of her effect on a man, if Corey knew women at all—and he knew women as well as he knew the art of boxing. She wasn't in his line, of course. Unless a man was on the Marriage Mart, schoolroom misses, debutantes, and such were like playing with fire. Corey much preferred to dally with women who already smoldered. But if, say, a man was thirty-five or so—the viscount was only twenty-eight—and he was looking to get legshackled, a fellow could do a lot worse.

As it was, sea-green eyes, adorable dimples, and petal-soft skin were exactly why chaperones were created. Which reminded him that his angel's was not doing a very good job of it. "I'll, ah, take over from here," he said, chivalrously relieving her of

30

the towel, and himself of dangerous thoughts as she wiped at the red streaks lower down his chest.

"I don't mean to sound ungrateful or anything, but isn't your companion being a trifle lax?"

"Nanny's nerves were overset so she took a sleeping draught, thank goodness. I mean, she needs her rest. There was a mishap with the carriage, and we had to walk a considerable distance this morning."

"Never tell me you are the Incognita in the ancient coach the fellows were snickering about before? They were calling you the Damsel, the Dragon, and Dobbin. That was you?" He laughed out loud, then clutched his side. "Dash it, I shouldn't have laughed."

Melody's chin was raised. Her tone was grim, "No, sir, you shouldn't have."

"Now you are angry. I'm truly sorry, Angel, really I am. Tell me what I can do to make things right."

How could she not forgive a silver-tongued devil with a ready smile and a black eye? She tugged his shirt around him better. "So you won't take a chill. And thank you, but unless you can play Cinderella's fairy godmother, wave your wand, and get my carriage fixed in a hurry, I don't think there is much you can do for me."

He laughed again, but much more cautiously. "I'm afraid I'll stay in your black books then, my dear, for your carriage won't be repaired anytime soon. Albert is the blacksmith!"

Chapter Five

The doctor came. Melody vanished into the bedroom.

It was a good thing Nanny had a heavy hand with the laudanum. And a good thing the doctor had some experience with ex-soldiers and dockworkers, or other patients with colorful vocabularies. And it was an especially good thing that Melody, behind the bedroom door, did not understand half of what she heard. No maiden's education need be *that* complete.

The doctor left, and Barstow and one of his stable lads helped Lord Corey down the hall, out of Melody Ashton's life. She wished she'd said good-bye.

Back in the sitting room she found no trace of the whole episode, no gory water or stained towels, no decanter, no battered but unbroken nobleman. There was just the faintest scent of brandy and male body—and Mrs. Barstow, clucking like a chicken that's spotted a fox near the henhouse.

"I just brought some fresh hot water, miss, in case you want to freshen up before tea."

Both sounded heavenly, but Melody thought of

her dwindling supply of coins. "Thank you, ma'am, but I didn't order tea, and we agreed not to be a further burden to you. Your giving up your rooms is far more than money alone can repay."

"Nicely spoken, miss. I told that clunch Barstow you were quality. But never you mind. It's all been taken care of by a gentleman whose name I don't recall so don't ask me."

Melody smiled. "You mean the one who wasn't here before?"

"Right. The one I'm to swear on my life you never spent the afternoon with."

"In that case, thank you, tea would be delightful. And please thank the gentleman for me."

"What gentleman might that be?"

"He'll be all right, won't he?"

"No one's ever cocked his toes up in *my* inn, miss. 'Specially not any handsome rogue what's too slippery for the devil to catch."

Nanny woke to the smell of fresh-brewed tea, lemon wafers, and buttered toast fingers with jam.

"You been behaving yourself, missy?"

"I haven't been out of these two rooms, Nanny."

Mrs. Barstow spilled the cream and had to go fetch more.

One night she was dreaming of balls and beaux; the next, fretting over her family's uncertain future. This evening, Melody dreaded blowing out the candle, for fear she would have nightmares of blows landing, bones breaking, blood and bruises and horrid yellow-purple, swollen skin. She didn't. She fell asleep with a smile, and a mind picture of a crooked grin and laughing blue eyes. She hugged the image to herself and never stirred till morning.

Mrs. Barstow brought morning chocolate, hot rolls, and the news that the coach would be out front in an hour. Albert's nephew and two of the grooms had been working on it since sunup, long before the bucks were up requiring their services. Melody was pleased to accept Mrs. Barstow's offer to help her get ready, saving her scalp from Nanny's ruthless touch. In forty minutes she was washed, dressed in a fresh gown, her hair pulled back in a neatly braided coil, her cape newly sponged and pressed.

When Melody reached for the reticule hanging off her wrist, Mrs. Barstow was having none of it. "Reckoning's been paid," she whispered for Melody's ears only. "Nothing improper in that, I made sure. Just his nibs's way of saying thank you."

Melody waited until Nanny went back to the bedroom to check that they hadn't left anything behind, for the third time. "You've seen him, then? He's better?"

"Cranky as a crab and uglier nor a pickled pig. He's down the hall in one of the private parlors where we moved a cot in to save him the stairs. It can't be what I'm liking, but he asks if you could stop in for a minute on your way out."

"It would only be proper to thank him for his generosity," Melody rationalized. Then Nanny clomped to her side in heavy boots. "But I don't think I can."

"That's been taken care of, too, miss." Mrs. Barstow turned to Nanny. "You know, I've been thinking of that mishap of yourn yesterday. A terrible thing, these ruffians on the road. Anywise, my sister used to be a prodigious needlewoman afore she moved away. Now her threads and such are in the attic, likely going to moths, for I never have time for it, more's the pity. I'd be pleased if you'd come choose what you could make use of, to make up for the delay and all."

Mrs. Barstow started Nanny up the stairs, nodding back at Melody toward the first door on the right. "Ten minutes, miss," she murmured. "And it's against my better judgment. But he's looking as harmless as a babe, so I suppose that's fair."

Melody hesitated outside the door. She really should not do this. Her reputation, her future—his practiced charm. She tapped lightly.

He was sitting, stiffly it seemed to her, in a high-backed chair. He was wearing a bright paisley dressing gown with a black velvet collar and gray pantaloons. The colors of the robe, which was open enough for her to see wide swatches of bandages across his chest, were as nothing compared to the colors of his face.

"Oh my," she said, going closer. "You shouldn't be up."

"And you shouldn't be here."

My word, Corey thought, standing cautiously. He must have taken a harder hit to the brainbox than he thought. Yesterday, with her hair down and her toes bare, his angel was a most appealing little baggage, and he had wanted—needed—just one more look at her dewy innocence to remind him that the world wasn't all hardened cynics. Today she was nothing more than a pretty schoolroom chit, all prunes and prisms, not a hair out of place, bundled sensibly against the cold. By all that was holy, even he had more conscience than to make mice feet of her good name, whatever it was. "You had better leave."

Of course she shouldn't be here. Any peagoose knew that. But hadn't he asked for her and arranged the whole elaborate scheme so she could come? Obviously, he had changed his mind. So had Miss Ashton. Instead of wishing him Godspeed and hoping that by some miracle this nonesuch would ask for her direction, she would stand tall—she had her shoes on today—and make polite inquiries as to his health, then return his largesse. A lady never let a strange man pay her way.

35

She pulled at the strings of her reticule—the weight of the thing was making it devilish hard to undo—and raised her proud chin.

"What the deuce is that thing around your neck?"

Drat Nanny anyway! She couldn't admit the muffler was her own cross to bear, so Melody answered, "It's all the thing, don't you know, my lord." But she showed her adorable dimples, and a lot of the viscount's good resolutions melted.

He raised the one moveable eyebrow. "Perhaps in Shavbrodia, my girl, but in London ladies don't pay attention to the weather. They are wearing the flimsiest of gowns, with the least underpinnings. Some are even dampening their skirts."

Her green eyes opened wide. "They are? Whatever for?"

He grinned. "Child, you have so much to learn. I only wish I . . . No, you had better leave."

"I am not in leading strings, Lord Corey. About your paying my shot at the inn, I do know that's not the thing." She couldn't get the blasted strings unknotted, and the wretched man was laughing at her! She stamped her foot in frustration.

He reached for the bag to help her, and exclaimed, "My God, what's in here? The thing weighs a ton."

She snatched it back, not about to reveal the reticule's contents, but he kept her hand in his, to her confusion. "If you must know, it's a going-away present from my schoolmistress."

"A fine instructor she must be, not teaching her young ladies about the danger of rakes." He was teasing her purposefully, noting her stress on the "going-away" part to distance herself from the schoolroom. He also noticed how the color came and went in her peach-blushed cheeks.

"School taught me everything I need to know, thank you."

"Everything, *mon ange*?" With that Corey drew her forward and brushed his other hand across her cheek and behind her head. He lowered his mouth to hers and kissed her, tenderly enough for his bruised lips, thoroughly enough to leave Melody dazed.

Now why the bloody hell had he done that? Corey asked himself. Most likely it was the same devil that had put Albert in his path: he just could not resist a dare. It would never do. The viscount shook himself, bringing his cracked ribs forcibly back to mind.

"Angel, Angel, you mustn't look at me all dewy and awestruck, or I'll forget I am a gentleman altogether. It was only a simple little kiss."

Her first rake. Her first kiss. The first time a second became eternity. And to him it was just a simple kiss? Melody sighed. "I suppose I have a lot to learn, after all."

"You'll get swallowed whole in the ton, else."

"I might never get to London." Never know another libertine, never feel that delicious tingling.

"Well, then your rural society, which can be even more moralistic. I really feel I owe it to you, to finish your education."

Melody felt that his kiss had opened more horizons than all the books in Miss Meadow's library. She sighed again.

His fingers stroked her hand, which was somehow still in his. "The first rule is no sighing; it gives a fellow notions. No, the first rule is never let a man get you off somewhere alone. Then you don't need any other rules. But if you should find yourself alone, say on a starry balcony, and the cur dares to take liberties with you, like this—"

This time the world stopped.

"—then you are supposed to slap him, like this." And he raised her hand to his face, but instead of the slap, her palm caressed his empurpled cheek.

37

The viscount took a deep, painful breath. "You're not a very apt pupil, are you, sweetheart?" He laughed.

He was laughing at her! "Of all the miserable—"

"That's it, Angel, you are supposed to be mad, not moonstruck. Here, make a fist, since your slaps would not precisely discourage an overheated beau." Corey's hands curled Melody's fingers into a ball, and he grinned at her. "Now pretend I am a randy buck toying with your affections."

She didn't have to pretend. She hauled off and swung at him, she really did. She missed, of course; he ducked back. But her reticule, with its roll of coins and hefty little book, swung right behind her fist—and it didn't miss.

Mingleforth's *Rules of Polite Decorum* came in handy, after all. *Now* Corey's nose was broken.

One other event interrupted Miss Ashton's journey home. Late in the afternoon, a shabby boy ran onto the roadway chasing a small dog, and Toby pulled back on the reins. The pup ran between the sturdy legs of Old Bess and Thimble and stayed there cowering, while the boy shouted louder, and Toby's hearing grew worse.

Nanny positively swelled in anticipation. Now here was someone she could intimidate. Here was a male, dirty, full of profanity, disturbing the right-of-way, and small. He was going to pay for all the indignities she'd suffered at his fellow men's hands. She grabbed the lad by the ear and jabbed him with her knitting needle. She called him a misbegotten whelp and a gorm-grown gallow's bait. She would have gone on for at least an hour, if Melody hadn't taken part.

At first Miss Ashton hadn't even stepped down from the carriage. She was too despondent to care about a foul-mouthed boy and his dog. But it was getting later, and other vehicles might come along,

38

so she intervened. At the sight of a reasonable face, the boy rushed into explanation: "It's me own bloody dog, and the old dungcrow's got no damn business akeepin' me from it. Bloody mutt were worritin' the chickens an' Ma says iffin I catch it, I can help drown the bleedin' bitch."

So Melody slapped the brat. Then she tossed a coin into the dirt at his feet. "There, now it's not your dog any longer. And if you are not out of here in two minutes, I'll send for the magistrate, you little muckworm." The boy grabbed up the coin and ran. Melody used a piece of cheese to coax the dog out from the proximity of Thimble's massive hooves. The little mongrel was ridged-rib starving, shivering, and filthy. It was young, mostly hound with something shaggy mixed in, and it licked Melody's hand in pathetic gratitude. She wrapped it in her wool muffler—with an I-dare-you look to Nanny—and carried it back to the carriage, where the pup had food and water from the hamper before falling asleep in its savior's lap. Melody promptly named her new friend Angel, then proceeded to dampen the poor beast with her tears.

Chapter Six

"*Y*ou brought home another charity case? For heaven's sake, Melody, *we* are a charity case! How could any child of mine be such a skitterwitted ninnyhammer? Where's my hartshorn? I need my salts. Perhaps a cordial."

Lady Jessamyn Ashton was reclining on the lounge in her bedroom, exhausted from the effort of offering her cheek to be kissed. She was interestingly pale, dressed in lavender gauze, and she fluttered a square of silk between her watery eyes and her ample bosom. With an air of die-away frailty, she asked, "Was ever a woman so beset?"

Melody poured out a tonic from the tray nearby. "Come, Mama, things cannot be as bad as all that. You sent me money for new clothes, remember?"

"A lady has to keep up appearances no matter what. Do you think I would let that harpy in Bath discover we are in Dun Territory? The woman has a wider correspondence than I do. Did, alas. I could not bear it if everyone in the ton knew we were below hatches. Could you sprinkle some rosewater on my handkerchief, dear?"

Melody did, and placed it tenderly across her mother's forehead. "But are we?" she persisted. "Are we below hatches?"

Lady Ashton tossed the cloth on the floor, dropping the role of tragedy queen with it. "Don't be such a gudgeon. We've been punting on tick for years. Now there's almost no income at all."

"But, Mama, the way you live, all the clothes and traveling, and my schooling, my allowance. I do not understand."

"Then you are a paperskull, Melody. The only hope we ever had was to find you a wealthy *parti*. The breeding was there, along with a modest dowry, thanks to Judith, and we made sure you had the education the highest sticklers demand in a wife. We encouraged the necessary connections, all those well-born girls at your so-fashionable school, all my so-called friends. Friends, hah! Where are they now, I wonder."

"Do you mean everything was for me to make an advantageous marriage? I thought I was to have a love match."

Lady Jessamyn gave that the consideration it deserved, none. "I researched the prospects for years before settling on Dickie Pendleton, whom I have been cultivating for ages now. He's an earl, and as rich as Croesus, they say, and needing an heir before he's too old to—before much longer at any rate. He wouldn't commit himself till your come out, of course, but we did talk settlements over Christmas at Sally Jersey's."

"Without . . . without even asking me?" Melody choked out.

"Of course, the man's the most sanctimonious Methodist in town, and I should have known he'd shab off at the first hint of gossip."

Gossip? Melody's head was already reeling, and

for a moment she wondered if there was talk of her indiscretion—indiscretions—at that inn. Rumor could not possibly have reached Copley-Whitmore, not if Nanny hadn't brought it, and there would have been a rare trimming indeed, in that case. Nothing was making sense! Setting aside the question of Lord Pendleton, forever, she hoped, Melody asked, "What gossip, Mama?"

Lady Jessamyn recalled her persona. She sniffled and dabbed at her eyes. "Ah, if only I knew. Not that it would have mattered either way. With no new money coming in, there isn't enough blunt left for a proper Season: renting a suitable address, throwing a ball, presentation gowns, you know. Mr. Hadley says no one will extend me credit." She pounded her fist on the table. "I should have made the stiff-rumped prig put an offer in writing! No, not Hadley, you twit," Lady Ashton scolded at Melody's gasp. Mr. Hadley was the family's aging man of business. "That twiddlepoop Pendleton. Not that Hadley was any big help. And stop pacing, it is wearing on my delicate nerves."

"Forgive me, Mama, but I just cannot comprehend the situation. We got along for years. What happened? I thought Aunt Judith left us in good stead, and the nabob was always sending money."

"Judith left us the house and its property, your dowry, and all those grubby little mouths to feed. My widow's jointure was barely enough to keep us in candles, without the other income. Then people started talking, invitations were withdrawn, checks stopped coming in."

"What checks were those, Mama? I never knew of any—"

"Didn't they teach you not to interrupt at that fancy place? When the money stopped coming ages ago, I wrote to the nabob, Sir Bartleby, that is, that we found ourselves in temporary embarrassment. Did he even answer? Hah! That's just like a man, underfoot when you least desire them, and least in sight during times of need. Don't tell Felice—the dear child has been such a help to me—but I think her father is not as wealthy as he pretends to be."

What a great match he'd be for Mama then, Melody thought. Out loud, she asked, "So what are we to do now, Mama?"

"Do? Do? How should I know? A lady of my tender sensibilities cannot be expected to deal with financial matters. That's a man's province, child. You'll just have to take it up with Mr. Hadley."

"Me? I mean I? Deal with your man of business?"

"Who else? I told you, you're the only one with any money. Heaven knows Hadley won't let *me* touch that dowry of yours. And dear, do try to do something about those hordes of children, and that dreadful Mr. Pike. Can you pour me out some laudanum before you go? Perhaps I'll write Barty again, after my nap. I'll ring when I need my writing case."

Mr. Pike, the constable? Melody shivered as she started to unpack her belongings, and not just because there was no fire laid in the grate and no maid to carry coals. There seemed to be a lot Mama had not told her, like those checks and the "other income" Lady Ashton glossed over, and rumors, and—ugh—Lord Pendleton. Well, her little chat with Mama relieved one of Melody's worries: she wouldn't be sitting around Copley-Whitmore for the rest of her days, moping over any toplofty aristocrat. No, she'd be trying to straighten out this mingle-mangle, if they did not all land in gaol first.

And then there were the children. Surely, Mama could not have meant that Melody was to take responsibility for the orphans at Dower House; surely, there was some provision for them. Wasn't there?

* * *

Mama's nerves recovered well enough for her to do justice to an excellent luncheon, and the meal encouraged Melody to hope the rest of the doom and gloom was as exaggerated as Lady Ashton's fragile sensitivities. The woman was tough as nails when she chose! The menu included poached salmon, mutton with parsleyed potatoes, tomatoes in aspic, and trifle for dessert. At least they still had Mrs. Tolliver to cook. No pureed peepers or chicken foot soup.

Unfortunately luncheon also included Felice, who would have been even prettier than Melody remembered, with her butter-yellow hair and perfect complexion, if not for the petulant twist to her rosebud mouth and the whine in her high-pitched voice.

"It's about time you got here to pull your weight," she greeted Melody before Lady Jessamyn drifted into the morning room. "I'm no paid servant to be fetching and carrying for your mother, you know. Why should I be concocting tisanes and matching threads, while you are having it soft in some uppity school?"

Melody's training at that same uppity school kept her from inquiring just what Felice was doing there at all. Miss Bartleby had been Aunt Judith's ward, and for as long as Melody could remember she had been bragging about going off to live with her father in India. If she was not going to join the nabob, why wasn't the ungrateful witch seeking a husband, a position or, by Jupiter, a broom? Mama seemed to enjoy her company, however, and the two must have memorized the fashion journals and the *on dits* columns together, judging from the conversation during the meal.

"A lady does not bring unpleasantness to the dining table, my dear." Lady Ashton rejected Melody's pleas to have some of her questions resolved. After luncheon, of course, Mama needed a nap; the strain of her day was so fatiguing. Felice disappeared without a by-your-leave, and Melody went in search of her answers.

Mathematics was not Melody's strong suit; obviously, it was not Mama's either. Lady Ashton's bookkeeping system consisted of a rat's nest of bills, receipts, demand-due notices, and more bills jammed into the pages of an accounts ledger marked Dower House Home for Children.

Melody sat at Aunt Judith's rickety old walnut desk, the dog Angel—now Angie at Mama's dread of the vicar's visit—lying under the desk with her head on Melody's kicked-off slippers. Newly washed and constantly refed, the pup's ribs still looked like a scrub board, and Melody was still her personal deity. "All that wriggling and tail wagging is fine," Melody told the dog, rubbing Angie's head with one bare foot. "But can you add?"

There were slips from mantua-makers and London linen-drapers, jumbled among those from every local merchant in Copley-Whitmore. None were marked paid. The rough sum Melody arrived at in her head was staggering; her addition must be at fault. She turned to the ledger.

On the last marked page, in the credits columns, were sets of initials, dates, and amounts, haphazardly listed in Mama's spidery hand next to the names of children Melody knew to be at Dower House. Heavens, Mama could not be sending the children out to work, could she? Five pounds for Harold. That would be Harry, who never seemed to stay at any of the homes or schools Mama found for him. Perhaps, Melody thought, trying to find some humor in this bumblebroth, Harry had turned thief at the age of twelve and was handing his bounty over to Lady Ashton. Ten pounds, four shillings for Philip. Dear Pip was quite Melody's favorite of the recent Dower House residents, a serious, studious lad of what? He must be all of fourteen by now, unfortunately rendered shy and awkward by a disfiguring port-wine birthmark on one side of his face, which also kept him from attending school, where other lads would make his life a misery. Regrettably, Pip was a natural scholar. The last time Melody was home he had already absorbed all the vicar's teachings and was devouring the library at the Oaks. Maybe Pip was earning his keep by tutoring, but fifty pounds for Ducky?

There was no polite way of putting it; Ducky was a wantwit. His moon face was always smiling and drooling, and he was happy to play with a wooden spoon or a shiny stone or a sunbeam. Nanny doted on him, finally having a baby who would not grow up. No foster parents would ever take him, nor little Meggie, the next entry. Why should anyone pay another ten pounds for a sickly, spindly slip of a thing? For each of Meggie's six winters, Melody recalled, there were fears for the little girl's life, and every minor childhood ailment almost carried her off. No likely family had come forth to adopt the twins yet either, the last entry. Laura and Dora were identical five-year-old imps who resisted all attempts to send them in different directions. Together they were hellions, often talking gibberish that no one understood, except the other twin.

Turning back toward the beginning of the accounts, Melody found many more listings in Aunt Judith's precise script. Some of the names were familiar from her own earlier years, many were not. Various notations indicated dame schools or seminaries. A few were marked His Majesty's Service or Trading Company; most of the latest were simply crossed through in Mama's wavery lines, as though Lady Ashton trembled to do it. Some of the monies cataloged were substantial, many were smaller amounts repeated over years. None of it made sense.

And the blasted dog had chewed up Melody's slippers.

Outside Dower House a sturdy, dark-haired boy was tossing a ball in the air. "What, sent down again, Harry?"

Melody and a chastened Angie had walked down the tree-lined aisle the Oaks was named for and through the home woods toward the smaller building that used to be the estate's dower house, which now was home to the orphans. That is, Melody walked. Angie hop-toed and scampered, woofing at every moving branch and snapping twig.

"I didn't do it, Miss Melody, I swear. Is that your dog? It's a prime 'un, all right. Can I play with it?"

Angie would not go near the boy, until Melody made it clear they were to be friends, at which Angie stole the ball and ran for the woods, to Harry's delight. Harry was chased in turn by an unkempt urchin in a bedraggled pinafore. The other twin had to be somewhere close. And Philip, sitting on the steps, put down the book he was reading to duck his head, take Melody's outstretched hand, and welcome her home, stammering.

"I brought you a book, Pip. McWorly's *Dissertations on Heavenly Bodies* was highly recommended at the academy, although I could not make heads nor tails of it. I'm sure you'll breeze through it, clever lad that you are." She ignored his blushes by kneeling down to the level of the pale little girl sitting next to him, all swaddled from head to toe in Nanny's woolens, with the palest of blonde curls peeking out of her cap. "Hello, Meggie. My, how big you've grown since last summer." For just a moment, as the child smiled at her, she was reminded of Lord Corey. Melody gave herself a mental shake. Only a noddy would see that rake's image in every innocent blond babe. Only a clunch would think of him at all. She went inside.

"Nanny, who pays for the children?" Nanny was feeding Ducky, who only wanted to play with the spoon, filled with porridge or not. Angie scrambled into the kitchen, her hound's nose leading her unerringly through the house to her mistress, or toward food, anyway. Nanny started to grumble when the dog licked up the spills on the floor, on the chair, on Ducky. But Ducky clapped his pudgy hands and grinned, so more food went into his mouth at a faster rate.

"A fine question to be asking, missy. Better you be asking who pays for the clothes on your back and the roof over your head. The children do, that's who. Who did, leastways. Rob Peter to play pool, like always."

"You mean I'm taking food away from the orphans?" Melody gasped at the thought.

"Not you, this rugrat you brought into my kitchen. He's eating the ham I was saving for the children's supper! You ever hear of mince-mutt pie?"

Chapter Seven

Felice insisted on accompanying Melody to Mr. Hadley's office the next morning. "Didn't they teach you anything at that place? A lady can't go traipsing off by herself, you know. Of course, schoolgirls needn't mind their reputations so carefully," she added spitefully, from her two years' advantage, as though no one would be interested in Melody anyway. If the little cat only knew of the interlude in West Fenton with that regular out-and-outer, her rosebud mouth would purse right up with jealousy and freeze that way, like a cod!

Of course, Melody was not about to mention West Fenton. "I don't think one need be so strict in the countryside. After all, I have known everyone hereabouts my entire life." She tied her bonnet strings and pulled on her gloves.

"I'll just walk along with you anyway, to be on the safe side. I'm anxious to hear Mr. Hadley's opinions."

She was most likely anxious to show off her ensemble. Melody was dressed for the early spring morning and the serious nature of her errand. She wore a serviceable blue merino gown with high collar and long sleeves, and a plain chip-straw bonnet. Felice, on the other hand, wore a flimsy short-sleeved, low-necked, Pomona-green striped muslin and a satin bonnet decorated with artificial cherries dangling charmingly just over her brow. The petite blonde tossed a fringed linen square over her shoulders as a sop to the early spring weather. Melody felt sensible, like a drab shopgirl or something.

"But I'll be closeted with Mr. Hadley quite a while, I fear, and you might find the wait tedious." That should take care of any notion Felice had of sitting in on the interview.

"No matter, I have some commissions for Lady Jess in the village."

More bills to run up, Melody assumed dismally. She was hoping Mr. Hadley would explain why they were saddled with such an ungrateful burden, along with everything else. Then she shook herself for being so uncharitable. After all, Felice was as near to an orphan as could be, abandoned among strangers by a father she never knew. Now it seemed he had even reneged on his financial responsibilities. It must be hard on Felice, so used to thinking of herself as a pasha's princess. Besides, living with Mama could not be easy. Just this morning her tea was too cool, her head was too achy to speak with Cook about menus, and her pillows needed turning, twice. Mama kept a little silver bell by her side, and by bedtime last evening Melody was having quite unladylike thoughts about the little chime. This morning Melody had feared she would never be on her way to town. Then she had the happy notion of offering Mama those Minerva Press books.

"What, those rubbishing gothic tales? Perhaps I'll just glance at them, dear, if you and Felice are both quite determined to leave me to my own devices. I

50

cannot read much, naturally, my poor eyes, you know. Were there any of Mrs. Radcliffe's novels?"

Mama was set for the morning.

Melody was wrong; Felice didn't want to come along just to show off her outfit and spend money. She wanted the opportunity to bat her eyelashes and smile coyly at every man they passed. The apothecary's boy out on deliveries was reduced to red-faced sputters; Mr. Highet sweeping in front of his haberdashery made such a low bow he almost tripped off his stoop. Even the spotty young curate tipped his hat and walked right through Mrs. Vicar Elroy's tulip bed. They nodded politely to Miss Ashton as an afterthought, if they noticed her presence at all. Melody felt like a paid companion!

Even Edwin, one of Mr. Hadley's assistants who had been a Dower House boy before going off to school and landing a position, greeted Melody punctiliously before turning to fawn over Felice. He passed Miss Ashton to another underling while begging to be of service to Miss Bartleby. Could he get her a cool drink or a chair, could he help with her errands? And this was the Edwin who used to sneer at Felice for thinking she was better than everyone else. Melody shook her head.

At least Mr. Hadley was happy to see Melody. He patted her hand and told her she was as lovely a young woman as he always knew she would be. Of course, Mr. Hadley was more than sixty, but his sincerity restored a bit of her self-esteem. His views on her current situation, unfortunately, did nothing for her state of mind.

"It's a sad day, my dear. I tried to warn your mother to set money aside, to get beforehand with the world. That's my job, you know, giving advice." He scratched his bald head. "Rainy days always come, you know."

"Just how rainy, er, how bad is the predicament?

51

To tell the truth, Mama's books made as much sense as Euclid."

Mr. Hadley polished his spectacles, not looking her in the eye. "In basic terms, Miss Melody, your mother has just barely outrun the bailiff. She made some poor investments, against my advice, I beg leave to tell you, and then, like many in the fashionable world, continued living above her means. Credit, you know. She was spending on her expectations, but expectations are not money in the bank, when all is said and done."

"That much I gathered from her records. But what I do not understand is what expectations Mama had. If not an inheritance from Aunt Judith, or settlements from my father, how had she hoped to afford to live the way she was? No one will tell me."

"The contributions, of course."

"You mean the money donated for the orphans?" Melody had a very uncomfortable feeling in the pit of her stomach.

"Oh dear, I thought you knew by now. You see, it started with your Aunt Judith, Miss Morley. She was a spinster lady, you will recall, with no family to speak of except your mother, who was at the time recently married to your father and living in London. Judith had the Oaks with its few acres, and a small competence, and was already responsible for Sir Bartleby's daughter."

"Felice."

"Ahem. Sir Bartleby's support included provision for your aunt, naturally, which enabled her to take in another unfortunate, ah, child. Your mother in London, meanwhile, met various ladies who, ah, wished to see such children given a better life than foundling hospitals offered. So, they became sponsors in the new Dower House Home for Children."

"Do you mean they made charitable gifts?"

"It was more than that. To sponsor a child, a

patron had to pledge to provide for that particular boy or girl through infancy and onward, right up to getting them started in a career or dowered to a respectable marriage. Other times the sums were provided to help the foster parents your Aunt Judith found, families who otherwise could not afford another mouth to feed."

"How kind of those ladies to make such a commitment."

Mr. Hadley took out a handkerchief and dabbed at this brow. "Ah, indeed. I helped draw up some of the papers myself. Now some of the sponsors chose to pay—ah, make their donations—monthly or yearly. Others made one large deposit to the Dower House account. Here is where it gets a bit ticklish."

That nasty feeling in Melody's stomach was arguing with her breakfast. Aunt Judith was a rigid moralist, who would never have touched the orphans' money. Mama could *not* have, could she? Melody was certain Mr. Hadley did not mean ticklish as in funny, but she had to ask. "How?"

"You see, it was understood with each contribution that your aunt, then your mother, was to have a share of the financial benefits, for their efforts and attention to the children. When there was a lump sum, an endowment if you will, the interest would accrue to Lady Morley, for her expenses in operating the home, et cetera. Then your father died and left all of those debts, and you and your mother came to live with Lady Morley. Slightly more of the, ah, principles were withdrawn. With Lady Morley's passing, I am afraid your mother became a tad careless with her bookkeeping."

"As in which was the orphans' money and which was hers?"

"Something like that. She did feel that by investing the principles she could increase the, ah, profits. As I said, the investments failed. All would

53

still have been well, however, if she had stopped spending, or if the, ah, gifts continued coming."

"But?" It was strange. Mr. Hadley kept mopping at his forehead as if he were overwarm, while Melody was chilled through.

"But recently the money has not kept coming. Your mother feels this may be due to certain rumors circulating in the ton."

"She mentioned the same to me. Do you have any idea what these stories are about?"

"I do not travel in those circles, of course. If I had to guess, my dear, I'm afraid I would have to say that people think your mother is stealing from the children."

There, it was said. Melody had refused to put the idea into words, although the notion had niggled at the back of her mind since seeing that ledger. Now she refused to believe it. "No," she firmly declared. "Not my mother. Mama is a lady."

Isn't she? a tiny voice asked. Melody overruled it and stiffened her already straight back in the hard chair. "We'll come about, you'll see. Mama mentioned that the dowry you hold for me, as trustee, could see us through this temporary setback, so I must ask you to release those monies to me."

"But, my dear, how will you contract a marriage, then?"

"I am afraid I am not likely to encounter eligible gentlemen in debtors' prison either, Mr. Hadley."

"But you are only seventeen, child. Your whole future lies ahead. You won't want to forfeit it now. Perhaps one of your schoolmates could invite you to town for the Season."

"What, shall I go off to enjoy myself, turning my back on my family and my responsibilities?"

The old man shook his head. Her mother surely would. "I cannot let you do this, my dear, but I respect your valiant sacrifice."

"Thank you for your concern, Mr. Hadley, but

54

what kind of future would I have if I could not respect myself?"

They compromised. Mr. Hadley would let Melody have half of the money Aunt Judith had put aside for her, if it stayed in her own hands. The chit had bottom, he acknowledged, and a sensible mind that wouldn't be sidetracked by fancy frills and furbelows. There was a lot more of Judith Morley in the lass than she knew. If anyone could get that house in order—and Dower House, too—young Melody was it. Too bad such weight had to fall on such tender shoulders. At least Mr. Hadley felt he could relieve her of one burden.

"Don't you go thinking that Miss Felice is another of your responsibilities. Judith provided for her, too, but the chit went through the blunt in one year, and some of those other monies we talked of, trying to nab herself a title, tagging along with your mother to those house parties and such. If ever there was a wench with ideas above her station it's that one."

"I thought the nabob, Sir Bartleby, was to send for her."

"We all did, but he hasn't been heard from. I thought for a while she'd make a match with young Edwin, but he wasn't good enough for her, nor were any of the local lads. She has her heart set on a London swell, it seems."

"She's very beautiful."

"And pretty is as pretty does, I don't need to remind you. Besides, what fancy gent is going to offer for a dowerless chit who cannot even dance at Almack's?" Mr. Hadley tidied the papers on his desk, pleased that the issue of Felice was dispensed with. He'd lost too many hours of work with Edwin's mooning after the heartless jade.

"But why wouldn't Felice get her vouchers?" Melody asked, confused. "I always thought Sir Bartleby was of the highest stare."

55

"That's because you listened to Miss Bartleby, I'll warrant. He only got knighted after years with the East India Company, you know, for lending so much of the ready to the crown. Bartleby wasn't married before he left the country either, and he left under some kind of cloud. You might say Felice was the silver lining."

Then again, you might say Felice was the dark shadow on a sunny day. Here Melody had her head full of important ideas: which bills to pay first, where they could best economize, how she could earn a living and see to the others at the same time. And there was Felice, grousing because Mrs. Finsterer would not let her put the purchase of a pair of York tan gloves on Lady Ashton's account.

"Can you believe the nerve? These provincial shopkeepers should be pleased to do trade with us."

"They would be more pleased to be paid what's owed them," Melody replied, sharper than she intended. Some of the other merchants must have been more lenient than Mrs. Finsterer, or more optimistic, or males, since Felice had a whole pile of packages. She was quick to transfer the bundles to Melody's arms, while retying her bonnet strings, and somehow that's where the parcels stayed.

"Oh, but now that you have settled with Mr. Hadley," Felice chirped, turning her brightest smile on Melody, "you can go back and reestablish our credit."

"I'm sorry," Melody told her, "but there will be no more credit." Truthfully, she wasn't sorry a bit. She wasn't even sorry when the sun went behind a cloud, and the underdressed, pouting, little blond tart shivered the whole way home.

Chapter Eight

$\mathcal{M}$elody was going to make this work. She had to; there was no other choice. So what if she knew nothing about holding household or raising children? She didn't know anything about pigs and chickens and turnips, either, and that was not going to stop her. She would just have to learn, she told herself with uncrushed youth's cheerful belief in invincibility, and the others would have to learn with her.

She made lists and talked to more knowledgeable persons: old Toby, Mr. Hadley, the neighboring landlord's bailiff, even a poacher brought to the house one dark evening by Mrs. Tolliver, the cook, to show Melody how to lay snares. And she enlisted the children, who were thrilled to help until their hands got blisters turning over a vegetable patch. Still, if the Morley-Ashton households were to become self-sufficient, everyone had a job to do.

Sturdy Harry was the biggest assistance, although he kept trying to convince Melody their best bet was to start a racing stable.

"I know you are horse mad, Harry, but hogs are cheaper to buy, less costly to feed, grow faster, and we can eat them."

"I know horses are expensive, but think of all the money left over from my schooling. That last place won't have me back, you know," he told her, grinning. "And the fire wasn't even my fault."

Philip volunteered his services as a tutor, to Harry's disgust, and to teach the younger children their letters, to save money there. "I—I'm not real strong like Harry, Miss Melody, b-but I am awfully good with figures. P-perhaps, that is, if you want, I could help with the b-books."

Now there was a welcome offer! After studying the accounts with Melody after dinner that very night, Pip even found a way to save money by paying the bills off in part, leaving some of their funds earning interest. "B-because the merchants will be pl-pl—happy to get any of what's due, and they'll see you mean to make good."

"I knew you were a downy one, Pip! Of course, I'll need you with me to explain it to them," she mentioned casually, starting another of her campaigns. Before he could object she went on: "I don't think I have the same grasp of finances you do. I'd only make a mull of it, you know."

Pip handsomely conceded that females weren't expected to understand such weighty matters, and yes, she ought to have a man, or a boy, at her side.

The twins, who were always filthy despite Nanny's best efforts, were naturally put in charge of the new pigs, once the pen was built. Then delicate Meggie, wrapped like a mummy in Nanny's knitteds, wanted a job all her own. She got the chickens and handled those eggs like fragile porcelain.

Ducky learned to weed, more or less, under Nanny's supervision. More weeds and less cabbage and parsley seedlings, thank goodness, Melody cheered. And Nanny, of course, kept her needles flying. With all the new wool, she declared, they wouldn't go cold for another three years. They might even try selling mittens in the village, come next winter.

Melody was determined that even the pup, Angie, would earn her keep. There were rabbits and partridge and pheasants in the home woods that could be better utilized on the home dinner table. Angie could scent food miles away—she was already *canis non grata* in the village—so all Melody had to do was convince the dog to help her locate supper in the wild. Of course, after Angie flushed the game, Melody had to shoot it, which posed a few obstacles of its own, considering Melody had never handled a gun in her life. She would learn.

Two other obstacles were not as easily overcome: Mama and Felice.

"My dearest daughter out there in the muck with pigs and chickens? My salts, quickly."

It got worse when Melody determined that the most money could be saved by combining the two households.

"Don't be a ninnyhammer, Melody. You cannot expect me to permit those, those *children* to come live at the Oaks, can you?"

"No, Mama, I expect you to go live at the Dower House."

"Oh, dear Lord, my heart. I'm having spasms, you sapskull, call the physician."

"Mama, we cannot afford to heat this pile, much less pay enough staff to keep it clean. The idea of an army of servants waiting on three women is absurd anyway, even if we had the means."

Tears did not work either, nor cajolery, nor guilt. "You are an unnatural child, trying to kill your own mother. I am not a well woman, you know. Living at the Dower House with the children, all the noise and *dirt* . . . I'm afraid it will be too much for me."

Melody wasn't budging, and she held the purse strings. She also hid that little silver bell.

"Don't give me that perishing cordial, you nod-cock, I need the brandy."

"I am sorry, Felice, but we cannot afford a dresser for you and Mama. In fact, the few servants we do keep will be too busy, so you'll have to look after my mother, help with her clothes and things."

Felice turned another page of the fashion magazine. "You cannot make a maid out of me, Miss High-and-Mighty. I won't do it."

"Then you won't eat."

Felice threw the magazine down and stamped on it. "My father shall hear of this!"

"Good, I'd like to have a few words with that gentleman myself. Perhaps he can advise me on some investments, if he ever reimburses the money spent on your behalf. Shall I show you the tally Pip made of that last stack of bills?" The beauty made no reply. "*Three* parasols, Felice?"

"I wouldn't expect a dowd like you to understand. They were for three different outfits, of course."

"But I do understand, Felice, and I sincerely hope you bought quality merchandise, for it will have to last you a good long time."

"You always were hateful, Melody Ashton, you with your so-perfect manners and your so-dignified airs. Well, you don't fool me for a minute; you're just jealous. You'll never get a husband, and you want to make sure I never get one! Why, even that windbag Lord Pendleton wouldn't have a managing female like you!"

Melody's innate honesty forced her to admit to the germ of truth hidden in the vitriol. Not that claptrap about husbands, of course, but the charge of jealousy hit home. All the attention Mama gave the other girl, all the stares from all the men, for all those years, hurt. Still, she could be fair. "You would be beautiful dressed in rags, Felice, and gentlemen will continue to offer for you, I am sure. Please believe me, I shall heartily wish you joy with whichever man you accept ... the sooner the better."

They planted potatoes and fenced in the chickens. The merchants were cooperating, and the two sows gave birth. Unfortunately, piglets could fit through gaps their lumbering mothers could not.

"Pigs like to wander," Toby informed Melody. So wires were strung.

"Pigs can dig." So boards were sunk.

Pigs could chew, and pigs could jump. Pigs could fly, for all Melody knew, and likely would before she found a way to keep them penned. So there were always little pink piglets in the garden, on the lawn, or down the drive, and almost always two identically dirty little girls chasing after them. Sometimes the boys joined in, and sometimes Angie, adding her baying to the giggling, shouting, squealing melee. They seemed to save the best, noisiest, muddiest pighunts for when Lady Ashton was taking her constitutional or when the vicar came to call. No one even bothered to hand Lady Jessamyn her smelling salts anymore; they went straight for the brandy.

Melody was practicing her shooting, using her father's old dueling pistol that Toby had taught her how to load and aim. The gun would be no good over distance, but in her careful reasoning, Melody felt she would do better to start with a stationary target at short range. Frankly, she wasn't sure she could shoot a bunny rabbit. There was a certain amount of pleasure, meanwhile, in the skill she was gaining.

She was concentrating on the day's target, a playing card, and never heard the man approaching till Angie's bark grew sharper.

" 'Ere, 'ere, call your dog off, miss."

"It's Mr. Pike, the constable, isn't it? How do you do, sir?"

Pike removed his low-crowned hat and bowed, revealing a rat-brown wig slightly askew on his head. "Aye, miss. They said as how you were the one I had to talk to, concerning the complaints."

"What complaints might those be, sir?" Melody asked, reloading the pistol.

"Well, ma'am, there's complaints from the shopkeepers about bills, complaints from the butcher about your dog, and complaints from the villagers about the bast—brats."

"Oh, those complaints." The man obviously had no sense of humor. He merely wiped at his pointed red nose, where another drip was already forming. "Yes, well, I believe I have accommodated the merchants, and Angie here has not repeated her foray to the village."

"And what about the youngsters? There's some as saying they belong in the workhouse."

"That's absurd." She looked at him narrowly. "Unless 'they' get a portion of the county dole for each resident there. Those children are my responsibility, not to be thrown on the parish."

"But law-abiding citizens are saying they're running around wild and unsupervised, and you're keeping freaks out here."

Melody drew herself up and looked down on the little man—they always were small, bullies like this. "Mr. Pike, those are lovely, happy children you are speaking of. They are well fed, properly clothed, and have lessons every day. I'll thank you not to call them names. Now if you are finished, sir, I have more practicing to do."

Pike rubbed his hands together. "You haven't answered all of the charges, miss." He edged a little closer, looking at her sideways. "Of course, I'd forget some of the complaints if you were to make it worth my while. A little snuggling might do it."

"Sir, you forget yourself!"

"No, I remember Miss Felice used to cooperate."

Why, that little yellow-haired baggage! Melody turned away and pointed the gun. "Mr. Pike, I am going to forget this conversation." She aimed at the card. "I suggest you do the same." And fired. She hit the card, the knave of spades, right on the nose. "Do I make myself clear?"

It was time to try Papa's rifle.

They harvested the first row of beans, sold some of the farrow pigs, thankfully before the twins could count, and Melody shot her first woodcock. Of course, she had to wrestle with Angie over possession of the bird, but she was working on the problem. Felice was spending more time in the village, fixing her interest on Edwin, Melody hoped, and Mama was resting, if not resigned. They were managing. Mr. Hadley told Melody she should be proud.

At night sometimes, though, when her body was exhausted but her mind was wide awake, and she only had Angie for company, Miss Ashton stared at the ceiling of her tiny room and despaired.

Should a person stop dreaming because no dreams have come true? Stop wishing when no wishes are fulfilled? Then where is the place for heaven? How can life itself go on without hope? It cannot; that's called hell. At the very least, one can hope for a sunny day or an end to rain. Small dreams, but fair odds, sooner or later.

And a young girl, even one with freckles from working out in the sun, should never give up her dreams. Sooner or later . . .

Chapter Nine

Sooner or later, a man has to pick up the threads of his life, even if his nose *is* crooked. Lord Cordell Inscoe, Viscount Coe, had stayed away from London for over a month. The first few weeks, of course, were not by choice.

"You take that deathtrap vehicle out of the carriage house, and I won't be responsible," the doctor announced when he came to the inn to do what he could for the viscount's nose. "One rut, one miscue to those fractious brutes you young blades drive, and one of those cracked ribs goes right through your lung. Then where are you? Lying in a road somewhere, gasping for air like a beached perch. And what did you say happened to your nose, anyway? You fell? Addlepated young fool, I told you to keep quiet. Lucky you didn't do yourself an injury right here, in Mrs. Barstow's best parlor."

Lucky? If the cantankerous old sawbones thought a broken nose was no injury, he should just get a taste of what it felt like. Coe had a mind to—

"Too bad I couldn't get here yesterday when it

happened. Mrs. Reilly, don't you know. For real this time, by Jupiter, great big bruiser of a boy, it was. Already set a bit, your beak, that is. I'll have to break it again, of course, unless you want to be sniffing at your right ear the rest of your days. This might pain you some."

If Corey didn't flatten the physician right then, it was because he was too busy picturing a slim, graceful neck between his hands.

So he stayed on in West Fenton for his ribs' sake, not eager for anyone to see him in his present condition anyway. Hostesses would faint, the fellows at the clubs would be merciless in their ribbing, without even knowing about the little girl who'd dealt the last blow, and his town house staff would wrap him in cotton wool. Corey thought for a moment of lying low as soon as he could travel to the little house in Kensington he kept for his convenients. He was not paying his current mistress Yvette for her conversation, however, and not being up to the obvious exercise, he might as well stay put.

Corey sent for his man Bates, his ex-batman from army days, now a dapper gentleman's gentleman, who took his stature from serving a pink of the ton. Lord Coe also notified his secretary to refuse invitations, forward important mail, and handle everything else. The viscount's affairs were well in hand, as they had to be, with him gone so long fighting old Boney. He trusted his bailiffs and his bankers and Mr. Tyler, who had been secretary to his father before him.

The first week Corey took laudanum for the pain; the second, Bates was hiding his master's boots to keep the viscount from overdoing. By the third week Coe was visiting Albert, playing cards in the taproom with the worshipful locals, and making a nuisance of himself in the stables, wanting to exercise the horses. Mostly, he went for walks and reflected on his life. Time and boredom will do that to a man.

The war was over, his part of it anyway, and maybe he *was* taking too many risks with his life. Maybe he should think about leaving more to posterity than a new driving record to Brighton. The viscountcy was secure, at least, in a sober cousin and his large, hopeful brood. Coe's personal wealth, the considerable unentailed property, would go to his beloved sister and her future children. Erica, Lady Wooster, was now a childless widow living in Bath, but she was only twenty-four, and that could change. Now that Corey had time to think about it, his heritage demanded more of him. He would just have to change his way of life—or find Erica a new husband.

London was a little thin of company when he finally got there, the Season not formally underway. The clubs seemed to have the same gouty gents sitting under a pall of smoke, the same glitter-eyed gamblers feverishly dicing away their patrimonies, and the same hard-edged tulips shredding reputations over cognac. The parks were full of dandies on the strut and hey-go-mad bucks on bonecrushers. Erica's first marriage was a joyless one, Corey thought regretfully, still feeling guilty for his part in arranging it. She deserved better.

With this thought in mind, or so he told himself, Viscount Coe went to Almack's. The beau monde's Marriage Mart worked both ways, he reasoned, and a gentleman on the lookout to become a tenant for life would more likely be found here than at, say, the Coconut Club or the Cyprian's Ball. If, while he reconnoitered the field of bachelors, the viscount's eye happened to glance to the rows of white lace decked debutantes, that was merely by accident.

As Lord Coe temporized for a stunned Lady Jersey, he was just popping by in case an old friend was up from the country. The elusive, reckless Lord Coe at Almack's surveying this year's crop of fledglings? What a tale to pass around! Reading her mind, Corey tugged at his neckcloth, an elegant creation it had taken him and Bates an hour to tie. It may be de rigueur to arrive at Almack's before eleven, and in knee smalls at that, and even to flirt with Lady Jersey, but dashed if he'd let the lady patronesses pass him off to every whey-faced chit and her eager mama. He was not about to give rise to hopeful expectations in any grasping woman's breast.

He had one dance with Princess Esterhazy before excusing himself. "I see that my, ah, friend is not here, so I'll just be going on. Another engagement, don't you know."

That wouldn't stop the rumors, not when his lordship kept scanning the sidelines.

She wasn't there, his green-eyed sprite, not that he would admit looking for her. She said she would not have a Season, but such a beauty deserved gowns and jewels and elegant waltzes—in his arms. After he strangled her, of course. He touched the bridge of his nose where there was and might always be a new bump, and smiled, causing one dumpling of a deb to nearly swoon with joy. The viscount did not notice.

This was absurd, he chided himself, looking for Angel amid such milk-and-water misses! Looking for her at all was foolish beyond permission. That's why he had purposely not asked Barstow for her direction, debating with himself whether Mrs. Barstow would have given it. Why, his behavior toward an untouched maiden was already reprehensible, and he was no closer to jumping into parson's mousetrap over a pair of green eyes and a captivating dimple than he was to . . . to asking that plump little chit over there for a dance. The wealthiest, most attractive, most alluring bachelor in many a year scowled and stomped out of Almack's. Miss Weathersfield fled in tears to the retiring room, while all the young sprigs of fashion wondered how they could get such interesting deviations in their proboscises.

At least Yvette could not be tarnished by his rake-shame reputation, Coe thought as he walked off his ill-humor on the long trek to Kensington. Hell, she'd helped him earn it, along with many of her sisters. Now it was time she earned that charming little bijou and the pony cart and the diamond necklace.

Yvette earned the matching bracelet, leaving Corey spent. Too bad she could not satisfy his mind as well as his body, but Yvette's talents did not include beguiling conversation. There was no friendly banter, no natural tenderness, or warm good humor. For the first time ever, Coe was bothered by bought affection. He went home early.

A few tedious weeks later, the best Viscount Coe had managed for entertainment was a green-eyed replacement for Yvette, some heavy wagers, and the idea of a house party at his property outside Bath, to liven up his sister's days. The best prospect he could come up with for a new brother-in-law was Lord Pendleton, and even Corey was hesitant about foisting the prosy bore on Erica for a fortnight. Then Erica wrote him a troubled letter, asking if he could help with a delicate matter. Her words spoke of adventure, danger, and intrigue, a menace to his dear sister's happiness, and a threat to the family name. What could be better?

It rained for four days. The viscount put up at Hazelton, a town about an hour from his goal, according to his maps. He had decided to keep this distance, not wanting his destination made public. He knew what a stir a nobleman and his retinue could make in a small village, which was precisely

68

what he wished to avoid in such a delicate family matter. He could not simply travel by horseback, for he needed the closed carriage, which meant a coachman, footmen, and postilions. A groom was necessary to look after his stallion, Caesar, tied behind. The viscount's man, Bates, refused to be left behind, saying: "Just look what happened last time, milord." So Hazelton it was.

It kept raining, however, and the only inn in town was damp. Corey's ribs ached, damn the quack in West Fenton. His man, Bates, came down with a cold, and the groom reported one of the carriage horses was off its feed. Blast this whole mission!

He set out finally on a high-strung gray stallion that hadn't been exercised in too long a time, down muddy roadways and up mired country lanes. He got lost twice and almost unseated once, to the detriment of his temper. At last he spotted a gravel drive, as per his directions, flanked by two stone columns with acorns carved in them. Original, he thought sarcastically, prepared to find nothing pleasing about this place. He was not disappointed.

The drive was rutted and weed choked under a canopy of ancient oaks. Last year's leaves formed a slippery roadbed of muck in places, and this year's leaves dripped water off Coe's beaver hat and down his collar. He hated it.

Caesar, meanwhile, hated sudden noises and small, darting creatures. So when the pig jumped out from the underbrush, and the grubby child darted after it inches from the huge stallion's nose, Lord Coe suddenly found himself seated in that same leaf-mold sludge. Corey held his breath and checked his ribs, while high-pitched voices chattered out of sight like monkeys in trees, for all the words he could distinguish. Only Lord Coe's dignity was injured, which the back of his fawn trousers would advertise nicely, thank you. Well, he wasn't turning back. He remounted and kept Caesar on a much tighter rein, swearing the benighted horse was laughing at him.

The drive ended, at last, at a large stone house set in an untended clearing. The windows were grimy, the steps hadn't been swept, and no one came to hold his horse.

"Hallo, the house!" he called, notifying the butler to send one of his minions. No one came. Corey could not very well leave Caesar standing untended, not with misplaced children and livestock popping up anywhere. "Hell and damnation."

"I say, sir, would you like me to hold your horse?"

Corey saw two boys dash toward the house. The speaker, a dark-haired, ruddy-faced lad with his knees muddied and his shirt untucked, was already fearlessly rubbing Caesar's nose. "He's a prime goer, I'll bet," the boy said, adding on another hurried breath, "I'm Harry, that's Pip." The other, sandy-haired lad, ducked his head and stood behind his companion.

Dismounting, Corey reluctantly handed the reins into Harry's eager, but grimy, hands. "You're not the groom here, are you?" he asked. No gentleman would let such a ragamuffin near his cattle.

"Oh no, sir," Harry replied, never taking his eyes off the stallion, "I'm one of the ba—"

Pip kicked him and came forward, eyes still on the ground. "We're b-boys from D-Dower House, sir." He nodded in the direction of a side path, inadvertently showing the splotched side of his face. Corey inhaled deeply, but his expression did not change from a grim, disapproving glower.

Just then the child with the pig came tearing around the building and down a path, pigtails flying, petticoats dragging in the mud, tongue running on wheels.

"What is she, a red Indian, or something?" Corey asked Harry, who seemed to have Caesar under perfect control, despite the screeching whirlwind.

It was Pip—what kind of name was Pip?—who answered: "She ... she's Czechoslovakian, sir." He turned his back on Corey.

That didn't sound like Czech to Coe, from his days of fighting with the allies, but before he could pursue the thought, Harry shouted out: "Hey you, you better get home and out of those dirty clothes before Miss Mel catches you. She'll take a stick to you, else."

Corey could not believe the manners of these boys. " 'Hey you' ?"

Harry wasn't fazed. "Don't know her name," was all he said, bending to find some fresh grass for Caesar. In fact, Harry didn't even seem to notice he was addressing a gentleman, much less a peer of the realm. For the first time in his life, Lord Coe's horse was getting more respect than he was!

The ramshackle place was even worse than Corey had expected. The children were unmannered, untaught, unwashed—and beaten, if Harry could be believed. The viscount marched determinedly up the path to the house, to be nearly bowled over by the same knee-high dust devil. He looked back at Harry, who merely shrugged as if to say, 'Women.'

No one answered the door, not even when Corey banged the knocker and shouted. The damned manor was locked up and deserted! He strode back down the path to look accusingly at the boys.

"Oh," Harry said, noting with surprise the viscount's irritation. "You didn't ask. They're all at Dower House. This place is for rent. Jupiter, you're not here to look it over, are you? By all that's holy, that would be famous! There's a bang-up stable that just needs some work, and I could—"

"Hold, bantling. I am here to see Lady Ashton, not lease her house." Corey noted Harry's crestfallen expression and added, "But you may walk Caesar here if your friend would be so good as to show me the way to the Dower House." There was

71

no reason to take his anger at the situation out on the children. After all, they were the real victims. He softened his tone toward the other boy: "Pet names are fine for the nursery, but between men I think proper names are more fitting, don't you? I am Cordell Coe."

Pip brightened instantly, forgetting to look down. "Oh, indeed, sir. I'm Philip. Philip M-Morley, that is."

"I am pleased to make your acquaintance, Master Philip. Perhaps you could tell me—"

Philip could not tell him anything. He was rooted on the walkway, his mouth hanging open in horror. Corey followed his gaze down the trail and almost choked. The tiny swineherdess had listened to Harry after all, about taking her clothes off and washing up. There she was, giggling on the path, as pink and shiny as one of her pigs—and just as bare.

Pip wanted to die. Whatever must this fine gentleman think? There was no doubt Mr. Coe was a gentleman, maybe even a lord. Zeus, maybe Pip should have been calling him 'my lord.' "M-M—Sir, th-th . . ." Pip just couldn't get it out.

Corey had turned his back on the little nymph, not so much from a sense of honor as an effort to hide his smile from the mortified boy. Somehow there she was, behind them now on the path, still as naked as a jay. The viscount turned his back again, then once more, before finally giving in to delighted chuckles. So there were two of the hell babes. Gads, how they would terrorize the countryside! When he could stop laughing, he patted Philip on the back in a comradely gesture. "Don't worry, old chap, I had a little sister, too." Of course, Corey's sister would never have shown even her ankle in public, and would have been on bread and water for days if she did.

Pip was comforted, nonetheless, and relaxed

enough to say, "Things are usually not this b-bad. Miss Ashton's out hunting, that's all."

So the person supposed to be supervising these waifs was enjoying herself riding to hounds. Corey had a few choice words to say to that harpy, along with his speech for the blood-sucking mother. In the meantime, this place was better than a farce. His ill-humor was in abeyance, and he was actually looking forward to whatever came next. Pigs, bare-bottomed moppets, abandoned houses, what could follow? Dancing cows and two-headed chickens?

The viscount was prepared for almost anything—except Felice.

Chapter Ten

$\mathcal{T}$he door opened at his knock, for a surprise. Corey expected a manservant or at least a maid, not the petite vision throwing him a pert curtsy. She was spring, in a daffodil-yellow gown with grass-green ribbon streamers tied just under full, rounded breasts. A tiny green cap nestled among curls the color of buttercups, and eyes like April mornings twinkled up at him over a rosebud mouth. Viscount Coe could feel the sap rising.

Philip scuffled his feet in disgust. This stranger was no nonpareil after all; he was just like every other moonstruck clodpole in the neighborhood. His mouth was gaping, and he was more tongue-tied than Pip at his worst. Over Felice! Hero-worship died aborning.

"I-I'll just go help Harry with the horse," the boy said, backing down the path and shaking his head. Wait till he told Harry what a looby the paragon turned out to be.

Pip's words broke the spell, and Viscount Coe recalled he was a man of the world, not a green schoolboy. Besides which, he was here on a mission. Business before pleasure, he pledged himself, but what a pleasure it would be. Corey withdrew one of his cards and turned down a corner to show he called in person. "I would like to see Lady Jessamyn Ashton, please."

Felice read the card. A viscount, delivered right to her door! And not just any titled nobleman, but one the *on dits* columns credited with great wealth and great success with the ladies. Felice did not need any stale London dailies to tell her why. The square chin, broad shoulders, and devilishly handsome grin told enough of the story. Now Felice merely had to rewrite the ending, which always termed Coe a perpetual bachelor. Not if she could help it!

"Won't you come sit down?" she offered, taking his riding crop and hat, and leading the way to a sitting room. Courtesy made him follow; the view from the back made him smile appreciatively. "You must be wondering where all the servants are. I don't usually answer the door myself, you know." She gave a tinkling little laugh, looking around for a likely spot to lay his things, as though she never had to worry about such mundane chores. "They are all . . . all given the day off. Yes, that's it. Lady Ashton is so generous, you know. There was a . . . a wedding in the village today." There, now her circumstances wouldn't look so no-account, and she'd even dropped a hint about weddings!

"I am sorry to bother you at a time when things are all at sixes and sevens, then," he replied politely. "And no, I shan't sit in all my dirt." Corey could just imagine this china doll's reaction to muddy stains from the back of his pants. He underestimated Miss Bartleby.

"Oh, we're quite informal here, my lord." She waved a tiny white hand around. The room *was* shabby, with bits and pieces of ribbons, colored

chalks, and picture books everywhere. Felice realized just how shabby and quickly disassociated herself from such pedestrian surroundings. "Oh la,
what you must think. These are temporary quarters only, don't you know, while the Great House"—
that sounded better than the Oaks—"is undergoing
refurbishing. The noise and the dirt would be too
much for dear Lady Jessamyn."

If Felice meant to suggest her own delicate sensibilities, she missed the mark, for Corey's eyes
were not quite so dazzled here in better light, where
that fresh blush on the beauty's cheeks appeared a
trifle too regular. The trance was wearing thin, under a chiming laugh that was beginning to grate on
his nerves like a dinner gong reverberating too
long. The boys had said the mansion was for let,
not under reconstruction, and if any army of servants had been next or nigh either place for months,
he'd eat his hat. Furthermore, who the hell was
this pocket Venus, and what was she doing here?

"If you could just give Lady Ashton my card,
Miss—?"

"Oh dear, how silly of me! I am Felice Bartleby,
Lady Ashton's ward. Actually, I was her sister Judith Morley's ward, and now that I am grown I suppose I no longer fit that description. Perhaps you
have heard of my father, Sir Bostwick Bartleby?
No? He is quite well known in the Crown Colonies.
As soon as he returns we shall be setting up household in London. Mayfair, of course. I'll be sure to
put your name on our list for balls and such." His
lordship did not take up that gambit, so Felice hurried on: "My, you must think me a sad rattle. It's
just so delightful to find a kindred spirit here in the
wilds. I'll take your card right on up to Lady Ashton and see if I cannot find where that naughty butler of ours hides the refreshments a gentleman like
yourself appreciates." She curtsied daintily and
minced out of the room, where she raced down the

hall, viciously kicked a ragdoll out of her way, and took the stairs two at a time.

"How many times do I have to tell you, Melody, my nerves—Oh, it's you, Felice." Lady Ashton stopped trying to hide the flask in the bedclothes. Since it was not yet noon, Lady Ashton was not yet risen. "I thought you were walking to the village to see if the new fashion journals had arrived."

"Yes, but we have a caller. You have to get up and come talk to him. Wait till you see those shoulders. Weston made the jacket, of course. He's divine."

Lady Ashton was studying the card. "Inscoe, Inscoe," she ruminated, tapping the card on her teeth. Jessamyn Ashton knew her Debrett's better than her Bible, and it took only seconds for her to place Lord Coe's family. She threw the card from her as if something with ten legs were climbing across it. "Is the constable with him?"

"No, he's by himself, and so exquisite. Do hurry!"

"Thank heavens he hasn't brought the magistrate down on us. Yet." She burrowed under the covers. "I won't see him."

"You *have* to see him. Otherwise he might go away!" Felice ruthlessly pulled back the sheets.

"Stop that, you ninny. He won't go anywhere. He's Erica Wooster's brother."

"He doesn't seem at all toplofty, and with his reputation he cannot be so particular."

"His reputation ain't to the point, and it's no worse than that of any other handsome and hot-blooded young buck on the town for a few years. These young rakeshames think all is well and good when their own pleasure is at stake, but let there be a hint of scandal near their womenfolk or their fine old family names, and there is hell to pay. No, I won't see any niffy-naffy lordling with his dander up."

"But what shall I tell him?" Felice wailed.

"Tell him ... tell him I am too ill to leave my couch; he has to see Melody. What's that you're doing with the decanters? You're not taking the good stuff? Oh, my heart, a pain right here ..."

Felice tripped back into the sitting room with a hastily assembled tray of Lady Ashton's finest alongside the children's luncheon dessert. She again urged the viscount to sit and take refreshment, for Lady Jessamyn was indisposed, and Miss Ashton was out and about.

"I thought she was on a foxhunt."

A foxhunt, when they hadn't kept more than a dray pony in years? Felice thought furiously, frantic to disinterest him in Melody before that marplot reached home. Not that Miss Bartleby could have anything to worry about. She patted a golden curl. If Lord Coe was one of those sporting-mad gentlemen who admired athletic pursuits in a woman, however, she would quickly disabuse him of that notion. "La, Miss Ashton is only out seeing about supper." There, let him consider Melody the drudge she was becoming.

Good, maybe someone was taking an interest in the children after all, Corey thought, while his palate reflected on the unlikely combination of well-aged sherry and molasses cookies. "I am relieved."

"You are?" Ah, then he was one of those men who believed women were too weak for lively activities and should merely be decorative. There was none weaker nor more decorative than Felice. She lay back on the loveseat and spread her skirts. "Oh, Miss Ashton is a veritable Amazon."

There was something about the way the chit posed herself that set alarm bells ringing in a wary bachelor's head. Coe had recently seen too many predators at Almack's not to recognize a shark circling for the kill.

"How thoughtless of me, Miss Bartleby," he said,

rising. "With Lady Ashton indisposed and the, ah, maids given time off, I should have realized you were unchaperoned. I wouldn't think of jeopardizing your good name, so I'll—"

"No, you mustn't leave!" The teeth were definitely showing. "Silly me. Of course, I knew you were a gentleman so I had nothing to fear, and now your scruples prove it. A woman cannot be too careful though, can she? I'll just go fetch us someone to play dogsberry"—that brittle laugh again—"while you pour yourself another glass."

Nanny was doing the wash in big tubs out back. Mrs. Tolliver and Meggie were up to their eyebrows in flour. Felice shuddered. "Looks like you're it, Ducky."

Ducky had found his calling. He crooned and rocked, ate cookies and drooled. He played with the silverware and sang *duh-duh-duh* to the viscount's pocket watch. He clapped hands and grinned and enchanted the bemused viscount with sticky hugs. There was no chance for suggestive innuendo, no coy flirtation, no accidental touches—the perfect chaperon. Until, that is, a desperate Felice started sneaking Ducky sips of the wine when she thought the viscount was not looking. When Ducky fell asleep on the sofa, his lordship rose to leave, and no protestations of Felice's could keep him. He was worried about his horse, Corey explained, and feared he had taken too much of Miss Bartleby's time as it was. Further, Miss Ashton was sure to be returning soon. Perhaps he would meet up with her on the path.

Felice held her hand out to be kissed. The viscount shook it, firmly.

Corey leaned against a tree, laughing at his escape. What a hurly-burly household it was, and if

79

that chit wasn't destined to be Haymarket ware, his name wasn't Cordell Coe. But it was, he nodded soberly, and he had a job to do. Naturally he felt like a fool doing it, tromping around the sodden woods looking for a woman he'd never met. His pants were muddied, his boots were ruined, his cravat was spotted with grubby fingerprints, and he swore to conclude his mission before luncheon so he would not have to come back to this raree-show another day.

He quickly tired of shouting "Miss Ashton," but he didn't want to startle her unawares at whatever she was doing—hunting mushrooms, the boys must have meant—so he whistled, feeling even more a jackanapes. At least it wasn't raining.

After four days of rain, Melody thought she'd better take Angie hunting before the hound lost whatever meager understanding she possessed about the purpose of the exercise. They had come to terms, more or less. Angie could race around yipping and yapping at anything that caught her fancy, as long as she stayed in view. She could sniff any tree or charge any bush. This took no training whatsoever, being the mutt's natural, ungoverned tendencies. If anything jumped, ran, or flew out of the shrubbery, Melody could shoot it. If the quarry slithered or crawled, Angie could keep it. The unorthodox method required no stealth or subtlety, just Melody's skill.

She had graduated to an old hunting rifle, a cumbersome muzzle-loading affair, which unfortunately had such a recoil that Melody was black and blue from practicing with it. Now she wore her father's dun-colored hunting jacket from the attics, with its extra padding at the shoulder. It didn't matter that the jacket had moth holes, or that it reached her knees and the sleeves had to be cuffed; the important thing was that she was protected

80

from more bruises. She wore an old slouch hat low on her head to keep her hair out of her eyes and unentangled in twigs, and the oldest, sturdiest dress she could find, an old black bombazine mourning gown that used to be Aunt Judith's. Rather than ruin any of her shoes, which were too expensive to replace, Melody wore a pair of scuffed workboots found in the stable. So what if they were too big? Angie didn't care.

The dog loved this game, with all the sights and smells. She woofed for the sheer joy of the thing. Melody kept training the gun just above and ahead of wherever Angie barked, concentrating. The girl knew she was an excellent shot, if she could only lift the heavy weapon, brace herself against the recoil, aim, and shoot in time. She also had to miss the silly dog, naturally. Miss Ashton set her entire mind to the task, blocking out everything but the dog's baying and the trigger.

There, Angie's yapping was frenzied. She must really see or smell something this time, just beyond those trees. Melody had to get nearer. Walking on the damp undergrowth, she raised the rifle, disobeying her own rules about taking a firm stance. Angie kept barking, Melody kept getting closer to those trees. Maybe it was a deer. Heavens, did she want to shoot a deer? Then whatever it was started out from behind the trees. Melody sighted down the barrel and squeezed back on the trigger.

The viscount came into the clearing where a dog was making a racket just in time to see an unholy apparition taking aim, not ten feet away. He did what any intelligent soldier would do: he dove for the ground.

Melody was so startled—it was him, wasn't it?— that she lowered the rifle and took a step back, onto a projecting tree root. Her foot slid, she rocked for balance, the gun went off. The recoil sent Melody flat on her back, the wind knocked out of her.

While she lay there, too dumbfounded to move, if she could, the viscount pulled himself up and stormed over to her. Befogged, she noted his hair was longer than before, likely to cover the scar, and he was not nearly as tan. He had mud in his boots and down his shirt collar and everywhere in between, and he was in a rage, too, towering over her. His face had improved immeasurably, except for the blood dripping from a crease along his cheek, and so had his vocabulary.

Corey did not seem to recognize her yet, which was not surprising in her disheveled state, but no matter, Melody thought, ignoring his tirade. He had come. By some wild and wondrous miracle, by some joyous, stupendous gift of fate, he had searched out her direction and come after her!

And she'd shot him.

Chapter Eleven

He never helped her up, that hurt the most. No, it hurt more that he never recognized her, when Melody believed she would know Lord Corey anywhere. He never assisted her to her feet, like a gentleman would have a lady, and he never waited for Melody to recover her wits enough to beg his pardon or offer to clean his clothes or have Nanny look at the wound. Before she could garble out even one word of apology or welcome, Corey was gone. He shouted back one final, inexplicable curse: "I would rather burn in hell first, madam, but I shall return to the Oaks at eleven o'clock tomorrow morning, and by God, Miss Ashton, either you or that gallows-bait mother of yours had deuced well better be there to receive me." ·

Mama was no help. She went into hysterics at the sight of Melody, ashen-faced and mud-covered. All Lady Ashton could howl was, "We're ruined, we're ruined."

"But, Mama, we were ruined long before I shot him."

Then Lady Jessamyn swooned. Possibly she passed out from the amount of purely medicinal spirits she had been imbibing for her nerves, but it was an honest faint. It took the efforts of Melody, Felice, and Nanny to revive her. Of course, Nanny's advice to prepare a speech for the gibbet did not hurry along the dowager's recovery.

"It was only an accident, Mama. I am sure Lord Coe will understand when he has time to reflect. We'll put on our prettiest gowns and ask cook to prepare a special tea and—"

"You widgeon," Lady Ashton sobbed into her handkerchief. "He's not here for tea! His sister was one of the Dower House sponsors. He's here about the money!"

That was indeed the worst hurt: Corey hadn't come to see Melody at all. He had come to accuse her mother of stealing from orphans. First, Melody felt like crawling under a rock. Then, she wished she *had* shot the bounder—not fatally, of course— for thinking such things of Mama. Finally, Melody decided she would just have to be as calm and dignified as possible on the morrow, composedly explaining the situation and her efforts to rectify it. . . . After a good cry tonight.

Lord Coe arrived in state. The villagers' talk be damned, he decided, and he was well past worrying over what his servants thought, not after arriving back at the inn looking as if he'd been set on by footpads. No loose tongues would wag once they were back in London either, not if his retainers wished to keep their positions. He acknowledged a touch of arrogance in wishing to intimidate these scurrilous females with his consequence, taking extra pains with his apparel, wearing dove-gray pantaloons and a new coat of blue superfine. His cravat was precise without being pretentious, according to his man, Bates, who was still ailing, but the diamond stickpin left no doubt as to his worth. Viscount Coe sat very much on his dignity, which ached after yesterday's debacle. That was the other reason his lordship chose the padded squabs of his carriage over Caesar's saddle. The plaster on his cheek also reminded him of the score to settle.

The stairs were washed and swept and there was Harry, scrubbed to an inch of his life, waiting to open the carriage door, then direct the coachman to the stables. Harry's eyes widened appreciatively at the well-matched bays, but he only touched his forelock to the viscount and stood aside.

Lord Coe's knock was answered immediately by a well-padded woman in spotless apron who curtsied, introduced herself as Mrs. Tolliver, the cook-housekeeper, and announced that Miss Ashton was expecting his lordship in the library, if he would please to follow her.

The hall was sparsely furnished, but someone had gathered armloads of wild lilacs, so the house bore their delicate aroma instead of the stale air of an unoccupied dwelling. Mrs. Tolliver stopped at an open door, announced "Viscount Coe, ma'am," and stood aside for him to enter.

He took two steps in and halted. No, it couldn't be. The exquisite woman rising to greet him, with her hair demurely coiled at the nape of her neck and a soft rose crepe gown . . .

"Angel!" he shouted.

Now the dog, locked safely away in the stable all morning, decamped when Harry opened the door. She raced across the unmowed lawn, through the overgrown herb garden, and in by the kitchen door, looking for her mistress. Then 'Angel!' someone called, and for one of the few times in her life, the hound answered to her name. With enthusiasm. Which left dirt, dog hair, and grass stains up and down the viscount's dove-gray pantaloons, along with a generous sprinkling of what is usually found on a stable floor.

So much for dignity, or Melody's intentions to soothe the viscount to a conciliatory frame of mind. He was in a royal temper, and not over a mere dog.

"You? You're Miss Ashton? Congratulations for making a perfect gull out of me! How could I have believed there was such innocence? You are no more than a lying, cheating bitch!"

"And how could I ever have thought you were a gentleman?" she yelled back. So much for quiet explanations.

"What do you know of gentlemen, you jade? I'll have you know I thought you were too pure to offer a slip on the shoulder!"

"You what?" Melody's screech brought Mrs. Tolliver running with a meat cleaver. She looked from her mistress, eyes flashing sparks from behind the desk, toward the viscount, who was still standing, his hands in fists at his side. The cook raised the knife and narrowed her eyes until Coe took the seat opposite Melody's, the old desk safely between them. When the viscount was settled and nonchalantly picking dog hairs off his jacket, Mrs. Tolliver lowered the weapon.

"I'll be back in a minute with the tea things," she told him. It was a warning, not a promise.

"You what?" Melody hissed as soon as Mrs. Tolliver was gone, leaving the door partly open.

"You heard me. I thought you were a lady. One doesn't make improper offers to females of breeding."

"Of all the disgusting, despicable—Why, I wouldn't accept such an offer if you were the last man on earth!"

"And I wouldn't make it if I were! You'd likely murder me in my bed while we were—"

Mrs. Tolliver brought the tea tray then and stayed to fuss with the dish of buttered scones. "One lump or two, my lord?" Melody asked sweetly.

Her face was flushed, and her hair was coming undone, and her chest was still heaving, and the viscount couldn't help thinking how she would look

86

in his bed after all. He sipped his tea and choked. The minx had put at least four cubes in his cup. Corey smiled for Mrs. Tolliver's benefit; he'd drink the sugary brew if it killed him. Yes, life would be interesting with Angel in his care. She might poison him, but he would never be bored.

"Another biscuit, milord?" Mrs. Tolliver offered.

"Yes, thank you. Delicious," he replied, but he was watching Miss Ashton lick crumbs off her lip, and his smile widened. His Angel, whom he had never managed to put out of his mind, was one and the same as the corrupt, conniving Miss Ashton. A fallen angel, indeed! As soon as this other matter was concluded . . . He replaced his cup on the tray.

Mrs. Tolliver left with a minatory glance at the nob who seemed to be devouring her mistress with his eyes. "I'll be just outside the door, miss."

Melody should not have had the scone, for it was stuck in her throat, or maybe that was a sob. She would not, not ever, cry in front of this imperious, sanctimonious lecher. She reclaimed her self-control, straightened her posture, firmed her chin.

"Now, my lord," she declared coolly, "now that we have positively ascertained that you have not come to Copley-Whitmore to offer me carte blanche, perhaps you will explain exactly why you are here."

"Cut line, ma'am. You know damn well I came for the child."

Whatever Melody might have expected, and truly she was beyond anticipating any of this improbable conversation, that was not it.

"You came to adopt a child?" she asked in disbelief. What would a degenerate seducer want with a child, and how could he think anyone would consider him a fit parent? "Why, pigs would fly before I let you near one of the little ones."

He colored at that, but replied, "Give over, do, Miss Ashton. We both know I don't mean *a* child, I mean *the* child you have in your greedy clutches."

"Greedy? Why, I'll have you know how hard I have been trying. I gave up my—"

One long-fingered hand waved dismissively. "Spare me the histrionics, Miss Ashton. I've seen how you live. I have also met your mother here and there over the years. I do not know what rig you have been running, but you will not get another groat from me or my sister. Nor will there be the least hint of scandal touching my family name."

"Oh, it's fine to drag my name through the dirt as bachelor fare, so long as no mud rubs off on you and yours. Is that it, my lord?"

"No, Miss Ashton, that's not it at all. Your family *has* no name to speak of, unless you consider blackmailer and extortionist enviable designations."

"Blackmail?"

"Please, Miss Ashton, that wide-eyed innocence won't wash; I won't fall for the same faradiddles twice. Now, I am growing weary of these little games, so shall we place our cards on the table? You have in your dubious care a child, a girl, I believe, whose provision my sister has been supporting with, I might add, ample remuneration for your debatable efforts. The point is moot. Such monies were not enough to satisfy you, and you sought to embarrass my family by publishing the child's existence, unless, of course, your silence was rewarded. Have I stated the problem succinctly enough? Here is an equally simple solution: you will hand over the child without any more roundaboutation, or I shall immediately bring charges against you and your mother for extortion, with your own letters as evidence. I believe blackmail is a deportable offense."

Blackmail? Melody sank back in her seat, trying to make sense of his words. That part about extortion had to be an error, a misunderstanding. There was obviously a child, however, whose very being must not be disclosed, or Lord Coe would not be here. The child was plainly a by-blow then, and—Poor Meggie. It had to be the wispy little girl with hair so light she'd reminded Melody of Corey instantly. Meggie's eyes were more turquoisy, she reflected, and the child's makeup held nothing of the rugged vitality of this man who sat at ease across from Melody, idly brushing at his waistcoat, waiting for her reply. How very sad it was for little Meggie to be the unfortunate bastard of such an uncaring, heartless libertine. She would have done better as an orphan.

"Well, Miss Ashton, if you have completed your survey, may I have my answer?"

"No. That is, the answer is no, my lord. I shall not put a small child into your care. Why, I don't think you even know her name."

His lordship looked away from those intent green eyes. "No, that was not in my information."

"It is Margaret. We call her Meggie."

"My mother's name was Margo. Blast it, stop looking at me like that. I did not even know of the chit's existence till two weeks ago!"

Worse and worse. "Let me understand. You abandoned your own flesh and blood like an old hat, letting your sister assume responsibility, and now you think you can just come fetch her as if she were a package lost in transit? And you call me names?"

"Confound it, girl, I am not going to sell my . . . my ward to white slavers, you know! I planned to send—to take her to my sister's old governess in Cornwall."

"Where she will be mewed up with an old woman instead of here, where she has playmates and people who love her. I think not, Lord Coe. Further, you cannot have considered the journey." She knew he hadn't, likely intending to ship a frightened, homesick waif off with servants. "Meggie has a weak chest. Would you know what to do if she

89

started wheezing at night or her lungs became congested?"

She knew dashed well he didn't, the little witch, Corey fumed. Oh, there were hired nursemaids and private physicians, and taking the trip in easy stages, which could take weeks. Weeks in a closed carriage with an ailing, tearful child who would most likely be motion sick the entire journey. Gads, what a coil. Still, he was not leaving any of his kin with these vultures. "I can handle it, Miss Ashton," he blustered. "Just what do you think I am?"

So she told him. She started with reckless reprobate and went on to debauched womanizer, with stops at self-righteous sapskull and buffle-headed bounder. She was paying him back for all of his hateful accusations and disrespect and a few shattered dreams.

The viscount responded in kind, to the mayhem this woman had brought into his life, as well as a few disillusions of his own. They were both on their feet shouting. Miss Ashton was pounding the shaky, old desk and ranting about kettle-calling, and his lordship was wringing an imaginary neck between his hands, raving about bedlamites and blood money.

Mrs. Tolliver slammed a tray of wine bottles and glasses on the desk between them and stood there glowering. "The twins have more decorum than you two," she muttered. "Lucky for you Nanny's not here. You're not too old to have your mouth washed out with soap, either of you. Such talk, Miss Melody!" She crossed her hands over her chest and positioned herself near the door, obviously on guard duty.

His lordship was restored to better humor by the humbling effect of old retainers, that and Miss Ashton's mortification at being caught out as a fishwife. She was blushing furiously, starting just above the rose crepe gown's neckline.

"So your name is Melody," he said pleasantly,

when he could tear his eyes away. "I wondered. Angel doesn't seem quite appropriate, under the circumstances."

"My name is Miss Ashton," she snapped back.

Corey raised one eyebrow in mild rebuke. He was doing *his* part to make polite conversation for her employee's benefit. He lifted his glass. "Melody suits you."

"Not at all, my lord." He wanted polite conversation; he would get polite conversation. "It was a conceit of my father's, who fancied he heard a nightingale sing on the day of my birth. I must be content he did not name me for the bird." She sipped her wine. "I myself have no talent in that direction. I was never permitted to sing in choir and was always delegated page turner at instrumental recitals. So you see, my lord," she said triumphantly, "you do not know me at all. Your impressions are quite, quite wrong. As are your accusations. You have tried and convicted me without a hearing. If it were up to you, I would hang."

"No, ma'am, hanging's too good for you." Then he raised his hand. "But hold, let us not go round Robin's barn again. I hoped to resolve this matter with the least bother to everyone, but I see it will have to be decided by cooler heads. There is a simple question of who has legal right to the child. I'll have my man-at-law look into it, and recommend you do the same." Now victory was his, Corey was sure. The weight of justice almost always came down on the side of money, power, and prestige. "I am confident they will find that no magistrate in his right mind would name a skitter-witted shrew and a schoolroom miss as legal guardians to helpless babes."

"And I am equally as certain no one would entrust the care of a guileless child to a—"

Mrs. Tolliver cleared her throat and jerked her head toward the door. The conversation was over.

Chapter Twelve

*M*ama was wrought. Not distraught or over-wrought, just wrought. "Do you mean all this time no one thought I was misusing the donations? And here I've fretted myself to flinders over nothing."

"Mama, blackmail isn't nothing." They were in Lady Ashton's bedroom, and for a change Melody was limp on the chaise after the morning's encounter with Lord Coe, while her mother paced in agitation.

"But I didn't do it, you goose. And how anyone could have thought I would is beyond me. Why, I've had more family skeletons locked away here than many a crypt, with nary a sound of rustling bones heard in the ton. I suppose that's why Lady Pa—ah, Lady Smith cut me dead at the Arbuckles' affair. After that a lot of my friends would not recognize me. I'll just have to write to Lady, ah, Smith and tell her that her little secret, or secrets, are safe with me."

"So the twins are bastards, too?" Melody asked weakly.

"Love children, dear, not that nasty term. And

the twins were to be the tokens of affection presented to a very famous general by his fond, but childless, wife. Unfortunately, the twins' conception did not quite correspond to the general's leave time, and the lady feared he would not appreciate the effort made on his behalf. One child perhaps, but two . . ."

Melody fanned herself with an issue of *La Belle Assemblée* nearby. Much more of this and she would be helping herself to the cordials. "Mama, are none of the orphans, ah, orphans?"

Lady Ashton stopped at her mirror to think, checking for new wrinkles. "We did have a boy once whose parents both died in an influenza epidemic. His grandfather didn't want a child around. I suppose he was the only true orphan."

"Then all of the others are love children?"

"Why, no. Ducky isn't, for one. He's a duke. Why do you think Nanny calls him Ducky?"

"Mama, have you been at the decanters so early this morning?"

"Well, he would have been. He could never have taken on the duties, however. Could you see Ducky in ermine at court? His parents had him declared incompetent and disinherited in favor of the younger son. All legal and all very quiet, and happy they were to get rid of him.

"Pip has quite legitimate parents, also, although I cannot consider them natural parents. We are used to dear Pip by now, of course, but he really is disfigured, you know. His mother took one look at the infant and went into strong hysterics. She said it was a mark of the Devil and refused to keep him. How one can refuse one's own flesh and blood is beyond belief. But she made her husband's life so miserable, down on her knees night and day, that he finally brought the baby to Judith."

There was a catch in Melody's voice as she asked, "Does Pip know?"

"Yes, his father told him. The man used to come visit. He'd cry and carry on about wanting his son at home, and then cross himself. Judith told him to send the checks instead."

"Good for Aunt Judith! But Mama, Aunt Judith was always such a high-stickler, how could she have, you know, taken in the by-blows?"

"Look at that, another gray hair. All this worrying is sending me to an early grave, Melody. What was that? Oh, the children. Well, Judith already had Felice, as a favor to the nabob. The mother left her on Barty's doorstep before joining a traveling company. He couldn't take a babe to India, naturally, and his family had just disowned him. As for the other children, it wasn't *their* fault, you know, that they should suffer for their mamas', um, minor indiscretions. Judith saw it as an act of philanthropy, as long as the children were handsomely provided for, of course. I mean, we could not afford to be that generous. The Dower House children were lucky in that their mothers chose to see them well cared for, if out of sight."

"Oh, so you and Aunt Judith were providing a public service?"

"Sarcasm is not becoming, Melody. We did nothing to be ashamed of, and we did find as many real homes for them as we could. Do you think the children would have done better in foundling homes? Infants there rarely make their first birthday; if they do, they are turned into thieves and pickpockets. What of a child like Harry, who was the chance product of a thunderstorm and a handsome Irish groom? Would you see him sold to a sweep or apprenticed in a mine? Should Meggie have been given to gypsies just because she was born on the wrong side of the blanket? And even Ducky, with his parents married at St. George's, in front of the entire beau monde, he would have ended up in Bedlam, or kept behind locked doors, if not for us."

"But couldn't their mothers keep them? Some of them?"

"Don't be naive, Melody. We are talking about well-born ladies, not peasant girls whose fathers find them a husband with the aid of a pitchfork. Ladies don't have a lot of options. Peers want their titles passed through their own bloodlines, not an Irish groom's. And if an unmarried woman is considered even slightly fast, she will never get a respectable offer."

Melody understood that fact all too well, not that she would ever tell Mama about her very dishonorable offer. She would have spasms for sure. "It's all so sad."

"Should the children never have been born, then? Or should moonlings like Ducky be put out for the wolves like the Romans did? Or was that the Greeks? I've never been sure, and I do not think there are any wolves in England anyway. No, high-bred ladies are permitted their genteel riding accidents, of course, but accidents cannot be counted on to cure all of these, ah, indispositions. The muslin company is luckier. They seem to have apothecaries and physicians who . . ." Lady Ashton finally realized she was talking to her own chaste young daughter who should know nothing of such matters. Of course, if other chaste young maidens knew a little more . . . "No matter. We were able to see to the ladies' needs: give them a nice quiet spot where they could say they were visiting a sick relative, and then assure them that their infants and their guilty secrets were both safe. Until now."

Lady Ashton had found a wrinkle that needed attention; she sat at her dressing table trying to decide which lotion to apply. It was Melody's turn to pace.

"So who do you think is sending demand letters to the parents? For that matter, who else had the information?" Melody was positive she could not clear their name without finding the one responsible. She didn't care if there was never another donation, and heaven knew they did not need any more "orphans." But, and it was a very important but, she just had to prove a certain judgmental viscount wrong.

According to Lady Ashton, Mr. Hadley held most of the legal documents, but he had been offering to lend money this age, rather than trying to collect his modest fees. Mama even suspected him of once having a secret *tendre* for her sister Judith. One could just as likely suspect Nanny or Mrs. Tolliver, which is to say, not at all. Both formidable women had been with the family forever, and both had pensions from Judith Morley put away for their old age, which was now. They chose to stay on out of love or duty, assuredly not for the profits. As for the orphans, and Melody refused to think of them any other way, they had the most to lose by such a scheme. Perhaps a maid had come upon Lady Ashton's records while cleaning, Melody suggested, and thought to better her position in the world by bargaining with the information. But Lady Ashton rejected the idea: the maids were all local girls who could not read. Besides, there were no records as such; Lady Ashton kept most of it in her head, to Melody's dismay. If Mama kept emptying wine bottles at such a rate, either the whole county and half of the next would be knowing her secrets, or they would be lost forever. Hopefully fuller documentation was kept with Mr. Hadley—and maybe some less scrupulous person in that office had access to them. Melody would have to check.

"Someone like Edwin? Hadley's been hiring Dower House boys since the start.

"Don't take on so, Melody. I'll simply write to all of the sponsors. We'll be merry as grigs in no time, and we can start planning your come out."

Somehow Melody did not think it would be quite that easy, not if any of the other patrons were anything like Viscount Coe. Which reminded her that she still had to deal with that implacable, infuriating gentleman.

"Mama," she asked, "who *is* legal guardian to the children? I'll go speak to Mr. Hadley tomorrow—you said he had papers and things drawn up—but can the viscount take Meggie?"

"Guardian? Let me see ... Judith used to have the children named her wards, so I suppose I inherited them along with the Oaks and the dower house. Later I recall Hadley suggesting a man be appointed as trustee, so I believe we entered Bartleby's name. I can't be sure. You know I am not good on details. Quite frankly, the issue has never come up. No one ever wanted one of the brats back."

Mama was fatigued after writing two letters. "Be a dear, Melody, and run these into the village. I want them to go out with the afternoon post. I shall complete more after my nap."

Melody wanted nothing more than to take a page from Lady Ashton's book and lie down with a damp cloth over her eyes. If she couldn't see the confusion around her, maybe it would go away. No such luck. Lady Ashton was suddenly concerned that the letters might go astray, that some miscreant would read the addresses. Previously she had entrusted the mail to the children, or Cook, or any passing carter making deliveries. No more.

So Melody trudged into town. The dog, Angie, followed behind her, still in disgrace. "No, you cannot come. Go home. Bad dog."

So the dog slunk along, further back, until she spotted a way to regain her favored post. What would appease Mistress more than supper, laid right at her feet? Unfortunately Angie's choice of easy pickings had other ideas. The prey, Mrs. Donzell's fat, furry, and much loved Persian cat, was sitting in the sun on the basket of folded laundry, while Mrs. Donzell hung a fresh batch.

So Angie had a row of claw marks across her snout, Mrs. Donzell had to do the entire day's washing over, and Melody had to promise one of the young porkers in recompense.

Harry secreted the squealing piglet away in a sack while the twins were at lessons, but Pip had been too diligent in teaching them their numbers. Laura and Dora were all set to raise a search party to scour the woods for their missing charge; Melody considered letting them go, then decided she couldn't be so craven. With great diplomacy and more trepidation, she explained about the cat, the wash, the damage. The dog and cat fight couldn't come close in volume or intensity to the twin tantrums Miss Ashton was subjected to. She only wished Mrs. Donzell were here to toss dirty wash water over these two creatures. Finally she had the girls quiet enough to listen to her speech that the pigs were, after all, not pets but a commodity. Everyone at Dower House depended on them, Melody said, and Laura and Dora nodded calmly.

Until Mrs. Tolliver announced ham sandwiches for lunch.

Like Chinese torture, the day kept dripping down more woes.

"I have settled with Mrs. Donzell, Mr. Pike," Melody told the constable when he caught up with her while she was checking on the hens, "so there was no reason for you to make the call."

The scurvy little man's watery eyes lit up. "More trouble with the dog, eh? I'll be having you up on charges of harboring a dangerous animal, I will."

Melody sighed wearily. "In faith, Mr. Pike, have you nothing better to do than harass honest citizens?"

"Honest, is it?" he needled, wiping his nose on

the back of his sleeve. "Honest folks don't go around shooting peers of the realm."

"Did that dastard bring charges then? I'll counter with trespassing, and—"

"Not yet he didn't, although there be a lot of talk Hazelton way." Pike laid his hand on her arm. "I just thought I'd renew my offer, put in a good word with the magistrate for you, don't you know."

Melody looked down at his hand, with its dirty, chewed fingernails and grime-encrusted knuckles. She spoke slowly: "Mr. Pike, if you and your filth are not out of here instantly, I shall go to the magistrate myself. I am sure Uncle Charles will be interested to learn how the county's business is conducted."

"Uncle Charles, is it?" he groused, but the hand was removed before another foul breath passed his lips. "You think to impress me, miss? Well, you won't get around old Frederick Pike so easy. I know what's what, and I knows you ain't above the law. Your fancy airs ain't worth pig swill. What'd you think, your ma found you under a cabbage patch? You're just another of the freaks and bastards she keeps around the place, and no better'n you should be."

If Melody had just slapped the makebate, she would have brushed through. Heaven knew the loose screw had been slapped many a time. What made it worse, and made Frederick Pike her enemy for life, was that she smacked him in full sight of Harry and Pip and Meggie. They could not hear the awful words, but they certainly had a good view of her hand flying forward, his head snapping back, and his rat-colored wig flying into the chicken coop.

Chapter Thirteen

Long journeys could be conducive to deep think-ing, especially if the carriage was well sprung and comfortable, the scenery was monotonous, and one's traveling companion had all the conversation of a plaster saint. Viscount Coe's man, Bates, wore the same long-suffering expression of many a martyr, but not a word of complaint would pass his lips. He would not mention two complete sets of fine cloth-ing, ruined, nor the boots he'd labored so lovingly over, destroyed, nor all of the extra work involved for a loyal retainer just up from his sickbed. Bates would certainly not comment on his employer's dis-tressing habit of having his face rearranged, nor the viscount's failure to discuss the circumstances of the past days with his devoted, faithful aide. There being nothing else on Bates's mind, however, he sat like a carving.

The viscount had a great deal on his mind, and except for an occasional sigh or sniffle from the wounded valet, he was free to let his thoughts wander. The coach headed toward London; Corey's thoughts wended back to Copley-Whitmore.

Melody. It did suit her. She was like a song that kept repeating in his head. He might not like the tune, nor admire its lyrics or tempo, but he could not forget it. The vision of an angel tenderly wiping his forehead fought with the picture of the fierce Miss Ashton nearly blowing his head off. She was magnificent in a rage, all fire and cutting ice, and she was adorable pretending to be a lady presiding at tea. A contrary animal, was his Miss Melody Ashton. Corey smiled, for there was no doubt about it, Miss Ashton was destined to be his. He could finally admit to the thoughts he'd held all along, from the first moment he had seen her at Barstow's inn: the viscount wanted that young beauty the way he'd wanted his first pony, with every fiber of his being. And now she could be his.

Lord Coe was not sure how he was to accomplish it, with so many guardians protecting the treasure. A man did not usually have to worry about seducing a woman with her mother nearby, much less a cook and a nanny, but he would do it. After all, Melody was not in any position to refuse. She had no name, no money, no future but hardship, and without his protection could be sent to gaol at any time.

Corey was not quite as certain of Melody's guilt as he had been. Oh, she had to be involved in the skullduggery to some extent, but she either had to be a consummate actress or the world's most inept blackmailer, and Lord Coe had difficulty believing either. Miss Ashton had to have known he would come down hard for possession of the child, but she never even opened negotiations. And there was that crack-brained notion of hers that the chit was his by-blow. A lot of men left their butter stamp around the countryside—not that he was one of them—without society's reproach and without their sisters

101

paying leech fees on them, to Corey's sure knowledge. Only a moralist or an innocent would have thought otherwise. Corey smiled again. Or a woman who had already been approached by a—what had she called him?—a vile seducer. He hadn't disabused her of either opinion, his pursuit or his paternity. The first was obvious, and the second was insurance if by some improbable odds Miss Ashton really was unaware of Meggie's parentage.

No child of his would ever be called by such a common-sounding name. Meggie suited an upstairs maid. Margaret was more fitting for a nobleman's daughter, and that's what Lord Coe would call the lass when he went back to fetch her. But what in bloody hell did he know about children anyway, and sickly ones at that? Corey congratulated himself that he hadn't done too shabbily with Ducky—talk about names for aristocratic offspring!—and he had actually enjoyed horse-mad Harry and serious Philip. Maybe children were not such an affliction after all. Even the impish little twins were appealing, making him regret not having a glimpse of his new ward. Erica would have wanted to know, he convinced himself. Of course, he would never tell his sister the chit was frail. He'd say she was delicate and sweet and pretty, but lively, just the way he imagined a daughter should be, now that he was imagining. If a man were to have a daughter, of course. Getting Margaret to Cornwall was still no attractive prospect, but a son of his own mightn't be such a bad idea, someday.

The trip to Cornwall might not look inviting, but the return to Copley-Whitmore did. As usual these days, Corey's mind quickly reverted to thoughts of Melody. As soon as he had papers in hand to guarantee Margaret's future under his protection, he'd see about offering a different type of protection to Miss Ashton.

Perhaps he should bring a gift when he returned,

something unexceptional for the mother's sake, to show that it was possible he had been overhasty in his judgments. It was premature for the emeralds those green, green eyes demanded. Lord Coe smiled on his side of the carriage, picturing Melody decked in emeralds and little else.

There, look at him grin, Bates grumbled to himself, sitting stoically rigid on the other seat. He's likely figuring a way to destroy more of his fine clothes.

Lord Coe's solicitor was not encouraging about speeding up the wheels of justice.

"No, a woman cannot adopt a child, or be named as trustee for a minor if property is involved. However, a man need only be named for the courts while the female is de facto guardian. Often the male dies, and no substitute is named. The courts are very overburdened with these matters, you must know. If there are no complaints, there is no inquiry.

"However," he went on, "in the hypothetical case you mentioned, there may or may not be accurate and complete filings whatsoever. Highly irregular situation from the start. I would have to direct a clerk to wade through court documents of the year and month in question. You don't have those details, my lord, for the, ah, hypothetical infant? In that case, I would send a man to the county of residence to search parish records, barring, of course, the cooperation of the *litage's* man-at-law. This could take time."

"If your man finds that the woman in question does have some trumped-up right to the child, how can that be overturned? Assuming for the sake of discussion, of course, that the person seeking custody is a legitimate relative of the child. Legitimate may be the wrong word. Blood kin, then."

"Quite, quite. Nearly every decision of the courts can be reversed, but often at unforeseen expense."

"Dash it, I'm not a nipfarthing! That is, the hypothetical gentleman does not consider the price of moral justice."

"Forgive me, Lord Coe, I had not meant mere financial expense, although justice is often hurried along by such means. I was thinking of the personal cost. If the gentleman in question were to present such papers to the higher court, seeking to rescind a legal adoption, there would have to be just cause, charges of neglect or whatever, an examination, proof of his prior claim, et cetera. There would be no way to keep said gentleman's name out of the public eye. The press, you know. I don't think that's what you want."

"B'gad, no!"

"Then I suggest I send a man to ascertain the details, and feel out the possibility of quiet negotiations."

Quiet negotiations, with Miss Ashton? Crocodile-legged sofas would get up and walk away first. Coe wished the man luck.

"I'm sure we can have the matter neatly wrapped up in, say, a month, my lord."

Coe gave him two weeks and left.

Two weeks before he would see ... the child, of course. Two weeks in London at the height of the Season, acquaintances everywhere, entertainments and invitations too numerous to count, and Lord Coe had nothing to do. Idly, he directed the coachman to drive to Kensington, too abstracted to recall that he'd given Yvette her *congé* and was now keeping a pretty little ladybird in rooms off King Street.

"But *mon cher*, you give Yvette permission to stay on here another month, *non*? Ah, you've changed your mind and wish Yvette to remain, *oui*?"

Non. But Corey could not come right out and say he'd forgotten and arrived in Kensington out of habit, not after Yvette's new protector had left in such a hurry, diving out the back door when Coe stepped through the front. Some protector. Now that Corey did remember dismissing Yvette, he also recalled leaving her a handsome enough parting gift that she need not settle for such a paltry fellow. He felt less gauche.

"I, ah, just wanted to talk. Is that all right?" He fully intended to pay for her time.

"Talk? You want to talk to Yvette?" She shrugged. One received strange requests in her line of work. "But of course, *cheri*, now that you have chased away that *chien*, what else is there to do?" She languidly bestowed herself on the divan, allowing the neckline of her robe to fall open. Not that the frothy, pink garment concealed much of Yvette's charms anyway, being nearly transparent.

Coe expected to be interested, and wasn't, to his own surprise. He still wanted to know her opinions, however, on matters about which he definitely could not approach females of his own class. It occurred to him that, man of the world or not, he was woefully ignorant about certain facts of life. "Yvette, what would you do if you found yourself with child?"

She looked at him as if he'd grown another head. *"Enceinte, moi?* With your child?"

"No, no, just a hypothetical child."

"Me, I do not know this hypothetical."

"Um, just the child of any man, no one in particular," Corey explained.

Yvette drew herself up, and her robe closed. "Me, I always know the man. I am not, how do you say, Covent Garden ware, going with any man for the price." Her price just went up.

"My pardon, *cherie*. What if, then, it were my child, or the man who just left? What would you do?"

"Me, I would not be such an *imbecile* in the first

105

place. But if, yes, if such a thing should happen, *incroyable*, I would take care of it."

"But would you discuss it with me, with the father? Would you hold him responsible?"

Yvette laughed. "Ah, finally I see. Some *jeune fille* is looking to net the so-handsome, so-wealthy *vicomte*. That is the oldest trap since the apple, *non*? No, *monsieur*, Yvette would not lay such a snare. That is not what you English call pound dealing, *n'est-ce-pas*? If I found myself in such a temporary embarrassment, I might ask *monsieur* for assistance, since you have been so generous, but no, I think not even then. I would simply get rid of *l'enfant* as soon as possible, if not before. A woman in my position cannot afford to lose her looks or so much of her time. The gentlemen, they forget, you see, if a woman goes visiting away too long. But no, no, and no, I would not spread a noose for one such as you, demanding marriage. Yvette knows the rules."

"Then I would never know?" Somehow the idea did not sit well with him.

"But what's to know? *Un homme* comes to Yvette for pleasure, not morning sickness and the shape of a cow. He has a wife for that. *Alors*, enough of this so-foolish talk you call hypothetical. Yvette is much better at the pleasure, *oui*?"

Oui, but not today.

Two weeks in town. Lord Coe had dinner at his club, checked the betting book to make sure his name wasn't in it, heard the latest *on dits*, and was happy his name wasn't among those either. Later he went to the opera, where his newest mistress—there, he recognized her in the first row of dancers—curtsied to his box during the tenor's solo. The bucks in the pit whistled till he bowed, and the turbanned dowager in the next box clucked her disapproval. "Disgusting," she declared loudly to the younger woman next to her, a washed-out wisp of

106

a thing in a faded gown that advertised a poor relation or a paid companion.

So Corey bowed to the matron and blew a kiss to the companion. After that they left him alone with his thoughts: of men like apes beating their chests, flaunting their possession of women, of women who had no knowledge of love, and women who had too much. He thought of men who craved heirs and begot bastards, and women who threw out children like the trash, women who feared losing their looks, ladies who feared losing their reputations, and a girl who truly seemed to care about the innocent ones. He thought about the children.

Dammit, why should he wait two weeks? He could help the solicitor's man check records, he could help sweet-talk the Ashtons into parting with Margaret. What a brilliant idea, and the one he wanted all along!

Corey almost convinced himself that he should be in Copley-Whitmore for the child's sake; it was his duty to ensure her welfare. Never before had duty and desire combined so happily

He left the opera house after leaving a check with the stageman. His mistress would understand. The green-eyed dasher could dance, but he bet she could not fire a rifle.

Bates was muttering over the packing—doubles of everything if they were going back to that hellhole—when the anguished letter came. Coe's sister, Erica, was in despair at not hearing from him and had decided to take matters into her own hands, despite his orders to stay away. The peagoose was going to Copley-Whitmore. She was leaving Bath in ten days. Blast, he had enough to worry over without another totty-headed female on his hands. She would only be overemotional about the child, possibly growing attached to the chit, and her very presence in that vicinity could give rise to the same conjecture he was trying to avoid. In addition, having his sister about would certainly cramp Lord Coe's efforts in Miss Ashton's direction. The mother and nanny and cook were bad enough.

Erica was usually the most biddable of females, Corey reflected, until she dug her heels in. Only once before had she disregarded his advice and look where that got her. Perhaps his advice hadn't been so fine, landing her with that mawworm Wooster, but Corey was young then and had done his best to see her settled before he had to join his cavalry unit. Age and good intentions were no excuses, he knew, and by Jupiter he was trying to make that up to her—if she would only stay out of it!

There was no dissuading her, Coe knew, although he wrote an impassioned letter anyway. Damn, she would be singled out in that backwoods neighborhood of dubious repute like a goldfish in a bowl of guppies ... unless Corey managed to muddy the waters. He interrupted Bates to order out his evening clothes.

There must be hunting or fishing, and assemblies at Hazelton, and picnics ... He could invite the Cheynes and the Tarnovers for respectability. Lady Tarnover had a stepbrother in politics. There was that prosy bore Pendleton, and Major Peter Frye, Coe's good friend, could be counted on to do the pretty. Frye had a ne'er-do-well cousin who was always on repairing leases. The basket scrambler would be sure to dangle after Felice and her tales of the nabob's money. Corey wondered who else might be at White's, who else would be interested in his sister or a fortnight's house party at a decrepit estate on the way to nowhere.

That climber Lady Ashton would be delighted with the company, Harry would be thrilled with all the horses, and Miss Ashton would be livid, which would be nothing new. No matter, Corey would have nearly a month to bring her round. Just in time for that little house in Kensington to be vacant again!

Chapter Fourteen

"*You* want *how* much for this wreck of a place, Miss Ashton? Perhaps you misunderstood me. I only wish to rent the Oaks for a month, not purchase it."

"I understood your wish, my lord, but not your reason. If you think to turn my family home into a place for your . . . your orgies, I won't have it."

"Miss Ashton, when I choose to hold an orgy, you will be the first to know."

Melody's furious blush reminded the viscount he had vowed not to rush his fences with her. "But the Oaks will take an additional outlay to bring it to the standards of a gentleman's residence."

"Gentleman, hah!" That was eloquent enough of Melody's opinion of the devilish rogue in front of her, his pale hair slightly tousled from the ride, his teeth gleaming in a bright smile, and his slightly crooked nose adding even more character to a face that—No, Miss Ashton told herself. This will never do. "The price is firm."

Lord Coe also recalled he had vowed not to lose

his temper with the prickly wench. "Very well, ma'am, I accept your terms, but it is highway robbery."

"Ah, that was one of the few crimes of which you have yet to accuse me. Let me see, there was lying, cheating, blackmail, wantonness, and attempted murder. Am I next to be called traitor to king and country?"

"I don't know. Have you been selling state secrets to eke out the egg money?"

"My lord, I don't know any state secrets, and I do not know what you are doing here." Melody had received the infuriating man's note asking to call, and she had met him outside, intending to be courteous but brief. Meggie had a legal male guardian, such as he was: old Toby had put his *X* on the paper under Mr. Hadley's signature. This blackguard standing close to her—too close—on the Oaks' front steps, dressed to the nines and obviously determined to tease her out of the sullens, was not entitled to Meggie, nor to any of Miss Ashton's good humor.

"I told you, I was concerned for the child's welfare."

"Gammon. The child is six years old, and you have never given a ha'penny's thought to her before."

"Ah, but you yourself reminded me so charmingly of my responsibilities." His smile broadened. "Furthermore, I did wish to apologize for that other day. Some of my charges may have been unfounded, some of my words hasty."

Some? Unfortunately, Melody had to admit that some were likely all too true. He was certainly being noble about it; she could be no less a lady. "And I, too, owe you an apology. It seems there may indeed be something untoward going on, so your concern was—is—understandable. Please be assured

110

that my mother and I had no knowledge of such a scheme, and we are trying to take steps."

His blue eyes fairly sparkled. "There, I knew we could see eye to eye about something! Now if we are decided that you aren't a blackmailer, and I am not a debaucher"—he thought he heard Melody mutter something about that wasn't what she'd decided at all—"might we call a truce and go inside where we could be more comfortable while we let the solicitors handle the question of the child? I really would like to discuss my plans for the house and enlist your aid in a scheme of my own."

Outside in the fresh air was close enough for Melody's comfort, but she could not continue to be so ragmannered in the face of his polished charm. She led the way to the library, and Angie came gamboling after the viscount.

Mindful of his buff kerseymere breeches, and Bate's sorrowful demeanor on learning his master's destination, the viscount commanded, "Down, sir!" in his best battalion voice.

"It's a female," Melody corrected.

"Figures," Corey replied, but his grin overrode the insult.

They were both amazed when the hound actually stopped frolicking around and flopped herself down at Lord Coe's feet. Impressed despite herself, Melody offered the viscount a glass of wine, and he drank in the sight of her in a muslin gown embroidered with violets, gracefully pouring. Her chestnut hair was neatly, severely bound; how he wished to see it loose and flowing down her back. Melody could feel his gaze bringing a warm flush to her cheeks, so she hurriedly took her seat behind the desk, folding her hands in front of her primly, expectantly. Neither one noticed the dog at Corey's feet, contentedly chewing the gold tassels off the lord's brand-new Hessian boots.

"You were going to tell me about a plan of yours,

my lord? One that might conceivably explain your wishing to rent the Oaks."

Corey admired how she looked him directly in the eye. For such a young chit she was remarkably self-assured. Of course, Mrs. Tolliver was likely nearby with a cast-iron frying pan. He smiled lazily. "I don't suppose you would swallow a tale about my appreciation for the scenery around here or my need to rusticate?"

Knowing from Felice that he was the *compleat* London beau and from her mother how many country estates of his own he had? Not likely. Melody tried to raise one eyebrow in mocking imitation of his own expression, and only succeeded in scrunching her face and making him laugh. It was a very nice laugh. Her own spirits lightened at the sound.

"There, I've made you smile," he said, as if he cared. "Very well, my sister wishes to see the child she has been supporting all these years. You'll acknowledge her right?"

"Gladly, and I would be happy to express my appreciation for her generosity and beg her pardon that someone has been trying to intimidate her. I am sure my mother would second that and extend an invitation, too. There is no need for you to lease the house." Or cut up Melody's peace, but she did not express that last thought.

"My sister has been blue-deviled lately, and I thought to invite other friends to keep her company, a regular house party, in fact."

"Here, with the children?" Melody remembered Pike's reaction to the orphans, terming them freaks and bastards; she was still agonizing over his specific insults to her. No one would do that to her charges. "I will not have the children laughed at or made the butt of tasteless jokes."

"And I would not have friends who did. There are members of the ton more eccentric and less amiable than Ducky, and many whose parentage does not

112

bear inquiry. You need not be such a tigress, rushing to the defense of her cubs. No one shall harm them. You have my word on that."

Why Melody should trust him was a mystery, but she did. In this, at least. She was not so sure about others of his motives, which prompted her to ask, "And this scheme of yours?"

"Requires your help, and that of the children, of course." He steepled his fingers beneath his chin and spoke in a low, confiding voice. "You see, I wish to find my sister a new husband and need to know if the prospective brothers-in-law like children. I thought to invite some eligible bachelors here, to gauge their reactions. Someone, I don't know who, said you could learn a lot about a man by watching how he treats children and d—Blast this mangy mutt! Look at my boots! Of all the poorly trained, evil-minded—I've a good mind to—"

"Children and . . . ?" she asked, laughing, and was pleased to see his anger turn to chagrin and then to the good humor that etched lines on his tanned cheeks and made his eyes sparkle. They both agreed the gentlemen would have ample testing ground. His lordship was willing, naturally, to pay for Angie's services as part of the experiment, once the hound had worked off her debt to his man, Bates.

"I am afraid poor Angie will be trying your sister's likely suitors for years, Lord Coe. But if I may ask, has Lady Wooster no preference in this matter?"

Interestingly enough, Corey felt like confiding in Miss Ashton, the same woman whom he had castigated as a lying jade not ten days ago. He did go on to tell about his sister, four year his junior, and how at an early age she had fallen in love with a soldier. Erica's soldier was a penniless second son with no prospects, except an imminent recall to service on the Peninsula. Lord Coe had found the two

113

together—Corey did not mention that he'd found them on the road to Scotland—and sent the young man off with a flea in his ear. The soldier was reported dead or missing shortly thereafter. Inconsolable, Erica went into a decline until a desperate Lord Coe sent her to visit her old governess in Cornwall, for he had to rejoin his own unit.

On Corey's next leave, Erica seemed apathetic, but resigned. She agreed to marry the man of her brother's choice, a solid, wealthy member of Parliament, an older gentleman who would cure her of those romantic flights and see to her welfare. Wooster turned out to be an ogre, who furthermore never gave Erica the children she craved. The only favor he did her was in dying of an apoplexy four years later.

"That was over a year ago, and now that she is out of mourning I want to make it up to her. I have invited an earl, a war hero, and a rising politico, all with impeccable lineage, substantial incomes, spotless reputations."

"But what about love?" Melody wanted to know. "Is there no place for that?"

"My dear, she is a woman of twenty-four summers, not that starry-eyed chit. She has had six or seven years since her childish infatuation, and she's shown no preference for anyone."

"But she was married for four of those years."

"What's that to say to the point? Don't be naive, Miss Ashton. Women of her class"—Melody noted he did not say "your class" or "our class"—"often find love outside of marriage."

"And that doesn't bother you? You would countenance her taking a lover, rather than marrying below her?"

"It's the way of the world, my dear."

It was tragic, that's what it was, and not just for this hard-hearted man's unfortunate sister. Melody vowed to befriend Lady Wooster and defend her against her brother's machinations, if the lady could not like any of his choices.

But what of Melody herself? Every word Corey spoke, every arrogant, aristocratic pronouncement of what was suitable for his family, cut like a knife into Melody's soul. Here he was, laughing with Melody, confiding in her, treating her like a friend, like an equal. But they were not equals and neither, it seemed, could forget that. Melody had no fortune or standing in the ton, her family name was stained with scandal, and now there were doubts about her origins. Oh, she'd hurried to Aunt Judith's family Bible as soon as Pike left, and found her birthday properly recorded. Was she truly going to be eighteen next month? She felt like eighty. But there it was, in Aunt Judith's firm hand. She was not just a foundling from the wayside. There was, however, no record of her parents' marriage. Melody knew there had been a runaway match—everyone seemed to know that—but was there never a wedding to legitimize her parents' love? She couldn't come right out and ask, Mama, did you ever marry my father? so she checked the local church registry one day when she brought flowers for the altar. Nothing. That's what she could hope for from Lord Coe and his sweet, teasing smile: nothing.

Melody was wrong, of course. Seeing shadows come to her eyes and detecting a quiver in her voice when she asked if he would like tea, the viscount was disturbed. He tried joking about the dog, enlisting Miss Ashton's sympathy for his sister, eliciting her advice about readying the Oaks. All he got was cast-down looks, monosyllabic replies, and deference to his wishes, no spark, no lilting laughter, no dimple. This quiet, humble, courteous Miss Ashton was not at all to Corey's liking. She even put the correct lump of sugar in his tea when Mrs. Tolliver brought the tray, nodded, and left. Was

Melody sad to think of strangers in her home? Was she shy about meeting the socialites he'd invited?

When Melody asked if he would like more tea, he absently nodded and held his cup out for her to refill. She had to come around the desk and stand close to him, where he could look up into her melancholy eyes. Hell and damnation, he hated that shattered look!

Therefore, while Melody poured, Lord Coe said, "You know, Angel, if you've had second thoughts about leasing the house, my previous offer still stands."

That was what Miss Ashton could expect from Lord Coe: a slip on the shoulder. She kept pouring the hot tea, while Corey was absorbed in watching the changes of expression flicker across her face, the brows gather, the green sparks shoot from her eyes, the lower lip thrust out. He kept watching. Melody kept pouring: over the brim, over the saucer, over his lap.

Bates was going to be *so* pleased. There was nothing to dampen a gentleman's ardor more than damp nether garments, especially on a long ride on horseback to a disapproving valet who was going to demand some explanation. Yet Lord Coe kept laughing out loud. By George, she was magnificent! What a mistress she would be!

Perhaps the wet unmentionables were interfering with Lord Coe's thinking, or he would have noticed the great gaps in his reasoning. Miss Ashton was such a delight with her candid charm, Corey was now convinced she simply could not be any kind of blackmailer. And there could be no hugger-mugger with the children's welfare either, she worked so hard for them. If money was in such short supply, Melody could have supported herself by going out for a governess instead of staying to feed the chickens. Only his Angel would turn down his generous offer, preferring to raise pigs!

Now, if she was not a criminal and not a liar, simply a gentlewoman fallen on hard times, then she was indeed a lady, a pure young lady not to be taken advantage of by rakes like Cordell Coe. If she was innocent of wrongdoing, she was innocent of immorality, and innocent she must stay. Reason be damned. Lord Coe was not thinking with his head, and lust knows no logic.

Chapter Fifteen

*W*hatever happened to the so-steady Miss Ashton from Miss Meadow's Select Academy, the one who never played pranks on the teachers or giggled in church or went into alt when Loretta Carmody's Adonis-like older brother took some of the girls out to tea? Sensible, mature Melody Ashton with nary a hair out of place nor an ungraceful gesture was long gone.

Melody felt as sensible as those dratted pigs who wouldn't stay in their pen where they were safe, warm, and well fed. She considered herself as mature as the twins, letting one man send her into a pelter with laughing eyes and roguish looks and suggestions—Well, suggestions that would have Miss Meadow frothing at the mouth. As for being neat as a pin, Melody had on an oversized apron, a borrowed mobcap, and had smudges of dust on her nose. She and Mrs. Tolliver were working with some village girls to get the Oaks ready for his lordship's arrival. In two days, the viscount would be bringing a chef, a butler, footmen, grooms, and his own valet, but Melody had decided that Lord Coe's servants would be as superior as he, and she was determined they find nothing to disparage in her family home. The paper was faded, and the carpets had bare spots, but at least everything would be cleaned and aired.

Melody whomped the pillow in the master bedroom again—his bedroom—and told herself she was being a perfect ninny to let anything about the man affect her so. He would come with his elegant guests, they would keep him occupied and amused, and she, Melody Ashton, would go about her own business, as far away from the disconcerting peer as possible. She would have more time to spend with the children and the garden, now that money was not to be such a worry and she didn't have to fret about putting food on the table. Mrs. Tolliver's niece Betsy was coming to take over cooking chores at Dower House, while her aunt stayed on as housekeeper at the Oaks, and Pip had the bookkeeping well in hand. Melody gave the pillow another hard whack. Yes, she would have plenty of time. It wasn't as if she would be socializing with Lord Coe or his fancy company. Earls—*thump*—and war heroes—*thump*—and diplomats. It was a good thing the ticking held on the pillow, and a good thing Melody Ashton would be seeing so little of that smooth-tongued rake.

"Not socialize with the viscount and his party? Melody, have you been working in that wretched garden again without your bonnet? You must be all about in your head if you think we can let an opportunity like this pass! Why, the Tarnovers and the Cheynes are the crème de la crème. And just think, young bachelors!" Mama was *aux anges*, going so far as to open a bottle of champagne to celebrate. Felice was in the village purchasing new ribbons for her gowns.

119

"But Lord Coe is bringing his own particular friends, Mama," Melody managed to interject. "He cannot wish three women thrust into their midst."

Lady Ashton ignored her. "We cannot invite the whole party here, of course, the children, don't you know. Melody dearest, you shall have to see about keeping the pesky brats out of sight. A picnic, though, would be just the thing. Yes, we shall invite Lord Coe to bring his guests to our picnic, for a start. Unless he asks me to be hostess for him, naturally, then we need not entertain at all. Yes, I think I may even offer, since it would seem peculiar to have another lady in charge at the Oaks."

"He is bringing his sister, Mama," Melody remarked. "Surely she will be hostess enough. And she is coming to see Meggie, remember."

"Don't be tiresome, Melody. And do put some of that strawberry lotion on your face. I swear, you'd let your complexion go all brown and freckled if no one took you in hand. Where was I? Oh yes, Meggie. I do hope she won't have the grippe, or anything, when Lady Wooster comes. You will be sure she makes her proper curtsy, won't you? And then say she has to have lessons or a nap or whatever. No one wants a child underfoot more than ten minutes. I do hope dear Lady Wooster is over her pet about those nasty letters. You did explain that we knew nothing about them, didn't you?"

"Yes, Mama, but I am not sure Lord Coe believed me."

"Of course he did, Melody. Why would he not? And Lady Wooster is a sweet woman, actually rather niminy-piminy if you ask me, so I am sure she won't cut up stiff. Exquisite dresser, too. I wonder if we can convince our viscount to throw a ball."

"Our viscount? Mama, Lord Coe is renting the house; he is not taking on the care and entertainment of three impoverished females. We are his

120

landladies, not his friends! Why, we are not even his social equals."

Lady Ashton was pouring the last glass. It would go to waste, else, all those lovely bubbles. "What's that? Not his equals? I'll have you know the Morleys go back to William the Conqueror, and your father's people were very well respected in Kent."

So well respected that they cut him off without a shilling for running away with Jessamyn Morley. And William the Conqueror also had camp followers. Melody's mother was seeing the world through champagne bubbles, bubbles that would be pricked at the first snub, or when the invitations did not arrive. Poor Mama.

"Perhaps we might see them at church, Mama," she offered. "Or now that we are above oars, perhaps we can contrive to attend the assembly at Hazelton." It was like talking to Ducky.

"Let me see, you'll need a ball gown, and we can all use new frocks for daytime. That new tissue seems perfect for the warmer months, and—"

"No, Mama. You put me in charge, remember? The viscount's deposit money has already been credited to the children's accounts." Melody might not be able to save her mother from making a cake of herself, nor from suffering cuts and setdowns, but she would not permit her mama to play fast and loose with their finances again. The money was in Melody's name, with Mr. Hadley as overseer, and most was earmarked for the children's educations or to restore their bank balances. No one would be able to accuse the Ashtons of living off orphans' shares.

"Not even Ducky's?" Lady Ashton wailed. "What could he need money for?"

"For his future, Mama, especially Ducky. He's never going to be able to earn a living or care for himself. Could you wear a new dress and gaily

121

dance knowing that someday Ducky might be homeless or hungry?"

Easily, but Lady Ashton didn't say so. What she said was: "You know, Melody, I was saving this champagne for your wedding. I'm glad I drank it now, so it won't go to waste."

Later that evening, after dinner and before bedtime, Lady Ashton was in the weepy stage of inebriation. Melody refused to make any push to attach a gentleman, her mother sobbed. She wouldn't dress in the height of fashion, she even intended to refuse invitations. Melody would never get married, the family would never be rich, Lady Ashton would never get to London again. There was no reason to save the champagne.

"How could you be such an undutiful daughter, Melody?" Lady Jessamyn whimpered into her lace handkerchief. "Now I'll never get to see you wearing the family veil I kept safe all these years."

Grateful for any distraction from the tearful diatribe that had been going on since luncheon, Melody asked, "What veil is that, Mama? I never heard of any family heirlooms."

Of course she hadn't. The jewels and portraits had been pawned years ago. One yellowed and frayed piece of lace wouldn't fetch a brass farthing at the cent-per-centers; now it was priceless.

Sniff. "Why, the veil my mother wore at her wedding, and hers before that. To think it will molder in the—"

"Did you wear it, Mama? Did you?"

Lady Ashton looked at her eager daughter in bewilderment. "Of course. Didn't I just say it was an heirloom?"

"But at your wedding, Mama?"

"Why are you such a slowtop tonight, Melody, when I have such a headache? Where else would I wear a wedding veil? And a beautiful bride I was,

122

too. The whole county said so. And to think you'll never—"

A wedding! "Do you know, Mama, I don't believe you ever told me where you and Papa were married."

"Oh, St. Sebastian's in Hazelton. Judith insisted the local chapel would never do. Are you . . . could you be interested in weddings? Oh Melody, dearest, please say you'll reconsider!"

Love. Marriage. A baby. What joy! Melody would certainly reconsider her position on meeting the houseguests—and the host. Mama drifted from euphoria to snores, while Melody wondered if there was a way to squeeze a new dress out of the account books she and Pip were so conscientiously balancing. Soon it would be time to sell the pigs, but no, Melody could not purchase a new gown when she'd denied Felice the treat that very evening.

Felice had been furious, accusing Melody of trying to snabble the gentlemen herself.

"All of them?" Melody asked, trying to tease Felice out of the sullens. "I should think with four or five bachelors, even I could not be so selfish."

"You'll never bring him up to scratch, you know," Felice bit back, and they both knew which *him* she meant. Melody blushed furiously and tried to deny any interest in that quarter, but Felice wasn't swallowing that gammon. "Women have been trying for years, fashionable, witty, well-connected women. And all with bigger dowries and better figures." She puffed out her own considerable charms, while Melody's confidence—and chest—caved in. "They call him the elusive viscount," Felice continued, "and his ladybirds are always the highest flyers. Why, his latest—"

Nanny was sitting in the corner with her knitting, and now she cleared her throat with an admonition to Felice to mind her tongue lest it turn black and grow warts and curdle milk. "For it's ugly is as ugly does." She went back to her knitting, a striped affair made of Mrs. Barstow's sister's remnants. Whatever the item was, it would soon rival Joseph's coat.

Felice went back to her grievances. "And I don't see why I cannot have a new gown, even if you aren't interested in making the most of the best thing that's ever happened in Copley-Whitmore. If you want to go around looking like a schoolgirl on holiday or a hired drudge, why should I hide my light under your barrel?"

Melody wished she had a barrel big enough so she could stuff the tiresome girl into it and mail her off to Sir Bartleby, wherever he was. She tried once more to explain that the money wasn't hers, it was to provide for the children. She should have saved her breath.

"I absolutely must have a new dress, Melody."

"Then you shall have to find the money to pay for it. Perhaps Mrs. Finsterer would let you help in the store in exchange for the material."

Melody might have suggested Felice appear in her shift for Lord Coe's guests, so shocked was the other girl. Her baby-blue eyes widened, and her rosebud mouth hung open for a moment, until she recovered. "What a tease you are, Melody," she tittered. When Felice realized Melody was not teasing, and not budging, she demanded a loan of the money. "My father is good for it," she insisted.

It was Nanny who answered: "Your pa's good for nothing but filling your head with moonshine," at which Miss Bartleby flounced off in a huff, leaving Melody to deal with the tea things and Lady Ashton in her cups.

"That one's got the pretty plumes of a peacock and the sharp claws of a hawk," Nanny warned. "You watch yourself there, missy."

"She's just spoiled, Nanny."

"Too many cooks, that's what it were. Lady Judith taking her in like the daughter she never had, doting like a hen with one chick, and that nabob with his promises, and then your mama . . . Why, that one's got less sense than the good Lord gave a duck."

"And me, Nanny? What about me?"

"You're in over your head for sure, missy. You're like to drown, too, less you learn to swim mighty quick like. There's big fish in that pond, child, what gobbles little minnows like you. Start paddling."

Chapter Sixteen

She was treading water, that's how Melody felt,
holding her breath and getting nowhere. Here she
was on the steps of the Oaks, lined up with the
others, like so many serfs waiting to pay obeisance
to a feudal lord. The village girls were hoping for
permanent positions, and Mrs. Tolliver had the
chatelaine of office in hand and the light of battle
in her eye, waiting for the uppity London servants.
Harry and Pip were combed and starched, Harry
restless and Pip tense and ready to flee, while the
younger children were back at Dower House with
Mrs. Tolliver's niece, Betsy. Felice was impatiently
twirling her parasol and tugging the neckline of
her gown downward. Nanny kept tugging it up, and
Melody feared the thin fabric would give out in despair. Lady Ashton, suffering the grandfather of all
hangovers, could barely stand. The sun was tortur-
ing her eyeballs, and if the pounding in her ears
wasn't hoofbeats signaling the viscount's arrival,
Lady Ashton warned, she was going to be sick. On
second thought, maybe she would be sick anyway.

All Melody could think of was the valet's reaction to that! She bit her lip and fussed with the ribbon threaded through her curls. What in the world would Corey think?

He thought she was enchanting, in her pale blue merino with a sprig of violets pinned to the neckline and her smile, hesitant but welcoming. The sunshine brought out all the red and gold highlights of her hair and added a natural glow to her creamy skin. The viscount also thought her graceful shoulders too slim to bear responsibility for the entire rackety group, so he proceeded to charm each and every one of the greeting committee, to relieve Melody of some of her self-assumed burdens.

He dismissed the hopeful maidservants with a smile and a simple, "If you satisfy Mrs. Tolliver, I am satisfied." For another of those smiles, Melody thought, the village girls would scrub the gates of hell if he asked. Mrs. Tolliver he introduced to his own major domo, who bowed ever so stiffly as he declared himself at her service. Mrs. Tolliver led the London staff away, happily murmuring, "At my service, why, I never!"

Melody thought she saw the viscount wink in her direction and decided the rogue was showing off for her benefit. Still, she breathed more easily.

Lord Coe turned to the boys and asked Harry if he would be kind enough to show the grooms around the stables and possibly help with Caesar. "The stallion gets restless in strange surroundings, and you seem to have a fine hand with him." No words could have thrilled Harry more; Nanny had to call him back to bow to his lordship.

"And Philip, my friend," the viscount said, shaking hands with the solemn lad, "I have a favor to beg of you, also. I brought some books with me that Lady Ashton will not wish mixed up with her own. Dry stuff, history and science, mostly. I understand you are familiar with the Oaks' library, so could I bother you to take charge of the collection, find a spot where they will be out of the way, or even make a list if you think it necessary? In truth, I cannot trust such a task to the footmen."

Pip did his best to stammer out that he would find the project an honor, not a chore. He gave up trying to express himself with manful dignity, when Lord Coe added: "Of course, if any of the volumes should be of any interest to you, feel free to make full use of them." Pip grinned like the young boy he was and flew after a footman toting a heavy carton from the baggage carriage.

Melody knew she was seeing a master in action when Corey bowed again over her mother's hand. "Lady Ashton, how kind of you to meet me in person," he said, still holding that hand, to Lady Jessamyn's giddy delight. "And looking lovelier than ever. Why, if I hadn't known Miss Melody was your daughter, I would have guessed—No, I shouldn't keep you standing out here in the hot sun, when I know your constitution is delicate. How thoughtless of me, after you have been so gracious in permitting me the use of your home. May I impose further by begging the pleasure of calling this afternoon? You see, I intend to plead for your assistance in entertaining my guests. Of course," he said, turning to Felice, "with Miss Bartleby nearby, I shall have to pry the gentlemen away to get in a day's hunting. *Enchanté, mademoiselle.*" Felice's hand was also saluted and also held longer than necessary, in Melody's estimation.

The viscount was instantly invited to take luncheon, tea, potluck supper while his own staff was getting settled in, anything the precious man desired.

"No, no, I must not intrude. And you, my dear Lady Ashton, must husband your strength for the houseguests. Would tea put too much strain on you?"

Would taking over Hercules's seven labors? Melody believed her mother would move mountains in order to have charge of the guest lists. An unsteady Lady Ashton tottered back to the Dower House, reciting names of local families and mentally eliminating any with marriageable daughters. Felice hurried after, most likely planning another stunning outfit to wear for tea. Any more daring and Corey would be served a rare eyeful, along with his watercress sandwiches.

Melody turned her attention back to the steps and Lord Coe's greatest challenge: Nanny. How infuriating that he found it so easy! All the viscount had to do was pull a bright red ball out of his greatcoat pocket. "Here, I brought this for Ducky. Do you think he'll like it?"

Nanny actually had to blow her nose! "No one's ever brought the tyke a gift." She snuffled, hurrying off to give her favorite his treat, leaving Melody in the selfsame situation she had vowed to avoid. How did it happen that she was alone with a practiced rake, a hardened charmer? She looked around to see if he was calling the birds out of the trees next.

Corey laughed, and the sound made her toes want to curl in her slippers, a not unusual reaction when he was close. "Don't think you can sweet-talk me so handily—" she started to bluster in defense, but he stopped her with a finger against her lips.

"Sh, kitten, I haven't said a word. Don't get your fur up, for I mean us to be friends."

"Friends?" she asked around the tingle in her lips. After what he'd last offered?

He took his finger away, reluctantly, it seemed. "It's possible, you know. You'll see. Trust me."

Trust him? She could trust a puff adder more! But his own sister was coming, and a friend sounded like a gift from the gods right then, especially a friend who was strong and kind and could

129

manage whole armies of eccentrics without losing that devil-sent smile. Melody nodded, but with reservations.

Corey was satisfied, for now. He stepped back. "I brought all the children gifts, but the rest are packed up somewhere, except for the ball and this." He pulled a tissue-wrapped parcel from another inside pocket. It was a small china-headed doll, all dressed in ruffled lace. "Harry helped me with suggestions the last time I was here. Do you think Margaret will like it? Should I have found something else?"

The foolish man was actually unsure of himself! Why did he think little girls would be any harder to wrap round his finger than big ones? Melody had to laugh. Obviously, Lord Coe was more used to buying his gifts at jewelers rather than toy shops. "She will adore it, my lord. It is the perfect gift. Why don't I go fetch Meggie now, so you can give it to her away from the others. Say a half hour for Nanny to make sure she is spotless?"

Lord Coe met them on the path midway between the Oaks and Dower House. Meggie was holding Melody's hand, hiding behind her skirts. Melody tried to make introductions: "Lord Coe, this is Meggie. Meggie, please curtsy to your . . . your . . ."

"Uncle," the viscount supplied; that was as good a title as any. "Uncle Corey." He knelt to the child's level, one knee on the ground—another pair of trousers ruined. He could see the moppet had that same pale hair of all the Inscoe clan and his sister's turquoise eyes. Below that, she was wrapped in a heavy wool scarf. He gestured to the wrap and asked, "May I?"

Meggie nodded solemnly and stood still while he unwound the muffler. Then, "My God," he said, "she's beautiful!"

"Of course she is," Melody agreed, not adding

that any child of his would have to be. He was offering the doll, and receiving fervent hugs and adoration in return. Corey's eyes seemed suspiciously damp, and Melody knew there was a lump in her own throat.

The viscount swung the child up in his arms and exclaimed, "Heavens, Miss Margaret, you and the doll together weigh less than a feather pillow! Why, we'll just have to fatten you up, won't we, so you don't fly away in the next heavy breeze."

"Oh, Uncle Corey." Meggie laughed. "I can't fly away!"

Corey held the child close and told her, "No, my precious, I'll never let you get so far away again."

Lord Coe was in love. Irredeemably and unquestionably smitten, and by a skinny six-year-old with silky hair and a gap-toothed grin. All his plans would have to be rearranged, and now he couldn't wait for his sister to get to Copley-Whitmore so they could discuss the alternatives. There was no way this little fairy child was being sent off to Cornwall.

Melody's opinions were changing, too. How could she deny him the child, or deny Meggie such love? If his lordship proved at all trustworthy, Miss Ashton would have to relent. Then again, if his lordship proved at all trustworthy, she would eat her bonnet.

Father Christmas could not have received a warmer welcome at Dower House that afternoon than Viscount Coe and his carpetbag. His lordship presented Lady Ashton with the latest London fashion journals, Byron's newest volume, and a box of candied violets.

"These are just tokens of my appreciation for all of the trouble you have gone through on my behalf, and the assistance you have so kindly offered," Corey told Lady Jessamyn. He also permitted her to gush on about her plans for his house party, without committing himself to any. "There are still ten days before anyone arrives, ma'am. I should like to consult my sister's wishes before I send out invitations."

He turned to Felice and bowed from the waist. "But if we do have an impromptu dance party, or attend the assembly at Hazelton, I beg you will save me a dance, Miss Bartleby. I am asking now, of course, to get a jump on my friends and to avoid the crush of all the local beaux. Perhaps you would honor me by carrying my small gift." Felice's present was a silk and bamboo Oriental-style fan, with a not-quite-naughty picture of satyrs and nymphs at picnic on one side. Felice practiced attitudes with the fan—coy maiden, blasé lady, sultry houri—until Nanny told her to put the fool thing down, she was creating a draft on the tea.

Nanny would not ordinarily have been at tea, but Lord Coe had asked that the children be brought down. "Even Ducky and those savage little twins?" Lady Ashton was as astounded as if he'd asked her to dine with Hottentots or headhunters. Either might be preferable, for all she knew.

But Ducky was content to sit in the corner and roll his ball back and forth between his spread legs, and the twins were soon fixed in another corner, jabbering away over their gifts. Corey had reached into his satchel and pulled out two big floppy ragdoll babies with painted faces and two packets of ribbons. He handed Dora the doll that was wrapped in a pink blanket, with a pink dress, pink booties and a pink bonnet; with Melody's help, he tied pink ribbons in Dora's hair. Laura received blue ribbons and the other doll, all in blue. "There now," Corey beamed, looking at the others for congratulations, "now we can tell them apart."

It did not take ten minutes before each twin wore one blue ribbon and one pink, and each doll wore half the other's clothes. Pip and Harry were in whoops until Nanny clucked at them; they returned their attention to their biscuits and to the viscount's wondrous bag. Corey shrugged good-naturedly and vowed to try again, even if he had to tattoo the little heathens. He found another strawberry tart and popped it into Meggie's mouth, where she and her doll sat on his knee. (Yes, they were a fresh pair of trousers, and yes, there was strawberry jam already on them. No matter, Bates had already given notice. Twice.) Finally taking pity on the boys, Lord Coe pulled out his gifts to Harry.

"I know you said you'd be content if I just let you care for Caesar and hang out around the stable. After lessons and chores, of course," Corey added for Melody's benefit. "But I used to love this book as a lad, and I was as horse mad as you, I'll wager. It's all about knights and their chargers." Although he thanked his lordship politely, Harry wasn't quite as keen on that gift as on the other, a genuine leather jockey cap, which he declared bang up to the mark, the best gift he'd ever received, and wasn't Lord Coe the most capital of good fellows, Miss Mel? Melody was thinking somewhat along the lines of Greeks bearing gifts, but out loud she agreed with Harry's enthusiastic praise.

Corey held a leather box out to Pip. "P-please, my lord. Harry said you b-brought all those b-books from London just for me. I c-cannot thank you enough n-now, so I c-cannot accept any more g-gifts."

"Well, Philip, that's a fine way to repay someone's generosity, denying him a promising chess partner." Corey opened the leather case and regretfully fingered the carved ivory pieces. "Are you sure you won't reconsider?"

Pip looked to Melody, who smiled her encouragement. "I suppose I might, sir. B-but only as a favor, you know." They all laughed, Pip, too.

Still smiling, Lord Coe said, "Harry, I thought you were a better conspirator! I hope you didn't tell anyone about the last gift." Melody held her breath while Corey gently lifted Meggie down and, standing, brought the tapestry bag over—to Nanny! Inside were four hanks of the softest angora yarn dyed a lovely green color. "Harry thought you could use a new workbag, Nanny, but I hope you can make something pretty with the wool." Only Nanny saw his wink or got a good enough look at the yarn's color to see it was the exact shade of Melody's eyes.

Tea was over; the gifts were all parceled out. "But Uncle Corey, didn't you bring a present for Miss Mel?" Miss Ashton could have throttled Meggie as almost all eyes turned to her. Mama was reading one of the journals and hadn't paid attention to anyone else's gift after hers, and Ducky had fallen asleep. The twins offered to share their dolls with Melody, the boys were embarrassed, and Felice snickered.

Her face aflame, Melody started to reprimand the child for her rudeness, but Lord Coe interrupted: "No, Meggie is quite right. It would have been unforgivable on my part to forget the indomitable Miss Melody, as if I could. To my sorrow, her gift was too big to fit in the bag."

And that was a relief to Melody, who feared for a moment that the unpredictable man was going to pull a jeweler's box from his pocket and shame her in front of the children with a courtesan's gift. Now she would have to wonder for another day what he could possibly get for her that was too large for his bag of tricks. It was a surprise, he said, that she would have to go into the woods with him the next morning to find. If he was planning anything untoward, wouldn't he just be the one surprised, for Melody swore to bring Nanny and Meggie and Harry and Pip and . . .

Chapter Seventeen

*A*dvance guards were dispatched. Melody sent the twins ahead along the path. Corey was delighted to see them each carrying a baby doll wrapped in its blanket, but for the life of him he couldn't remember which twin had pink and which had blue, not that he could rely on their keeping the designated colors anyway. He held his finger to his lips and shook his head, so the twins skipped back to Melody all giggly that they knew a secret, and she did not. Melody wasn't surprised that her scouts' loyalties had been so easily subverted and did not even think of sending Meggie to spy. That chit was firmly in his lordship's pocket, dancing ahead with a basket of sticky buns to offer him as a midmorning treat.

Corey stood in the clearing, sunlight on his pale hair, his coat slung over a tree branch, and his white shirt open at the neck. Melody caught her breath, reminded of her first sight of him in Barstow's inn yard when she thought he looked like a sculpted god. The crooked smile he wore today was all too human and all too manly for her suddenly racing heartbeat. In his hands, when her eyes got past the broad shoulders and the tanned vee of his chest, was her gift: a lightweight, twin-barrel, nearly recoilless, modern rifle, with embossed silver plates on the stock. A lady's hunting weapon, and all for her! To think that the last gift Miss Ashton had received was Mingleforth's *Rules of Polite Decorum*—and she had hit Lord Coe with it! Tears came to Melody's eyes, and she fumbled for her handkerchief.

"Well, I am glad to see that at least Harry and the twins liked my gifts," Corey teased to give her time to recover. Harry was wearing his cap and had likely slept in it, and the twins were clutching their baby dolls. They were, at any rate, until one of the dolls started to squeal and kick, demanding to be set down. First one and then the other piglet ran off, bonnets and all, the twins, Harry, and Angie in chase behind. Melody's troops were deserting her, and so was her willpower to resist Corey's enchantments.

"If this is some kind of bribe, my lord," she began, only to be brought up short by his laughing denial.

"What a suspicious lady you are, Miss Ashton. Didn't I tell you to trust me? The gun is only a gift, to show my appreciation for all you've done, and to atone for whatever aggravation or distress I may have caused you. I thought all women liked gifts."

Melody glanced quickly to Meggie and Pip; they were happily setting up the painted cloth target Lord Coe had also brought. "But it is much too costly. I cannot accept—"

"Now you are sounding like Philip. Don't be a peahen, Angel, I bought it for my own self-defense. Can't have you blundering around so close to the Oaks with that unwieldy antique you were trying to use. I thought I could show you how to shoot."

He thought he might give her pointers, did he? Melody walked over to the round target. "Come away, children, Lord Coe is going to teach me how

136

to use the gun." Philip cleared his throat, and Meggie started to say, "But, Uncle Corey—" until Melody clapped her hand over the child's mouth.

Corey demonstrated how to load the rifle, speaking simply enough for Meggie's understanding, then paced off a short distance. No need to tax her skill, he said, just hitting the target would be enough for starters.

"Oh dear, yes," Melody agreed, trying to recall even half of Felice's affectations. Perhaps she could develop the other girl's knack of looking up at a man and batting her eyelashes. No, Melody was too tall. Instead she stood limply, permitting the viscount to position her hands properly on the rifle. Then he stood behind her, his arms around hers, holding the gun up. Oh dear, indeed! What had she gotten herself into?

Her back was against his chest, her cheek was brushed by the thin fabric of his shirt sleeve, her fingers were wrapped in his, and she was enveloped in the fresh lemon and spice scent of him. Melody never noticed that the viscount's voice was a trifle ragged as he tried to remember the instructions for aiming a rifle. Instead, she noticed how his words rumbled in his chest and how his breath ruffled the hair near her ear, so close to his mouth. Why, if she turned slightly . . .

"And squeeze back slowly on the trigger like . . . so."

The gun's boom brought Melody back to earth, that and the need to make sure her knees were still supporting her when the viscount withdrew his arms to check the target.

"We'll have to work on your aim, I'm afraid, if you can miss at this distance."

Aim? Had she been aiming? Melody smiled sweetly and wondered if she could try the next shot by herself, to get a better feel for the weapon, she said. The rifle was so light she overcompensated, and her shot hit the outer ring, which his lordship thought was just wonderful. He winked at Pip, who almost choked.

Melody fumbled the reloading, and then asked Meggie if she could spare two of the sticky buns.

"Shouldn't we wait for after the lesson, Miss Ashton?" Corey prompted.

"This is the lesson," she replied. "Ready, Pip?" She raised the rifle and called "One." The toss. *Boom* "Two." The toss. *Boom*.

Viscount Coe threw his head back and laughed, bowed to Melody, and brushed crumbs off his shirt.

If the viscount's intention was to confuse Melody, he succeeded. He did not behave like any London beau she imagined, idle and bored, spending hours over his dress and food. Nor did he seem to seek out low company for carousing or gambling. He acted the gallant flirt for Mama and Felice, the affectionate uncle to the children and, as promised, the warm friend to Melody. She just could not figure out why.

For the next few days, the viscount was everywhere. He gave the twins and Meggie turns riding in front of him on Caesar and oversaw one of his grooms' instruction of Harry on a docile mare. He asked Lady Ashton to accompany him on calls to the local gentry, in his carriage, of course, the one with the crest on the door. He played chess with Pip and discussed the boy's reading; he partook of make-believe teas with the little girls and make-believe teases with Felice. When he came upon Melody and Harry trying to mend the hogs' pen, again, he took off his jacket and started pounding fence posts. Corey could have called for one of his grooms instead of getting his hands dirty, but he pounded away in the hot sun until those pigs wouldn't have dared escape. He did not have to take Ducky for a ride or sit on the floor rolling balls with him for hours, and he did not have to accompany Miss Ashton when she went hunting.

138

Corey did not even bring along a gun, he showed that much confidence in Melody, but he did have some hints about training Angie, like leaving the impossible mutt home. The viscount wasn't patronizing at all about the woods lore he could teach Melody from his own experience, claiming he was only passing on the information because he was fond of rabbit stew. Naturally, he had to be invited to supper.

Lady Ashton was no longer wilted, Meggie was getting tan from following the viscount around all day, Pip was losing his stutter. The Oaks was getting ready for company, and Melody . . . ? Melody was feeling safe and warm and comfortable in his lordship's presence. At least she no longer turned to blancmange when he brushed close by her, or not often anyway. But why? When a spider cast its web, maybe it was looking for a place to dangle, not just a passing meal. When a noted rake cast his spells, maybe they were innocent, not necessarily insidious. Melody thought they were both likely instincts: the spider just spun, rogues just charmed, because it was in their nature. Well, she could admire a web for its dewdrop-diamond artistry without becoming any libertine's tasty morsel. But what a tempting trap, if trap it was.

Was it possible for a spider to build such an intricate, sticky web that it got stuck itself? Corey Inscoe came back to the Oaks every evening tired, dirty, and satisfied, to his own surprise. He played chess with Philip, raised Bates's salary, and relaxed with a glass of brandy on the library's leather sofa after everyone else had gone to bed, content to watch the dying fire and idly turn pages of his books. There were no balls, no all-night revelries or card parties, no greedy mistresses—and he did not miss any of it. At least not the greedy part.

Lord Coe still wanted Melody, uncomfortably more than ever. He had returned to the Oaks determined to use the time to his best advantage: to show Miss Ashton he was not a fribble and gain her trust. Hell, friendship between man and woman was just a temporary detour on the road to seduction, wasn't it? The only problem was, he liked her.

The more Corey saw of Miss Ashton, the more he admired her. Not just her beauty, although sometimes the sight of her, even ankle deep in pig wallow, made his breath catch. It wasn't as though she was exactly pretty; that little mantrap Felice was far more comely in the fashionable sense. But Angel had a freshness, a glow, and that dimple he'd move mountains and pig manure just to make appear. She would not go to fat like that rounded Miss Bartleby either; her shape when Corey had held her and the rifle in his arms offered promises—and another sleepless night if he didn't concentrate on Scott's latest epic.

There was more. He loved her affection for her ragged band and her loyalty to her rag-mannered family. She was honest and open. Why, if she disagreed with him, she would shout or throw things; she wouldn't sulk or cry or snipe at a fellow for two days after. She was intelligent and well read, interesting, and a good listener. She was not afraid to get her face in the sun or her hands in the garden. And she laughed. Not the simpering sound well-bred ladies were taught to make, but genuine, unaffected laughter. All in all, the poor confused viscount mused, Miss Ashton was everything a man could want—in a friend.

What a dilemma . . . and what in heaven's name was going on in the nether regions of the house? The servants had been dismissed an hour ago because his lordship saw no reason to keep them standing around yawning just to light his way upstairs, so no one should have been in the kitchens. Someone was, from the noise, and not making any secret of it either. Corey stepped to the desk and took his pistol from the top drawer. His soft slippers made no noise as he prowled down the hall.

"I am sure there is a good reason for this," he drawled from the kitchen doorway. "But do not stop what you are doing. Let me guess."

Melody nearly jumped out of her shoes at the sound of Corey's voice. Then she turned the color of dough that had been left out too long. Gads, what a hobble this was, finding herself exactly where she should never be, alone with a man—a semidressed man, at that, in his paisley robe—in the middle of the night. Her shaking hands continued their motions of scraping plates of food onto old newspapers, folding the papers, and putting the bundles into paper sacks. She knew her hair was undone, but at least her green cloak covered her and her lawn nightgown from head to toe. That fact gave her enough confidence to say, "Couldn't you just go back to bed and forget about me?"

"That's a contradiction in terms, Angel. I haven't been able to do it in months." He grinned when he saw the color rush back to her face but decided to stay where he was for the nonce, casually leaning against the door frame, out of respect for her temper and her aim. "I would have been within my rights to shoot you, you realize," Corey observed, putting the gun into his pocket. "Although I wonder if a person can be charged with breaking into his or her own house. Somehow I wouldn't have thought robbery would be your next foray into crime. Then again, most burglars head for the silver and jewels, not the pantry."

"Oh, do stop, you wretched man. You know it is no such thing. Mrs. Tolliver left these plates out for me to take."

"In the middle of the night? Now why, I wonder. Could it be that Miss Ashton is too proud to borrow food?" His voice grew softer, more coaxing. "You

141

know, Angel, if things are that bad at Dower House, we can still make some kind of arrangement. . . ."

Melody looked from the plate in her hands, veal marsala, to Lord Coe's paisley silk robe. No, she would salvage whatever dignity remained to her. She raised her chin in that gesture Corey prized, like a grande dame putting down an encroaching caper merchant.

"Yes?" he prodded, just to remind her he had the upper hand. After all, it was his house, albeit rented, his food, and her cork-brained scheme, whatever it was.

"Do you know that your French chef is the most haughty, self-important man I have ever known?"

"And here I thought I was. But no, I don't believe I had that impression of Antoine. Of course, I seldom converse with the fellow."

"Well, he is. You'd think he was the nobleman, not you. He has no concept of money and no respect for others less fortunate."

"Was that meant to be an indictment of the entire peerage, or just Antoine?" There was the dimple. Now that it was safe to get nearer, Corey started carrying the empty dishes to the sink.

"You see? Antoine wouldn't touch the dirty dishes, either. He has an assistant just to hand him things and clean up after him. But that's not to the point. The fact of the matter is, Antoine refuses to serve less than four courses, with removes, at a viscount's table. Anything less would be beneath him, or you. But you are only one person until your house guests arrive, and most of the food goes to waste since the servants have their own dinner before. And Antoine absolutely refuses to re-serve leftovers. That would be a sacrilege."

Corey was grinning by now. "Yes, I see the problem. But why couldn't one of the footmen bring the food to Dower House so you don't have to sneak around at night?"

"Because Mrs. Tolliver asked very nicely the first night, and your precious Antoine refused."

"He what? I'll—"

"He refused to let his labors, his artistry, his magnificent creations, his *leftovers*, go to feed the hogs."

"Ah yes, the pigs. I should have known. But what shall I do about it?" Corey asked. He was chuckling as he lifted two of the filled bags and her lantern, now that Melody was done. "If I order him to cook less, you'll have less food for the hogs, and if I order him to give them the remains, he'll either quit or feed me pig swill."

"Not to worry, I am teaching the twins French. Antoine will hand over the food just to get—What are you doing?"

Corey was raising her hood and holding the door for her. "I am seeing you and your booty safely home."

He wouldn't listen to her objections, and he wouldn't go back midway. In fact, Lord Coe walked Melody right to the kitchen door she had left unlocked in the back of Dower House. There he hung the lantern and handed her his two bags of foodstuffs, wondering how the pigs would feel about the glazed ham. With his two sacks and her two packages, Melody could not reach to open the door. "My lord?" she whispered.

"Thief-takers always get a bounty," he answered, and took his reward, while she had her hands full and her mouth open. Pinwheels, cartwheels, catherine wheel fireworks, Melody's senses were swirling and smoldering from his kiss, when Corey pushed her inside and closed the door behind her.

That was not a friendly token of affection at all. No friend's handshake ever left Corey Inscoe sweating and shaky, nor caused yet another restless night.

Chapter Eighteen

*W*hy bother going to bed if you know you won't sleep? Lord Coe threw another log on the library fire and picked up his book of Scott's ballads. He must have dozed off, dreaming of heroes and wars and crowds screaming, for the noises stayed in his mind when he jerked awake. The fire was still high and banshees were still wailing. It was all of a piece, the viscount figured, taking the gun from the desk again, that the blasted house would be haunted; nothing about the place seemed to fit his notions of reality. The sounds were all too real, however, and coming from the front door. Fiend seize it, what if Angel was back, hysterical and seeking revenge? Let it be a banshee.

It wasn't. If there was one other feather-headed female in the world beside Miss Ashton who believed Dower House actually was, is, or should be, an orphanage, Lord Coe had missed the woman by minutes. What she left was tucked in a basket, crying as if the hounds of hell were after it.

Coe gingerly picked up the infant—no, he picked

up the basket—and the wailing stopped. He carried the whole thing back to the library to set it down while he considered his next action, and the shrieks started again. Not a slow learner by any means, the viscount hefted the basket and did his thinking on the move. Not that Corey had a great deal of deciding to do, for there was not a soul in his house who would or could know what to do about a screaming infant. Mrs. Tolliver went home evenings, and Bates would likely reenlist if Coe so much as asked him to hold the blasted thing so the viscount could dress. There was no hope for it, Corey and the baby would have to make their way in the dark, in still damp soft slippers, back along that wretched path, praying Miss Ashton was yet awake. He juggled the basket from arm to arm, trying to shield his candle and avoid jagged stones. Hell and damnation, he never should have left London!

The light was on in the kitchen, thank goodness. He looked dubiously at the item in the basket, wondering if he dared chance putting it on the ground in order to knock. The thought of facing an abruptly wakened household of screeching, swooning women was less appealing than facing Boney's cannons again, so he sacrificed his manners and his foot and kicked at the bloody door.

Melody was still wearing her green cloak when she opened the door, and Corey could see that her eyes were red rimmed from crying. Damn and blast, he thought, it needed only that!

"Don't you dare even think about—" Then she took a better look. "What in the world do you have?"

"Well, it's not another shipment of pig feed, ma'am. And no, it is not more evidence of my debauchery." Melody's bruised lips were enough of that! Corey avoided her eyes as he walked past her into the kitchen. "Some fool woman left it on my doorstep by mistake. Here, you take the little blighter."

Melody was even then lifting the infant out of the

basket and cooing to it. "Why, what a beautiful baby! And look, Corey, the clothes are fine white lawn and silk embroidery. This isn't some beggar's foundling. Maybe someone in the village will know what happened to the poor mother, that she would leave her baby."

"But that's tomorrow. What will you do tonight? I'm warning you, it does nothing but scream if you put it down."

"Poor dear is most likely hungry. There is no waking Nanny so late, and Betsy has gone home with Mrs. Tolliver, but don't worry, I have been around infants all my life. I know what to do. Here." She moved to hand the child to Corey, who jumped back as though it were live coals in her hands. Melody laughed. "I cannot warm the milk or find the bottles and those leather nipples Nanny used to have unless you take the baby. Or would you rather I put it back in the basket and chance waking Mama or Felice?"

Corey held his arms out, like a prisoner awaiting shackles. "No, silly, here," Melody instructed, cradling the babe in his arms against his chest.

While Miss Ashton bustled about in cabinets, Corey examined the scrap of humanity he held. "You know, she's not so homely after all, now that she's stopped squalling. She's got the prettiest smoky blue eyes."

"All babies have that color eyes at first," Melody called from the pantry. "But why do you suppose the baby is a she?"

"She's so light and pink and dainty. Look at those tiny hands."

"But all babies start out so sweet and delicate," Melody explained, coming over to look. "You're right though, she must be a girl; she's already smiling at you."

"Uh, Angel," he said, holding the baby out, away

146

from the wet spot down the front of his robe, "I think it's time we found out for sure."

No one in the village knew anything about a baby or a lady in distress, Betsy reported later that morning, but that sharp-nosed constable Mr. Pike was sniffing around about it, and he promised to call at the Oaks that afternoon to take the infant to the county workhouse and foundling home. Not if she could help it, Melody vowed.

Unfortunately, no one else thought she should keep the baby. Nanny shook her head and kept on knitting. "I'm too old for a young 'un, missy," she admitted, "and Ducky is already as much as I can handle, and he'll always need me. Don't look to your mama neither, for she's always been too busy being a lady to be any kind of mother. I can't figure she'll change now. Tigers don't change their spots, you know."

Lady Ashton merely asked if Melody had checked the basket carefully for an envelope or a bank note. Without compensation, the waif was just another orphan, and what did Melody think this was, a charity home? Felice, of course, had no time before the viscount's house party to tend to anything but her wardrobe and her complexion. She would not even hold Baby, for infants were so messy.

Harry moaned, "Not another girl!" and even Pip tried to show Melody in the books that they had no money for a wet nurse or a milk cow. Mrs. Tolliver had too many chores as it was, and Betsy too many mouths to feed at home, with her Jed out of work now.

Only Meggie agreed with Melody that the baby should stay with them. She even tried to give the infant her doll. "Because I have Uncle Corey, and Baby has nobody."

Mr. Hadley was no help. "No, my dear, I cannot sign the papers for you. It would be a life sentence, and the remnants of your dowry would never see you or the babe above dirt-scratching poverty. What you want is a husband, girl, to give you children of your own! If you take this infant you would never have such a life, for no man would want such an encumbered female. And think of your reputation. All the evil-minded gabble mongers would spread it about that the babe was yours, then you would be subject to every kind of insult known. No, I am sorry, I cannot let you take on another burden. Find a rich man, Melody, then you can be as generous and warm hearted as you please."

Melody did not feel warm hearted; she felt absolutely pudding hearted at the thought of facing Lord Coe again after last night, after that kiss. All she had to do, however, was ask him to sign some papers.

Unbelievably, he said no.

"I'm sorry, my lord, perhaps you did not understand. I am not asking you to support the child or anything, just become the guardian, the male guardian, of record."

He was pacing around the library in beige whipcord pants and a serge jacket, thinking furiously. If Melody had another child, an infant at that, she would never come to London. Besides, she was too young to have such cares by herself. Damn it, he wanted to make her life easier, not more complicated. "I'm sorry, Angel, I did understand you, and I cannot do it. You've been at such pains to bring home to me my responsibilities. I couldn't just sign a document and walk away. She would be my ward forever! My way of life, my habits and interests, they just do not include babies. I don't even know what I am to do about Meggie, ah, Margaret."

"I haven't yet said you could take Meggie."

"And if you are thinking of offering me Margaret in exchange for the baby, it won't fadge. You are too young, and you cannot afford the infant." He stopped his pacing at her protest. "No, don't tell me about all the girls who are married with two babes before they are sixteen. Half of them are dead before they are twenty, and they have husbands to care for them. You cannot do it alone, and I won't help you."

Melody was stricken. So the hero had feet of clay after all. Why, oh why had she let herself forget he was nothing but a pleasure-seeking reprobate? "Spoken like a true nobleman," she sneered. "As long as you are comfortable and your peace isn't cut up, you'll write a check and consider yourself the most generous of fellows."

Corey's jaw was clenched, and Melody could see a muscle flicking at the side of his cheek. She didn't care; her own hurt and disappointment were too great. How could she ever have considered him a friend, and more than a friend? She continued: "I suppose you have your own standards, noblesse oblige and all that, until someone asks you to get your hands dirty."

"I have got my hands dirty, Melody." His voice was low, controlled.

She remembered him helping with the fence posts, carrying dirty dishes, holding sticky hands. "When it suited you, my lord. Thank goodness your true care-for-no-one colors showed before I made even more of a fool of myself. I was right the first time, you are nothing but a heartless flirt playing fast and loose with every woman who comes your way."

"Not every woman," he said with a deep breath, coming closer to where Melody stood fighting her tears. He stroked her cheek once with the back of his hand. "Come, we will work this out. My sister will be here soon, and Lady Cheyne. Between them they must know of someone who is pining away for just such a pretty little babe. Less than a week, Angel."

They did not have a week. They had less than ten minutes before Coe's butler announced there was a person, not a gentleman, mind, but a person, zealously and stridently demanding to see Miss Ashton.

Coe raised one brow and told the butler to show

149

the person in. "Unless you wish to be private, Miss Ashton?" Melody quickly shook her head no.

Pike waited for an introduction to the London toff and waited to be offered a hand to shake or a chair to sit in. He was going to have a long wait. His weasel face turned red, and he retallied all the insults he'd received at Miss Ashton's hands.

"I got you now, Miss High Boots," he crowed. "Waylaying a ward of the county and interfering in the rightful disposition of a minor under the laws of the king's justice. And I got papers."

Corey looked at Melody for an explanation. "It seems Mr. Pike, our local constable, gets a fee from the county for each resident of the local almshouse, which he also manages."

Pike never noticed how the viscount's eyes narrowed at the information. Pike was too busy demanding the vagrant child be instantly handed over to his legal care. Melody looked from his runny nose to his dirty hands to the hairs growing out of his ears and swore she wouldn't let him touch one of her pigs, much less an infant. If Baby had to stay at the county farm, temporarily only, then Melody would bring the child there herself. Pike waved his papers, and Melody crossed her arms over her chest. He threatened to have her arrested, and she offered to accompany him to the magistrate that very minute. Then Pike laid a hand on Melody's arm. Now that was a big mistake. Before he could say jack rabbit, the constable's feet were dangling inches off the ground, and his bony Adam's apple was bobbing over a rock-hard fist wrapped in his dingy shirt collar. An ice blue stare bored into Pike's watery eyes with the promise of unimaginable mayhem.

"The *lady*," Coe rasped, "said she would bring the child tomorrow. Was there anything else?"

Still dangling like a bunch of onions hung to dry, Pike gabbled out, "No." Nothing happened. "No, my lord."

Corey drove Melody in his curricle, a groom up behind, the baby in her arms swaddled in the multicolored blanket Nanny declared finished for the occasion. They hardly spoke beyond her softly voiced directions, and soon enough they reached the dry dirt track leading to the grounds the county set aside for its orphans and elders, its sick, drunk or crippled, its indigent homeless of whatever variety.

There were barefooted children poking in the ground with a stick and a scabrous old crone trying to get water from a well. A woman in a faded smock on a stool near the door coughed and coughed and coughed, and a bundle of rags issued wheezing snores. A man wearing the faded tatters of a uniform, with one leg and a crutch, stood propped against the wall.

While the groom held the horses, Corey helped Melody down. She clutched the baby more tightly to her shoulder.

"Who's in charge here, soldier?" the viscount asked the one-legged man, who merely jerked his head toward the house.

Inside was worse. The filth, the stench, a child wailing, people sprawled around like so many discarded scarecrows. "Who's in charge?" Corey asked again, and a scrawny hand gestured to a rear door. The soldier had followed them in, and now he added, "Dirty Mary keeps tabs for Pike, when she ain't shot the cat. She'd be in the kitchen cookin', if you can call it that."

Dirty Mary was facedown at the littered table, the bottle in her hand dripping onto the floor, where roaches and a toddler crawled. The one pot on the stove was scorched, and whatever it contained smelled so rancid Melody had to put her hand over her mouth. Corey led her out, keeping his arm around her and the baby. Unchecked tears streamed down her face.

"Were you on the Peninsula, private?" Corey was asking the soldier.

"Aye, servin' my country, and look what it got me." There wasn't even bitterness left in the man's voice, just resignation. He spit on the ground.

"Would you work if you could?"

"Aye, if anyone would hire a cripple, I'd work."

"Would you wash and sweep and carry water and see that these people get fed and bathed and, by Harry, treated like human beings?"

The veteran made a harsh sound in his throat that might have been a laugh once. "And who would pay for food and clothes and soap and medicine, eh, my lord? Pike?"

Corey reached into his coat for his wallet and pulled out a handful of bills. "I am paying. Pike won't be back, but you can be sure I will, with the magistrate. I was on the Peninsula, too, private, and I was proud of all the men who served under me. If a man let me down, he was out. Understood?"

The soldier saluted neatly. "You won't regret this, sir. And God bless you and your missus."

Corey helped Melody back up into the curricle and gently wiped her face with his handkerchief, then brushed her forehead with his lips. He peeled the blanket away from Baby's face and reached one finger to that so soft cheek. Tiny fingers wrapped around his.

"We have to see the magistrate anyway; a few more papers won't matter. But it's only temporary, mind, so don't get attached to the brat. And we'll do it my way. That means a wet nurse and a governess for Meggie and the twins while we're at it. As soon as my sister finds her a good home, Baby is going, is that understood?"

Melody gave a pretty good imitation of a salute, considering her eyes were watery and she had a baby in her arms and a big grin on her face. The soldier and the groom cheered.

Chapter Nineteen

*L*ord Cordell Coe was an experienced rake; Miss Melody Ashton was a green girl. She never had a chance. On the ride home from the poorhouse, waiting in the magistrate's parlor and showing Baby off, Melody admitted defeat. She tried to tell herself that her heart would not be broken when he left for London to resume his raffish ways. Her head told her it was too late, so she surrendered. Her virgin *heart*, that is. Melody acknowledged to herself that she loved Corey Coe and had a snowflake's chance in hell of changing his lust and liking into something else.

Melody conceded about the governess also, although Corey had been dictatorial and high-handed about hiring someone. That, too, was part of Corey's appeal, she realized, because he was right. Melody really was too busy with her chores to devote hours and days to lessons, especially when Corey expected her to mediate between Antoine and Mrs. Tolliver, to look over menus and invitation lists, bedchamber choices, and flower arrangements. The viscount did not wish to see his sister bothered with such details in a strange house for so short a time, if Melody wouldn't mind. As for Pip continuing to hold classes for the children, Corey declared that out of the question. The boy had too fine an intellect and had to be sent to school. He could study for the law or banking, where he could make a fine living for himself, or even the Church if he chose.

"And just how do you propose convincing Pip he would be happier among strangers? I have been trying for ages."

Corey just gave her one of those superior grins and said he was working on it. So Melody magnanimously yielded the point, but kept arguing until Corey practically demanded she find a suitable person immediately. Miss Ashton smiled, with no doubt that before too many days had passed she would see Miss Chase, her favorite young schoolteacher from Miss Meadow's Academy, here at the Oaks, willy-nilly. That was the way Lord Coe operated: he never seemed to be in question about what he wanted or scrupled about his means to get it. Miss Ashton could very well take a few pages from his book. She was young and lost in love for the infuriating man, but she was learning. . . . And she still had a few weeks to go.

Late that night, rocking Baby and wondering if the viscount was having as hard a time falling asleep as she was, Melody thought she heard noises downstairs. She went to the head of the stairs, intending to catch Harry on his way back from raiding the kitchen. But a light was coming from the little study where she did the books, so Melody picked up Baby and her candle, and went down to tell Pip to go to bed; he would ruin his eyes reading so late. Angie never stirred from her place at the foot of Melody's bed.

When Melody got to the bottom hallway, softly calling, "Pip," the other light went out. "I know you are there, you clunch, so light your candle and come upstairs." Nothing happened until Melody reached the study, when someone rushed behind her, shoving her into the desk, which toppled over. Melody protected Baby, but her candle went flying, right onto the pile of papers lying scattered around from the desktop.

"Help!" Melody screamed. "Harry, Pip, hurry. Fire! Up, everybody, up!" She dashed back up the stairs, nearly tripping over a frenziedly barking Angie, handed Baby into the first pair of hands she saw—Felice's. Meggie and the twins were shaking Nanny awake. As soon as Melody saw the children, Nanny, and her mother on their way out, she raced back to the study, where the old drapes were well caught, and one row of books was starting to burn. Pip was pulling them off the shelves and stamping on them, but Harry was standing in his nightshirt, open-mouthed, saying, "I didn't do it," over and over.

Melody shook him hard and shoved him out the door. "Get to the Oaks, Harry, get help. And take Angie. Her barking will get them up quicker." Melody picked up a rug and started beating at the flames.

Pip pulled the desk chair over and stood on it to tug the burning curtains off their rods, while Melody yelled that he was too close to the fire; they could let the whole place burn rather than take chances.

Then someone was pouring a bucket of water on the draperies, and someone else was shouting orders, and soon there were so many people in the little room that Melody could not breathe, for the smoke and the confusion. She dragged Pip out, past the row of men, some still wearing their nightcaps, who were passing pails of water from the pump in the kitchen to the men in the smoke-filled room. Outside, Nanny had the little girls and Ducky in a cluster, and someone had put a blanket down for Lady Ashton to be prostrated upon, with Felice nearby retucking her guinea gold curls under a lace cap lest they get sooty. The dog was tied safely, but unhappily, to a tree.

Someone, the butler, Melody thought, handed her and Pip cups of water, and she drank thirstily, then went back inside after ordering Pip to stay with the smaller children.

Melody had to see if the men were winning or the fire, so she pushed to the head of the row and took her place, handing the heavy wood buckets to the viscount. She did not even know whether he recognized her or not, under the soot and smoke. He just kept encouraging the men to keep the water coming. Then, just when she was getting into the rhythm of the pass: turn, lift, turn, hand the heavy bucket to Corey, take back the empty, turn, hand it to the man behind her, the viscount swung around and stopped to call, "That's it, men. Fire's out, we can—"

Turn, lift, turn, hand the heavy bucket to—At least the bucket missed him.

Corey insisted they all stay at the Oaks.

"But your guests, my lord," Melody protested.

"Won't be here for a few days, by which time we can have Dower House cleaned and aired. I won't have you or the children breathing that unhealthy smoke. Furthermore, the Oaks is large enough that my guests will not be disturbed, nor are they paltry enough to be overset at sharing the house with a parcel of children." Corey had his doubts about some of the guests, that stodgy Pendleton, the dirty-dish cousin of Frye's, and Lady Tarnover's cabinet-aide stepbrother, but if they didn't like the noise and confusion of Melody's brood, they knew the road back to London, or Lord Coe could show them.

Lady Ashton and Felice naturally reclaimed their former rooms as if by right, the older woman bravely waving aside Lord Coe's sooty offer of assistance up the stairs. She would survive, Lady Ashton supposed, if someone could just fetch her some laudanum, and some hot water, and a little brandy to get the smoke out of her throat. The younger children and Nanny were put in Bates's care, to escort to the old nursery and make sure they had everything they needed. When Melody handed Baby to the impeccable valet, the viscount took one look at his former batman's expression and reminded Bates that they shot deserters.

The viscount's staff was thanked prettily by Miss Ashton and practically by Lord Coe with a keg of ale, then Harry, Pip, and Corey followed Melody to the kitchen for a general cleanup and application of the salve Mrs. Tolliver kept on a shelf. Bates had earlier brought down a dry shirt for the viscount, an armload of extra nightshirts, and a dark maroon velvet robe, which Corey draped over Melody's shoulders. It smelled of him, all lemon and spice, and trailed on the floor.

Melody and the viscount had a few minor burns, but Pip had been closest to the fire at first. He stood bravely while Melody dabbed at his face and hands. "Do you think we should send for the doctor, Corey? What if he is left scarred? Oh Pip, you were so brave, and you knew just what to do!"

Lord Coe turned the boy's face toward the light, the better to examine the burns. After what he had seen in the war, these were not so bad, and most were on the side of Pip's face discolored by the birthmark. "Leave the boy be, Angel. I think he will be proud to wear a few scars, won't you, Philip, when you go off to school in the Fall? You can tell the other lads what a hero you were."

Pip turned even redder, gulped, and nodded. Melody hugged him, careful of the burns, and sent a smudge-faced smile in Corey's direction, which had his lordship wishing the boy to Jericho. Pip did not comment, but he thought it peculiar how his lordship insisted on the formality of Margaret and Philip instead of pet names, but would call Miss Melody by her first name, or even the dog's name! Pip would never understand adults.

While Melody's attention was on the other boy, Harry was raiding the larder, fixing himself some bread and jam, wedges of cheese, sliced chicken, and blueberry pie. Corey found three more plates and a pitcher of milk.

With Harry's hunger partly eased, his curiosity needed satisfaction.

"I bet it was Pike who did it. What do you think, my lord? The front door was locked when I went to get you, so he must have used the window. It was open, wasn't it, Pip? Did you notice anything else, Miss Mel?"

"Is Pike that stupid, then?" Corey wondered, slicing the pie. "I thought I made it fairly plain that I'd beat him to within an inch of his life if I ever saw him in the county again."

Melody shook her head. "He's stupid enough, but not brave enough. Somehow I do not think it was Pike in the room with me. I do remember the window open a crack, but it was a warm evening, and I may have left it that way myself. And the kitchen door is always off the latch anyway. Maybe it was just a burglar." Melody did not think so, remembering those papers spread out on the desk, Mama's letters and ledgers, but she did not want to discuss her fear that the blackmailer was back looking for more information, not in front of the boys. Corey nodded in understanding; they would talk more later.

Meanwhile, Melody had a few questions of her

own: "Harry, why did you keep saying you didn't do it? *I* lit the fire with my candle when I fell, and I knew you were asleep in bed when I called out, so why did you think I was accusing you?"

Harry chewed and swallowed first, mindful of his manners, then said, "They always blame the bastard. Ouch." Pip must have kicked him under the table. "Uh, pardon, Miss Mel, Lord Coe. It's just that at all those schools, whenever anything happened, that's who got called up first. Sometimes it was easier to admit to whatever they wanted you to confess so you'd get sent home. Otherwise they'd get around to deciding to beat a confession out of someone, and you know who that someone was going to be."

Melody put her glass down. "Harry, surely things were not so barbaric! I couldn't let Pip go if I thought—"

"Philip is too smart to get into those situations, Melody," the viscount interrupted before Philip could change his mind. "In addition, he'll have my recommendation, which will ensure him a measure of respect. I think Master Harry was not such a scholar, and perhaps not always so innocent." Harry just grinned around a mouthful. "What I would like to know is why you did not simply say you were an orphan, Harry?"

"Why, that would be lying, my lord, and maybe even putting a curse on my parents. My mum is a fine lady, Miss Judith once told me, and pays for my keep. She never had to, you know. And I've even got a father somewhere. He was real good with horses, too."

"You never contact your mother, do you, Harry?" Melody asked uncertainly.

"Oh no, Miss Judith told me I never could, or she'd stop supporting me. I would have to be 'prenticed out then, or sent to the factories or mines. 'Sides, I don't even know her name. I always figured, though, that if things got really bad around here I'd find out and ask her if she needed a new groom."

Corey choked on a piece of pie, and Melody decided it was long past time they were all upstairs. They needed baths, and Baby would be up early, and they would have a great deal of work, getting Dower House back in order.

Corey disagreed. "You three heroes shall stay abed till noon if you wish. Mrs. Tolliver can look after Baby until the nursemaid comes, and I shall send the village girls to help your Betsy with the cleanup. Margaret and I shall manage to collect the eggs and feed the chickens without you, and Bates, I am sure, will be happy to assist the twins in feeding the pigs, if Master Harry here leaves them anything to eat."

"Old fussbudget Bates would never go near the pigs," Harry jeered.

Pip added, "Or near the twins."

Corey was pulling back Melody's chair so she could rise without tripping over the robe. "He gets to choose: the twins or Baby."

Lord Coe was more confused than ever. The woman he found more desirable than any in his life was two doors down from him. She would get out of her bath all rosy and warm—Zeus, he could just visualize her long legs and narrow waist—and she would put on *his* nightshirt. And her mother, her mother, by Jupiter, was *one* door down! Nobody's mistress had a mother! Hell, nobody's mistress had a houseful of orphans or chickens or pigs. None of which meant a tinker's damn, because Miss Melody Ashton was, in fact, nobody's mistress.

Nor was she likely to be in the next few days, with her old Nanny telling her to eat her greens, the village girls having a hundred questions, that impossible mother demanding Melody wipe her brow with lavender water, some brat or other wanting a story. Worse, if Melody Ashton was not to be under his protection, then she was going to need protection from him and his reputation.

Corey was finally forced to the reluctant conclusion that Miss Ashton was not a bit of muslin after all. She was, indeed, a marriageable female, if a gentleman were so inclined, of course. He wasn't. Therefore, the viscount would not let himself be alone with her, or let his eyes watch her every graceful movement. He did not tease, did not brush against her by accident, he didn't even insult her once in the next three days.

Melody couldn't understand the viscount's coolness. He was polite, he was proper, and he could have been a parlor chair for all the affection he showed. After their shared experiences and the understanding she thought she had read in his clear blue eyes, suddenly he was a stranger.

Melody just couldn't figure it out until Dower House was nearly restored and Corey offered the ladies his coach for a trip to Hazelton to purchase upholstery fabric for new drapes. Mama and Felice were thrilled, especially when the viscount insisted on accompanying them and bespeaking tea at the best inn the town had to offer while Melody and Betsy were placing their order.

The fabric they selected was less dear than Melody had budgeted and temptingly near some lengths of damaged goods the linen-draper was trying to sell cheaply. All those fashionable ladies were coming to the Oaks, and it was Melody's own money, after all, from the dowry Aunt Judith left for her. She skipped all the rationalization; maybe the viscount would smile at her again if she didn't look like such a schoolgirl. The purchase was quickly made, a cream-colored silk shot with flecks of gold and green with only small water spots on one edge.

Next, Melody had one more brief errand before joining the others and watching the viscount fawn over Felice. She wanted to stop into St. Sebastian's, Melody told Betsy, to see where her parents were married. While Betsy had her own notions why her young mistress was interested in churches and weddings, Melody was checking the church registry.

There was the record of her parents' marriage, and there was the reason for the viscount's coldness. Melody laughed bitterly, thinking one might say she had been premature in her hopes for the regard of such a proud man. One might also say she had been premature in this marriage, if one were very, very polite.

Love. Marriage. A baby. But not necessarily in that order.

Chapter Twenty

There were good surprises in life and bad surprises. Finding a truly excellent old sherry that Lady Ashton had overlooked was felicitous. Finding that Miss Ashton's mutt was still prone to accidents in the house was not.

The new governess, Miss Chase, was a decidedly happy surprise for Lord Coe; realizing how much he missed the Ashton ménage when they moved back to Dower House was not. After a timid introduction, the schoolteacher from Bath turned out to be a pleasant, soft-spoken young woman who calmly tempered Felice's coyness and Lady Ashton's self-absorption. She and Melody shared a genuine affection, and the children were quickly enfolded in that warmth. From what Lord Coe saw of them, anyway. Now that Dower House was habitable, and Miss Chase had taken over the classroom with more formal notions of schooling, Corey saw very little of the youngsters. Astonishingly, he missed going up to the nursery in the evenings to watch Baby sleep or help read bedtime stories. He missed seeing Philip in the library at all hours or Harry in the stables.

What Corey missed most, of course, was Melody, and that was not a surprise to him at all. In fact, he had missed her before she left. While he was trying to maintain the proper distance, Miss Ashton had added miles. She was cool and aloof, conversing with Miss Chase instead of him whenever possible at meals, busy with the house or the livestock or restoring her papers to order other times. And no, she never needed his help. It was as if she were never home when Corey called, although he could see her, talk to her, almost touch her if he dared let himself, to shake sense into the peagoose. He was the one being careful, being protective. Why was she treating him like he had the pox? Didn't she know it was the man's job to back off a relationship grown uncomfortable? No woman had ever turned from Corey Coe, and it was a shock to find how lowering the experience was.

Even Bates noted his master was unusually blue-deviled and attributed the viscount's moods and megrims to postbattle fatigue, after the infantry's retreat. That would soon change, of course, with the arrival of real houseguests. Neither Bates nor Coe's London butler considered the Ashtons or the nursery party to be worthy company, although Bates had been caught out teaching Pip the proper way to knot his tie, and the starchy butler's white gloves were often sticky.

Corey decided he hated surprises. The incompetents in the Peninsular Campaign were always planning grand surprises for the Corsicans, and Lord Coe still carried the scars. When he was four his father had promised him a special birthday gift, then handed him baby Erica instead of a pony. Now that very same sister, the one for whose sake he'd gotten into this mess in the first place, wrote that she would have a surprise for him sometime after her arrival. Corey should set aside another bedchamber. If Erica thought to lecture him on his duties and then parade another empty-headed chit in front of him like a filly at auction, she was in for a surprise herself: she could very well share her room with the wench. He wouldn't. Damn and blast, Erica was supposed to come, select one of the gentlemen, and be happy ever after. Corey did not want any surprises.

Now even Lady Ashton was plotting some disaster in the guise of a treat. She had come to the library earlier, interrupting him in some notes he was making for his steward in Kent, begging another bedchamber for yet another uninvited houseguest.

"Not that Barty's not invited, oh no. I have asked him to come many a time," Lady Ashton gushed over the sherry Corey was forced to offer. "He's been gone so long, you know, and now his ship will dock any day. The letter must have gone astray, for I wrote him of our little difficulties some time ago, but you cannot care about that. It's just that I cannot see him staying at Dower House. Not that I would mind having a man around the house, what with fires and people breaking in. But it's the proprieties, you know."

She tittered like a debutante, making Corey wonder what kind of queer nabs this Sir Bostwick Bartleby was, not to be trusted in the house where his own daughter lived, with Lady Ashton and Nanny. He knew there was some irregularity about Felice's birth, that the chit had never been presented in London, but he never cared to nose about for all the details. If the old roué approached Melody . . .

Lord Coe's face must have given away his thoughts, for Lady Ashton hurried on: "Oh, you mustn't think the worst of Barty. He's as sweet as a lamb."

A lamb that would be the black sheep in a family of cutpurses, likely, Corey thought, twirling his pencil.

Lady Ashton changed tack. "The Dower House is

165

so small, you know, especially now with that Miss Chase among us, and the infant and its nurse. . . ."

Weren't the governess and the servants safe from the man? Corey would be damned if he wanted the bounder around his sister.

". . . And right now dear Felice is the tiniest bit put out with her dear papa. As much as I hate to say it, I think we might all be more comfortable if you could see your way to giving him room here."

"Wasn't he supposed to be coming to take Felice to India with him? I would have thought she'd be happy."

Lady Ashton emptied another glass and fluttered her kerchief. "There's the rub. Dear Barty wrote that he wants to settle down here in England. A new beginning, a new family . . ."

A young wife. Corey got the picture and knew what it meant to Felice's future, and Melody's. The pencil snapped in his fingers. "I could see where Miss Bartleby might be downcast, but won't the nabob, ah, Sir Bartleby make provision for her?"

"He won't countenance her going to London until he has a respectable wife, he writes. The old scandals, don't you know. And he did mention how he thought she must have been a trifle extravagant recently, the naughty puss. I'm sure he'll come around, you know, if only . . ."

If only he is not subjected to a spoiled brat's tantrums, Corey concluded. He could well visualize life with a disgruntled prima donna like Felice, and he almost pitied the man.

Then Lady Ashton spoke the fatal words: "And if everything works out, I think we may have a happy surprise for you. Melody won't have to worry about this old house anymore, or all those children. We'll all go to London."

So this selfish, silk-clad sot was promoting the match, was she, to feather her own nest? Corey would give the old rakehell house space, all right. He'd keep him so far from Melody the dastard wouldn't recognize her if he passed her on the street!

There are certain surprises that are known as ambushes. A weathered soldier learns to anticipate them, and a determined bachelor, hardened after a few Seasons on the town, knows the forewarning signs.

When no one was supposed to be in a bachelor's rooms, yet by odd scents and little rustlings someone unmistakably was, that spelled trouble. When the bedcurtains on the big four-poster were pulled shut in the daytime, only disaster for the unwary could lie within, the type of catastrophe that usually ended in screams, tears, hysterical mothers, and weddings.

Corey stayed in the doorway, mentally calculating the odds of this being another housebreaker. Nil. "Oh drat," he exclaimed loudly, "I forgot my book." He noisily walked down the hall, hiding behind a chest of drawers on the other side of the stair landing. Nothing happened, and the viscount was going to feel like a perfect fool if one of the maids found him skulking behind the furniture. He walked just as noisily back to his room. If the occupant of his bed was one of those same village girls hoping for a promotion, he could send her off with a smile and a smack to her bottom. But what if the intruder were, say, Felice, feeling ill-used and cast-off by her father, who saw a way to guarantee her own future? Ambitious and spiteful, Felice could never stand to see Melody take precedence. In one underhanded masterstroke, the golden diamond could capture herself a fortune, a husband, entry to London's most select doors, and a title, if Corey Coe were fool enough to get caught.

Zeus, what a hobble. He didn't want to embarrass the chit by calling for Bates or put off the inevitable by leaving, so he stood where he was and called, "If you are not out of there by the count of ten I shall fetch the housekeeper."

Nothing but sniffles came back to him. Hell and damnation, he thought, tears! Corey strode over to the bed, threw back the drapes, and started to bellow, "Get out of there this instant," when he realized nobody was in the bed at all. "What in blazes?"

Then two small, dirty, tear-streaked faces poked out from under the bed, and a little voice whimpered, "We're sorry, Lord Corey."

And another finished. "We didn't know it was your room."

Now Corey truly felt like a jackass, suspecting threats to his freedom the way a middle-aged spinster saw ravishers behind every bush. The only real menace he saw was explaining to Bates how there came to be so many dirty footprints on the bedcovers, as he gathered the twins close to him, propped up by the pillows.

"I am sorry I yelled at you, moppets. Now what is the problem? Running away from Miss Chase, is it? I thought you liked her."

"It's not Miss Chase," one twin started.

"It's Miss Mel," the other ended. "She wants to send the pigs off to market."

"To be killed."

By George, Corey was in trouble now. He took a deep breath. "But sweethearts, you knew the pigs had to be . . . sold. Pigs go to market, that's what they do, the same as little girls go to classes."

"But some pigs are too special."

"And should be kept home, with their friends."

Corey squeezed the girls closer. "Let me see, you don't want to keep all of the pigs, just a special—how many?" Each twin held up one finger. "Two. That doesn't seem too unreasonable. What does Miss Melody say?"

"She says we haven't enough money to keep any."

"Except the mama pigs, who will have more babies."

"But it won't be the same."

Tears started to fall again, and Corey had to shift

to find his handkerchief to blow noses. "But what can I do? Miss Ashton hardly ever listens to me, you know, and I think she would take it amiss if I told her not to get rid of the very favorite pigs. It's her business, after all. And I know she won't let me pay for their keep as I do for Baby."

Four big brown eyes looked up at him. His collar was tight. "I, ah, suppose I might tell her I need some special pigs for my country property. I could purchase the pigs from her, and then, ah, ask her to keep them awhile till they get bigger. Of course, I would have to rent some land back from her to keep them and pay for their food. Do you think she would swallow that?"

The viscount was nearly smothered in pinafores and petticoats. "I only said I would try, brats! But hold there, I want something back from you two hellions." Corey got up and went to his dresser. He fumbled in the carved wooden box that held his rings and fobs and came back with two pearl stick-pins, a black pearl and a white pearl. "What I want is a promise that you'll wear these for me, and mind you each only wear the right one. No one else has to know which is which, except us, if we are to be partners in this pig business. Agreed?"

The twins exchanged looks. "But Nanny won't like it."

"Us taking more presents from you."

"You just ask Nanny to tell you about casting pearls before swine, for you are my pearls beyond price. Now, how about if Dora has the dark, so I can remember that way? Laura will have the light." He pinned them on and kissed each forehead. "Now, let's go see if we can convince Miss Ashton."

"But what about the pigs, Lord Corey?" they chorused.

"The pigs? You mean the pigs are here, under my bed?" Two nods, two gamin grins. "Why, you little hellborn babes, I have a good mind to teach you some manners!" He picked up one of the pillows from his bed and started chasing the nearest giggling, squealing little girl, then the other. When Bates and the footmen came with milord's bath some few minutes later, they were still at it, with flying ribbons and braids and feathers all over, and piglets rooting in the middle of the viscount's bed. Bates fainted.

The twins were so happy, Melody did not have the heart to deny them. "But there is no question of your paying for the pigs, my lord," she told Corey when the girls went to put their pets in the pen.

"No, there is not," he agreed, flicking a stray feather off his sleeve. "And I expect you to charge at the same exorbitant rate you got for the house."

"My lord, I do not put a price tag on everything."

"No? That's not the impression I got from talking to your mother. Rich old men, houses in London. If that's not mercenary, I don't know what is."

"And I do not know what you are talking about, Lord Coe. I think some of those feathers must have addled your brain. And I shall not let you buy those pigs."

"Miss Ashton, you are the most exasperating female I know. You'd rather starve than take my money, for which, incidentally, I made a deal with the twins so cannot renege, yet you would sell your very soul for pinchbeck security. Don't do it, Angel."

Then, instead of hurling missiles or insults, Melody did a very surprising, uncharacteristic thing: she burst out crying and rushed up the stairs where Corey could not follow.

Lord Coe really, really hated surprises.

Chapter Twenty-one

It was a house party from hell.

The first guests to arrive were Marquise and Lady Cheyne. Lady Cheyne took one look at Baby, being walked in a pram by the nursemaid, and decided Baby would make an admirable addition to the cricket team she was building. Lord Cheyne adamantly refused, declaring that their hopeful brood was large enough as is, and he had been considering his friend Corey's invite as a second honeymoon. The happy couple retired to their suite to discuss it and were not seen again for days except for meals, although loud noises could be heard now and again coming from their rooms.

Next came the Tarnovers, with Lady Tarnover's stepbrother, the politician. Lady Tarnover had deduced, somewhere midjourney, that she had not suddenly developed motion sickness but was indeed increasing. Her husband's solicitude set her teeth on edge, but if he was not within earshot she alternately complained or wept, which did little for Lord Tarnover's peace of mind.

The early arrivals reinforced Lord Coe's convictions that the state of wedlock was more a life sentence than a comfort and joy. Marriage was looking no more appealing than ever. Corey might be confused, and he might be disturbed, distressed, and altogether discombobulated, but he could always walk away from the situation, find a new bird of paradise and resume his carefree London life—as soon as this wretched gathering was done. Corey could not even find peace and contentment in his books, for the petty bureaucrat had taken the library over for his private study. Government business, don't you know.

Then Erica appeared, *sans* companion, nor would she deign to identify the unspecified houseguest.

Lord Coe kissed his sister warmly and made her comfortable in the sitting room, but warned her that he would put up with no matchmaking on her part. "Don't think to trot out some fubsy-faced female like you did in Bath. This party is for your benefit, not mine."

"My benefit? I don't understand. I thought you were inviting your old friends the Tarnovers and the Cheynes, who have been out of town so much lately." She patted smooth a coil of pale blond hair, very much like Corey's without the sun streaks, then her eyes narrowed. "Just who else have you invited, brother?"

Corey adjusted his collar and straightened his neckcloth. "Just a, ah, few others. Lady Tarnover's stepbrother was staying with them; he's something or other in the government. I couldn't very well not invite the man, could I? And did you know Peter Frye is thinking of selling out? He is nearly recovered from that last wound, so I thought he might like some fresh country air and exercise. Fellow officer and all that. He always admired you, you know."

There was a very pregnant pause. "And one or

two others," he muttered. "Frye's staying at his cousin's, and Dickie Pendleton's been hanging around the clubs. Poor fellow had no place to go."

"That's because no place is good enough for that stuffed shirt. However did you get him to come here?" His sheepish look was answer enough. "Oh, Corey, you didn't dangle me as bait, did you? That man has been looking for a female worthy of carrying on his elevated bloodline since before I was out!"

"Well, yours is every bit as elevated as his. You have a handsome fortune and, if a mere brother may say so, you grow more comely each year. I'm pleased to see you out of mourning, my dear, and I like that new way you have of doing your hair."

"What fustian, Corey, as if you notice how I fix my hair! You needn't hand me Spanish coin either, brother, because that horse won't run."

Then, as Corey lounged against the mantle under the portrait of Melody's Aunt Judith, his meek and mild sister proceeded to blister his ears. "You listen to me, Cordell Inscoe. I am not seventeen anymore, and you do not have the ordering of my life. You nearly destroyed that life years ago with your good intentions and your self-styled superiority. I was too young to fight you then. I can only forgive you now because I know you acted out of love and what you thought was for the best. But it wasn't, Corey, and I shall never let you come the heavy with me again. For all I love you, you can be autocratic and overbearing, you know."

"It has been mentioned. Also pompous, conceited, and a few other choice epithets you would doubtless consider good for my soul." He grinned ruefully.

Erica nodded. "I am sure that was a woman speaking, and someday I would like to meet such an astute and intrepid female, but for now, you seem to have invited every eligible *parti* you could get your hands on. I refuse to have anything to do

173

with them, Corey. I have plans of my own—no, I shan't discuss them now, until I see the child—so what are you going to do with all of your bachelors?"

"You need not worry about the numbers being uneven, the place is swarming with females, some of them even astute and intrepid."

"I am intrigued, brother, but now might I see Margaret?"

"I sent one of the footmen over to fetch her as soon as you arrived. But just remember what I said about any prospective mantraps, Erica. That guest you invited sleeps in your room."

Erica smiled, the same slow smile Corey had that started at one side of the mouth and worked its way around. "I'll remember, brother dear."

When Melody brought Meggie to the Oaks, she wanted them both to make a good impression. She need not have bothered, for Lady Wooster had eyes for no one but the child—turquoise eyes, the same unusual, lovely color as Meggie's.

"Oh," was all Melody could find to say, in view of the knowing grin on Lord Coe's handsome face.

The other houseguests drove up after lunch, and the fiasco was truly underway. Erica had, as promised, no interest in the assemblage, only wanting to keep the child near her, the child who was her duplicate in miniature. The rest of the company was too polite to comment, naturally,.but Lord Pendleton's nostrils were seen to flare. When he realized he was expected to dine with the outré females from Dower House, his nose practically twitched like a rabbit's. He would not permit himself to be anything less than polite, of course, not even when Lady Ashton, with rouged cheeks and high-pitched, girlish voice, had a few too many refills of wine with her dinner and fell asleep over the sorbet.

Although he did not necessarily immediately comprehend what he saw, Major Peter Frye was a practiced observer. He considered how things stood with Lady Wooster, and he noticed how his friend Corey devoured the exquisite Miss Ashton with his eyes. Major Frye looked further afield for congenial conversation.

To Lord Coe's rather jaundiced view a few days later, it therefore seemed that things could not have gone more awry. The married couples were either bickering or in their bedrooms making up. Instead of finding a husband, his sister had found an illegitimate daughter she refused to part with, and of her prospective suitors, Lord Pendleton now had a permanent tic in his nose, Major Frye had transferred his attention to Miss Chase, the governess, and the politico had fixed his interest on Harry, of all things! At least Frye's cousin Rupert was taking on the role Corey had mentally preassigned the loose fish; it had only taken Felice's usual boasting of her father the nabob for the cawker's ears to perk up and his affections to be engaged.

Now the house was overrun with local gentry leaving their cards and paying calls, provincial beaux making calf eyes in the wrong directions, matrons pretending not to notice Lady Wooster and her butter stamp. This had to be the worst idea the viscount had ever had! Through it all, Corey had no one to laugh with, no one to help bemoan his matchmaking efforts, no one to share his concern over Erica and Meggie. In this whole crowd of people, Lord Coe was the loneliest he had ever been. His angel was gone, and he had no way of getting her back while this gypsy circus was in town.

Melody felt invisible. No one paid her any attention in the glittering crowd when the entire party from the Oaks was invited to Squire Watson's to partake of local society. Then she felt naked, as if they all knew her secrets, about the blackmail and the misused funds and her irregular birth. They were too polite to take notice, as with Lady Wooster and Meggie, but they knew. That was why the men ignored her and the women were either distantly courteous or outright unfriendly.

Melody could not have known that the local swains took one look at Viscount Coe's proprietary glare and decided to keep their distance, no matter that Miss Ashton was the most fetching thing the county had seen in ages. The older gentlemen felt it was safer to do the pretty with the married ladies and widows, the younger to get up harmless flirtations with that bit of fluff Miss Bartleby. Miss Felice was totally ineligible, of course—their mamas were frightfully provincial about such matters—but at least a chap could ask the little beauty to take a stroll in Squire's rose garden without fearing a heavy hand on his shoulder or that dagger stare in his back.

As for the women, there wasn't a female in the place who didn't see which way the wind was blowing. The single ladies hated Melody instantly for having won the race before the starting pistol was even fired. The matrons were taking a wait-and-see attitude. Not all was smooth in the courtship, obviously, but the whole shire was aware how the handsome viscount had been turning the countryside on its ear, firing constables, refilling the poor box at his own expense, and seeming pleased with these small diversions like supper at Watson's, and him a fine London gent. If ever a buck was marking his territory, the good ladies decided, it was Cordell Coe. For some reason, the viscount's suit wasn't prospering, despite the time he'd put in making up to those strange children at the Dower House, petting the calf for sure. None of the dowagers could figure it, unless that Melody Ashton had more hair

176

than wit. If she was their daughter, they'd shake some sense into the chit all right, for scurrying away like a frightened rabbit whenever the viscount approached, sitting in corners or talking quietly with his sister and that mousy Miss Chase. Lady Ashton never noticed, acting more the debutante than her daughter, fluttering around in her gauze and trailing ribbons. The other ladies, meanwhile, found the muddled wooing better than a Minerva Press romance and were content to sit back and watch.

Melody thought she was keeping busy, seeing Lady Tarnover had a pillow behind her back, moving the Madeira out of Mama's range, reassuring Miss Chase that she was not making a romance out of whole cloth, that Major Frye truly appeared smitten. No, he would not mind that Miss Chase was dowerless.

"For you come with a fine mind and gentleness of spirit he cannot help but appreciate. And my understanding is that the major has an easy competence of his own. He has even undertaken some of the expenses of refurbishing the workhouse, I understand."

"Yes, he wants to do more for the returning injured veterans. What an admirable, high-minded gentleman he is," Miss Chase said with a sigh. "If I could only prove worthy—"

Melody cut the self-doubt off in midstream. "Isn't it fortunate how things have worked out? I was so despondent that I could not offer you a position in London as my companion, and now see, you are near to making a wonderful match right here in Copley-Whitmore."

"I know I have you to thank, Miss Ashton. Even if . . . if nothing comes from Major Frye's attentions—a female in my circumstances, you know—at least I am out from under Miss Meadow's thumb. Lady Wooster wishes me to continue on with her and dear Margaret, and I would be more than pleased with the position."

Just then the gentlemen were rejoining the ladies, and Melody could see Major Frye headed in their direction. She diplomatically got up from the loveseat next to Miss Chase and said she thought Lady Wooster was beckoning.

That lady did indeed pat the sofa next to her, while Squire's wife saw her two spotty daughters fixed at the pianoforte, one to play and one to sing, for the delight of the guests not participating in the card games at the other end of the room.

"My dear, you are to be congratulated," Lady Erica said, nodding in the other couple's direction. "I think your Miss Chase is just what Peter needs, now that he has seen the world and war." Melody would have denied any credit for the match, but Erica continued. She spoke softly, not to intrude on the duet presently unraveling *Greensleeves*. "Now what about your own prospects? Forgive me for being outspoken, but Meggie adores you, so I feel like one of the family, and I sincerely hope for your happiness."

Erica also cared deeply about her brother's happiness, and she believed the two were intertwined, if only Corey would stop acting like such a nodcock. Why, right now he should have been sitting beside this intriguing miss, instead of trying to play a hand of whist and watch her every move out of the corner of his eye at the same time. Erica hoped the cocklehead lost.

Melody hid her embarrassment in polite applause for the sisters and smiled when Felice arranged herself prettily at the instrument's bench. Rupert Frye jumped up to turn her pages, and Felice proceeded to trill an Irish ballad.

"She is quite talented, don't you think?" Melody suggested.

"Quite," Lady Wooster answered dryly, noting

178

the doll-like blonde's arch look up at Rupert and her simpering smile for the rest of the company. "That one will see to her own interests, but what about you, my dear?" she persisted. "Do none of the gentlemen here please you?"

One pleased her all too well, in his dark blue superfine stretched across those broad shoulders Melody could see from here. Those were fruitless yearnings, however, so she answered Lady Wooster as honestly as she could: "I do not seek to marry, my lady. I find my independence comfortable and would not wish to become chattel to some domineering, high-handed male."

So the clunch had already made mice feet of it, his fond sister concluded, having no trouble recognizing Corey in Miss Ashton's description. She would cheerfully have strangled him for that shuttered look on the poor girl's face, but he was her brother and only a male, so what was one to expect?

"But a woman can only find security in marriage, and true fulfillment," Erica tried for her brother's sake.

Melody was astounded. Here was this woman, a widow who had flatly rejected the suitors her brother had brought for her perusal, who had a child born out of wedlock that she was determined to have by her side, who flaunted all of society's strictures, and *she* was advocating the married state!

"Forgive me, my lady, but I understood your own marriage was not entirely happy."

"Oh, that was my second marriage," Erica answered airily, applauding the end of Felice's performance. "Wooster was a pig."

"Your second? Then you were married before? And Meggie is not . . ."

She never got to finish the flood of questions or get any answers, because as Felice stepped down, that nasty, spiteful little witch tittered that it must

179

now be Miss Ashton's turn to entertain the company. Miss Bartleby knew well that Melody had no voice and could barely read the music, but her nose was so firmly out of joint that Felice determined to depress Melody's pretensions once and for all. Little Melody thought she could choose the ripest plum, did she, cozying up to his elegant sister in that insinuating way she had, leaving the gleanings to Miss Bartleby? Even the lackluster governess had attracted a wealthier, handsomer *parti* than ne'er-do-well Rupert!

At first, with all eyes on her, Melody just blushed and demurred. Then, when Felice called, "Oh come, Melody, don't be missish," Melody apologized to the company and sweetly advised them that she was looking to their well-being, for she had no musical aptitude whatsoever.

Felice issued the coup de grâce: "I thought all young ladies of breeding had musical talent."

It was Lady Ashton, after a few too many cordials, who mumbled loudly enough for everyone to hear, "That couldn't be true, Felice dear, or you'd—"

She was interrupted by Lord Coe. Throwing down his cards, Corey strode over to Lady Ashton and took the glass out of her hands. "What Lady Ashton meant to say was that Miss Melody's talents lie elsewhere."

The entire company was still; this was better than a Punch and Judy show. Melody was somewhere between horror-struck and hysterical. Lady Wooster patted her hand nervously.

"I am certain Miss Ashton is too modest to blow her own horn, unlike others, but she is a crack shot. As a matter of fact, to repay your generous hospitality and for your entertainment, I should like to invite everyone present to the Oaks in three days' time for a picnic and a rifle tournament."

The women were delighted at the idea of a picnic,

and the men were curious. It was Lord Pendleton, not surprisingly, who pointed out that it was not at all the thing for young ladies to be competing with weapons. Archery, perhaps, but never rifles.

Lord Coe grinned and his eyes sparkled. "Who said anything about the ladies competing, Pendleton? I will back Miss Ashton against any of you gentlemen!"

Chapter Twenty-two

How could he have singled her out that way in front of everybody? Melody would have done better to have thumped her way through some scales or sung Ducky's favorite nursery song, if she could have recalled it at that awful moment. She remembered the tune fine, now that she was home in her own bed. She also remembered every eye at Squire Watson's gathering being fastened on her, some in pity, some gloating at her discomfort. If she had just thought to recite a poem or something, her embarrassment would have been over by now, instead of having to be gone through again in three days' time, in front of the same group of neighbors and London sophisticates.

Melody's cheeks burned at the very thought of putting on a demonstration of marksmanship, having gentlemen wager on her prowess. She may as well tie her garters in public! If Miss Meadow got wind of such unladylike behavior, she'd choke on a macaroon and go off in a purple apoplexy. Even Miss Chase, when applied to before bed, considered the situation unfortunate but unavoidable without making the viscount look no-account. A shooting match was not what one could like, the schoolteacher declared, but if Miss Ashton was going to do it, Major Frye wanted inside information to know what odds to back, and even Miss Chase had an extra shilling or two.

So much for responsible advice. Miss Chase was correct, however, about the viscount. He had stood up for her after Felice's troublemaking pronouncement, at least temporarily directing attention away from Miss Ashton's shortcomings. Therefore, she owed him the rifle match, even if it labeled her a hoyden.

Then Melody sat up amid her rumpled bedclothes and laughed. How could she lose her good name when she never had one? She had just been whining to herself how the world and Copley-Whitmore considered her no better than she should be, with all of Mama's "minor indiscretions." Let them. Melody Ashton was going to stop feeling sorry for herself and start having a good time. The London guests would be gone all too soon, and there would be little enough joy after that. If one in particular of the town crowd chose to place his wagers on her skill, meantime, Melody vowed to do her damnedest to see he won.

He liked her, he really did. He had stationed footmen around her house at night to guard against another intruder, and he'd made sure that Lady Tarnover's stepbrother did not stay around to cut up her peace of mind. The man had to return to London, pressing government business, don't you know. Melody had it from Harry, who heard it from one of the stable lads, that it was more like a rock-hard fist pressing up alongside his chin that sent the man scurrying. Of course, Corey could have been acting for the children's welfare in those instances, but he had given Felice a biting setdown on the ride home from Squire's, saying he would rather see the infants at his lawn party than a malicious shrew set on embarrassing his friends. Felice fled in tears, and Melody was still cherishing his words. Friends. She fell asleep with a smile on her face.

The next days were too busy to get into flutters over the match, anyway. Melody did not even have a chance to get Lady Wooster aside to ask for an explanation of that lady's enigmatic remarks about an earlier marriage. "You'll see," was all Erica laughingly teased before she tripped off to hand out the formal cards of invitation. Lady Tarnover offered to do floral arrangements, and Lady Cheyne took over Baby's care so the nursemaid could help Betsy and Mrs. Tolliver with the extra baking and cleaning. Additional staff was hired from the village, along with carpenters to erect an awning over the south lawn, in case of inclement weather. The gentlemen were hunting one day, fishing the next, to provide more delicacies for the tables and to get out from underfoot. Melody spent hours consulting with Antoine, and then she, the children, and Angie went berry picking, flower gathering, pig washing. Felice sulked, and Mama was prostrate from the exertion of checking the wine cellar.

The day of the picnic dawned on a perfect spring morning, crisp and clear and smelling of new-mown grass. The sky was as blue as Lord Coe's eyes, and the bird songs were as joyful as Melody's mood. She put on her prettiest gown, the white muslin with the violets embroidered on the bodice, so that no one could find fault with her dress. It might not be as suitable for target shooting as her father's padded hunting jacket, but what a figure of fun she would look in that! No one laughed at Miss Ashton today. They all thought she looked exactly what she was: a beautiful young woman very much in love with the man who made her eyes sparkle with his compliments and her dimples appear with his teasing and her cheeks turn rosy when he took her hand in his to greet the arriving guests. As for Corey, he had given up on his determination to keep his distance. One glorious smile from Melody had melted all resolve.

"Come," he told her, "for you are surely hostess here today. Not only is it your house, but I know I have you to thank for making it a delight for my company. I am disgustingly proud of you, Angel, and you haven't even fired the rifle."

No, but she was already reeling from the recoil.

Melody decided she was having the very best day of her life. The house was glowing, the lawns looked like a fantasy from Araby with cushions and rugs spread around, and the menu would have shamed a Carlton House dinner. Meantime, the children were as shiny and polished as the silverware and on their best behavior. Ducky sat on a cushion under the awning with Nanny knitting nearby, and everyone stopped to bring him a tidbit or a flower. Lady Cheyne sat with him and Baby and taught the little girls how to make daisy chains to wear in their hair. Harry presided over the refreshments table, and Pip was deep in conversation with the vicar and Mr. Hadley. Even Angie's coat gleamed from a brushing, and the favorite pigs wandered around, ribbons in their tails and soon collars of flowers around their necks. No one mentioned the you-know-what roasting on a spit for supper after the shooting, when the twins would be back at Dower House.

Melody's heart soared. When Corey served her himself from the food tables or brought her a cool lemonade or tucked her hand in the crook of his arm as they strolled among the happy, complimentary crowds, she felt as if she was two feet above

185

the ground. What crowds? Melody only saw his smile.

When it was time for the tournament, some of the guests, especially the older women from the neighborhood, chose to stay behind on the comfortable cushions and lounges set out. Mama was napping. Felice and Rupert were off on a stroll, and Lady Erica Wooster was nowhere in sight. To no one's surprise, Lord Pendleton loudly disdained to take part in such a rackety pastime. Melody did not call him a rasher of wind as she wanted to, for trying to ruin her lovely day, or accuse the pedantic popinjay of defecting rather than be proved a failure at what he himself considered a manly art; she merely directed him toward another path through the woods, where she was sure the scenery could not help but please.

The rest of the company followed Melody and Lord Coe along the path to the clearing, where chairs had been arranged a safe distance from the targets and tables had been set out with chilled wines and lemonade. Corey took charge, directing the contestants into groups and distances, ladies going first. There were three women beside Melody on the distaff side: Squire Watson's eldest daughter who giggled nervously, the Marchioness of Cheyne, and Lady Tarnover. The local lass was a passable shot, hitting the target with her four attempts, but the two London ladies were poor marksmen at best, leading Melody to think they were taking part merely to keep her from being singled out. She smiled her appreciation for their thoughtfulness as she stood to the firing line.

Melody's first shot was wide, catching the target on the outer circle. She could hear wagers being called, Lord Coe being teased for his boasts. She settled her mind to the task at hand and hit the center blue circle with her next three tries.

Laughing, Corey took the rifle from her. "Sweetheart, it's obvious you'll never be a gambler. You're supposed to lose the first round to make the odds go higher."

"But the ladies shoot at close range," Squire put in. "I'll still take her on."

Two of the local youths stepped forward and the rest of the houseguests. Major Frye winked at Melody when he took his turn, getting two of his balls into the blue. Lord Cheyne had the best round, and only one of the local boys managed to hit the target all four tries. The other retreated to good-natured hoots and whistles and Miss Watson's ministrations.

Lord Coe refused to take a turn, declaring himself impartial judge. Everyone laughed, and Melody felt her face grow warm. For the next round the target was moved back, and Lord Cheyne was declared winner among the men. Then the marquise and Melody took turns alternating their shots, both scoring four bull's-eyes. Wagering grew more enthusiastic.

"Much more distance would be unfair to Miss Ashton, with her lighter rifle," Corey declared, "so I propose a change in the procedure to moving targets. What say you, Cheyne?"

His lordship was game, so they called intermission while Pip practiced throwing wafers in the air, and the men cheerfully argued over Melody's advantage with the lighter weapon versus the male's natural hunting instincts and years of practice, to say nothing about wars and such.

Before they could resume the match, Lord Pendleton came blundering into the clearing, all red-faced and out of breath, his hair in disorder for the first time in anyone's memory, his clothing looking dampish.

"This is the most ramshackle household it has ever been my misfortune to visit, my lord," he in-

187

formed his host and anyone standing nearby. "I shall inform my man to commence packing immediately. You'll understand, of course, this is not what I am accustomed to, nor what I was led to believe. In fact, I feel you were entirely unprincipled in your invitation, and I shall therefore be forced to sever our acquaintance. Good day, my lord." He stomped off.

Corey shook his head. "I wonder what bee that fool got in his bonnet now?"

"I, ah, think I can guess, my lord." Melody hesitated, not sure of Corey's reaction. Pendleton was a guest, after all. Corey's raised eyebrow bid her continue. "Judging from the path his lordship took, I believe he may have come upon the twins, who begged to be allowed a visit to the pond on such a lovely day. The water is quite shallow and sunwarmed, you know."

"Yes, Miss Ashton? You interest me."

"One can only assume from his lordship's, ah, distress that he did indeed encounter the twins, who were most likely swimming. They swim the same way they do everything, boisterously and with great enthusiasm."

"And au naturel if I don't miss my guess!" Corey laughed out loud. "What a sight it must have been. I hope those bare-bottomed little urchins soaked some of the starch out of his stuffed shirt, but I doubt it."

"Then you aren't sorry to see him go?"

"Heavens, no. I am only sorry you had to be insulted by the prig."

Melody smiled. "Don't be. I told him which path to take." Corey smiled back, raised her hand to his mouth, and tenderly kissed her fingers.

Major Frye coughed and called for the match to resume. Melody's fingers tingled, and she missed the first wafer. Cheyne missed, with no such excuse. Squire and Lord Tarnover were busy making side bets, and Corey stated that he would cover any and all.

"Come on, Angel," he encouraged, and she never missed another.

After three or four of Melody's dead hits, Lord Cheyne cheerfully conceded, but Corey asked Melody to continue, just to show the company he had not been idly bragging of her skill. Harry loaded, Pip threw, and Melody hit anything at which Corey pointed. Then he was declaring her the winner and ordering champagne to be poured and placing a thin gold victory circlet on her curls. If anyone was thinking of other gold bands, they were too well-bred to speak their thoughts aloud.

Squire Watson wanted to know what Coe would have done if one of the men had been triumphant.

"I've seen most of you gentlemen shoot, remember, so I was not worried. However, if the little lady was having an off day or something equally as unlikely, for instance the sky falling in, why then *I* would have challenged the winner myself. Have to keep the house honor, don't you know."

Everyone was laughing and calling for a match between Corey and Melody, and she was looking at him speculatively. She had never seen his lordship shoot at all.

Melody was never to have her curiosity satisfied, because just then Corey let out an oath. The stem of the wineglass snapped in his fingers, and champagne spilled on the lace cuffs of his shirtsleeves. His face lost all color, as if he had just seen a ghost.

He had.

The whole assembly turned to follow his gaze, where Lady Erica was slowly walking up the path with an officer in scarlet regimentals at her side. He was seen to be limping, and his arm was across her shoulders. From the expression on the soldier's face when he looked at Corey's sister, his arm was not there just for support. Meggie danced along beside them.

When they were close enough, Lady Wooster announced: "Ladies and gentlemen, may I present Lieutenant Bevin Randolph, late of His Majesty's Second Cavalry."

"I thought you were dead." Corey spoke before anyone could greet the new arrival.

The young officer looked Lord Coe in the eye and addressed him as if no one else was there. "I was. That is, I was declared missing and presumed dead. When I recovered and found myself in a French gaol, I had no way of communicating with our forces. Later, too late, I was released only to discover that Lady Erica had been married. I know who to blame for that."

Corey, too, seemed to have forgotten the eager-eared audience. "You were gone, man. And you were young and penniless besides. I couldn't let my sister waste herself on—"

"On a mean-spirited old man who made my life a misery?" Erica put in. "Who wouldn't let me see my own daughter?"

"*My* daughter," Lieutenant Randolph bit out. "And I will never forgive you for that, my lord, nor for the way you settled matters between us in Scotland. You would not listen to reason, not even your own sister's sworn oaths that we were on our way back from Gretna, not on our way there. You knocked me unconscious and had me trussed like a hen, to be shipped out to my unit. My lord, you cost me seven wretched years, for each of which I have been waiting to do this." And he pulled his fist back and struck Lord Coe a smashing blow to the jaw.

Corey wasn't expecting the punch, wasn't even thinking of anything but what a fool he had been. His feet went out from under him and he hit the ground, hard. One minute Corey was seeing stars, the next Melody's green eyes, deep with concern.

190

He stayed where he was, finding the cradle of Melody's lap much more comforting than getting up and facing the avid crowds or his sister's long-lost love. While Melody used Corey's neckcloth to dab at the blood dribbling down his chin, Corey felt his jaw—nothing broken—and said, "Welcome home, Lieutenant Randolph."

Erica smiled and tossed her handkerchief down to Melody. "I can see you have gained a little sense in all these years, brother. We'll continue the discussion later, if you don't mind." She turned to go, the scarlet-clad officer's arm back around her. "Oh, there was one more thing," she said, giving Corey back his own one-sided grin. "I have had the lieutenant's bags brought to my bedchamber. Those were your instructions, weren't they?"

Chapter Twenty-three

"*W*hy didn't the silly widgeon say anything for all those years?" Lady Ashton wanted to know. She had Melody pulling out every gown in the wardrobe. The nabob had finally arrived. Melody was trying to explain why they should put Sir Bartleby up at their own house rather than impose on Lord Coe and his sister at such a sensitive time.

Mama had slept through most of the startling events of the picnic and had seen nothing of the Oaks contingent for the whole day and night after. Brief close-mouthed calls from Lady Cheyne and Major Frye told Melody little, for if either of the visitors to Dower House had any more information about Lady Wooster's marriages, they were not discussing details, out of courtesy to their hosts and friends. Rupert came to call on Felice, but since he hardly knew the time of day, Melody did not believe he could shed any light on the situation. Who would tell such a rattlepate anything?

Melody had been wondering if she could call at the Oaks that morning, just to see how the viscount was getting along, of course, when Lady Wooster, or Mrs. Randolph as she must be, hurriedly came to call. Erica begged Melody's pardon for causing a scene and for keeping her in the dark. Now Melody was trying her best to explain the delicacy of the situation to her mother. It was like explaining diapers to Baby.

"Nonsense," Lady Ashton declared, making a face at the purple satin gown Melody held up for inspection. "They have a house full of guests right now. One more won't matter, and Barty don't stand on ceremony. No, that one won't do. I look like someone's mother in it."

Melody blinked. Mama *was* someone's mother, hers. Because of that, Melody felt she had to save the older woman from a possibly deserved setdown. According to his sister, Lord Coe was already nursing a dreadful sense of ill-usage along with a bruised jaw.

"But Mama, with Sir Bartleby at the Oaks, they will have to invite us to dinner; that's at least five strangers they would be wishing to Coventry, and Lady Erica is top over trees as is."

Lady Jessamyn shook her head. "Foolish beyond permission."

"Lady Erica? I think she was worried over the lieutenant's reaction to Meggie, that's why she did not want to tell anyone in advance."

"No, you peagoose. That gown. I look sallow in yellow. Whatever possessed me to purchase it? What was that about Meggie? They are going to take her off our hands, aren't they?"

"Yes, Mama, but Lady Erica could not be sure, earlier. When Lieutenant Randolph finally wrote to her, after he learned she was widowed, he knew nothing about a child. Once Lady Erica saw Meggie, though, she never wanted to part with her daughter again, so she was going to go live in Corn-

193

wall where no one would know the child wasn't Wooster's."

"But I thought you said she was married to that soldier, Melody. Hold up that pink sarcenet again."

"She was, but she had no papers to prove it, and if he chose not to acknowledge Meggie, she was going to reject him, despite all the sorrow. But he adored Meggie on sight and wants them all to emigrate to Canada, away from any gossip. There was another dreadful row, it seems, for Lord Coe wants to set them up in London, so he can share Meggie with them. Lieutenant Randolph refused to be so beholden to the viscount, but I believe they have compromised on some plantations Lord Coe owns in Jamaica, where Bevin, that's the lieutenant, will act as his agent. Of course, Corey made Bevin swear to bring his family back to visit. I'll miss Meggie, too, won't you?"

"The magenta? No, it's much too puritanical. I bought it when I was hoping to impress that toad Pendleton for you. Isn't there a figured silk in that closet?"

Figured? The gown had cabbage roses down its length. Mama would look like walking wallpaper. "No, I don't see it. Perhaps it got left at the Oaks by error. What about this pretty lavender India muslin? It would be perfect for a small dinner here, just the family, you know, to welcome the nabob, ah, Sir Bartleby home."

"Melody, you try my patience. I have not seen Barty in almost twenty years except for the twenty minutes when he first arrived. Do you think I am going to entertain him at this dowdy place and have those little monkeys hanging off him all evening? No, I am going to welcome him home to *my* home, in style, where there are enough rooms that we can have a private tête-à-tête if he desires. Without dog hairs on the furniture and infants bawling and

Nanny's needles going click-click-click every blessed minute."

Obviously, Melody was missing something here. "Mama, isn't Sir Bartleby coming to fetch Felice?"

"No, didn't I tell you? Barty is going to settle in England. He's discussing it with Felice up at the Oaks now. I don't know what's to become of the chit, after all the high expectations she had. I just don't think London will accept her, but I couldn't make her see that she'd do better with that nice boy Edwin at Mr. Hadley's office. Rupert Frye is an ivory tuner if I ever saw one, and after your father, I know the breed. He's only hanging about for the money, 'pon rep, which Barty ain't about to hand over to some here-and-therein knight of the baize table. Barty didn't get to be a wealthy man by bankrolling basket scramblers. Maybe he can make Felice see sense, for he doesn't want her living with us."

"Us?"

"Perhaps I should wear the ecru lace. That high waist won't show what he needn't see, although I've kept my figure well enough, wouldn't you say, Melody?"

"Us, Mama?"

"Of course, Barty always did like his women plump. Do stop that goggling, Melody. You look like a goldfish. Us. Barty and I, together as we should have been these twenty years past."

Twenty years? "But what about Papa? I thought you were so in love, marrying despite your families' opposition."

"In love with that feckless Ashton? Oh, he was a handsome devil and had a title, and we did think his father would come around in time. But I married the useless lobcock to spite Barty, pure and simple. We had an understanding, but he refused to give up his opera dancer till the wedding. That was Felice's mother. I wouldn't set the date with

195

any faithless whoremonger, so there was a big row-dydow right in the park. I was very young, of course. Got straightaway into James Ashton's carriage and convinced him how romantic it would be to flee to Scotland. I didn't know he found it politic to leave town right then because of the duns at his door. He thought *I* had money. Romantic, hah! The inns were damp, his horses were bone-rattlers, and we had hardly a pound note between us."

Melody sat down, dumping her mother's dresses off the chair and onto the floor to do so. "You eloped to Scotland like Lady Wooster? I thought you were married in Hazelton. I saw the marriage records there."

"We had to come live with Judith when I found I was increasing. Ashton was below hatches, for a change. Judith called the Scottish wedding a heathen rite and insisted on a grand, public, religious ceremony for the neighbors' sake. She also insisted on taking in Felice when the opera dancer left the chit on Barty's doorstep and his parents washed their hands of him except for buying his passage to India. Judith did it just to spite me, I always thought, though sometimes I suspected she had a soft spot for Barty herself. I tried to love Felice like Judith did, for Barty's sake, you know. The child could have been mine, but I was always glad she wasn't."

Neither woman heard Felice's soft steps outside Lady Ashton's door. Lady Ashton was searching out kid gloves to match the ecru gown, and Melody was too busy in her mind, blowing notions of her parents' storybook love affair to pieces like the wafers in the rifle tournament. They did not love each other; they were adolescent fools who spent years regretting their hasty vows. But they were married, over the anvil or not, long before Melody's appearance. She wasn't a . . .

"How dare you, Melody Ashton!" Mama was

thoroughly indignant, and not just because her dresses were on the floor. "What kind of woman do you think I am? I'll have you know your mother is a lady!"

The nabob was a caricature, thought Corey, in his upward-curving, pointy-toed slippers, baggy trousers, billowy silk robes, water pipe, and more rings than Rundell's. He was outspoken, overfamiliar, overweight. How could it be that Melody was too busy getting ready for this overstuffed mushroom to so much as inquire into Corey's well-being? She had to know his phiz would only frighten the children if he came to Dower House, so obviously she did not care. Hell and tarnation, now Corey had to entertain her would-be fiancé. If the blighter didn't stop puffing smoke in Corey's face and didn't stop crowing what a fine figure of a gel she was, he would be out on his fat ear in jig time. By Jupiter, Lord Coe knew what a fine figure Melody had, and the idea of this sausage-fingered caper merchant so much as touching her made the rest of his face look as bilious as his injured jaw.

"Do you think she'll have me? I mean to do it right this time, don't you know," Sir Bartleby was nattering on.

"Do you mean to say you've proposed before and been turned down?"

"Aye, but she was just a wee lass then, and I botched it. She asked if I'd be faithful, and all I could swear was that I'd try."

Corey could well imagine Melody's reaction to a philandering husband. "And now?"

"Oh, now I'd lie. Bostwick Bartleby don't make the same mistake twice, you know. Of course, it would be easier if I could see my little girl settled first, so as I can get on with my courting without reminders of past lapses, heh heh. I don't suppose you'd be interested? A fine gent like yourself needs a pretty armful to—"

"No."

"Aye, it's a sore shame, it is, but the chit's birth is against her. Of course, I intend to come down heavy for the right man."

"If I loved your daughter, sir, her birth would not matter tuppence. Without love, all the gold in Asia could not make me a tenant for life."

"Aye, Jessie warned you were a toplofty devil. Don't see what you young 'uns are about, dallyin' around, not that I did so well in my salad days neither. Still, there is Felice to consider. A rare handful, that puss. Pretty as can stare, too. No way I can take her to London with us, her being the image of her mother. Ah well, take one hurdle at a time, I always say. What about a toast? Here's to successful wooing."

Corey nearly gagged.

Antoine's fine dinner stuck in Melody's throat. She would tell Corey, she should tell Corey, but how *could* she tell Corey that she was not baseborn after all? A lady did not simply approach a gentleman after dinner and announce that she was not a bastard, that her birth was every bit as good as his own, and therefore . . . and therefore what? And therefore he could tender an honorable proposal? Therefore he was free to love her as she loved him? Melody could sooner take her slippers off and dance on the tabletop through all five courses and removes.

The nabob would likely applaud, the old roué. If that overfed philanderer pinched her one more time or patted his lap for her to sit, Melody would box his ears. Could that enormous rock pinned in his cravat be a real ruby? No wonder Corey was scowling, the way Barty and Mama were carrying on like turtledoves right at his table. Perhaps this evening was not a good time to seek a private conversation with the viscount anyway.

As soon as the gentlemen rejoined the ladies after dinner, a still glowering Corey asked Miss Ashton to attend him in the library on a business matter. Miss Ashton took one look at his forbidding expression and thought she had better remain with her mother, in case that lady's delicate constitution required a daughter's care.

"Your mother is as delicate as an ox," Lord Coe declared, grasping Melody firmly by the arm and leading her from the room. "And she has as much motherly instinct, if less sense. If I don't miss my guess she and that court card pasha will be off for a stroll in the rose garden shortly to decide your future."

Melody certainly hoped the infatuated lovebirds would get on with the formalities and make the announcement soon before she sank with embarrassment. The viscount nodded curtly to his sister, who was trying to hide her smiles behind a fan. Erica smiled encouragement to Melody.

"Mama is just a trifle excitable, my lord," she started to say when they reached the library.

"My stallion is a trifle excitable, too, Miss Ashton, and I keep him on a short rein. No, don't get in a dudgeon. I did not mean to insult your mother, and if I have to wish you happy, then I shall, although I wish you will reconsider."

While Corey poured them both glasses of wine Melody told him, "But, my lord, I have nothing to say in the matter."

"I cannot believe that of you. You have been the most outspoken, managing female of my acquaintance." He held up his hand. "No matter, that is not what I wish to discuss. Another blackmail letter has been delivered to my sister this afternoon."

Melody was shaken by that. "Oh no! Just when

199

Lady Erica seems to be finding such joy. Who could be so cruel? How did the letter come?"

"Sip your wine, Angel, you look too pale. No one shall harm Erica or Meggie, have no fear. The letter was in the basket with all of the other post and notes from the locals thanking us for the picnic. No one recalls the letter in particular. That's not important, nor is anyone's getting wind of Erica's so-called bigamous marriage to Wooster. It will be a nine days' wonder in London, till something else comes along. Erica wishes to forget about the threat and let the blackmailer do his worst. I spoke to your mother earlier, and she told me to let it drop, also. She seems to feel the nabob would know how to handle any awkwardness that might come up about the money or extortion threats."

"But we have to catch the criminal! There are other people who could be threatened, and people would keep on thinking it was Mama who's the villain."

Corey smiled for the first time. "I knew I could count on you, Angel. I, too, would like to see an end to this business, and I do not want to see my family affairs published in the broadsides if I can avoid it. Now that I have your permission, I can proceed to lay a trap for our scoundrel."

"Wonderful. When and where? What shall I do to help?"

His lordship sat back. "But, Melody, an outlaw rendezvous is no place for a lady."

"Don't be cork-brained. Of course I must be there."

Corey got out of his chair and came around to her side of the desk. "No, my dear. I know you are pluck to the backbone, but there could be danger."

Melody stood, too. "You know very well I can protect myself. I am going." Her determined chin came up, and for once Lord Coe was not amused.

"There are other dangers. There could be a messy

200

scandal with bailiffs and magistrates. You are not going, that's all." He pounded the desk for emphasis.

"I know what it is," she declared, pounding right back. "You don't trust me!"

"Hell, woman, it has nothing whatsoever to do with trust. I am trying to keep this thing quiet." His fist came down again, hard.

"Quiet!" she shouted. *Wham.* "What do you think I am going to do, yell it from the rooftops that you are planning to catch a thief?" *Wham.*

"You've already just notified the household and half the countryside, blast you for an interfering shrew."

"And blast you for an evil-tempered tyrant. I am going!"

"No, you are not!"

Now by this time the poor old desk was rocking. Pencils had long gone flying, papers were scattered. One more solid blow should see the decanter overturned. That final whack came as Miss Ashton turned to leave: "Then I hope the thief shoots you, and you die and go straight to hell." *Wham.*

Corey grabbed the decanter just as the door slammed behind her. "And I," he said to the empty room, looking down to see his lace sleeve trailing in the spill from the upended inkwell he hadn't caught in time, "hope the nabob has a very patient valet."

Chapter Twenty-four

So he didn't trust her, did he? Well, Miss Melody Ashton would just show that smug son of Satan a thing or two! She would take her good name, her first-ever silk gown, if she finished sewing it on time, and she would go to the assembly in Hazelton with the rest of the Oaks party—and she would flirt! Now that she was to have her dowry restored by the nabob, either out of generosity or a desire to get her off his hands, she could even simper like a debutante at her come-out. Yes, that's what Melody swore to do. She'd had enough lessons from watching Felice, and even from observing Mama flutter around Sir Bartleby. Melody would giggle and bat her eyelashes and hang on some man's every word, stars in her eyes and . . . and rouge on her cheeks. She would go find herself some nice lad who liked children and dogs. Perhaps a modest landowner, or even a farmer, anything but a sophisticated man of the world whose emotions were as shallow as his hedonistic life. Her beau would have kind eyes and a pleasant face, but not be so attractive that he had an elevated notion of himself. He would have a sturdy, pleasant build without looking like some god every woman had to worship on sight. He would laugh and dance with her, and never, ever think that Melody was a liar or a cheat or a light-skirt.

That's what she would do, go find herself a husband. Why should Melody Ashton sit home on the shelf with only her dog for company? She was barely eighteen, and she had never been to a real ball. Just because some toplofty lordling did not trust her, she did not have to sit home weeping like some third-rate Juliet. Melody wiped her eyes. Trust him, he had said. But the trust was not to be reciprocal, it turned out. He wouldn't even tell her how he could suddenly tell the twins apart. He wasn't even her friend, and her dog was a more loyal companion. She sewed faster.

Melody's dress was finished on time, if her new mantel of cold-blooded manhunter wasn't. The gown was exquisite, falling in graceful folds that hugged her slim, striking figure. The bodice was a little lower than Melody was used to, but Mama assured her she would be out of the mode in a high-necked creation. In fact, there had simply not been enough fabric. That was why the sleeves were mere puffs, and the skirt was narrower than Melody would have liked. Tiny green leaves had been painstakingly embroidered over the cream silk wherever there was a water stain, and an ivory silk rose with three green leaves was fixed at the décolletage, bringing her charms to immediate attention. Another rose was fixed to the gold victory crown on her head, with her chestnut curls, shining from every potion known to a houseful of women and a great deal of brushing, gathered up and threaded through the circlet to fall in waves down her back. That was no angel's halo tonight, but the golden lure of a temptress.

The children were awestruck, even Pip beginning to realize how grown men could make such mooncalves of themselves. Mama never noticed Melody's appearance, fussing with her own before Barty's arrival, but Felice said something cutting about sparrows dressed up as swans, so Melody knew she must look as good as Harry said, bang up to the mark. Even Nanny said she'd do, and she'd better not. Nanny's gift of a gossamer-stitched shawl, made from the viscount's green wool and draped charmingly over her arms, made Melody feel even more like a Siren and less like a schoolgirl— if only her knees weren't turned to pudding.

The nabob simply pinched Melody's cheek as usual when he came to collect them, having quickly learned that Lady Ashton grew liverish if he paid fulsome compliments to any other female, even her own daughter. Instead of going into raptures over Melody's appearance, he bowed at the shrine of his ladylove's beauty. Mama's chest inflated with pride. She did not even hear her cavalier's corsets creak. She had found the cabbage-rose gown after all and made a perfect match to her gallant in his yellow pantaloons, red-and-black striped waistcoat, puce brocaded coat, and enough gems to make a dragon drool. If Mama looked like wallcovering, Melody decided, then her new steppapa-to-be looked like upholstery. That thought carried her to Sir Bartleby's hired coach, where she took her seat between Felice and Miss Chase. The governess had been convinced to attend the assembly, thus stretching the conventions, only after Melody's nervous pleas for moral support at her first ball, combined with Major Frye's entreaties and her own heart's desire. The major was waiting with the two carriages of the Oaks party at the main road, so they could all travel together for safety on the hour-long journey.

The hour was too short for Melody, who worried

that no one would ask her to dance. No matter, she wouldn't remember the steps anyway. Or she would stumble, or her hair would come undone, or Mama would overindulge in the ratafia. A thousand things could go wrong, like Viscount Coe not noticing her.

She need not have worried. Melody drew his eyes like the only candle in a cavern, except there were acres of people between them, many women more sumptuously dressed, most with more jewels, fuller figures, or more confident smiles. She was the only one he saw.

By the time the viscount could get to her side, the orchestra was tuning up for the first set. Damn, he thought, he was too late. That fat old fop would have her first dance for sure. Corey could not turn back without looking churlish, so he continued to where Major Frye and his cousin Rupert had joined their ladies. Corey was resigned to having the first dance with Lady Ashton. After the usual greetings, however, when he bowed over that overdressed old beldam's hand and requested her company for the opening quadrille, the nabob got piqued.

"Here now," he huffed. "That little lady is mine. I've been waiting twenty years for this dance, and I don't mean to be cut out by any jackanapes in funeral garb. This newfangled style of only wearing black and white must go with the sober-sided way you do your courtin'. Get on with it, lad, and leave Lady Jess to me. Frog bonnets, boy, the gel's like to die of embarrassment if you don't stand up with her."

The old fool was after Lady Ashton all along, not Melody? Angel wasn't going to marry this over-blown bank account? The smile that broke over Corey's face could have lighted the darkest night. It did for Melody, blushing furiously, when Corey turned to her and said, "In that case, may I have the honor of the first dance with the most beautiful woman here tonight?"

"Can't," Bartleby called back over his shoulder. "I already do."

At which Peter Frye, taking Miss Chase's hand, chivalrously countered, "No, I do."

And his cousin Rupert, standing by Felice, could do no less than repeat, "No, I do."

All those "I do's" were sounding remarkably like a death knell in Corey's head, and the icy hand of fate was tapping him on the shoulder. No, the hand on his shoulder belonged to Jamie Murdock, begging an introduction to Melody. Murdock was a London acquaintance with a country estate somewhere hereabout, the viscount recalled. He was also darkly handsome and the very devil with the ladies. "No," Corey answered, sweeping Melody away on the first strains of the dance.

This was not Miss Ashton's longed-for country swain, no biddable boy who would never shake the foundations of her very being. This was Corey, and Melody shook. She floated into his welcoming arms.

The quadrille required concentration and movements between the other couples in their set, leaving little time for conversation. The viscount did manage to ask how long Lady Ashton and the nabob had been keeping company.

"Forever, it seems. Can you believe it? He really is a very kind man, and Mama seems much more lively since his return. I don't know how I can learn to call him stepfather, but I shall try."

"Has an announcement been made then?"

"Look at them. I think that is declaration enough." If the same could be said for another couple whose eyes never left each other, whose hands lingered over every touch of the dance's movements, then the local gossips could save another note to the London papers. Melody just kept floating.

When the next figure brought them together,

Melody felt she had to ask: "What about the letter? Have you captured the criminal?"

Corey did not want to argue, not now. He simply answered, "Sh, not tonight." Melody was content.

After the dance and a walk around the room on Corey's arm to greet the guests from the Oaks, Melody was pleased to accept the offer of Major Frye for the next set. Then she danced in turn with Lord Cheyne, Lord Tarnover, and Sir Bartleby, who performed every dance like an Irish jig. She was happy to sit out the next set with Lieutenant Randolph, whose injuries, he said, precluded taking the floor with the show of grace her beauty deserved.

"How gallant you are, sir, when you must know my toes are in agony and desperate for a hot soak."

Then it was time for another magical interlude with Corey, and her feet stopped aching. Dancing on clouds was never fatiguing. She wished it might be a waltz, on this her night of firsts, but the waltz was not yet sanctioned in the rural fastness of Hazelton. Corey handed her off to Major Frye, for his second dance, and excused himself. Perhaps the men were tired of their duty dances and were getting up a card game, Melody considered, for Lady Tarnover was sitting with Lady Cheyne on the sidelines, their husbands nowhere in sight. Now that Melody thought about it, Lady Erica and her soldier were no longer among those sitting on the gilt chairs, either. Melody looked around during the dance to note that Felice and Rupert must have gone out to the balcony, silly chit that she was, without a care for her reputation. Mama and Sir' Bartleby, who should have been watching, had eyes for no one else. Melody shrugged. It was not her concern, not tonight. . . .

After the dance, Major Frye led her toward the chairs where Miss Chase was now sitting, mentioning something about Squire Watson and a horse for sale. Melody's eyes narrowed. Not tonight? Then why was every one of the viscount's friends missing? Why all of a sudden were local gentlemen stumbling over each other to get to her side, when all evening they had been kept at a distance by Corey and his guests? They may have been the landed gentry and country squires she thought she wanted for a biddable husband, but not tonight. She made some excuse and followed Major Frye across the room.

Melody dashed into the ladies' withdrawing room and searched hurriedly for her cloak. Nanny had insisted she bring the green velvet so she didn't get her death of cold in that skimpy dress on the ride home. Now Melody wanted the wrap to pull over the white of her gown and her hair for some cover of her identity. She did not spot the cloak immediately and was afraid she would lose sight of the major if she dawdled. The night was warm enough, at least.

Frye was headed toward the rear of the assembly rooms, down an alley toward a building under construction. Melody waited until no one was nearby to see her, then ducked outside and around the other side. She could circle back without being seen by Frye or—yes, there was Lieutenant Randolph in his scarlet jacket, propped against a lamppost across the street, nonchalantly blowing a cloud. His back was facing her, so she darted into the shadows of the dance hall and sped down the dark corridor between it and a neighboring building, ignoring scurrying noises and the fact that her white gown was trailing in the alley's filth. She stopped when she neared the new structure, squatting behind a pile of bricks. She picked one up, just in case. The new building's framework was partially completed, but open enough for her to see Corey with his fair hair standing behind a half wall. He was making no effort to conceal himself or stay in the shadows;

he just stood there, his shoulders drooped, his head down.

Cautiously, Melody approached. "Corey?" she whispered, in case the trap was still to be sprung.

Lord Coe spun around. "You jade," he snapped out, grabbing her by the shoulders and shaking her till her teeth rattled. "What did you have to come back for, to gloat? Damn you, I let you get away once, now what am I supposed to tell the others?"

Melody tried to pull away from the madman; his grip was like iron, and he kept shaking her. "What happened? Did you open the satchel and discover the fake bills? Did you think you could just waltz back here and come the innocent with me? I saw you, damn your hide, in that blasted green cape of yours. You fool, couldn't you even have worn something less distinctive? What if Cheyne or Tarnover saw you in the street, you could end up in goal. Damn you, Melody Ashton," he cried. "I would have given you anything. You didn't have to steal it!"

"You *let* her get away? You idiot!" Melody had to break loose to go after the criminal. When she threw her hands up to break his hold, she forgot about the brick in her hand, truly she did.

Some few minutes later, Coe managed to pick himself up out of the dirt and give the whistle signal to his friends, who finally gave chase, after they stopped laughing.

The posting house, that had to be the thief's destination, Melody thought as she ran down Hazelton's main street. The dastard, she alternated, thinking she was it! The ball was the perfect time for such evil-doings, with so many people inside, no one out to see a lady in a green cloak. No one but a pig-headed jackass, she amended.

Melody's breath was rasping in her throat, and her toes were truly aching this time, for light dancing slippers were never meant for this hurrying over rough cobblestones and uneven plank sidewalks. The pain in her side was growing, and she would never forgive that miserable makebate if the thief made it to the London coach, whose tin horn was just sounding as it entered town from the other direction.

Just a block or two from the posting house, Melody spotted her own green cape. She used her last burst of energy to close the distance between herself and the small female figure and her hustling companion. Wrapping her knitted shawl around the brick she still carried, Melody shouted out, "Stop right there, Felice, or I'll shoot."

Felice dropped the satchel and raised her hands, but Rupert hesitated. "You know I won't miss at this range," Melody reminded when he looked like he would snatch up the bag and Felice and make a dash for it.

"You wouldn't shoot," Rupert sneered.

"No, but I would," said the familiar, deep voice at Melody's back amid the pounding of many feet.

Chapter Twenty-five

$\mathcal{E}$verything was tied up neatly, and everyone's future was settled. Everyone's but Melody's.

Felice and Rupert were being sent off to Canada with those tickets Lieutenant Randolph had bought in case he and Erica had to flee the country. The nabob wept into his yellow handkerchief when he brought Melody the news the next morning. Major Frye had quietly shepherded Sir Bartleby, Mama, and Miss Chase from the assembly, giving out that Felice had taken ill, and Melody was waiting with her in the carriage. Felice was not there, of course, and Melody had had to explain to the others. Mama swooned and Sir Bartleby blamed himself.

"It's all my fault for making so many promises. I never knew what to do with a chit except buy her things, you know."

Lady Ashton roused herself enough to go *tsk*. "Fustian. The girl was just like her mother, greedy and selfish through and through. How could she have done such a thing to me?"

"She said she wanted to get away," Melody explained, "where she would not always be the second-class, second-rate bastard stepdaughter. And she had no sympathy for the other parents who tossed their children away like handing castoffs to the ragman. She must have been bitter for many years. She also admitted she was downstairs the night of the fire, looking for more names."

The nabob had gone back to the Oaks to write one last check to his errant daughter. He stayed until the details were all worked out, and he could report back to Melody. She patted his beefy hand, and he blew his nose. "That man Hadley had to be called in this morning to transfer monies and things, and it seems the young fellow Edwin he took into his office was helping Felice gather the information. He says she made him believe some of the children just wanted to know their real parents' names. I don't know, the cub could have been under her thumb the same way I fell for her mother. I said I'd give him a chance after Hadley was all for throwing him out. Send the cawker to India to my partners. Always opportunity for a likely lad."

"That's very kind of you, sir. I don't think Edwin was truly dishonest; Felice was just so convincing."

"Call me Barty, m'dear, and perhaps you won't think I'm so kind when I say that we won't be going to London after all. Your mother is such a delicate little flower, you know, and this has been an ordeal. I'm thinking of taking a house in Bath or Brighton for the summer, as soon as she is well enough to travel, so my Jess can recuperate. Would you mind very much, m'dear?"

"Of course not, sir, ah, Barty. I think that is an excellent idea." It would be even better if the two were married before they went to scandalize another town, Melody thought, but she only agreed. At least Mama needn't be around when people started to ask about Felice. Melody had a hard time convincing Sir Bartleby that she had no regrets over London and no intentions of playing dogsberry to the lovebirds in Bath. "I am still needed here, you know. The children."

But Meggie would be leaving shortly with Lady Erica and her husband. Lord Cheyne had bowed to the inevitable, of course, so Baby would also be going when the house party broke up in a day or two. Pip would be off to school in a matter of weeks, and Harry was begging to be allowed to travel to Ireland, where Lord Coe had a cousin managing a racing stud for him. The cousin had written offering Harry a place, if he wanted to study hard to be a horse trainer. There was nothing the boy wanted more, and Melody could not deny him, no more than she could have kept Meggie from her parents or Baby from an idyllic home.

Miss Chase was staying on for a time with the twins. She was paid through the quarter, she said, but Melody suspected from the governess's placid smile that Miss Chase was biding her time while Major Frye settled with the War Office. Melody had an inkling he was thinking of relocating in the neighborhood where he was so involved with the poor and the returning veterans. She would not be at all surprised if he and Miss Chase decided to begin their family with a pair of irrepressible imps.

So everything was settled, and everyone had what they wanted. Except Melody, who would have Nanny and Ducky and a lot of pigs. And Angie. No one was likely to fall in love with the dog and beg to carry the mutt away, not the way Melody's luck was running. What she also had was a big bouquet of white roses with a card that read, *Please forgive me.*

In addition to the flowers, Melody had the memory of Corey softly kissing her last night in the streets of Hazelton, before he sent her off with Major Frye while he dealt with Felice and Rupert.

He was leaving in two days. Roses and remembering were not enough to last a lifetime.

She gave him another day before taking matters and a leather-covered box into her own hands. She did not stop in the parlor to greet the company or wait for the butler to announce her. Melody marched straight through to the library and plunked the box down on the desk.

Corey jumped up at her entry, took one look at the glitter in her eye and quickly moved the cognac decanter and glass out of her range. If he had been sipping courage from the bottle, it did not help his appearance any. One side of Lord Coe's jaw was purplish-yellow, while the other side was raw, red, and partially covered with sticking plaster. There was no way he could shave around that mess, so he had a seedy, shady look despite his elegant clothes, not helped by the dark circles under his eyes from another sleepless night, or their slightly bloodshot appearance.

Melody refused to be swayed by sympathy. Her heart was hardened against this rogue. She snapped open the lid of the leather case and announced: "Since I have no father or brother to defend my honor, I hereby challenge you to a duel."

Corey shook his head to clear it. God, she was magnificent when on her high ropes. No other woman of his experience could be so feminine and alluring, while behaving like a veritable Amazonian warrior, and sounding like a peagoose. "What about the nabob?"

"He has enough burdens to bear. This is between you and me, an affair of honor."

"Not even an affair yet, sweetheart."

She ignored the interruption. "Your evil intentions have been clear from the first. You have toyed with my affections, compromised me more times than I can count, even kissed me in public."

"And in private," he reminded.

Her cheeks reddened, but Melody was not finished. "You frightened away my beaus so I could not make a respectable match, and you cast slurs on my integrity. I demand satisfaction."

"I apologized for that, Angel. It was the blasted green cape."

"You didn't trust me even before that. If you had let me help set the trap none of this would have happened."

"I only wanted to protect you."

"You didn't trust me."

He ran his fingers through his hair, disordering the careful arrangement. "I never trusted any woman. What can I do to make amends?"

"You can meet me in the woods clearing, unless you are afraid."

He raised one eyebrow. "Ah, a challenge match. I confess I am curious, too, about which of us is the better shot."

"No, my lord, not a contest of skills, a real duel."

"You mean like between gentlemen?" The thought struck Corey as funny, and he chuckled.

Melody did not see the humor. She picked up the half-full glass of cognac and tossed it in his face. "There, isn't that the way gentlemen do it?" She stood with her arms crossed, while he mopped at his face with the ends of his neckcloth, painstakingly tied in the *trône d'amour* for the occasion.

"I should have known I couldn't get through a conversation with you with my wardrobe intact," he muttered into the linen. "But I do wish you would be more considerate of poor Bates and my pocketbook. I am already paying the man thrice what he is worth, just to soothe his nerves. I suppose it's a good thing you didn't slap me with your gloves. Knowing you there would likely be rocks in them." Corey reached over and took Melody's hand. He lifted it to his mouth and gently kissed the

215

turned palm, then he placed one of the pistols in it. "Here, Angel, you know I cannot shoot you. Do your worst. I deserve it."

Melody looked at him, all rough and disheveled, then at the gun in her hand. Her lips trembled. "I cannot."

"What's this, Angel, tears?" Corey took out his handkerchief and blotted at her eyes, his hand tenderly cupping her cheek. "You don't want to shoot me, sweetheart, but you don't want to marry me either, you know. I am just not husband material. You told me yourself. I am autocratic and dictatorial, and I would be jealous, possessive, and overprotective. You would hate it, just like you hated my not wanting you to help catch the blackmailer. I would want to wrap you in cotton wool, to see you safe."

"Why? Why would you care so much?" She stared intently into his eyes, looking for the truth.

"Because I lo—like you. We are friends."

"You let your other friends come into danger. You love me," she rejoiced. "I know you do! You are just afraid to admit it."

"Of course I love you, my Melody. You are the song in my heart, but . . ." But those carefree bachelor ways had been making one last desperate stand, thus the bottle and the bleary eyes. Without her, though, there would be no music for his soul to dance to. "But I shall try to make you a good husband."

Melody turned away so he could not see her smile. "You have not asked me yet, my lord."

His hand on her shoulder turned her around. "Do you truly love me, Angel?"

"Of course I love you, silly. I love you too much to let you grow into a grumbly old bachelor with no one to tell you your faults and no grubby children to lower your consequence."

He kissed her then, not as he would have wished,

due to his scratchy beard and sore face, but softly, a gentle promise. When he stepped back, still holding Melody in his arms, her green eyes were shining like emeralds in the sunshine. "I love you so much," she told him, "that I thought I would die if you went away."

"I was never going to leave without you, my adorable goose." And he kissed each eyelid for emphasis.

"But were you thinking of marriage this time?"

"Of course." She was grinning so he had to add, "You will just have to trust me on that. I take it that my suit has been accepted?"

"Hmm, I don't know," she teased. "Just how bad a husband did you say you would be?"

"Wretched. I am grouchy in the mornings, and I toss the blankets around all night. You would never need to worry about my straying, however. I'd be too cowardly to look at another woman, knowing your aim. But come now, madam, give me your answer. You have already shot me and doused me and subjected me to every indignity known to man. You have broken my nose and my chin. Don't say that you are going to break my heart, too?"

"Never." And this time her lips carried the promise. "Never, my lord, my love, my life."

Epilogue

$\mathcal{T}$he bride wore ivory satin and an antique veil. She carried a bouquet of pink carnations, blue forget-me-nots, and yellow columbines. The identical flower girls wore matching dresses, one pink, one blue. Another little girl was dressed in yellow and carried the train. The bride's mother wept.

The bridegroom wore white satin knee-breeches, white satin swallow-tail coat, white brocade waist, and snow-white linens. His valet wept harder.